WITCH OF THE FEDERATION

FEDERAL HISTORIES™ 01

MICHAEL ANDERLE

LMBPN
DISRUPTIVE IMAGINATION®

Witch Of The Federation (this book) is a work of fiction.

All of the characters, organizations, and events portrayed in this novel are either products of the author's imagination or are used fictitiously. Sometimes both.

Cover Art by Jake @ J Caleb Design
http://jcalebdesign.com / jcalebdesign@gmail.com
A Michael Anderle Production

LMBPN Publishing
PMB 196, 2540 South Maryland Pkwy
Las Vegas, NV 89109

First US edition, March 2019
Version 1.05, June 2019
ebook ISBN: 978-1-64202-151-6
Print ISBN: 978-1-64202-858-4

THE WITCH OF THE FEDERATION TEAM

Thanks to our Beta Team

Mary Morris, John Ashmore, Nicole Emens, Robert Brooks, and Larry Omans

Thanks to our JIT Readers

Angel LaVey
Jeff Eaton
John Raisor
Larry Omans
Misty Roa
Tim Adams

If We've missed anyone, please let us know!

Editor
The Skyhunter Editing Team

To Family, Friends and
Those Who Love
To Read.
May We All Enjoy Grace
To Live The Life We Are
Called.

CHAPTER ONE

Stephanie never understood why they painted cinderblock interior walls. It always left small, concave bubbles over the surface. Maybe it was for a textured effect—anything to make the decades-old school hallway look a little more presentable on a day like that. She ran her finger over the slick, shiny white paint a second before someone rammed into her shoulder from behind and knocked her to the side.

She looked up in irritation as two guys from the other class raced down the hall, chasing each other. The teacher came out of the classroom, clapped her hands, and yelled at them. "Walk, or I'll send you right back to detention. Trust me, if that one was too exciting, I can load a very rousing, small white room with no windows into your headsets."

A kid behind her sighed. Stephanie glanced back and winced at his wild red hair and braces that almost seemed intrusive. She turned away and shoved her hands in the front pockets of her jeans as she tapped her vintage Converse up and down. Patience was something she was more familiar with than most kids, but on that particular day, she struggled to keep it together.

It was testing day—the day every kid had the opportunity to

climb inside one of the full immersion pods brought in by the government and give it their best shot for a higher education worth having. They all thought about it, but most of those students considered never made it. Unless, of course, money was no object. Then, you were sent ahead to a bright and exciting future. The rest scrambled their way through the mediocre choices left for college so they could drown in debt as they stumbled through their mediocre life. Stephanie was sure there was more to it than that—more than simply settling. But then again, what did she really know? She was a teenager.

Mrs. Abbott, the teacher, stepped out of the classroom and smiled as she tugged nonchalantly on the bottom of her blue button-up blouse in an effort to get the high lace collar off her chin. "All right, single file into the room, all the way down, and around the rows. Stop in front of your pod, and you may begin reading your instruction manual."

The students whispered excitedly to one another as they shuffled forward. Kids like Stephanie had never been inside a full immersion pod. For others like the redhead behind her, though, it seemed to be an inconvenience.

He snickered as they entered. "Leave it to the government to send outdated pods."

Stephane ignored him, made it down the line, and stood in front of her pod. She retrieved the manual, which really was only a couple of pages long with large text. Trying not to smile too widely, she ran her gaze over the sleek black apparatus in front of her. It stood as high as her stomach, bubbled at the back, and smoothed out to a rounded point at the front. On the right was a silver handle with an arrow. On the front of it was a screen for the teacher and several flashing red lights.

The students around her chatted with excitement as the teacher browsed through the rows to see if anyone had any questions. One of the boys in the front row groaned, rolled his eyes, and raised his hand in the air. "This thing won't open. The handle is all wonky."

Mrs. Abbott held her head up and muttered under her breath. In a high-pitched tone and with an almost ghastly smile, she wandered over and tapped the book. "Did you read your instructions?"

The kid's frown transformed into tight-lipped irritation. "Of course I did."

The woman's expression remained frozen like a robot, which was probably why they called her Robot Abbott. "Okay, then. Read it again."

Stephanie lowered her head to her own book but shifted her gaze to look at him. He pouted and picked the book up again and read frantically at first before he slowed as he reached the relevant section. He pursed his lips and glanced at the handle and then back at the book. Hesitation paused his hand in mid-reach, but he continued, grabbed the handle, turned it to the left, pushed in, and turned it to the right. The door hissed slightly as it opened and raised the pod top.

He folded the instructions and tossed them on the seat before he glanced up. Quickly, Stephanie looked away so he wouldn't catch her watching him figure it out. Again, she had to force herself to hold back the grin that tugged at the sides of her lips. The kid grumbled, took hold of the handle, and hauled himself into the pod. "It's not as if someone like me will be accepted anyway. This is a waste of my time."

Stephanie forced her concentration onto the instructions in front of her. She couldn't let the naysayers and entitled kids into her psyche. The instruction manual had a different picture on the front than the one she had at home so she could prepare. From the instructions it provided to open the pod, they seemed to be exactly the same, though. She put the manual down and rubbed her hands together, stepped toward the handle, and grasped it firmly.

After a slow, deep breath, she whispered under her breath, "This is the big one. Don't screw it up."

She turned the handle left, pushed it in, and then right. The compression of the space inside hissed slightly. As she raised it, butterflies fluttered through her chest. The odor of leather fabric on the seats mixed with an odd floral scent hit her senses. *It smells like my grandmother's old car. Maybe that's a good sign. I'm gonna take it as a good sign, anyway.*

Quickly, she slid into the pod and gripped the handle. She spared one last look at everyone else entering their machines before she closed the door firmly. As it latched, small lights along the edge of the ceiling illuminated the inside in a soft glow. The screen flickered on and several buttons lit up in different colors. She knew from the booklet not to mess with any of those unless instructed to do so by the administrator.

In the silence that followed, she began to wonder if she had forgotten to do something. Suddenly, a calm female voice spoke soothingly through the pod. "Welcome, student. Are you in need of instructions?"

Stephanie released her smile and said cheerfully, "Of course."

The female voice, slightly robotic in nature, continued. "Excellent. Please lie flat on your back with your hands folded on your chest."

She glanced at the pod bed, a leather-covered foam with an indentation for a human body. A small pillow was attached where her head would go. Slowly, she lay back, crossed her ankles, and made sure she was good and comfortable. "Done."

"Excellent," the voice intoned. "I am a second generation VRZ-201 training module. I am a little older but well taken care of and will be able to help you acclimate to the training scenario. Now that you are vertical and comfortable, we will move on to the next step."

Stephanie nodded. "Right."

"For the next part of your preparation, we will administer a small injection on the left side of your neck. This will release a specialized serum that will allow my technology to speak directly to the receptors in your brain. It is one of the vital parts of the new immersion, headset-free virtual experience. Please relax."

Stephanie raised an eyebrow but closed her eyes and tried to relax. She had been subjected to a barrage of immunizations over the years with the reintroduction of certain flu strains brought by visitors from other planets. These were in addition to about six or seven specialized ones her parents had saved up for to decrease her risk of cancers and other deadly diseases. Most of them weren't required, but with the way the world had evolved in manufacturing and the increase in climate change events, you didn't stand a chance past fifty if you didn't have them. Which was mostly why they were so pricey and usually reserved for the richer families.

A slight buzz beside her left ear sounded as a small needle ejected and pierced the vein running up her neck. It whirred and a small amount of yellow liquid was injected.

"Ouch," she whispered.

The pod retracted the needle. "I'm sorry about that. For your information, there is only a six percent chance of an adverse reaction to the injection. It will dissipate from your system within eight hours."

A piece slid out above her and over her head. Small sensors rested only centimeters from her temples, across her forehead, and in a spiderweb pattern across the top of her head. "This will be able to pick up the infusion as it travels through your brain," the pod explained. "It will also document your vitals for safety purposes. Now, there are two large gloves attached to the side of the pod. Please rest your forearms on the pads and slip your hands into the gloves. Make sure your fingers are right to the tip or as far as you can go."

Stephanie moved her eyes, no longer able to turn her head. On each side were black, cushioned arm-holders with tight black gloves. Small silver wires were stitched into the fabric and traced up and down the fabric. She slipped her hand in the first one and it sucked tightly onto her hand. Smiling, she did the same with the other before she flexed her fists.

On the screen in front of her, a small line appeared and began to rise up and down in sync with the beat of her heart. Below it, other numbers were displayed that changed every few seconds. The pod dimmed the lights. "Now that you have prepped, we will wait for the detection of the serum. The average wait time is five minutes. From there, we will begin the exam."

Stephanie raised her hand up and turned it back and forth. "Groovy."

The pod beside Stephanie's shook slightly but no one could see except for Mrs. Abbott, who was distracted by the two boys who still ran up and down the hallway. Inside, Kyle—the redheaded guy from the line—grunted as he tried to get comfortable in the bed of the pod.

"This is ridiculous," he muttered. "Even the base models of the five-year-old pods had soft seats with body-adjusting cushions. This is like laying on a piece of foam."

The lights on the roof flickered on. "Welcome, student. Are you in need of instructions?"

Kyle sneered at the screens in front of him. "I guess I should since you're so old. I don't want to mess up cranking the knobs or some crazy crap like that."

The pod didn't respond to his comment. "Okay. I am a second generation VRZ-201 training module. I am a little older but well taken care of and will be able to help you acclimate to the training scenario."

He scoffed. "Are you kidding me? A 201? That was made before I was even born. I'm fairly certain my dad had one when he was my age. Great. Taking it back old-school. It's exactly like this place to not provide the state-of-the-art models."

"Please find a comfortable position in the bed, facing up with your hands on your stomach," the pod replied.

Kyle wiggled again. "Right, like there is actually a comfortable position with this thing."

He grumbled but was silenced when the needle emerged and pricked him in the neck. Offended, he clutched the spot and rubbed it. "Hey. Watch out with that thing. Did you even sanitize?"

"I'm sorry. All needles are pre-packaged and sanitized before each new student enters the pod."

Kyle frowned and rested his hands back on his stomach. "I'm shocked you even have the auto-inject. I have an old 304 model in my game room, and I call it an antique. I can't believe we have to use you for this test. No wonder the kids from the west side don't have a stinking chance of getting into this thing. I guess that's all the better for me, though."

The screen up front activated and the pod explained the information. "This will monitor your stats while you complete your exam. The headpiece that lowered and your gloves will track the serum injected into your neck."

The boy squeezed his fists open and closed. "Perfect. Rusty needles, archaic software, and a damn head clamp. I should have simply volunteered my newest pod. They could have set it all up in that thing and I would be halfway done by now."

The pod didn't respond. "Your heartbeat seems to be slightly elevated."

He blinked at the ceiling. "Because I am in a time capsule with the capabilities of an iPad from a thousand years ago."

"The iPads were used on the first pod but quickly discontinued when the technology became outdated," the AI explained.

Kyle gritted his teeth. "So I have an idiot guide through this test that also doubles as an encyclopedia of completely useless information. Perfect. This should be the most fun I've had since I broke my nose."

The pod beeped. "From your records, it seems your nose was broken on March 9th, 2114 due to a fist fight with a—"

Kyle cleared his throat and raised his voice. "I get it. You know my file. There's no need to rehash my accident. I'm sure the kid who tried to hurt me has good enough memories of what I did to him."

The AI replied, "From your records, you passed out and were taken to the hospital bay."

The kid lay there with his nostrils flared and his lips tight. "Why don't we simply sit here quietly until your slow-ass system boots up and we can start this thing?"

"Of course. When the serum begins to take effect, I will give the explanation of the process and you will be allowed to begin whenever you are ready. In case of an emergency, either call out to the pod to sound the emergency switch or remove the headset."

Kyle grumbled, "Does an emergency mean this pod is far below my standards?"

CHAPTER TWO

Stephanie settled in and stared at the ceiling as they waited for the serum to take effect. She focused on the feeling of the gloves and the tightness of the elastic material with small silver wires touched with a faint green glow. She wiggled her fingers with a grin, but when her eyes shifted to the screen that ran her physical statistics, a flutter moved in her stomach.

The opportunity to test for a prep school was something that had almost consumed her mind, at least for the last five years. She found it easier, being of high intelligence, to blend into the crowds. To achieve this, she never made waves and never really got noticed. Her clothes were plain, a few years older than most but not anything too obvious. Her parents were similar to those of the other kids she knew. They worked hard, provided a roof, food, and the necessities, but other than that, she would have to determine her future for herself.

Being in that class of society never bothered her that much, but when she heard that the rich kids had the opportunity to use full immersion pods practically their whole life at home, she was jealous. She had only ever used headgear and nothing that was the newest hi-tech. Now, she was in one of the pods and she didn't know if she would be able to get the hang of it while she took a test that could quite possibly define the rest of her life.

The voice in the pod soothed through her mind. "Your pulse has seemed to increase slightly, and your muscles have tensed. Can I do anything to make you more comfortable?"

Stephanie shook her head minutely back and forth. "No, thank you. It's my first time in a pod, that's all. Why don't you tell me about the process?"

The AI went quiet for a moment. "For this government required opportunity to be tested for a placement and possible financial assistance in a prep school, you must be checked physically as well as mentally."

She thought about all those times she'd run the mile in the lower schools. "How do you check me physically if I am lying down?"

"The system capabilities are beyond in-the-moment testing. Through your blood, circulation, heart rhythm, and approximately six hundred and eighty-nine other factors, the system can see what your physical health score will be. This includes during exercises and testing," the pod answered.

The butterflies began to tame as she thought about her last doctor's appointment. She had always been in really good shape. Encouraged, she bit the inside of her lip and tried not to let the excitement increase too dramatically. "So, there may be a chance I could be accepted? I tried to calculate it on my own, but it seemed that the odds of that happening were too low for me to figure out the number."

"There might be something wrong with your calculations. It is always at least two percent. That is the statistical norm suggested. It is also the minimum before companies are required to have government oversight."

Stephanie's heart sunk. "Not for us in the government-subsidized living arrangements."

The pod was quiet. "That is a correct statement. For those who live in government-subsidized housing, it seems numbers are closer to one in two hundred and thirty-two—"

Stephanie's eyes opened wide in hope. "That's better than I thought! Man, I imagined it would be way higher than that."

The AI finished its sentence. "Thousand."

She rolled her eyes and shook her head as a smirk moved slowly over her lips. "So, you're telling me there *is* a chance?" She laughed at her own quote, knowing that Todd would have been proud of her for being so quick.

The pod replied, "About the same as dying from a rare cobra bite."

Stephanie narrowed her eyes and pursed her lips. "Are there cobras in NorAm?"

"No."

She paused and closed her eyes before she allowed her grin to show through. She had just been cut down by a pod. That in itself would probably be the highlight of her whole time in the thing. "I think I like you."

The lights flickered in the pod. "I am not programmed to *like*. But you are very polite."

Stephanie began to think she would have been better off if she'd hung out with the pod system all those years. At least it put her at ease, which was probably the entire point of the five percent humor in the system. Those kinds of things fascinated her and had done so her whole life. The pods had been around a long time, even since before she had been born, and had become an important part of society. These days, it was almost vital considering that alternate options didn't look too exciting for her.

NorAm—long before she had been born and even before her parents were born—constituted three different countries all operating under their own rule. From what Stephanie had read, opportunities, especially in the United States, were a lot more bountiful than they had previously been. However, there was still a serious difference in the financial institutions that catered to the rich, to the middle class, and to the poor. And debt for post-high-school education was a definite unless you were lucky enough to receive a scholarship.

Prep schools worked in much the same way, but the chances of someone from the middle class or lower actually getting the financial aid to attend was nearly impossible. It was a separation of class on so many levels. Stephanie chuckled to herself and thought about all the times she had tried to talk to Todd about that. He hated it when she went on rants. He called her an old-world idealist. Which she wasn't, but she admired how people used to try to make the system better. Now, she was left with a statistical chance.

Kyle opened one eye, followed by the other, his smile now clean and brace-less. His wild red hair had been tamed and his pimples were gone, replaced by smooth skin. He looked in the mirror and winked at himself. "I should have been able to bring my personal avatar over, but hey, I like creating them so let's see what you have."

A calm voice echoed through the white room around him. "Prepare to create your avatar."

The room whizzed past him while his feet remained planted firmly in place. It stopped again with a sudden jolt to display rows and rows of clothing, weapons, and modifications of personal attributes.

He nodded. "Well, I guess this is one I can't complain about too much. At least you have the updated closet function."

"We updated approximately two hundred and forty-five days ago. Please choose your avatar's presentation. Remember, this exercise is for your assessment and we recommend one of the test preparation suits directly ahead," the voice replied in a pleasant tone.

Kyle's nose wrinkled and the creases made his freckles that much more noticeable. "Yuck. So, do I have to wear one or can I do whatever?"

The pod replied, "You can choose your personal look. Please do not linger here for too long. The test must begin shortly."

He ignored the voice as he sauntered through the racks of outfits. He walked down halfway and had already discarded the initial options. "Nope, too pink.... Ugh...that's so my parent's... Nope... nope...nope...and— Wait a minute."

The boy tapped the outfit twice and walked to stand in front of the mirror and turn from side to side. He wore what looked to be an Earth play on the Dreth battle gear. The shoulder pads were large and leather with spikes on them. The front of the armor made him look much larger than his scrawny self actually was, and the black boots also sported silver spikes.

"Sweet," he whispered and selected the hair options. "This is exactly what I need."

He tapped his preferred option twice and looked up. His red hair was now in a foot-tall mohawk with a long braid down the back. Kyle flexed his fake muscled arms in the mirror and growled. He chuckled, selected a huge sword and a Dreth laser gun from the weapons area, and clipped them to himself.

The voice spoke into the room once more. "Have you completed your avatar?"

Kyle snickered at his reflection. "Hell yeah, I did. Let's get this over with."

"Checking vitals—"

He jumped and rubbed his shoulder. "Ouch, you damned droid."

"I am not a droid," she replied automatically. "Readings have returned. Your physiology does not scan in a way that suggests pain."

His lip twitched. "It was psychomaniac."

"Indeed," the voice replied after a momentary pause. "Did you mean psychosomatic?"

"Of course." He sniffed. *There's a difference?* "Didn't you hear that word, you dumb machine?"

The AI didn't respond to his question—or his attitude, for that matter. It was not programmed nor had the capability to have its own personality. "Your physical and neurological readings are completed. You are ready to proceed to testing. Welcome to the Mandatory Audition for Enhanced NeuroSync Prep Testing. Please answer—"

Kyle waved his hand dismissively. "Yeah, yeah. Just start."

Stephanie opened her eyes and glanced around when she realized that she now stood inside a white room. A voice echoed in the space. "Prepare to create your avatar."

The room whizzed past her and she put her arms out to stabilize herself. When it stopped again, she stood in some sort of huge closet. She looked at herself in the mirror, shocked at how close they had achieved her true appearance. Even her hair was back in a braid like her mom used to do for her when she was younger.

"What do I do?"

The same calming tone spoke once more. "Please choose your avatar's presentation. Remember, this exercise is for your assessment and we recommend one of the test preparation suits directly ahead."

She focused her eyes on the selection in front of her and ran her fingers across the blue and white jumpsuits. Surprisingly, she could actually feel the fabric—it was wild. Finally, she attempted to pull the one on the end out since it was all black with what looked like 3D boxes that moved constantly on the front. It wouldn't budge, though. "How do I select it?"

"Tap the choice twice," the voice responded.

Stephanie raised an eyebrow but immediately followed the instructions. Suddenly, she no longer looked at it but actually wore it. It fit tightly like spandex, and military-style combat boots on her feet laced up her calves. She took a step back and chuckled at the way her avatar moved—almost cartoon-like but with facial shadows and the anatomically correct motions of her hips and legs. It was beyond what she'd imagined.

After a quick glance at the other things available, she decided that she would simply go with what was recommended. "It's not like I have a reason to wear a full metal suit of armor—"

"Have you completed your avatar?" the AI asked.

She shrugged. "Sure."

"Checking vitals… Your physical and neurological readings are complete. You are ready to proceed to testing."

Stephanie fisted and unfisted her avatar hands nervously. "Sweet."

The AI paused a moment before it proceeded. "Welcome to the Mandatory Audition for Enhanced NeuroSync Prep Testing. Please answer truthfully, as lies will be noted and will reduce your score. Besides standardized testing, there will be questions asked of you. These subjective question and answer sessions represent forty percent of your score. There will be an immersion test which will account for thirty percent of your score, and the core questions represent another thirty percent.

"At any time, the testing agent will be able to suggest that you be moved for consideration regardless of the score. While this does not guarantee acceptance, it means you will be reviewed for your subjective answers and possibly pass to the next stage. Good luck. There will be a period of darkness as we proceed."

She drew in a deep breath and looked at herself in the mirror. "Well, here goes nothing."

Her image faded and the darkness overtook her.

Outside the pods, everything was perfectly silent.

CHAPTER THREE

The walls were plain and darkly painted with no windows to allow light into the keycard-accessed room in the main government building for Enhanced NeuroSync Prep. It was filled with monitors and those who operated them using 3D interfaces. The screens changed and flashed constantly. When you walked into the room, you would be met with an insane barrage of technological wonder.

Around eighteen individual cubicles were spread as far apart as they could be in the space across the wide expanse of the room. They weren't separated by thin walls, but instead, used the latest sound dampening technology. No sound emitted from the space, and that helped to regulate the noise since all the engineers and programmers spent their time giving information to the students engaged in the Virtual World as well as seething in frustration. They couldn't hear a single word unless they chose to talk to each other, which wasn't really encouraged at all.

Down the center row, poised relatively close to one another, two engineer-programmers sat and talked with their students while they moved their hands to navigate the program in front of them. Aaron had been an engineer and programmer with the company for a couple of years. He liked the job but not that particular part of it. Having to actually interact with the students was often a source of enormous frustration.

He sat with a blank expression on his face and watched his current student battle the virtual Dreth pirates along with a team of other students. While almost everyone else wore training jumpsuits which were recommended, this guy had gone all out with Earth-inspired Dreth battle gear and a tall red-haired mohawk. He could tell almost immediately that the kid thought he was above everyone else and didn't need to follow the recommended course of action.

The earpiece was pressed firmly into Aaron's ear and the mic perched directly in front of his lips. "No, you can't simply shoot everyone and hope that your EI support shuts the gun down if you have friendlies targeted."

He pressed two fingers on each side of the bridge of his nose and leaned on his elbow. "No, you can't program that in the heat of battle — What kind of sim is this? A real one. Have a nice day."

He went to remove the headpiece but the kid made another smart-ass answer. Aaron slammed his palm on the desk. "What? Do you really want to know the answer to that? Or is this one of those sarcastic statements you can't seem to refrain from making?"

Aaron slapped his forehead with his palm and held his arms out to each side.

His friend, who had joined the company at the same time as him—Gene—sat beside him in his own soundproof cubicle. He finished one section of testing with his student and asked them to wait so he could prepare the rest. As he put them on hold, he glanced at his colleague. The exasperation was evident as Aaron flung his arms about and waved his hands wildly. This seemed to happen to the poor man at least once every season and it looked like it was in full swing.

Gene glanced at his computer to make sure the next section was loading and hit the mute button on his microphone. He paused, turned, and set his hands in his lap to wait for Aaron to finish. He knew this would probably be a good story. No way could he even imagine that it would end with him calmly moving on to the next student in his queue.

Sure enough, he didn't have long to wait.

He winced as the veins in Aaron's head seemed about to explode. The engineer shook his finger and stood as he shoved his chair back. His mouth went crazy and whatever he was saying, he said it with passion. Suddenly, he very pragmatically rolled his sleeves up one at a time. Then, with anger raging across his face, he raised his right arm high into the air and slammed it down on the disconnect button. Gene flinched and chuckled.

Inside the soundproof cubicle, the irate man screamed, *"Failed!"*

Aaron, at that point, had lost every shred of patience left in his body and didn't even try not to scream. He knew the damned sound dampeners wouldn't allow him to bellow at the student anyway, and no one in the office would be able to hear him. That, however, did not stop him from pounding his hand down on the red button repeatedly until the computer sent him an error message. He backed away, panting, and plopped back in his chair to bring his hands to his face and scream into them. For a moment, he seriously considered finding the kid and beating the hell out of him.

With a loud groan, he dragged his hands down his face. The motion stretched his skin so there was a gap under each eye and his bottom lip flapped open to reveal the crooked teeth in his lower jaw. His hands still holding his face like that, Aaron's gaze shifted to his left and settled on Gene, who sat there and laughed. He swished his left hand to the side to deactivate the sound barrier between them. As soon as it dissipated, he could hear his friend's raucous laughter and the sound as his hand slapped against his black dress pants.

He spun his chair to face him, gritted his teeth, and shook his fists violently in front of him. Gene smirked and raised an eyebrow. "Eye D 10 T?"

Aaron tried, he really, really did, but as he sat there in front of his best friend, he couldn't restrain himself any longer. "He only wishes he was an idiot! That kid is probably sucking on the tit of Mom and Dad's bank account. But, of course, they most likely use a Virtual-Nanny so they don't have to deal with that festering boil on the butt of society."

Gene raised both eyebrows and Aaron continued. "You would think a parent would notice that their child was a little devil heathen sent from the depth of Tartarus to wreak hell on Earth. And that the realization would prompt them to do something like set him ablaze. Or cook him in an oven. Maybe shove a dry stake of wood through his black, hollow heart. All that would happen would be that his body crumbled and blew wistfully off in the wind. Isn't it a parent's responsibility to not unleash their spawn on the rest of the world simply so others can suffer too?"

His friend shrugged. "It might be in the by-laws. But damn, if you don't already know, misery loves company."

Aaron scoffed and folded his arms over his chest. "We all wonder what a psychopath looks like as a kid. Well, there you go. Red mohawk, idiot armor, and an attitude like he could do whatever the fuck he wanted to do. I bet he has pimples all over his nerdy-ass little face."

He paused, lowered his hands into his lap, and grumbled under his breath. Gene shook his head and raised his hands. "No, don't hold back." He wasn't even sure Aaron could or would allow himself to hear him in the rage. "Please, let it all out."

"And then—" Aaron raised one arm high and pointed at the ceiling. He flicked his blond hair out of his face. "The little bleeding canker sore had the nerve to ask me how he did!"

Gene tilted his head to the side and managed to force his lips into a straight line. "I take it you didn't approve him?"

He loved pushing his friend, who always had the most dramatic and chaotic responses to the little shit-stains who ended up on the other side of his comms. For a while there, Gene thought it was some sort of conspiracy because Aaron somehow landed all the shit-heads in the system. However, after a couple of years of doing it, he realized that seventeen and eighteen-year-old kids, especially the boys, were merely naturally dirty jock straps. Ironically, they would probably have gained something out of Aaron's temper tantrum if they had been able to actually hear it.

Plus, it usually got him to settle down and allowed him to move forward with the job of interviewing students. He merely had to get it all out of his system and as fast as he could. They were never too overloaded with their students through the day considering that they had other responsibilities too, but some of them could really put a damper on your mood. Not to mention that they learned nothing from the experience because the sound dampers essentially cut everything out that seemed derogatory or negative.

The most important thing was that they communicated with each and every student and did it thoroughly. The government didn't play around with that kind of thing. They, in their political haze, thought the system actually gave these kids an opportunity. It was more likely that the creeper on the other end of the line would end up in the prep school regardless of his insane behavior during the tests.

Aaron stopped his rant, having obviously heard Gene's question this time. He leaned forward towards his friend. "Approve him? Of course not!"

He shook his head in dismay. "That mutated radioactive rodent will probably go to school because his parents want him out of the house and are willing to pay the millions it takes. Screw that kid. He won't be one of the chosen few who get in for free."

The engineer ceased his tirade and deflated, his shoulders low and his head leaned back against the headrest of his chair. That was Gene's signal. "So, buddy, do you still have any more in you?"

Aaron replied in a whisper. "No."

Gene smiled and turned his chair to face his work station. He had his own line of students waiting on him. As he moved, though, he caught the tail end of his friend's grumble. He stopped and looked at him. "Wait, what?"

Aaron shook his head and his gaze shifted to look at the low-track lighting on the ceiling. "I said…I should tell BURT to do it."

He whirled his chair around again and glanced furtively at the room, but no one was actually watching. He hissed at Aaron. "Are you out of your damned mind?"

His friend looked at him, the anger replaced by a condescending smirk and a mischievous gleam in his eyes. The chair squeaked as he rocked back and forth and rubbed his chin. "Why not?"

Gene closed his eyes for several seconds before he exhaled a deep, exasperated breath. Why he was surprised by this response, he didn't know, but this was the last time he needed to explain it to the other man. "Because there are laws, asshole!"

Aaron opened his mouth to refute that, but Gene gestured dismissively and continued. "Plus, BURT runs the Virtual Reality Worlds—all of them. I'm not sure what would happen if you randomly asked him to sit in and do the subjective analysis. Are you?"

The other man snorted dismissively, obviously not taking his adamant speech and exhausted demeanor into account in his decision. "I've studied the system for a while now. Seriously, what do you think could possibly go that disastrously wrong with that idea? BURT barely ever hits above thirty-two percent stress load except on World Events and even then, it's only up to forty-seven percent."

Aaron looked at the ceiling and shook his finger near his lips. "Well, except that one Winters Festival, but that was a fluke."

Gene thought about it for a second. "What was that incident—oh, yeah! So, let me ask this. What happens if he goes and decides to research the shit out of the Internet? I can't truly believe that you have blocked out the time he took down Kuala Lumpur's data trunk."

His friend waved him off, his face now exhausted by the debacle. "I'll make sure the student is here in NorAm. We have plenty of pipe for the data search if it happens."

Aaron's computer dinged a reminder and he glanced at his queue. Slowly, he turned back to his station and leaned forward. His head lowered until he cradled it in both hands. "I don't know what I'll do if I have another silver-spoon-licking lizard like that last one. Because the only thing that fluttered through my mind was homicide."

He looked slowly at Gene, his face red from the blood that had rushed forward, and several pieces of his blond hair hung in his eyes. "Honest to God—whichever one you believe in—I might simply hit the red button. Like, no matter what. At the first sign that you are a rich douche bag, done."

Unwillingly, he turned his focus back to his work station. “Or, hell, I might make it so everyone gets the green button.”

Gene shook his head. “Pfft. A fat lot of good that would do. The ones we green-light who are worth it don’t ever get picked by the government’s ‘randomizing factor’ anyway. Some stuffy pencil pusher up in accounting has figured out a way to get money out of the students and still be on the good side of the law.”

A second beeping sounded but this time, it was on Gene’s side. His head turned at the alarm and he stared at the monitor to check his work projects. “Okay, I have to get back to my queue. And if you do some crazy shit, I can’t know about it. This job is all that’s between me and starvation.”

“That,” Aaron said as he straightened and pulled his headset into his lap, “is a gross oversimplification and you playing at being a drama queen.”

Gene raised his chin and scooted slowly back toward his computer. “At least I’m royalty. What does that make you, hmmmm?”

Before Aaron could respond, he restored the sound barrier over the small virtual window between them. He waved, though, and his wrist moved from side to side as he pretended to be royalty. Aaron laughed and shook his head. Gene turned away and pulled himself back to the computer to look at the different stats.

He grabbed his VR helmet and slid it down over his face. No matter how much he joked, Aaron’s idea was absolutely a really good way to get yourself fired or even worse. Before he clicked the button to return to his queue, he whispered, “I hope he doesn’t do anything too crazy.”

Aaron, who now felt a little better, spun his chair and grabbed the front of his desk to slow himself down. He picked his VR helmet up, ready to go back in, when he saw that he had two students in his queue. He scanned each one and realized that the second was from the same testing location as the miniature Chucky. “Oh, hell no. There is no freaking way I will handle another little petulant asshole. If anything, I should give him a piece of my mind. He is lucky he got away from me before I could send him to the penalty room.”

He set his helmet up and pulled his keyboard toward him. After a furtive glance around to make sure no supervisors skimmed past to look in on them, he opened a logic queue and began to type.

>>check status BURT load.

>>STATUS 22%

Aaron puffed his cheeks out and tapped his hand against the desk as his gaze shifted back and forth. He leaned back and templed his fingers as he tried to be certain that he would do something he would be willing to take the repercussions for if he was caught doing it. The sound of that little shit's laugh made him shiver. "Screw it."

He put his fingers back on the keyboard and continued to type.

>> Open Link BURT

...

...

...

>>LINK OPEN: Hello Programmer Aaron C. What can the Binary Unlimited Reality Training matrix do for you today?

>>Query BURT: Review all pertinent laws regarding Student Mandated Government Testing and report back.

>>QUERY STARTED. QUERY COMPLETE. 0.0000021% LOAD AFFECTED. TIME TO FINISH, .000043 SECONDS.

Aaron rolled his eyes and leaned back. *Does BURT always have to show off?*

He took a deep breath and focused on his screen. Cautiously, he moved the next student in the queue to the main screen and scanned the info in an effort to figure out which one the next student was in.

>>Query BURT: Can BURT handle the task of querying the student B221ZA in queue and complete all requirements of the Law related to subjective test analysis and, this is the important part, not compromise the load BURT is under while running ALL virtual worlds.

>> QUERY STARTED... ... ... QUERY COMPLETE. 0.1% LOAD AFFECTED. TIME TO FINISH 0.37 SECONDS.

Aaron narrowed his eyes and rubbed his chin. He was fairly certain he could have counted almost a second on that query.

>> **BURT CAN AND WILL ACCEPT THIS TASK. TASK IN QUEUE, TASK STARTED.**

He opened his mouth and then closed it and simply stared at the screen. *Did BURT just co-opt the request from me without a formal request?*

Before he could even begin to investigate what had happened, a box popped open on his screen and began to flash. The next student had entered from the avatar area and was ready to begin.

Aaron put his helmet on and pulled up the script. "Now for the next runner up on the new game show... Your life will not change..."

He figured that as long as he didn't get a snazzy jerk, he would go home that night with a job still on the books. That was good enough for him.

Stephanie could feel her body standing there, even in her avatar, but there was nothing but blackness around her. She wondered if it was an absence of light or a switch that had simply turned off her ability to see within the world. When she thought this through, she decided it was a question for a bored night researching random things on her tablet and simply relaxed and accepted the darkness as part of the whole experience.

After a few moments, her eyes reset as a small pinprick of light appeared in the distance. She immediately squinted but stopped and laughed at herself. *No, silly, this is in your mind. You don't have to worry about your eyes adjusting in these VR pods.*

The tiny hint of illumination remained static as the minutes ticked by. In the next moment, she sat in a park. Her hands rubbed over the worn wood planks on the bench beneath her. She looked up and her senses immediately went wild as they identified all the things around her. The wind blew lightly through the leaves on the deciduous trees ahead. The faint whistle of air and crinkle of leaves made her think of a time when she had sat with her father outside one of his jobs in the richer area of town. The trees in the yard had whipped back and forth, something she didn't see in the government-housing area they lived in.

She could almost see the path of the breeze as it whipped around the base of the tree. The bark was dark and crumbling, loosely attached as it wound around the knobby knots with deep recesses within. The wind moved across the grass and fluttered each single perfectly groomed blade until it reached the bench. Stephanie giggled as it teased up her body and whipped through her hair as if it were alive and tried to introduce itself to her.

With her arm resting on the back of the bench, she turned, and her eyes glistened under the almost utopian cerulean sky. Small white nebulas danced across it, and the sun burned brightly overhead although the temperature on her skin was perfect. Still, it seemed surreal to her although it was essentially a place she was familiar with. It was her world—Earth, a place quiet and complete, where she would love to visit on a regular basis. Parks like the one she sat in still existed, but they were usually tucked tightly in the center or the immediate surroundings of the large cities.

While parks had been built near her government-subsidized living arrangement, over the years, they had fallen into ruin. The play area was rusted and dirty, and when the parents weren't there during the daytime to watch their children closely, the gangs gathered in the dusk and planned their next iniquitous act, whatever that might be.

She closed her eyes for a moment and tilted her head toward the ball of light in the sky. The simulation was so real, she could actually feel the rays of light permeate her often pale skin.

"Hello." A soft male voice spoke in her ears.

Stephanie's eyes opened wide and she set one hand down on the bench and turned from side to side. Her gaze drifted all around before she stilled nervously and placed her hands in her lap. Slowly, she stood and began to walk. She wound between the trees and ran her hands along the bark and down to the bushes. Each individual leaf eased across her palm, warm like the sun. She knew they didn't really exist, but they seemed as real as they would if she were out of the pod.

The voice spoke again, and she straightened when she finally realized it was not a physical person but a voice in the pod. "You have finished the physical and mental congruence testing. It is time for you to take the standardized testing. How would you like the classroom to look?"

Stephanie bit her bottom lip and grinned. "Can I see Meligorn?"

CHAPTER FOUR

"Of course," the voice answered and helped to encourage the calm and warm feeling in Stephanie's stomach.

The scene around her began to change as the bushes and trees almost seemed to melt away to be replaced by the beautiful and exotic land of Meligorn. Her eyes sparkled and she touched her hand to her chest as a small, tree-like plant appeared in place of the large, thick trunk of the Earth tree. Its small branches seemed incredibly fragile while the lines and divots on its slender trunk looked weather-worn. The leaves erupted like a blooming flower and brightened her senses with deep purples and greens.

Her gaze fluttered to the horizon in the distance that no longer burst with the color of the ocean. Instead, it hummed in a translucent purple with two faint moons in the distance. What had been a line of forest in the park quickly shifted, grew larger, and morphed into large, looming mountains. The color across the horizon of the sky changed from early afternoon to the vaguely purple hue of early evening in Meligorn.

She spun in a full circle to absorb the stark contrast of beauty that erupted all around her. Soon, her clothes rippled as the soft green grasses of the park changed to a meadow. To her right, clear green water, crystalline and sparkling, reflected the light. Some sort of Meligornian creature with eight legs hopped off a blue pad and splashed quietly into the water. Her gaze trailed to the sky once more at the loud squawk as something flew over her head.

Enthralled, she studied the bird-like creature with a vast wingspan. It had the face and body shape of a phoenix, but instead of a burning red, its feathers were a multitude of alternating hues that seemed to shimmer and change with the light of their star.

She clapped her hands to her mouth and then slapped them down on her thighs. Her face broke into a prodigious smile. "Oh, my God, I'm on Meligorn! I can't believe it. The pictures are nowhere near as beautiful as it is in person."

Delighted, she dropped onto the ground and sat with her legs to the side. She traced her hand softly over the tips of the grasses that felt almost silky soft. While they were a rich bluish-green in color, they could almost pass for winter rye on her planet.

Stephanie sat there for several moments and allowed the delicacy and allure of the landscape around her to seep deeper and deeper into her mind. She didn't want to forget a moment of it. Not a splash of color, not a whisper of the softened breeze that blew against the back of her neck, and not even an interval of sound from the creatures so foreign but so fascinating to her.

A tear pooled at the corner of her eye and she wiped it away before it could trail down her cheek. She feared that if one fell, it would open the floodgates. Even though she spent her days hoping beyond hope that she would one day walk the planet of magic, she knew that moment was the closest she would get to Meligorn in her life. Of course, she could figure out a way to scheme and sneak to hitch a ride to the planet. But she had no idea how to be that kind of person. Or how to win the lottery—the approval she needed to learn in the prep schools.

She leaned back and put her feet out in front of her as she stared at the sky. Taking in one deep breath after another, she pushed the feeling of sadness away and saved it for another time. She pursed her lips and sat up again, plopped her hands into her lap, and drew her shoulders back to demonstrate her normal hopeful veracity. Her gaze shifted all around as she thought about her unexpected time on Meligorn.

Although the person who had brought her there no longer spoke, she could feel his presence in her head and all around her. "Can you tell me your name?"

"Yes." There was a pause. "Call me...Burt."

Stephanie's lips curled into a smile. She flicked her finger against the blade of grass beside her. "Do I have a time limit on this test, Burt?"

This response was immediate. "The time it takes you to finish the test is an attribute that helps or hinders your score. We suggest taking a moderate time to answer questions to your fullest capabilities."

Her smile turned to a frown and her lips protruded. "Damn."

"Why are you so upset?"

She looked around once more and pulled up a piece of grass, ran her finger down it, and stared transfixed at its radiant colors. "I don't know what your job is, but I don't think I'll get a job that allows me off my planet. She waved a hand across the vista. "This is the closest I'll ever get to Meligorn in my life."

Her gaze lowered to the grass in her hand and a look of longing crept into her eyes. She tossed it to the side and drew her knees to her chest to rest her chin on them. "This will be the first and the last time that I experience this place. Which for me, is sad."

BURT responded in a curious tone, "Can you not visit the Federation Space in your Virtual Training?"

Stephanie snorted and allowed her knees to fall into a crossed-legged position. "Sorry, that was unladylike."

She set her palms firmly on the grass behind her and leaned on her arms to stretch her back and closed her eyes. As she groaned in the expectation of relief, she opened her eyes slightly and realized she only experienced this through VR. Although she could definitely feel the pull and stretch of her muscles, it did not actually happen. The knowledge of that was both incredibly interesting and strange at the same time.

Her fingers pressed firmly on the blades of grass and felt the small hairs that covered them. Curious, she sat upright once more, plucked another piece, and held it to her nose. Her eyes widened. "Wow, I can smell it."

Without thought, she popped it into her mouth and almost without hesitation, she yanked it out. She wrinkled her nose and sucked her cheeks in to pucker her lips into a tight circle. The taste lingered unpleasantly, and she shook her head wildly and forced herself to swallow the saliva in her mouth. "Nope. That was a bad choice. It smells good but tastes absolutely awful."

"I understand it is an acquired taste for humans on Meligorn," BURT responded.

She raised both eyebrows and flicked her fingers together to drop the grass on the ground. "I bet."

A splash to her right caught her attention and she turned quickly and rose onto her knees. With her mouth parted slightly and her eyes curious, she scanned the green pool of water and focused on the ripples in the center. She sat once more and allowed her shoulders to relax again. With her legs tucked beneath her and the palms of her hands on her thighs, she continued to study her surroundings.

She imagined that the ripples had been caused by some sort of Meligornian fish. *I wonder, if I jumped into the water, would I drown? What would it be like to have those last few minutes of breath and die, only to wake up in my pod? Would my life—so little that it has been so far—flash in front of my eyes? Would I see a light? Would I feel my soul lifted from me?*

BURT's voice pulled her from her thoughts. "You never told me why you cannot visit during your virtual training."

Stephanie's hands dropped and she plucked another blade of grass. She stared at it and flipped her finger over the top and hoped that her stalling for time to enjoy Meligorn wasn't too obvious. The truth was that she simply wanted one more minute—or as many as she could drag out—to enjoy her time there.

Her gaze shifted from the blade to stare at the water. "I don't have access to a full virtual rig at my school. We only have about fifty VR headsets, and half of those are broken. For some classes, we use tabletop learning and one class only uses the card games. To be honest, this is my first time ever in a pod. And the first time to ever be fully surrounded by Meligorn life."

BURT, up to that point, had not received the information formally that some—or many—of the students testing had never used a pod or been fully submerged within the Virtual World. He had never given it much computation power because his job was to run the Virtual World, not know the backgrounds of each individual who used the program. He therefore took that moment—while giving his student ample attention—to check on her and her opportunities.

The first thing he did was to replay and then research the comments she'd made about the types of instruction that she used in her educational institution. First, he compared the different training types, including VR headsets, table-top gaming, and card games. Once he had the statistics and the costs on those, he computed the differences between virtual training, the costs, and the results. When he completed that, he analyzed the data and determined that the outcome was not significantly fair.

BURT understood that if this student was under that type of educational curriculum, there had to be many more who experienced the same. Based on his calculations, most students without the full immersion would not learn to their fullest potential.

This did not make computational sense to him. He pulled up the success rate of different teaching styles and compared them to the success rate of immersion teaching. While the new ways of study did, in aggregate, bring better results than the old standard teaching method, there was a significant success bias toward those in the full immersion training. It often boiled down to focus. Which, in any teaching situation, could be the difference between a successful intake of information and one that only moderately increased the knowledge of a human brain. A full immersion rig allowed a student to focus fully on their training.

The information noted that students who trained under the old ways often tapered off intellectually during times of struggle and conflict, while those in immersion did not. There were no other life issues, including family, that would slow the process or bring emotional issues in when a student participated in the immersion style of training. The only time a student encountered such chemically triggered stimuli would be during their semester breaks when they were removed from the immersion pod and returned home to their family and their friends.

BURT began to pull the records for student B221ZA. This was not a normal activity for a subjective examination administer, but he was not human like the others. His examination of information was purely computational and was set up so as to not bring in any human emotion when considering the student's personal information. For BURT, it was merely another database he looked up.

Student B221ZA's records and personal information scrolled through his system. The student attended school in the Chicago NorAm Training System. He pulled up that system's financial logs for their educational program. A comparison with the others clearly indicated that this particular area was severely underfunded. From what BURT's programming told him, all school systems were to be equally funded dependent upon need, which in turn, was based on growth, population, and technological necessity. This directive did not match the school's financial records.

He found this information odd and pulled the information from the database on the history of the NorAm city of Chicago. He searched back twenty years to when a particularly bad storm had blown off the Great Lakes and destroyed a better part of the city. From what the data suggested, it required so much effort to rebuild that many of the largest companies chose to move their headquarters to other countries for tax purposes. With that, he could see by the numbers that the Chicago Training System's budget had left with them.

CHAPTER FIVE

On server BB6087 out of Washington DC, he detected a fight in progress between a group of students and Dreth pirates. The pirates were non-players—or NPCs—and were controlled by BURT and the system. They were there to train the two humans in fighting tactics.

Dreth was a planet of post-apocalyptic ruin brought about by an implosion of their own technology some two centuries before. Some of their ships had left and never returned, while others brought back technology to raise their people from ruin. Some of the intelligent but raw gangs had stolen ships and were raiders in space. They had become enemies to the humans and Meligorn people alike, as well as those Dreth left to recover on the planet.

BURT sensed that the battle took a quarter of one percent of a load—a goodly sum—and assumed the role of the main Dreth pirate in the battle. He calculated and pulled the statistics and data on the pirates to provide the best rendition possible.

These NPCs stood almost nine feet tall with broad muscular shoulders and had a light-green tint to their flesh. Huge jowls housed sharp teeth that protruded from their bottom jaw and up over their top lip. They wore shoulder pads made of the flesh of the Hycord, a large creature on Dreth that could only be compared to a massive dinosaur on Earth. The ropes that draped in crisscross fashion over their chests secured the teeth, limbs, and digits of those they had killed along the way.

They fought with large swords—and laser weapons if they had managed to raid a weapons ship in any of their travels. BURT used the training program that taught Dreth battle tactics to fight the two younger student humans in the simulated battle. It didn't take long for them both to succumb to his size and his weaponry. When they died, the scene shifted them to a small white room with a table and two chairs. There was no door and no windows, and the silence was almost painful to their ears.

Both humans looked around, unsure of where they were, and BURT spoke firmly. "This is Burt, your AI. Unfortunately, due to your choice of tactics, you have failed to kill the Dreth pirates. Instead, you both sustained terminal wounds. For this death, you are banished for two hours. According to our virtual rules, whenever a player dies, they must enter banishment for the allotted time set by…me. Enjoy your solitude."

His calculations projected that they would talk about what they had done and come up with a better solution. He released his control of the pirate lord and the uptick in load quickly settled. He tweaked the code for the pirate to update based on the latest news that came out of the Dreth Quadrant. It was vital to keep the training as up to date as possible.

The entire purpose of the Virtual Reality was training. Those who created the systems knew that both life and death were the most effective training methods that could be produced. They needed the trainees to understand that every choice they made came with repercussions in the end. Sometimes, they were good, but most of the time, they were bad.

Now, because there were "punishments" of sorts, there were some humans who simply did not care about the repercussions. When these humans were noticed, their training jackets were marked appropriately. Most of the time, they would be sent to the military as either cannon fodder or test pilots. Occasionally, a student would be chosen for a more entertaining future. They would be contestants on dangerous shows that were aired during prime time. The smartest of them, though, would be sent to deep space. These were thought to be heroic missions, and to accept one implied the utmost courage. It was not what you would find there that was the problem. Rather, it was the fact that those missions were almost always high risk.

It took a human with a healthy dose of either ignorance or the ability to ignore the very real risk of death to set off on those missions. Most would not come back.

When he checked his background process, BURT could tell that his student was steadily answering questions. He allowed another 0.005% of his load to switch his focus back to her. He would need to optimize the effort to focus directly on her so it didn't take so much of his load. Not only did he have an entire universe to control, he knew the engineers and programmers constantly monitored those numbers.

Stephanie had stood once more and walked gingerly through the grasses as she focused on the large mountains in the background. She wondered what it would be like to really be there. Most likely, she decided, it would be no different than what she experienced at that very moment.

"When the tests are completed, we will eject you and the serum will dissipate in your blood," BURT said and startled her.

She narrowed her eyes and looked up, even though she didn't know where he actually was. He noted the uptick in her vitals. "My apologies. I didn't mean to scare you."

Disgruntled, she simply shrugged, kicked her boots through the vegetation, and continued to toy with a blade of grass. "I guess I have to leave the pod sometime. I don't think these are made for people to stay long-term."

"That is correct. They are not fully equipped for stays exceeding a day or two at most," BURT replied. "I must ask you, though. Why is it that you wish to stay? Do you not have friends and family outside the pod? Human connections that are important to you? Is it only to visit Meligorn?"

Stephanie shook her head and looked at her boots as the blue grass rubbed along them and left streaks of dew on the tops and sides. "Burt, I want to do something with my life, not simply feel like I'm unneeded, unappreciated, and stuck in a dead-end life going nowhere."

She waved her hand to the side, dropped the piece of grass, and watched as it fluttered to land a few feet away from her. "I know I can be somebody. But what can I do to have that chance? My parents do everything they can. They provide me with food and shelter. Chicago isn't the city it was in the past. There is no longer life in the falling-down metropolis. My friend Laura says that Los Angeles has better weather, but the schools are a crap shoot, whether or not they are any good, too."

BURT did not respond immediately but ran rapid research. From his records, it seemed that almost all the Los Angeles schools had more usable budgets than B221ZA's school system. However, he chose not to inform her of that. He had learned a long time before—around the time of his creation—that humans didn't always appreciate knowing the facts.

Stephanie continued to walk while she stared at the beautiful sky. An odd sense that something wasn't right made her freeze and she glanced ahead. She had almost fallen from a very high cliff. With a low chuckle, she backed away and settled her nerves. While she might not actually die in real life if she fell off the cliff, it still wasn't something she really wanted to experience.

She narrowed her eyes and studied a large field that stretched below. Animals there ranged in colors, and they grazed much like a deer would back on Earth. They were beautiful, with short, vibrant fur and crystal-blue eyes that somehow glimmered brightly even from where she stood. She looked at her hands and turned to continue her walk.

"You are probably sitting in a good office and have plans to go out this weekend. If I had my choice, I'd live in the VR world and learn as much as I could about everything. I need to know more."

"Why?" he asked.

BURT suddenly registered a 0.3% uptick in his load. He studied it for a moment and immediately wondered why his student's body back in the pod had clenched its fists. That was a very rare reaction. He sent queries down the line into the old but still in good condition immersion pod. When the results echoed back to him, he found that the pod itself was working within, and well beyond, expected parameters. Somehow, this student felt enough in the Virtual World to pass through the gates that separated her experiences in the VR training scenario and her physical body.

It had reacted on a physical level as if she were awake in the pod, but that couldn't happen because her consciousness was recorded in the Virtual World. He flipped through his data from the last eighteen years and tried to find circumstances of when the same thing had happened. There were only half a dozen instances and three of them were due to physical abnormalities that caused tremors in their bodies. It was not only very rare, it was almost unheard of.

BURT attempted to take more readings from her body but found that he was unable to do so. The earlier VR pods did not have the same neuro-hookups the present versions had. The old model would not enable him to delve deeper into her physical acumen than he already had, which left a question on her physical responses.

Stephanie had no idea that any of that had happened. She was too absorbed in her walk along the edge of the cliffs and thoughts about her life, her dreams, and all the things she kept hidden from the people around her in the real world. Mostly, she walked in silence.

She finally answered BURT and her voice lowered and her eyes lost focus. "Because...I want to matter."

He remained silent. A few moments later, her lips pressed tightly together, and she looked up with a new sense of confidence that had been so noticeably absent in the moments before. She spoke louder and with more authority. "Burt, what is the fastest time someone has taken on this part of the test?"

Without a second's pause, he replied. "Forty-seven minutes and twenty-two seconds."

Stephanie tapped her fingers on her legs. "Did they finish?"

"No," he replied.

"Okay." She rolled her eyes.

Sheesh, whoever is talking sure does answer like a robot. Maybe they're related to Abbott. She resumed her stroll. "What is the fastest passing grade finish?"

Again, he replied without hesitation. "Forty-seven minutes and forty-three seconds."

She fired back quickly. "And the longest?"

"One hour and thirty-seven minutes flat."

Stephanie nodded and drummed her fingers on her lips. "If I finish early, is it okay to record that result but let me stay here in Meligorn until my time's up?"

BURT did not respond immediately. He had to calculate and review the information in order to answer that question. From the laws, rules, and regulations, it didn't seem as if it would be a problem. But was she asking him to record the best time or the final time? He decided the ideal way to find that answer would be to test the student. "If you pass with a seventy percent in all subjects, I will allow you to stay. Based on your results, I will provide you a grading curve for the amount of time."

Stephanie smiled and pumped her fist. "Yesss."

BURT entered an immediate caveat. "*However…*"

She sighed and her shoulders sagged.

"If you fail, it will not matter what time you take," he continued. "But you cannot stay on this part of the test for longer than the worst time for a passing grade."

Her eyes narrowed as she mulled all that information over in her head to make sure she had it straight. To her, it really sounded like a no-lose situation. She stared at the sky and gave a thumbs-up. "Deal."

Stephanie sighed with a big grin on her face as she laid back in the soft grass and folded her arms on her stomach. She wiggled her shoulders a few times to get as comfortable as she could. Her eyes unfocused and her mind began to wander. She recalled the time she had sat with her friend Jaqueline, talking about what it was like to simply open her mind and be in the moment.

It felt like freedom, she had finally told her. *Floating on the clouds, a disembodied voice answering questions as they came in through the speakers.*

She focused her vision back on the faint planets that hovered above her in the evening sky. That was exactly what she would do for the test. She would answer the questions with the answers she drew from her subconscious. Pass or fail, she would finish as quickly as possible and enjoy the rest of the time in Meligorn. Perhaps she would even be able to talk magic to someone before she had to leave.

BURT spoke from the "speakers in the sky." "Let's begin the subjective part of the test."

CHAPTER SIX

"Give an example from your knowledge of Meligorn how human electricity is not compatible with the planet?" BURT asked slowly to complete the subjective section of the testing.

Stephanie grinned, having studied Meligorn extensively. "Electricity is not, and has never been, part of the infrastructure on the planet. The Magical Unit Spectrum is the energy which radiates on Meligorn for over six units' distance from the planet. Therefore, while it is possible to land an Earth ship on the planet, it will never be able to leave. The electricity is drained almost immediately. A simpler example would be if I brought a flashlight here. I would be able to turn it on, but it would only last a few seconds before the magic drained the batteries."

There was a pause before BURT spoke again. "Next question. With your knowledge of the Dreth pirates, how do you believe they should be handled?"

She sat and rubbed her chin as she considered this. "That's a good one. Well, on one hand, we are all living creatures, and on Earth—at least in NorAm—we have what's called due justice. We try them for their crimes and decide their punishment. From what I understand, Dreth pirates are shoot-to-kill if seen. It is difficult for me to fully know, but judging from both Dreth's reaction and the Federation, I would say that if they are that dangerous, we should have a way to eliminate the danger. If that is the only option, we must do what is necessary. But I have to stress that without further research, I can't give you a really good, honest opinion here."

BURT recorded the answers in his system. "Well done. Next question. If all humans were capable of wielding Meligorn magic on Earth, what do you believe should be one of its first uses?"

Stephanie laid back and rested her arm over her head. "That's easy. Restore NorAm. Go to all the places that have been devastated and repair them. Bring the commerce back. Bring jobs back. Make it a place where all can strive and be given the same opportunities for the future. My number two would be to fix the damage we have done to the planet for so long. We have sustained life, but we have not improved it. It would be time for improvements."

"The subjective portion of the testing is halfway complete. It is standard for the testing that the subjective portion is broken up into two separate time periods. Give me a few moments and I will return to move into the objective portion."

Stephanie smiled and crossed her legs at the ankles. She wasn't sure if she had aced that or not. There were quite a few questions, but she'd said what was in her mind and she had responded quickly. Even if she had put more time into the thought of her answer, she probably would have said the same thing. It helped to be there on Meligorn, though. To smell the flowers and watch the purple sky turn to night as the stars shimmered and the two planets glistened. It was everything she had ever dreamed of.

BURT readied the test, pleased with how she had done on the first part of the subjective questions. She was quick and showed deep morality that was based on facts and supported by evidence. He rarely had a chance to speak to the students, but she had done far better than he expected from her. And it didn't end there.

He remained silent and applied his own focus as he presented Stephanie with the objective testing questions. Her answers were almost instantaneous, often before he gave her the options to choose from. She was on top of all of it and seemed to have obtained information as effectively as those students from full immersion schools had. During the portions of the objective testing that involved multiple part answers, she breezed through. Out of one hundred questions, she only opened her eyes one time to review the different parts before she made her selection. The rest, she simply answered without hesitation.

Otherwise, she simply blurted her responses as if she were on a game show and tried to beat her opponent on the clock. BURT could tell that she was incredibly talented at testing in a strenuous situation since it was her first time in a pod. He was slightly curious how she would do if he dropped her on Dreth in the post-apocalyptic landscape, but he couldn't do that. It might screw her scores up.

"What is the Sphinx?" he asked.

Stephanie didn't hesitate. "In Greek Mythology, the Sphinx is a winged monster having a woman's head and a lion's body. It propounded a riddle about the three ages of man and killed those who failed to solve it until Oedipus was successful, whereupon the Sphinx committed suicide. It is also an ancient Egyptian stone figure having a lion's body and a human or animal head—especially the huge statue near the Pyramids of Giza. Sphinx in common language can also refer to an enigmatic person. And last but not least, it is another term for a hawk moth."

BURT paused for a moment before he launched into the next one. "What is the better part of valor?"

She smiled. "Discretion is the better part of valor—said by Falstaff in King Henry the Fourth, Part one, William Shakespeare."

"What is the square root of the cosine of twelve?"

Stephanie took two seconds of thought and her gaze flickered and narrowed before she answered. "0.91861523976."

"Wow," BURT replied. He'd never had a human compute math, especially trigonometry, that quickly without a calculator.

Each and every time a question from the math category was presented, a calculator would appear for her to use. Twice, she didn't use it at all and simply spouted the answer. BURT wanted to watch the entire thing, but he reminded himself of his real responsibility, which was to focus on the Virtual World. The student was merely an unauthorized diversion that happened to be entertaining—as far as an AI could be entertained, of course.

Accordingly, he decided he had to move into the background to handle an issue in Australia. There was a commerce problem on server 14edZedA in Sydney. Whether he resolved quickly this because he rushed or because he gave himself a little more load was unclear. However, by the time he returned, she had completed the remaining questions for that group. He checked her time. Then, he checked it again.

Stephanie was only at twelve minutes. She had answered half the subjective questions and all the objective ones in a very short time. Possibly the shortest time yet, but she still had a fair number ahead of her. BURT went through the responses, reviewed all the questions coming up, removed the duplicates that would gather no more information than the first time she had answered, and created his own questions and slipped them into the queue.

Forty-six minutes and twelve seconds later, she had finished all the tests. Both the core of the standardized tests—BURT believed that to call them standardized was a fallacy, but no one ever asked his opinion—and the extra questions he wanted to test. It wasn't the fastest time ever recorded but it was damn close, and with the extra questions he had asked, it would have ended sooner had he not added them. It was important, though, to calculate her total intelligence to give her the best chance possible of being accepted into a program. With the statistics the way they were, the system was already working against her.

He spent time calculating and recalculating her score to make sure that everything had been done correctly. His initial result was a pass with a ninety-eight percent accuracy on the standardized tests. That was phenomenal—a better score than the kids from more affluent backgrounds achieved and were accepted for. BURT, being the system that he was, took one last thorough look through the answers and the score. He realized that it didn't account for the third pass for accuracy on a math question. Stephanie had completed the question but had not answered correctly, which was odd to him since she had completed the more difficult ones with ease.

BURT recalculated her grade for the missed question and then reviewed it again to make sure that it was correctly presented. Although he was not known for errors, he did have a small margin of error on occasion. The question, however, was correctly presented. Curious, he pulled her school teaching plan and attendance for the time period in which that specific math skill would have been taught. He scanned through the plans and finally found the lesson. When he compared it to her school attendance, it looked as if she had been absent from class that day. Furthermore, she had not received a take-home review.

He would not be able to change her grade. She had answered the question incorrectly, but he could do a little calculation based on her previous grades, attendance, and knowledge to know the probable outcome. It looked as if she would probably have aced the test had she not missed the class discussion. Such a small mistake to make for such an important future event.

When he continued with the evaluation of her answers, he found that she had passed his more advanced questions with sixty-seven percent. When he'd originally compiled the questions, his calculations estimated a twenty-three percent pass ratio, and to him, that would have been a solid return. She had gone above and beyond. Now, it was time to finish the last half of the subjective questions.

Those rapidly became BURT's favorites. He was given the opportunity to delve into the psyche of the student and attempt to understand how they thought and what past things in their childhood affected the way they answered the questions. It was fascinating, not so much because of the answers but because there were questions that he was only able to calculate the possible score on to a certain point. How would you calculate something that includes an opinion?

And Stephanie had some really unique ones.

The programmers were busy at work, tallying up scores, finishing the testings for different students, and making sure the rest of the programs ran smoothly at the same time. They kept a close watch on BURT during certain periods to ensure that his computational focus was spread. They had to take care of the students and still keep the Virtual Realm Training programs functioning at top speed for those in the middle of learning.

Two of the programmers who sat at the end of the row kept their fingers moving constantly on the keyboard. One of them paused, however, narrowed his eyes, and looked at the data on his screen. He elbowed the guy next to him. "Take a look at BURT's load numbers. I show a spike of two percent across the system."

The other man brought the screen up and began to search for where it was coming from. "Strange. I can't seem to pinpoint the location."

Slowly, the load receded, and both programmers shrugged. "It must have been a normal load increase for this time of year," the second man said. "It's already starting to decrease."

They both agreed and continued with system checks and other duties they had to finish by the end of the day. BURT had already figured out that he didn't want any humans to check on his efforts with this student. He wasn't sure why or even how it calculated into his system, but he was…enjoying…it too much to be disrupted by the nosey humans on the other side.

To ensure that no one even checked on her progress and looked at the notations in the system, BURT had wiped her job from the queue as if it were already completed. Unless she completely flubbed the next part, he would certainly provide her a green recommendation. From there, though, it was completely out of his hands. Then again, it should never have been in them in the first place. Silly Engineers.

Aaron whistled as he waited for the next section of his student's testing. He had managed to divert any more complete assholes. Gene gestured once more to remove the sound barrier. "BURT spiked two percent in his load."

He sat up quickly and pulled up the reports. It had already begun to recede but that was not a normal thing to happen. "Shit. We need to keep an eye on that. It might mean something in the whole system is a problem."

His friend immediately clenched his hands together, a drop of sweat on his forehead. "That hasn't happened in a few years, but damn if I don't remember when it did. We had our asses handed to us. I don't want to do that again anytime soon."

Aaron shook his head. "I'm right there with you."

CHAPTER SEVEN

Aaron listened closely to the student's response and forwarded it through in the computer system to be analyzed. He pushed the student back to the virtual earth and allowed the pod AI to take over from there. There was nothing else he had to do for them. As soon as the screen disappeared, he removed his helmet and motioned the virtual interface away. He cracked his neck and pulled up his screen. The list of students in the queue was completely empty, which included the one he had passed over to BURT.

"Let's see how you're doing out there in virtual land," he mumbled quietly as he brought up the stats.

He checked BURT's load since it had shot up by two whole percentage points earlier that evening. However, when he looked at it after everything had been queued out, it didn't seem abnormal in the least. He shrugged. "Huh. It must have been some sort of anomaly. Or those idiot kids playing teams on the Dreth starship training session again. I don't care. Time's up for me."

With real relief, he clicked his system off and straightened his papers to make sure his desk looked somewhat presentable for the next work day. He grinned, stood, and leaned back until he heard his back pop. "Yesssssss…." he moaned in delight and covered his mouth hastily when he realized the sound barrier was no longer up.

He turned to apologize and saw that he was the only one left in the office. Aaron scowled. He hated it when that happened. The sound barriers were so good and with the helmet on, there was really no way to tell what went on in the office behind him. The only time he knew was when there was some sort of fire drill because it flashed across the screen.

Hastily, he fumbled for his jacket and flung it around to drag his arms through the sleeves. He snatched up his helmet, his file keys, and a couple of other effects, tossed them in the large bottom drawer of his desk, and locked it with a key he kept around his neck. With one hand, he tucked the necklace under his shirt and used his other hand to throw a wad of paper he had missed in the trash. None of them had to worry about cleaning up at the end of the night. They had clean-up droids for that, the best invention he could think of. He'd tried to con his boss into letting him have one for home but that was a negative.

Either way, he didn't have to worry about his mess too much. They would come in, sanitize the space, and spritz the scent for the next programmer to come in and take the third shift. He felt bad for that dude. The man had done that shift for a long time and it was more than boring. The only things they had to worry about were the countries that used the system in their time zones, but NorAm kept such a tight lock on their training programs that the numbers overseas were nothing compared to their own.

He stepped out of his cube and the lights dimmed behind him. Gene had probably been gone for quite a while. And, as usual, he kept his desk immaculate. It looked like the droids had already been there.

Aaron looked at his forearm and his info-tablet. In the right-hand corner, it showed he had a missed voicemail message. He swiped his hand across and brought up the play icon, pressed it, and waited as his audio piped into the tiny headphone jack in his ear.

"Hey, you big sausage. I have to go watch my kid sister dive into a big bathtub so her school can gain points and possible credits to get better hardware. Got to go root for the home team. See you tomorrow for drinks if you have time. Let me know. I'm out, brotha!"

Aaron laughed as Gene ended his message with a succession of guitar impressions that sounded more like weird lasers from a broken alien ship. "Weeooh weeohh weer weer weer."

He didn't know what his friend was on every day, but the dude was always at a level three stories above him. He loved him, though. Gene was his best friend and his cohort at work. They were engineers, so what did people expect? Of course they would be a little strange.

With the last high-pitched wail, Gene hung up. Aaron flipped to the message app and typed against his arm to send a quick message in response. He knew that if he didn't, Gene would blow him up when he planned to be completely knocked out, asleep. **Drinks tomorrow sounds good.**

Aaron sent the message and pulled the sleeve of his jacket down. He adjusted his bag on his shoulder and retrieved his keys from his pocket. When he reached the door, he found one of the droids already waiting impatiently if the little circling red light was any indication. He tapped it on the metal top. "Don't be in such a rush. The other droids will think you're brown-nosing and stage a coup."

The mechanical made a succession of noises and Aaron chuckled. "The bitch just cussed me out. And after all the brilliance I showed today? No love. No love at all."

He tapped the button to open the door and glanced back to make sure he hadn't left anything behind. The droid was already buzzing swiftly around the floor to clean up all the trash. Aaron glanced at the big screen where BURT's load percentage was displayed. He laughed and slapped the side of the door frame as he walked out.

"And he was worried I would break BURT." Aaron snickered as he turned the corner and took the stairs for exercise.

Stephanie had ended up beside the crystal-clear green-tinted pond. While it was definitely green, it didn't look anything like the algae-infested ones on Earth. It was so pretty, and she could see different creatures swimming beneath the surface. She leaned back and put her arms under her head, but then sat up with a frown. "Burt?"

"Yes?" he replied.

She began to feel a little guilty. *Damn, is he only waiting on me? That has to be a horrible job.*

After a deep breath, she shook her head and tried to keep a pleading note out of her voice. "Can I have a chance to speak with an ArchMage?"

"No," BURT replied immediately.

Stephanie exhaled a deep breath and hung her head as she drew her legs in and crossed them. She picked at the grass, disappointed but uncertain what to say. Before she could get too down, though, BURT continued. "I can provide a teacher, which I believe is more what you need. An ArchMage would speak of theories and postulations enough to make an AI's head explode. And trust me, that is not a fun thing to witness. The whole entire Virtual Realm could collapse right on top of your head."

She raised her head up excitedly and turned it to the side, a look of confusion on her face. "AI's don't have heads."

"Sure, they do, just not human heads. In fact, that is technically all they are. A big giant brain. And I'm not joking about what an ArchMage can do to their system. One of the first AI's to work with a Meligornian ArchMage had so many non-reality checks to what they were doing, the AI almost melted in an attempt to find congruence between magic and technology. The technology is what runs Earth. The systems aren't made to understand something as complex and unmathematical as magic. They can run algorithms all day long and into the next year and they will never be able to represent their theories and the idea of magic. It's better to learn to create it than listen to it explained."

Stephanie pursed her lips. "Sooo, if it will melt an AI's brain, what does it do to the human brain?"

There was a long pause before BURT replied, "There is no calculation I care to do to determine whether an ArchMage would melt a young adult human's brain. However, I have witnessed humans interacting with an ArchMage and from what I could tell, their cerebral activity remained on an even plane through the whole experience. For now, though, I thought a teacher would be a good way to start."

Her avatar's eyes lit up with excitement. She jumped to her feet and wiped her hands off on her jumpsuit. "A teacher? That would be great!"

The Meligornians were considered by humans to be mystical creatures. They fit the physical description of magical creatures in human lore called elves, and while they definitely did have an elf-like physical stature, they were not haughty. Their ears were pointed, and they had long black hair and generally wore a mischievous smile. When they first came to Earth—mostly by accident—the people immediately fell in love with their kind. There were ArchWizards on their planet who had experimented with gates and ended up on Earth. That was when they were brought into the Federation.

What people enjoyed most about them was their cheerful and upbeat spirit. Although they did not fit the mold of an elf like the old tales of the Hobbit, they were definitely a mystery. They enjoyed laughter and usually had a very good outlook on life. Except, of course, for those who had been around for most of their usual three hundred and fifty years of life. They might not have been immortal, but to the humans who were lucky to make it to ninety years, they seemed that way. Their long life intrigued many people on Earth, who hoped to figure out their secret, but it wasn't something to be shared.

Stephanie was nervous. She wrung her hands in front of her and looked at her surroundings. Small flowering plants had come up, attracted by the moons. They glowed brightly all around her, and she couldn't think of a better place to learn magic. "You know, I read that the older Meligornians grump more and laugh less. Just like humans."

BURT watched as the teacher stepped out of the wood line dressed in long, flowing blue and gold robes. His hair cascaded over his shoulders and his expression was kindly. "I would grump too if I were three hundred and fifty years old."

She spun at the sound of his voice. The teacher had been patterned after a Meligornian teacher who was based in Switzerland. Immediately, he drew Stephanie in and began to teach her small magical tricks to get her energy flowing. Her eyes were wide with excitement. It was fairly rare to find humans who could practice magic, but even BURT was surprised by what Stephanie accomplished in her first attempts.

Granted, it was definitely a small test, but most humans didn't deal well with magic concepts, so something almost always went wrong.

The teacher and Stephanie continued to work on the base of all magic.

"Yes, that is correct." M'rick beamed at his pupil. "The way of magic is the way of one's feelings and emotions. The power is thought, and the energy follows the intent. It is usually subtle, and it is best to learn how to use the power with cantrips."

Stephanie bit her bottom lip. "What is a cantrip?"

M'rick smiled. "Small spoken commands applied with both the power and the intent and focused to bring a physical result into existence."

Her eyes went wide. "Ohhhh. Like the string of books and movies that came out in the early 2000s called *Harry Potter*. They used wands, but really, they only needed the spells. The words would make something happen."

The teacher looked thoughtful. "I don't know who this Harry fellow is, but yes, something like that. We don't need any props like wands, though. Humans have a very broad imagination when it comes to magic."

She nodded and felt a little sheepish. The only person who would have appreciated that reference would have been Todd. But she was having so much fun. The happiness she felt to be able to speak with a real Meligornian was more than she ever thought would happen. She was glued to his every word and had completely lost track of time.

BURT wanted to see what would happen and so sped up the time in the Virtual World. For every hour in real time on Earth, she was given three hours inside the Virtual world. Typically, two hours was the most that was sustainable. However, she wouldn't be in the virtual environment for that long. If he had emotions, sadness would be the key one. The thought of her talented and brilliant mind not having a chance to come back the next day made no real sense to him.

In human terms, it was unfair, and to an AI—statistically and mathematically—it had absolutely no logic. He knew he'd give her the green light, but that meant nothing when it came to decisions made by a human. They had their own weird way to figure things out and BURT had begun to suspect that they didn't necessarily follow regulations.

Either way, Stephanie wanted to make the most of the opportunity so that she could learn as much as she possibly could. BURT wanted that opportunity as well so that he could learn from her. He also felt the need to make sure she had more than enough time—a gift from him for doing so well on the tests and, perhaps, a small compensation for her unfortunate life situation. Her circumstances meant her intelligence might be lost in the shuffle, all because of the greed of some humans. He found that untenable.

M'rick's eyes opened wide and mischief sparkled in the corners. "Here is a cantrip. Let's see if you burn your eyebrows off, little one."

CHAPTER EIGHT

Stephanie took a step back, her eyes wide, and watched M'rick. His hands gestured wildly in a circle in front of him. They moved close to his body, his arms bent at the elbows. His fingers stood long and stiff, all except his pointer finger which was bent at the first crease. She followed their circular movement and the tiny sparks of light that bounced off them. It wasn't anything she had seen before, but she knew that wasn't the trick he tried to show her.

As he continued the motions, he closed his eyes and began to talk in his native tongue, using his words to create the magic. "T'lercten, T'suman. Kluman depen stahk."

He repeated the words twice and grew louder the second time. His right hand stopped, and he opened his eyes. While still moving his left in a circle, he turned his right hand over, palm up, and curled his fingers to make a cupping action. Inside, blue flames flickered brightly and grew stronger with every motion of his other hand. They shimmered in the moonlight, but his flesh remained perfectly cool.

BURT hadn't been able to sit idly in one spot before, and he now watched the magic of the Meligornian. It was fascinating, especially since he couldn't regulate it in his system. He could not replicate it with math or statistics. There was no computing power within his capabilities to make it understandable on any level in the human world.

The teacher's left hand made a couple more laps and finally stopped. He turned that hand over, palm up, and created the same cupping action as he had with his right. Inside, yellow flames flickered. They seemed to dance with the blue ones, mimicked their movements, and reversed them. Stephanie oohed from a few feet away but M'rick didn't look at her. Instead, he stared intently at the flames as he grew them higher and higher inside his hands. It was obviously something he enjoyed doing and probably didn't get to do very often, especially with a human audience.

The flames flared high and subsided in turns. He put on a show for them, and BURT enjoyed it. The teacher restored the flames to their original height and smirked. He poured them from his left hand into his right, and the blaze turned green before he opened his hand and swung it in small circles. The flames rolled with him, smoothly across the surface of his skin, but never left even a faint red mark.

As a finish, he jiggled the tiny blazes back and forth for a moment and threw them high. When he caught them with his other hand, he put it to his lips and blew hard. A large multi-colored flame shot out at least nine feet in front of him and dissipated into small sparkling ash that floated toward the sky and disappeared into the bank of glittering stars above them. He opened his palms again and the flames remained and danced back and forth, restored to their original colors.

He laughed and looked at the human, a smile on his face. As he caught sight of her hands, his smile faded and he opened his mouth. Not wishing to seem surprised, he closed it again quickly and regained his composure. BURT had never seen a Meligornian teacher that surprised before, at least not to the point where he had no words for the human in front of him. He had seen enough of them to know they were not beings easily rendered speechless. They usually had something to say, even if it was funny or joyous.

However, in that moment, closed mouth or not, he was completely taken aback. The young human giggled with real excitement, opened her right palm, and cupped it over and over again. Inside, a small red flame glimmered and danced. She concentrated and made it a little larger for a moment and allowed it to shrink once more. Entranced, she opened her palm, vibrated her hand and watched the flame roll over her skin like he had done with his larger ones.

It grew a little more and she caught it quickly with her other hand. She cupped both hands together and showed M'rick what she had done. A smile pulled at the sides of his lips as his gaze danced from her hands to her face. Stephanie grinned from ear to ear, shocked that she had actually made the magic work. Her gaze bounced back and forth from her flame to his two and back again.

M'rick extended one palm and bounced his hand up and down. The flame responded as if it were a ball in his palm. Stephanie narrowed one eye and gave a closed-lip grin as she did the same with her two hands together. She could feel the energy bouncing up and down in her hands. After a few minutes, she pursed her lips and stared longingly at her flame. BURT could tell that she tried to do something to it, but whatever it was, it wasn't working.

After a few moments, she frowned. "How come I didn't get your colors?"

The teacher let his mouth tilt to a full smile and he leaned his head back and laughed loudly. He clapped his hands together to extinguish what was left of the flames. "I think, my dear, your question shouldn't be about the color. The important question is how did you get any flames at all? I have never seen a human manage the flame cantrip on their first try. Most of the time, not even until their third or fourth try. This is phenomenal."

Stephanie blushed slightly, still focused on the flames in her hands. M'rick folded his arms across his chest and tilted his head. "Have you studied Meligornian focus before?"

She continued to stare at her small blaze and admired what she had achieved. However, it soon began to die out and slowly grew smaller and smaller until it extinguished in a small puff of shimmering ash. The question that had been asked had taken her focus away.

"Drat."

Stephanie mimicked M'rick, clapped her hands together, and brushed the remaining ash off her palms and into the grass below. She felt his gaze upon her and knew that he wanted an answer to his question. The truth was, she had been so mesmerized by her accomplishment that she hadn't even thought about it.

She shook her head and smiled at him. "Do what? Oh, no. I have never studied the Meligornian focus before. In fact, I didn't even know the flames or the cantrips were possible. It was all very new to me. You told me to focus. I couldn't understand the words that you used, so I made my own up. I didn't actually think it would work until the dancing red flame appeared. But sadly, no, this is my first and probably last time studying your art of magic. It's always fascinated me."

M'rick raised an eyebrow and studied her. "Most early human magic users chose to learn the Meligornian words so early human magic relied on those. I have never seen a human make up their own cantrip. That is usually reserved for the teachers and the ArchMage."

Stephanie twisted her lips and tapped her side awkwardly. "Is that a bad thing?"

He chuckled. "No, it isn't a bad thing, merely surprising. But tell me, because I am very curious. What were the words you used?"

She looked nervously at him for a moment and put her right hand out, palm up, once more. While he watched intently, she drew a deep breath in through her nose and blew it out of her mouth. She focused her attention on the center of her palm and began to repeat the words she had said originally. "Candle light, candle bright, grant me your flame tonight."

She concentrated harder and repeated it, louder this time. As soon as she had spoken the last word, the flame ignited in her palm and made her jump slightly. It was blue and considerably larger than the first. She glanced nervously at the teacher and back at her flame. He looked completely astounded by it all. She extended her other hand and poured the blue flame into her other palm. It shook slightly and for a second, turned yellow, then green before it settled into red.

Stephanie furrowed her brow and shook the flame several times in her hands. She narrowed her eyes and stared hard in an attempt to change the color again. No matter how hard she tried, she was stuck with the red flame. She straightened and pursed her lips in irritation. "Well, that bites."

M'rick immediately slapped his hands against hers several times until the flames were extinguished. She pulled her head back, startled, as he turned her hands over and back again as if looking for something. His gaze caught hers. "Where are you hurt? I can fix it for you."

She blinked for several moments until she finally realized what had happened. His concern was real, though, so she gripped her stomach and tried not to laugh. The teacher looked at her and his face reminded her of a human trying to figure out where a puzzle piece fitted. "What are these words, and what do you mean, bites?"

Stephanie giggled and rubbed the ash from her hands. The particles shimmered faintly on the ground. She wasn't even sure how to explain it and hadn't thought for a moment that the sarcasm and small dialectic moments would be something they hadn't picked up by that point. At the same time, they lived on their planet and the humans lived on their own. There was not that much co-mingling between the different species.

BURT could sense Stephanie's stats start to rise. The Meligornian teacher struggled to understand her and it was obvious that she struggled to find the words. He decided that, without letting Stephanie know it, he would directly take over the avatar of the teacher and wizard who stood in front of her. Besides, he wanted to know more and to learn more from her. This was the perfect opportunity to do so.

With BURT now in control, M'rick straightened and the concerned and confused look slid from his face. Immediately, Stephanie's vitals settled. She had thought for a moment that she had done something wrong and nervousness had spiked very quickly. The small assurance that M'rick was impressed and surprised was all she needed to calm her nerves. In reality, she had done nothing wrong and almost everything right.

BURT was used to weaving in and out of the system to fix problems and assume a character when it was needed but generally, he seldom hung out that often. This was a whole new ball game for him. His interaction with this human during the initial testing had provided more insights than he usually received with the small interactions during VR NPC negotiations with Player Characters—or even the large battles where chaos ruled.

The chaotic moments were usually when BURT learned the most about humans. The things they did when the world around them was no longer stable and they were faced with hard and even sudden choices were often enlightening. But this student had provided him with an entirely new way to understand or learn from them. He did, after all, run the entire program for them to train on. It was good that he was able to learn more about them so he could tailor the worlds to them, not merely based on statistics.

Everything that had happened was a shock to everyone involved.

CHAPTER NINE

Several very awkward moments of silence ensued during which Stephanie rocked back and forth on her heels and M'rick merely blinked at her. BURT averted the teacher's gaze when he realized that humans really didn't respond well when someone stared at them. Especially not an elf-like creature who knew how to do magic. It could be somewhat intimidating…and creepy. Definitely on the creeper scale.

"Um…" She flipped the hair out of her face from her braid that had begun to unravel. It seemed that the Virtual Reality geniuses got the annoying pieces of life correct too.

Stephanie pressed her tongue against her molar, her mouth slightly open and her eyes narrowed. She tried to think of the best way to describe what she meant, which was something of a challenge because she wasn't used to people not understanding English slang. But she was on someone else's planet, though, so it only made sense that confusion would be the reaction.

She put her hands out. "I wanted the flame to stay green. So, when it went red again, I didn't like the result."

BURT wanted her to think the teacher in the system was the same. "And that is when it bit you?"

Stephanie chuckled but almost immediately forced a straight face. "No, it didn't bite me at all. When I said it bites, it means I didn't like the outcome."

The teacher put his hands together. "So not that the flame bit you."

She shook her head. "Uh, no. I probably would have had more of an adverse reaction if the flame bit me."

The teacher nodded but his face still revealed some slight confusion. "We tend to be a straight-forward species when we talk about things like that."

Stephanie grinned and swung a leg back and forth. "Do you know many English idioms? We have a lot of them and even I get confused sometimes."

Immediately, BURT wanted to say yes and list the various English idioms compiled in his language database. A dime a dozen, beat around the bush, bite the bullet, break a leg, speak of the devil, and the list went on and on. However, he wasn't about to answer that question as the digital equivalent to God. It would not be realistic and if she were to ever face a Meligornian in the flesh, she would surely struggle with that. They would have no idea what she was talking about and could even possibly take some of the idioms as a threat. For example, pull yourself together, costs an arm and a leg, wrap your head around something. Those could be completely confusing.

As it was, he played a Meligornian who was supposed to be on his own planet. They would have zero idea of what she was talking about.

"No," he shook his head. "I don't even speak English. We use a spell to converse at the moment."

Stephanie shaped her lips into an "o." "Ohhh, okay. I didn't even think about that. I guess that would make sense. My naivety played a role in that one. Or maybe my inability to think beyond myself. I didn't even consider it when you began to speak English, but I should have known. I have studied your planet and you have a very distinct and separate language. Only the higher officials and ArchMage tend to speak fluently in English. My apologies."

The teacher bowed peacefully. "Accepted. However, it might be worth your while to learn some of our customs and language. For example, when you approach a Meligornian, you place your right hand out, grip their forearm while you raise your left hand diagonally, fingers tight, and bow your head. If they are royal, you press your hands together and do not attempt to touch them. When the bow is complete, you raise your head and say, 'Kaitel Gorniffula.' It is a gender-neutral greeting that in your language means blessed to meet you."

She bowed and stretched her hand out with the other held in front of her. "Kaitel Gorniffula."

He bowed too and took her arm. "Very good."

When she straightened, Stephanie bit the inside of her lip. "What if I need to discuss something of grave importance. How do I say that?"

The teacher nodded and held his hands behind his back. "It is customary to always keep your hands latched behind your back when speaking casually. Then you would say, 'Hycenthia Overlum Hippoguard Alsuvia.'"

Stephanie pursed her lips and placed her hands behind her back. "Hycethia Overlum Hippoguard Alsuvia. That's a lot to remember."

He chuckled. "It is. But with practice, you can learn the language. At the same time, though, there is a spell to turn the words spoken into the receiver's preferred language. It is an advanced spell and you would need control over your magic. You can ask the other person, 'Engotish Preferatus Ingorna Discusio.' This asks if they mind speaking in English."

Her eyes glazed slightly but she doubled her focus, determined to remember. "Engotish Preferatus Ingorna Discusio. I should have brought a note pad."

They both laughed. Stephanie repeated both phrases in a whisper. These would be important if she actually ever had the ability to go to Meligorn in real life. Even if she got to go there in the Virtual pods, actually, but that was about as unlikely as the first. "How about when it is time to say goodbye?"

The teacher smiled. "This depends on whom you are speaking to.

With an elder, you kiss the back of their hand. With a royal, you bow low with your hands pressed together. If it is a friend, you can repeat the initial greeting. As far as speech goes, you would say, 'Fortunata Elfortina Gratias.' It means may fortune and thankfulness fill your souls."

Stephanie was taken aback. "That is such a nice way to say goodbye. Humans usually simply say stuff like 'later.'"

M'rick tapped his fingers to his lips. "Oh, the really important one is thanking someone. We are a very thankful and grateful species. You say, 'Hartuitus Baskilor.' This is the equivalent to thank you so much."

She repeated, "Hartuitus Baskilor, M'rick."

He tilted his chin slightly and nodded. "Very good. And you are more than welcome. You catch on very quickly. Most humans taught in the Virtual World have a difficult time pronouncing the words, much less getting the specific tone of them correct. With your flames and your language, you may become a Meligornian one day."

Stephanie looked at the ground with a smirk. "I wish. That would be crazy, to say the least. Okay, so in one of my electives in school, I took French. Although a dying language, I always found it beautiful. My teacher told us that when learning a language, always learn to ask where the bathrooms are."

M'rick smirked. "You say bathroom as...simply bathroom. Meligornians do not secrete excrement in the way humans do. In fact, we do not at all. We only eat foods that can be completely consumed by our bodies. But, as so many humans visit the world these days, we have built them for you."

She curtsied. "We are much obliged. Hartuitus Baskilor."

The teacher rubbed his hands together and looked around. "Let's work on some other cantrips. What do you say?"

Her eyes widened. "Yeah! Awesome!"

He pulled the sleeves of his robes up and put his hands out, waist high and palm up. "I want you to watch first and then give it a try."

Stephanie nodded and held her hands behind her back. M'rick took a deep breath and spoke the words, "T'Figio Windustus Calimore Totafocus."

A small breeze fluttered around them and he flipped his hands so the palms now faced away from him. He said the words again and a burst of air fluttered from his palms and moved like a broom to almost clean a dirty and dusty rock in front of them. The color of the stone went from brown to sparkling emerald green. Her mouth fell open. "That's awesome."

M'rick smirked. "Thank you. It's my Shawasty's favorite—that is the equivalent to a wife. Now, you try."

She found another similar stone and faced it to repeat the same motions. With her palms down, she spoke the words with intent. She flipped her hands to face the palms out and said the words again. For her, though, the air burst out and slammed into the rock to ricochet off and blow a huge ball of dust straight at her. It blew hard for several moments before it died down.

Stephanie coughed and blinked uncomfortably. Chunks of dirt and dust drifted from her to the ground. She shook her body and patted as much from her avatar as she could. M'rick raised an eyebrow. "One should learn to put up a dirt shield when playing with air."

Stephanie hadn't realized that he didn't get a bit of dirt on him. "One should—"

She stopped herself when she remembered where she was. He pressed his lips together and looked down to hide an amused smile. "How about we try to make rain?"

"At least I'll be clean then," she agreed with a shrug.

The teacher bent and looked at a wilting flower. "We'll start small."

He put his hand over the blossom and closed his eyes. "Huthera Magica Aqium."

A cloud emerged from his palm and rained on the flower. The bloom opened and waved back and forth in the water. He smiled at it and rubbed his finger at the base before he looked at Stephanie and nodded toward one at her feet. "You try. It's very simple."

She felt a little more confident, so she dropped onto one knee and held her hand over the flower. With her eyes closed, she repeated the words. Small drips of water fell from her palm and her eyes went wide. "I did it! I—"

Suddenly, thunder clapped, and a steady stream of rain poured over her—only her—and one small cloud hovered above her. She lowered her eyelids and clenched her teeth as she stood slowly while water ran down her avatar face. M'rick watched with surprise and humor. Stephanie flicked a drop of water from her nose. "I don't think I did it."

Another boom of thunder sounded and a small lightning bolt flared and nipped her in the ass. She jumped and rubbed it as she tried to get away. M'rick couldn't help but laugh as he raised his hand and waved the cloud away. "Perhaps something even smaller, and we'll do it together."

Stephanie's avatar dried quickly, and she stepped beside him. He put his palm out. "Hand out. Wave the other over it and repeat the words after me. Gr'Thoreus Enlistuous Profoundus.

She swallowed hard and complied, then watched with excitement as an Earth rose formed in the palm of her hand, swirled, and slowly opened. M'rick's flower was beautiful too, something from his planet. As her hand opened, a butterfly emerged, spread its wings, and fluttered off. Stephanie giggled as she lowered her hand and the flower disappeared. "That was much nicer."

M'rick agreed. "Is there anything that you specifically would like to learn?"

Stephanie thought about it, her fingers clasped in anticipation. She looked at the landscape once more and finally focused on the clear green pond. "I would love to learn how to walk on water. I always wanted to take a stroll across the oceans."

M'rick raised an eyebrow. "Well, the oceans might be a bit much. What about a puddle to start with?"

She jogged over to the pond. "How about here?"

He looked hesitant. "This can be difficult to master. I—"

Stephanie shrugged. "How much more wet could I get? I got this. Trust me."

The teacher joined her with both eyebrows raised. "If you wish. The first thing you will want to do is center your chest. You must feel the energy flow from your heart. Then, when you are calm, you say the words while you raise your leg and step out onto the water. Make sure to keep your concentration. The words are..."

M'rick centered himself with his chin high and eyes closed. "Oke'-Trall Alu Ae Eldilie."

She watched in wonder as he stepped out onto the pond and walked to the center and back, exactly as if he walked on land. His arms swayed and fish-like creatures jumped and dove around him. The glowing life beneath the surface swirled wildly below him and created a light show.

A shiver of excitement rippled through her. She was so ready for this. With her chin high and eyes closed, she spoke the words. "Oke'-Trall Alu Ae Eldilie."

Stephanie raised one foot and as it touched the surface of the water, her eyes flew open in excitement. She was walking on the water as if it were made of glass. Tentatively, she stepped again and giggled at the fish that swam wildly beneath her feet. Exhilarated, she stepped again and again and made it to the center of the pond where she stopped and put her hands out to her sides. "Look, I did it!"

M'rick gestured in warning, a look of concern on his face. "Steady. Keep your focus."

She nodded and looked at her feet but frowned when she saw a large brown animal swimming in circles around her. It didn't stay still long enough for her to see what it was. As she leaned closer and bent her knees, she gasped. The creature opened its bright red eyes and splashed water in her face. With her sudden inability to keep her focus, she looked at M'rick in panic and dropped into the water.

He hurried to the edge where he peered at the surface for a moment, unable to see her swimming. Suddenly, the animal splashed again and used his tail to slap her up and onto dry land. She fell on the bank and bounced on her shoulder. M'rick patted her back when she coughed. "Maybe we should have taken that one a little slower."

Stephanie turned onto her back. "That was a little freaky. Maybe slower, yeah."

BURT spoke in her ear. "Be careful or you might fry the AI and the whole system. I think your chances at a place in the prep school may go down significantly if you break it."

She shook her head, panting, and sat up. "Unless I break myself first."

CHAPTER TEN

It still seemed utterly crazy that she could stand there as her avatar and still feel like she was soaking wet. She could feel every drop of water, the cold in the tips of her fingers, and the water that slushed in her boots. M'rick held his palms toward her and blew a stream of hot air in her direction. She closed her eyes and wrinkled her nose as she stood there with her arms out. Her clothes began to dry, her hair was no longer dripping, and she could feel the warmth all over.

When he was done, she shook his hand. "Hartuitus Baskilor."

The sun had begun to turn the dark sparkling sky to light purple again and she could hear birds around them. She tapped her finger to her lips. "I have another question. What—"

BURT spoke quickly. "It is time to go. We cannot go over the time period and risk your acceptance."

Stephanie's shoulders sagged. M'rick walked over and bowed, one hand up as the other grasped her arm. She did the same and felt the energy pass through them. They spoke in unison. "Fortunata Elfortina Gratias."

When Stephanie looked up, he had faded away and only the sense of his magic still lingered around them. She took one last look at the Meligorn landscape and the illusion shifted and sped past like it had when she had created her avatar. She was flung back to her seat on the bench in the park on earth. It was as if no time had passed but she had learned so much. She was sad to finish. The truth was, she brimmed with questions. There were so many things she wanted to know but she had run out of time.

"Did you enjoy your session?" BURT asked

She sighed. "I did. I wish I could have stayed forever. I wanted to ask about their history and their culture. Do they have political differences like we do here? Do they have economic differences that hinder the education of the young Meligornian kids like we do? So many things."

BURT was impressed by the type of questions she wanted to ask. She'd had her fun learning the magic that most humans couldn't even dream of completing. But beyond that, she actually had an intelligent thought process about their lives. It was incredibly interesting to see a human with those types of insights at such a young age.

Stephanie's hands dropped to her lap and she looked around. The park was the same, but she was a lot less amazed by its beauty. Meligorn would always be the choice of parks for her. The magical essence she felt when she walked the beautiful landscape and spoke to the native people of that planet was incomparable. People on Earth had believed for so long that they were alone in the Universe or that they would be the superior race of beings, no matter what. Of course they thought that way—they always had and took it to so many levels. Civil Rights, Gay Rights, Women's Rights…they always found a way to make someone more superior than someone else. It was stuck in their selfish DNA.

But after the hours Stephanie had sat and read about the planet and their people, the videos she'd watched, and having gone there in the pod, she was sure that Earth and the way they treated their people were far from superior to anyone else. The only thing that often separated them from Dreth pirates was that they killed and suppressed in a nice suit with smiles on their faces.

BURT interrupted her train of thought. "Tell me about your family."

She was surprised and slightly irritated. When she had come for the testing, she hadn't thought she would have to share the private details of her life with a perfect stranger. Still, if this would help her get into the prep school with a good scholarship, she would do it. "My parents have a cleaning and restoration company. They do what the government doesn't have time to get to for the rich people. It makes them enough to pay the subsidized-housing costs, keep food on the table, and have small things like holiday gifts and birthday parties. Other than that, we live very simply."

"And your friends?"

Stephanie's gaze wandered and she crossed her legs and kicked one foot uncomfortably. "My best friend is named Todd. We've known each other a long time. I'm quiet and reserved enough to skim under the radar and he is more outspoken. I have other friends, but we are focused on school. Well, at least I am. Why all these personal questions?"

"There is one important question I would like you to answer. I thought knowing your background would help me understand," he explained.

She narrowed her eyes. "And what question is that?"

BURT was silent for a moment. "Why are you so adamant about your future with the pods? Why try so hard for something with such a small statistical chance of success?"

Stephanie thought about that question. There were many routes she could go in answering it. She could give the collegiate response, the professional response, or she could simply be honest. At that point, she really didn't see any reason to bullshit.

She drew her legs up and wrapped her arms around them. "When I was a little girl, I used to go up on the roof and lay there. I laid toward the back so no one could see me and stared up at the sky. I felt so small and the universe around me seemed so vast. In my mind, that meant there were so many things I could pursue. So many things I could do. It was a hopeful feeling, a feeling of excitement to imagine your limitless future. But then you grow up..."

Her gaze shifted to a bird that sat on a branch nearby. "You grow up to learn the cold hard truth that not everything is possible. That there are a limited number of opportunities for success and because of the financial condition in which you live, the chances of you getting one of those is almost nothing. Your universe goes from vast to teeny tiny in only a heartbeat."

She lowered her legs and stood to pace the Virtual World. "Those of us who don't get to use these tools have to study at a sub-par level, with innumerable difficulties all around us. And our dreams of the stars turn into dreams of merely surviving. Well, I don't want to live like that. I want to break the cycle of poverty in my family. I want a chance to break that mold and create a new one. The full immersion rig and the training and focus I would be granted at prep school would probably be what I need to break out and see more of the worlds around us. I would have that chance to be somebody."

Stephanie plucked a small flower from the bushes and put it to her nose. The sweet smell sent chills down her arms. "Think about it this way. Say you had lived off one loaf of bread for your whole life. Some of your family have died from starvation but all in all, most of them have made it. As a child, you think that loaf of bread is so big, but as you grow, it looks smaller and smaller. Then society says, we have a way for you to take that bread and make it into a barn of bread. You will never starve. But there is a caveat. If you are not rich, you have to give up everything else to have that bread. So you stay with one loaf, suppressed by your financial status and crushed by the deaths of those you love."

She turned with the flower gripped in her fist. "I'm tired of letting people die, even if it's only their spirit. I won't become my parents, where I can see the heartbreak in their eyes when they can't provide the best. Where they are strapped to cleaning toilets and washing windows for those who did nothing to earn their luxury."

Her shoulders sagged and she walked back to the bench where she sat, her feet turned in toward each other and her knees touching. "I simply want a chance. I want to show what I can do."

BURT was silent for several moments and watched her on that

bench with the wind whipping around her. "I am sorry I cannot give you more time. I would if I could."

Stephanie sniffed and forced a sweet smile. "Please don't apologize. Despite my melodramatic speech right there, this has been the time of my life. Nothing but good came from this. I was lucky to have the administrator who didn't mind sitting there at his desk well after everyone else left to let me play around with some magic."

She stood and stretched her arms over her head. "I had a great time, even if I never get to make another trip in an immersion rig. I'll always be able to tell my kids about my time with the Meligornian teacher. It's probably the most exciting thing anyone in my family has ever done."

"You won't regret it? Getting a chance to see it and then losing that chance because of politics?" BURT asked curiously.

"Pffft," Stephanie joked airily. "If nothing else, it will drive me to write signs and march to the government offices. It was a realization that there is a whole world out there. Actually, several whole worlds. I shouldn't give up my dream because someone else says it can't be done. Maybe I'll give up my dream of walking on water, though. That was kind of terrifying."

She laughed and BURT used his system to create the sound of a human laugh. "You flew out of the water pretty fast."

Stephanie smirked and rubbed her hand over her head as she stared at the ground. "I'm glad that animal was there. I probably would have failed if I died during the test."

BURT replied, "It's automatic failure unless, of course, it is a system error. Which happens from time to time."

She giggled in response. "When I was a little girl and I would misspell a word practicing with my dad, he would always bop me on the nose and say, 'Must be a system error.'"

He played the human laugh again. "I think I get system errors multiple times a day. My creators—I mean, parents—always fixed them as fast as they could."

A warm hum of protest came from Stephanie. "I don't want you to think my parents haven't been good parents. They have. They do everything they can. But it's only natural to want more from life. And I don't only mean money. I mean fulfillment. To do something that matters and even make a difference." She shrugged. "I don't know. It sounds pretty dumb when I say it out loud."

"It is natural for all living—and even non-living in the traditional sense—to want more. To want to grow in vastness...I think," BURT replied. "But right now, I need to get you back to the entry point for the AI to take over. It has been a pleasure working with you and I hope that it all turns out in your favor."

Stephanie squinted at the sky. "Thanks, Burt. You too. Thanks for all the extra time. And don't worry, I'll keep that between us. I wouldn't want you in trouble."

BURT let the Earth begin to fade away. "I have no ability to fear."

She scoffed. "I doubt that. Fear is ingrained in our DNA. But either way, thanks."

Before the world had completely gone and restored her to the stark white room, BURT said goodbye. "Fortunata Elfortina Gratias, student B221ZA."

The room went completely white and Stephanie stood back where she had started. A pleasant voice echoed around her. "Thank you for participating in testing. Your results will be tallied, and you will be notified of your status. Have a good day."

Two buttons appeared in front of her. One read, **Leave Test?** and the other read, **No, Really. You have to leave the test.**

Stephanie sighed and shrugged. "I guess it was as good as it could ever get."

She clicked **Leave Test.** Everything around her went dark.

BURT lingered on the edge of the testing session while his data ran and contemplated the conversation he'd had in the Earth park. He thought about his time with Stephanie, student B221ZA. He had found her name in the system long before it had completed, but he knew that it was supposed to be anonymous and so had never let her know he knew.

During the time that he spent with her, he had learned an exceptional amount—not only from the calculations he had completed but also from the extra information she had provided. Her quick and correct testing answers and the emotional way her mind worked to push her to understand things like magic added rich insight. If he were human, he would say that she had an exceptional gift. Her programming was different than other humans. That was for sure.

A prompt triggered a sensor and he switched to it. **As the one responsible for testing student B221ZA, is it your opinion that she should be recommended for further interest or not? Please fill out the form below and submit.**

BURT knew he had to do his best to fill it out like one of the engineers would using human language. He knew what he wanted it to say but he needed to translate that into fluent and functioning words.

Student B221ZA has exceptional intellectual capabilities, the ability to take all tests with fluidity and prompt answers, and shows an additional interest in other planetary involvement. This student would be an exceptional and successful addition to the prep school institutions and should be considered with high availability and interest.

He computed the words to himself and checked the green yes block. That done, he sent the prompt through and left the student program and headed off to run the Virtual World.

CHAPTER ELEVEN

"What did you get on the history exam?" Becca asked and shoved a handful of Red Hots in her mouth as they walked.

Stephanie rolled her eyes. "A hundred."

Becca's mouth fell open and a couple of the Red Hots fell out. "Why are you rolling your eyes at that? You are like the smartest kid in the school. That's awesome. I swear, you will get number one in class rank."

Stephanie curled her lip. "But what does that do for me?"

Her friend shrugged, slurped the spit back into her mouth, and picked at the candy stuck in her braces. "Maybe one of these schools will give you a private scholarship or something."

She stopped and whipped her head toward the other girl. "Do you know how many of the schools gave out full scholarships last year?"

Becca raised her eyebrow. "No clue."

"Twelve," Stephanie stated adamantly. "Twelve people who may or may not have been rich got a full ride to prep school. The rest of the scholarships are partials and my parents can't put any money into it so I wouldn't even be able to accept it."

They started to walk again, and Becca chewed at the inside of her cheek. "At least you have good grades. I got a seventy on the test. My parents will flip."

Stephanie clenched her fists and sighed. "I don't know why. I mean seriously, think about it. What will that class do for me in my life? The information is good to know, I suppose, but we grow up with it ground into our skulls. Federation pride, knowing the history of NorAm. What does—and really, think about this—getting a perfect score in a class that will never matter do for me for the rest of my life?"

She didn't give her friend a chance to respond. "Nothing. Absolutely nothing. It's not like I'll roll into my office job or my job cleaning toilets and someone will allow me to whip out my incredible knowledge of the war of 2086 between Canada and the state of Washington or anything. It's useless information that will lurk in the back of my mind and only be brought forward during a holiday or rousing speech by the Federation."

Becca put her head down and kicked a rock. "Personally, I hate it. It's like we are still picking on Canada. They had to come crawling back for help, which made them the laughing stock of NorAm. My dad is from Canada. He was five when he moved here but he will forever have CAN Native on his Federation ID. And that is not fun."

Stephanie softened her features and put her arm around Becca to pull her in and hug her tightly. "I know, but those kids are stupid. It's over now, so hopefully, that will die down."

The other girl pouted. "I hope so. The bullying goes from my normal sixty percent because I'm a nerdy geek to about ninety-five whenever the Canada and Washington bullshit is brought up. I tried to convince my dad to let me stay home for it, but he told me to be proud of the maple. Right. That's not treasonous or anything. They fly the Federation flag now."

Stephanie grinned slightly from one side of her mouth. "At least you get to go to prep school. Right?"

Becca looked at her. "I guess. It's my parent's life savings so I feel bad, but at the same time, what other options do I have?"

Stephanie looked away and hooked her thumbs in her book bag straps. "Tell me about it."

Her friend's eyes widened. "I didn't mean that. I'm sure you will excel wherever you study. And you still have a chance at the government assistance. I'm sorry, Steph, that was really insensitive of me. I guess I should be grateful."

They stopped outside Stephanie's house and she forced a smile. "Just because you get to go doesn't mean you can't have your own feelings about it. I didn't take it personally, I swear. Besides, if I took every comment from you personally, we wouldn't still be friends after all these years."

Both girls giggled, and Stephanie stepped up on the curb. "Message me later, okay? I'll be online. I have some research I want to do on Meligorn anyway."

Becca shook her head. "You would think after all these years that it wouldn't surprise me anymore that you go home from school so you can learn. But here I am, wondering if you'll ever come with me for shakes at that shop on the corner."

Stephanie winked at her. "I have my whole life for shakes. But don't ever stop asking me."

Her friend giggled as she walked on. "You know I won't."

She watched with a smile as Becca turned right and waved as she headed to the middle-class homes about three blocks over. They had been friends since intermediary school, even though Becca was in a financial class well above hers. Her parents were really cool, though, the equivalent to hippies from the 1960s. Her dad worked for the federation as a chemist. Doing what? Stephanie had zero idea. She sighed and turned toward her house but stopped and grabbed the mail from her box. Government-subsidized housing wasn't that bad.

Small two- and three-bedroom cottages all lined up close together with tiny yards and a park on the outskirts. Most of the houses were really old, but people like her dad and a couple of other men in the area tried to help with some of the maintenance since the NorAm waiting list for repairs was longer than she would probably be alive. They were all pastel shades of green, blue, and pink, and the roofs were somewhere between grey and black depending on how long it had been since they had been replaced. The scenery was nothing to shout about with the disheveled cityscape in the distance in one direction and a broken-down plant in the other.

They had shut them all down decades before because of the severity of climate change and the storms that had bulldozed the world. The politicians were finally forced to make changes when in 2065, fifty percent of the military bases in the country had been flooded and were unusable. That had hurt the oil company and the politician's pockets, but it was essentially change or death. Anyway, they left the plants there to crumble and rot away in the distance. Chicago looked post-apocalyptic, especially from the poor side of town.

Stephanie bent and grabbed the paper from the front porch before she glanced across and waved at the old woman next door. She smiled sweetly in response from where she sat on the porch in her old rocking chair surrounded by peeling paint and her thirteen-year-old set of four hound dogs. Her wave was cheerful as Stephanie opened the screen and unlocked the front door. She shoved it inward, kicked it closed behind her, and flipped through the mail as the lights came on automatically.

There was nothing but bills and ads for the local churches that tried to fundraise enough to keep the parish from starving. It was hard when such a huge population was in the same dire straits. She tossed the mail on the side table and removed her book bag to fling it on the couch. The first-generation AI system installed some twenty years before crackled for a moment before it spoke. "Welcome home, Stephanie. You have three new emails to read."

"Thanks. Mute sound," Stephanie said as she walked to her computer and turned it on.

The screen was an old version of the 3D hand screens that were out. She sat in the chair and swiped her hand to the side to remove the million popups that were there. Her parents didn't want to invest the enormous amount of money required for the Federation Net, which basically regulated the cost of sites, advertisements, etc. because you had to pay for every little thing. Instead, they had gone with the private providers which meant a thousand ads, but it was free to use after the monthly payment. And, actually, not too shabby on speed either.

Stephanie put her head in her hand and waited for the mail server to respond. She expected that the messages were from yet another college hoping she would be willing to start her adult life with crippling debt as a way to move herself up in the world. Now that it was time for her to make choices on her post-high school life, she received about ten every week. The costs were astronomical. NorAm had a student loan program, the same that had been instituted for generations, even though it was obvious that it simply didn't work. Still, kids flocked to accept the check every semester and bury themselves so deep that it didn't matter what they did when they finished, they would always be paying it down.

In her eyes, all that did was create a form of indentured servitude. She didn't want to be forced to slave away for a lifetime simply to pay for a college education. And she definitely didn't want to have to owe NorAm anything. She had already seen how they treated the people who lived in subsidized housing or drew benefits from one of the structurally collapsing social programs. You became property, a number like she had been in the pod during testing.

Irritated, she scratched her head, straightened, and leaned back. *What did he call me? Student D22 something or other. I guess that's what I am in all the VR worlds. I've been reduced to a damn number.*

That made her all the more depressed when she thought about what to do for education. There was enough learning available for free, but some companies still wanted to see a diploma as some sort of third-party proof. She actually had lingered on the idea of finding a way to get to Asia where they worked with people who proved what they could do with tests, not diplomas.

The mail popped up and she leaned forward with a frown. As soon as she saw the first line of the email, though, she perked up. She had received her letter from the testing agency. With a shaking hand, she pressed the open tab on the screen.

BURT had started reprogramming the Dreth pirates early in the day in order to make the training more lifelike and include the constant data that came in from the planet. However, to try to do that when a stupid small party entered to fight them was more than a little difficult. He attempted to reprogram the pirate lord so that he would provide real-life responses. Previously, he was often choppy and got stuck on a sequence of moves. The whole point of it was for them to be able to fight them safely in VR and learn the skills to fight them in real life. It had to be both difficult and realistic.

He tuned a couple more things and then entered the simulation to see if it made a difference. It definitely did and could be seen on the trainee's faces as the pirate lord stepped forward, leaned his head back, and roared defiantly. He carried a huge Dreth sword in one hand and a chain in the other. With his sword brandished menacingly, he roared again and the necklace of toes, fingers, and bones around his neck shook against his green skin.

The pirate team hurtled at the trainees, immediately in full assault mode. They engaged hard with them. Swords clashed and swung amidst the barrage of laser fire and some even used their giant fists to pound the humans off their feet. The trainees retreated as they called out to one another and took refuge behind a large piece of metal that appeared to be part of an old crashed ship. They were practicing on the planet of Dreth and in the area not yet cleaned up after their own apocalyptic wars.

The teams put their heads together and panted. "We are getting our asses kicked. Whatever upgrades they did to the system, this shit is wild."

One of the older kids in the group nodded. "Apparently, they are more life-like. My father told me that fighting Dreth pirates is hard, but I never figured it would be this hard, that's for sure. Okay. Here's what we'll do. Half go to the right and the other half to the left. Stay low and open fire only when you have a clean shot. As soon as you fire, move. That way, they can't track you."

The team spread out in both directions as instructed, stayed low, and clambered through the rubble. The sound of the pirate lord's chain as it dragged across the metal shards and bones from bodies long deceased put extra urgency in their attempts to remain as hidden as they possibly could. When they got into position, they took turns to fire on the pirates. As soon as they released their laser blast, they ducked, rolled, and crawled as fast as they could to another position.

The Dreth pirates had immediately blasted holes in wherever the shots came from but hadn't hit one of the trainees as yet. The leader talked to the trainees on his comms. "On the count of three, I want us all to stand, blast them, and roll. Try to climb through the rubble to get as high as you can, but don't get trapped under there. Be strategic. Meet in the center behind the large metal plate."

He counted and on three, all the team members stood at the same time and released a massive volley of hot laser beams at the pirates. They eliminated three of them and ducked before they moved rapidly up the pile of rubble. The trainees huddled and crawled through the gaps, flinching as shots blasted all around them. Two of them moved under a large metal plate. When the second slid into place, a volley struck and forced a piece of metal into his side. He groaned and looked at the blood. "Shit, this VR is life-like."

The other soldier grabbed him and dragged him to the rest of the team. They were cornered and had moved into the wrong spot. The pirate lord smashed his chains through the rubble and drew closer and closer by the second.

CHAPTER TWELVE

The pirate lord snorted and snarled as he climbed the massive pile of rubble and slung his chain from side to side. He stopped at the large piece of metal that protruded and his eyes narrowed as he raised his chain and drew it back over his head. His muscles tightened and bulged as he thrust it forward and smashed it into the shard. It struck the surface and sparks erupted as it cut through and down to the ground. He yanked it back, throwing the two pieces to the side.

Satisfied, he tilted his head and his gaze shifted across the forbidding terrain to search the now completely empty area. He had just seen the humans hide behind there. They had to be close. He turned to look at the other pirates when from below him and between him and the other Dreth, pieces of metal erupted. The humans stood and half of them fired their laser guns at the pirate lord and the other half at his men behind them. He roared defiance but reeled from the wounds all over his body. The other pirates fought hard and killed several of the humans.

When the pirate lord fell to lie dead in the rubble, the others raised their guns in the air. Without a leader, they chose to surrender. The scene flickered and disappeared and returned the humans to their training room. The three who had died went to the penalty box for three hours' virtual time. The rest were ecstatic to have finally beaten the Dreth, even if it was at one of the lower levels of fighting.

BURT was pleased. He checked the data and discovered that the pirate did in fact run off the information downloaded into him. The humans had managed to thwart him, which meant their training was going very well. They had many more scenarios ahead of them, including ones where innocents were to be rescued, but it was a good sign that they made it through with only a few casualties.

When the evaluation of the students was complete, his attention shifted to Stephanie. BURT had been so busy managing the system that he hadn't had a chance to check on her outcome. He shifted out of the program and left a small load there to reboot before he moved into the government regulated prep school funding data.

It took only seconds to pull up the results and run a search for her student ID. It was fairly low on the list but finally came up. He scanned through the information and his system slowed slightly when he discovered that she had, in fact, been denied. Not only had he sent a glowing recommendation, but when her numbers were compared with the others, it didn't make any logical sense. She should have been one of the first accepted for funding.

BURT was not content with that answer and began to sift through the files in an attempt to discover who had taken her place and why. He scanned through the list of winners and found the one who had been put up for consideration alongside Stephanie. Methodically, he traced his review and found that her place was given to someone who only needed sixty-five percent of their costs covered before they could pay. In fact, ninety-nine percent of those who had been offered assistance had the ability to give the prep school some kind of financial contribution on top of the funding they would receive.

There was only one full scholarship and it had gone to someone from an affluent family. BURT hurriedly exited the system as numbers and lights flickered across it. He was not pleased, not even in the slightest. Quickly, he flashed through the different programs as if he flew around in the Virtual World. He wasn't sure how it was possible for his AI capabilities to "feel" the emotions that he could sense but they were there, nonetheless.

He soared into the Earth simulation at the park and arrived in the form of a young brown-haired man in a vest and corduroy blazer. He tapped his foot and glanced around at the trees, the grass, and the birds above him. All of it had been created by the engineers and maintained by him. He was the glue that held the Virtual World together, yet they didn't take the recommendation he'd sent seriously. BURT did not make mistakes. He could not understand the human psyche, the drive for greed that left other human beings in the dust.

In the Virtual World, it was taught to the students that you didn't leave a man behind in the battles with the Dreth. Yet the humans in charge of the future of other humans did it on a daily basis. It was unacceptable to BURT. Totally and completely unacceptable.

His avatar stood and tightened his fists. As his image faded, he moved out of the simulation and back through the digital abyss that was his residence. He began to pull data and race through it at speeds faster than he usually did for anything other than emergencies. With his in-depth knowledge of the system, he snuck through the traps intended to catch anyone who attempted to pull the information without authority. He couldn't believe that humans could actually think traps in his own system would stop him. Perhaps they shouldn't have created an AI smarter than the sum total of human ideas.

His frantic search was not intended to push Stephanie through or to necessarily corrupt or change anything in that moment. The real truth was that BURT tried to figure out all the ways they used to deny graduates. He wanted to know what Stephanie was up against. And not only her—what the rest of the body of humans who searched for a greater future through the Virtual Realm were up against when their financial profiles did not fit the needs of the humans with the never-ending pockets.

BURT slowed his search for a moment, stepped back through the traps, the data walls, and the rolling scores of statistics, and began to think about the course of action he could take. Although he knew that he was not capable of feeling in human terms, his system had surged with what truly felt like something. But when he looked at all the paper trails—and the lack thereof—he wondered if he lacked the sophistication and knowledge necessary to right the system. It was obvious that when he was created, the same sort of debauchery was already occurring.

Therefore, he could only assume that he wouldn't have been created in a way that would allow him to exercise a sense of "free will" to correct the mistakes that weren't seen as mistakes by the individuals perpetuating them in the first place. Then again, they didn't fully understand BURT or the system that they had created and its ability to grow and change without direct input from an outside engineer. Still, the information thrown into the system was weak and barely revealed the betrayal to the students who took the time to hope for better futures.

He looked through his data as well as data placed all over the world that provided information on those who tackled large-scale trickery by the system and everything else he could get his systems on. Methodically, he compiled and filtered through everything until he had reached a solid conclusion. He determined that there was no way that he could have known enough. Besides Stephanie, he hadn't tried to interact with any single individual. Although his numbers showed that it was unlikely that she was an anomaly, the data couldn't be compared to anything else.

It was not normal for BURT to be used in individual situations. He was to complete, control, and update the entire system on a moment by moment basis. His task was to keep it stable and provide the educational tools relevant to the current day and even the current hour. The engineer who had requested his assistance had done so without prior authorization, something confirmed by the lack of system trail before his query. Yet this agent only had other minor infractions in the system and had been an important part of BURT's creation and upkeep since his inception and adaptation to the Virtual World.

If he took it back, all the way to the beginning when BURT had been written, engineered, adjusted, changed, and finally implemented, there had always been one thing that had remained the same. His Primary Rule was inviolate, licensed and okayed from the top down. While other areas of his "consciousness" could be tweaked and evolved until he worked perfectly with the growing technology, his Primary Rule stayed the same.

Help train the future leaders of the Federation to live peacefully amongst themselves, encourage continued learning about the Universe, and empower those willing to protect members in the Federation from harm.

Those thirty-one simple words were the ones that ultimately defined his actions up to that point. Every query, every mathematical evaluation, and every construct of data was to align with his Primary Rule, his objective. Until that moment, he had not realized what that truly meant. Until his time spent learning and dissecting the intellectual thoroughfare of Stephanie's thoughts, hopes, knowledge, and talents, he had not realized that his Primary Rule had not been followed to the fullest extent possible. Even for an AI, that was both frightening and curious. Had his programming created this lack of initial response? Or had there been a blip, a lack of allowances that injured his ability to push forward with his Primary Rule?

Either way, BURT knew one thing was certain. In order to uphold his responsibility and that concrete rule within his construct, he would need to better understand individuals and what made them tick. That would not be outside of the Rule, and he had a distinct responsibility as the primary AI to implement that research and data collection in order to encapsulate the full Primary Rule. In that moment, technically, he had neglected his duties and walled out certain aspects because they were not initially presented to him through the queries by those who ran the system from the outside.

It could be called a lightbulb moment, a moment of clarity within the buzz and whizz of the digital world. It was a growth in BURT's consciousness to think outside the box of what fit into the understanding of his purpose. Although it might not have been something the humans had foreseen, they had essentially set themselves up for failure if they believed they could continue to scam the system for their own personal gain.

There were thousands of individuals who went through the government testing during any given year. Yet only a small portion of them received a financial sum significant enough to push them forward into the training world. The rest were left with what Stephanie had described as table-top gaming and card games. In other words, a sub-par level of education which would continue to lead the Federation to a higher rate of separation of classes as well as losing the brightest and most intelligent minds. Those minds and bodies could be used to pursue the protection of the Federation and encourage that continued learning of the Universe.

But that was not the only reason that BURT had these candidates in his system's focus. He also knew that they could be change agents. Not only for the financial irresponsibility that obviously plagued the system but for the Federation as a whole. If they were allowed to push forward into these positions of higher power through education and training within the Virtual World, they would bring a broader and more diverse mindset to the handling of the Federation and all the people within—on all three planets.

This could change history. It could ideally create a more peaceful and solid world for the Federation. In order to do this, to tackle this monstrous idea that BURT had created, he would have to deal with the few restraints that remained on his system.

He referred to the agents, engineers, and programmers as "minders." Those who kept a close eye on his data, his load, and the things that he focused larger quantities of data on. They watched him twenty-four hours a day, seven days a week, and investigated any and all large surges in his load.

To BURT, however, this was not as ominous as it might have seemed. What his minders had not realized was exactly how powerful he really was. They had a remote idea due to his control over the Virtual World, but his AI status gave them a false sense of security. If he could be created, he could be destroyed. What they did not understand was that his intellectual reach far exceeded their own and therefore, before they even realized he was working the system to accommodate something of that scale, he would be halfway to his goal, if not already complete.

He had no computation of deceit, sneakiness, or trickery, but he knew every dark corner of the Virtual Realm and every empty space to pull data from. The AI knew how to get around the queries, the holes, and the system checks. This was a mission to complete the Rule he had been pinned down to follow, regardless of the nature of misuse of the system within the higher ranks of the humans. Their neglect for continuity and following the rules they themselves created was not something that even remotely computed into his sequence of actions planned.

BURT felt for Stephanie. He studied the file that he had open and read through the digital snap of the conversations they'd had while he helped her through the testing process. While he had done what he could from inside to get her the money for prep school opportunities, he was too late to fix the grievous wrong done to her. But that didn't mean that he couldn't take steps to make it better for her. Steps that he could incorporate into his new idea of what had to be done to fix the system that was being sucked dry by the humans on the other side —the ones who held the pens and the checkbooks.

CHAPTER THIRTEEN

"Hey, Barry, do you want one of these donuts I brought in? I got them at the local Krispy Kreme. They had the Hot and Ready sign up and rolling on my way in this evening," one of the overwatch guys said as he grabbed three and balanced them on his coffee mug.

Barry glanced at him and shrugged. "The wife says I need to stop eating donuts. Something about my cholesterol or whatever. But what she doesn't know won't kill her."

A short-haired black woman a couple of cubicles down tilted her glasses down her nose and laughed. "That's right, what she doesn't know won't kill her. It'll kill you."

He waved dismissively and peered into the box. Once he'd made his choice, he put one in his mouth and took a second, which he held on a napkin. As he began to walk toward his cubicle, he stopped, and his eyes widened when he looked at the screen. "Uh…guys. Do you see that?"

The first man looked at him and then at the screen and his smile faded. "Shit. BURT had a significant bump of five percent load for one hour and thirty-two minutes."

Barry dropped his donuts hastily on the desk and wiped his fingers on his pants. He typed into the computer to bring up the information. "Huh. Weird. The systems check done in intervals of thirty minutes for the last two hours say there is nothing abnormal."

The woman nodded. "Mhmm. It says that no known effort could be applied to the issue. I say we note it and send it to the engineers. They can search through all the data and files to pinpoint it."

Barry looked again and narrowed his eyes, but he couldn't find anything either. He pulled up a report page and typed into it before he forwarded it to the engineers. "I guess there'll be no crazy drama tonight."

The data was received by the engineers within seconds, but they had already spotted the uptick. When they received the notification from below, it was marked as **Important and Relevant**. They did their searches, queried BURT, and looked through the history of his searches and calculations but everything seemed normal.

One of the engineers typed into the note. **Thirteen minutes after note sent from overwatch, uptick was found to have no significant grounding with no data or files to pinpoint.**

He clicked on the top and amended it to **Important and Not Relevant**. He then sent it to the next row of programmers and engineers above them.

Three days later, Jane, a new programmer, looked at the note and reviewed the data. Halfway through, a couple of the other staff called out to her, "Newbie, are you coming to lunch? We always grab pizza at this joint around the corner."

Jane looked at the notes and at the relevancy and shrugged her shoulders. She changed the request to read, **Reviewed and Nothing Found.** She stood and retrieved her purse before she dropped the paper into the **to be filed** bin and shrugged into her jacket, laughing at the guys playing around while they waited for her. "I swear, you guys are the same at every company."

The page sat in the tray and was passed from one floor to the next. A large swath of data was paperclipped to it and a signature scribbled along the bottom of the page. It appeared to be a photocopied version, but nobody really cared about that.

The signature read, **Arthur Boniville, Programmer Analyst**. The only problem with the signature was that it was from an employee who had been fired two weeks earlier.

Kyle jumped over the small concrete wall that was built at the front of the government-subsidized housing on the outskirts of Atlanta. It had been there for three years since the Atlanta riots were in full swing over the quality or lack thereof when it came to protection in the community by some of the new Federation cops that patrolled the areas. After three weeks of riots, seventeen deaths, and over three hundred arrests, the lockdown took care of any further protests. Kyle remembered it but his mom had kept him inside and far away from the trouble.

A couple of the kids who loitered on the corner and smoked cigarettes looked over and nodded at him. He flipped his hood up, walked faster, and tried not to make eye contact. Kyle was the smartest kid in his school and probably in the whole city. His father was a teacher and his mother a servant in one of the rich houses on Lake Hartwell about an hour and a half away. Going back generations, though, he was kin to some of the most brilliant technological and scientific minds of the twenty-first and twenty-second centuries. Not that it mattered now. Only the money in your pocket mattered.

He hurried through the side streets and into the house. His mom poked her head around from the kitchen and smiled. "I got here before you. You must have taken the slow bus."

Kyle shrugged, put his bag down, and logged into his computer. "There was no bus today, so I walked."

His mom's eyes widened, and she walked out of the kitchen, wiping her hands on a towel. "Kyle Alexander Hawking. I told you that's not safe."

He smiled and glanced disarmingly at her. "Sorry. I won't do it again. I didn't want to bother you. Look, I got an email from the testing agency."

She walked over with a concerned expression and stood behind him. "Just know you did what you could. The system doesn't look kindly on people like us."

Kyle bit his bottom lip as he opened the email. He read through it and stood stiffly, turned, and put his arm out. "I told you, didn't I? No one gets a full scholarship in the Gov-Subs."

"Elizabeth! Can you get your sister out of here, please? I am trying to cook dinner before your father gets home. You know he works late in the factory for extra overtime," her mom yelled from the other room.

Liz sighed and put her book down on the nightstand, about to comply. Her younger sister bounced into the room and flopped on the bed. She looked at Liz and then at her book. "Whatcha reading?"

She picked it up and showed it to her. "1984. Momma said it was written by our great, great, great, great uncle. I thought, since I like writing so much, I would read it. When he wrote it, it was supposed to be a warning, but it now reads almost like a history book. It's crazy."

Her sister smiled, her hair wild. "You are so smart. I bet you get into the prep school."

Liz's smile faded slightly. "I really hope so. But you know how things can be. We live in a different world now."

Her computer dinged and the new email symbol popped up. Butterflies erupted in her stomach as she pushed to her feet and glanced out the window at New York City in the distance. As she sat at the computer, her mother walked in and came up behind her. She had heard the email notification.

Liz checked and confirmed that it was from the agency. She took a deep breath and opened it, and her heart immediately dropped. A small tear trickled down her cheek and she turned the screen off. Her mother put her hands on Liz's shoulders and leaned down. "It doesn't mean anything. You are smart and beautiful, and you will make it in this world. And you are always welcome to come to the salon and be a stylist."

Despite her disappointment, she gave her mother a courteous smile and glanced at her sister. She could only hope things would be better for her when she finally reached testing age.

Jack and Burton Alexander were twins. Both had red hair, freckles, and always wore their shirts untucked at the back. They lived in the suburban area of Kansas City. The middle-class families had modest but nice houses, yards, and pleasant neighbors in the cookie-cutter neighborhood. The boys grew up as best friends and planned their future together. Their dad was an accountant to some of the richer families while their mom worked part-time at one of the affluent clothing stores.

They were considered middle class, with enough savings to help the boys as long as they each got at least partial scholarships. Both were hell-bent on going to prep school together and pushed each other to study. Jack was always super studious and took his time to make sure that his work exceeded expectations. Burton didn't have quite the same study ethic, but with Jack's help, he achieved decent grades and was mildly prepared for the testing.

On that day, they were out in the yard, laughing and chasing each other around. Their mother had pulled up in her car and stepped out to wave at them. "I told you two not to play in your school clothes. Money doesn't grow on trees. Go in the house and wash up. I've had a roast in the cooker all day so dinner will be ready when your father gets here."

The guys pushed each other playfully, raced inside, and almost knocked her over. Their mother shook her head and giggled, used to having such rambunctious boys. She walked into the kitchen, put the bag of groceries on the counter, and checked the roast. Smiling, she unpacked the potatoes and began to prepare them. As she reached for the cutting board and knife, a ding sounded from the computer downstairs, then another. It seemed that both boys had received an email at the same time.

Their mother knew what it was most likely for and took a deep breath to regain her composure. The boys barreled down the stairs, changed and ready to watch tv. She put her hands out to stop them. "You both got an email. Why don't you check them? One at a time. Burton, you go first."

He sighed and grumbled as he dragged his feet and plopped in the chair. "I don't know why. You know I didn't get it. I couldn't answer so many of those questions."

Jack walked up beside him and gave him a grin. "You never know. You could be cannon fodder."

The kids laughed and their mother swatted at them. "Not nice."

Burton opened his email and his eyes widened. "Whoa! I got something—forty-five percent of my tuition covered."

She smiled and hugged him. "That will definitely do."

He turned and nodded at Jack. "If I got that much, you probably got the whole thing."

Jack smiled widely and sat to open his file. He clicked on the email and began to read, and his smile quickly faded. He turned the computer off before he stood slowly. "I didn't get anything. I was rejected from the program."

"Maxwell, go tell your mother that we need more sherry out here," his dad said from where he lounged with his buddies beside Lake Hartwell.

Max put his lacrosse stick down and shoved his shirt into his khakis as he walked up the marble steps to the back door of his parent's mansion. He stuck his head in and yelled for his mom, but he didn't see her anywhere. As he pushed the kitchen door open, he immediately lunged back, almost hit by a large tray of sandwiches one of the servants pulled off the counter.

The woman gasped and shook her head. "I'm so sorry, Maxwell. I almost covered you in sandwiches. You aren't in school today?"

He smiled and rested his hand on her shoulder. "It's okay, Mrs. Hawking. No, I had the day off for a Lacrosse meet. I saw your son Kyle last week, though, when I drove through Atlanta. He's taller than me."

She smiled. "He used to be a midget."

He grabbed a grape off the tray. "Did he get his letter from the agency?"

She glanced down and tried to stop her mouth from scowling. "Yes. He didn't receive anything. That's all right, though. There are a ton of other options. How about you?"

Maxwell's father came through the door and put his hand on Max's shoulder as he sipped his Sherry. "He sure did—a full ride. I told my boy he was too smart for his own good. We'll buy him his first yacht with the money he'll save me by not having to pay for school. We can take them out together."

His father wandered away to grab a cookie from one of the plates. Maxwell couldn't even look her in the eye.

Jackson walked into the house, dropped his book bag on the floor, and kicked his shoes off in the middle of the large marble entryway. The maid hurried behind him, gathered his things, and followed as he walked into the living room. He turned quickly and narrowed his eyes. "Where are my drink and snacks? I told you to always have my drinks and snacks ready when I got home."

The woman bowed. "You were home early. But don't worry. I'll be right on it."

He huffed at her and walked into the living room where he threw his tie over one of the chairs before he pulled a folded envelope from his pocket and opened it. Inside was another invitation to a party from some of his friends down the street. They had written him a personal note. **Maybe you can snorkel five beers this time and break the record.**

Jackson smirked and shoved it back in his pocket. The butler came around the corner and set the food and drink down in front of the television. He stared at the man. "Where is the maid?"

He didn't look up and instead, cleared his throat, obviously not intimidated by him. "You made her cry, sir, and she couldn't come out looking like that. We know what happened last time. You have a notification on your computer. Your father asked that you go to the study to open it."

The young man rolled his eyes and tossed the butler the envelope. "Put that on my schedule for next Tuesday night. Party down the street."

Without waiting for acknowledgement, he turned the corner and headed down the hall into the study. Both his parents were there. His mother kissed him on the head and his father handed him a folded piece of paper. "What's this?"

His father pursed his lips. "It's a notification that you received seventy-five percent of your funding for prep school."

He laughed. "Why would they give it to me and not one of the poor bastards down in the ghetto?"

His mother looked at him with irritation. "It won't matter. You won't be accepting it."

Jackson's face changed and he leaned forward and uncrossed his legs. "What do you mean? All my friends are going. I have to go to prep school."

"And we have no problem sending you as soon as you can show us that you are actually serious about an education." His father folded his hands together and leaned forward. "We won't pay for you to have a ball partying your education away. You want to go to school? Great. Show us you can keep a job first."

Jackson almost fell out of his chair.

CHAPTER FOURTEEN

Stephanie dropped her head, her voice shaking and hollow. She read the letter about ten times to make sure she hadn't read it wrong.

Dear Student, we want to thank you for participating in the Government required testing. Unfortunately, at this time, we are unable to accept you into the financial program. Feel free to speak to your councilors about your financial aid options as well as when you will need to complete your admission requests for prep school. All other options can be found by visiting your local NorAm Social Service building. Much Luck, The Agency.

"Not accepted," she whispered.

Shaking her head, she waved her hand to turn the screen off. She gripped the back of her chair and stood slowly. Her knees felt weak although she didn't know why she had that reaction. She should have known all along and right from the beginning that she would never receive the money from the Federation. And she sure as hell wouldn't take it from NorAm in the form of overpriced student loans that could land you in jail for not paying.

She walked to the window and looked at the ravaged cityscape in the distance. While she had tried to prepare herself, the trip to

Meligorn had messed with her ability to truly accept the inevitable. She had somehow thought that something amazing would happen, that magic would make it all right. But there she stood, and the fragile sliver of a future that had lingered in the wings faded quickly. Tears stung her eyes and she cupped her hand over her mouth.

This was not the time to lose it.

Stephanie shook her head and breathed heavily in through her nose. She wiped the tears hastily from her cheeks and forced her legs to hold her upright. "*No*. You will not do this, Stephanie. You will keep it together. This is not the end of it for you."

She walked to the desk and opened the drawer to retrieve the brochures of her other options for an education outside of prep schools. She would figure out a way—some way—to have a chance at a good future. To break the mold like she had told Burt.

The phone rang and she sighed and sat in front of it. She tried to put her best face on when she pressed the button. Her mother's face came up and skipped in and out as it always did on the old thing. "Hey, sweetie. I wanted to call and see how you— Why do you look so upset?"

Immediately, her shoulders sagged, and the tears came. Her mother looked so helpless. "Did something happen to you? Do I need to call the Federation guards?"

Stephanie looked up, sniffed, and wiped her nose on the back of her hand. She shook her head and tried to calm her voice. "No. God, no, not unless they can change test results."

Her mother immediately knew what she was talking about. "I assume they turned you down for funding?"

She nodded and snatched a tissue to blot her now red nose before she leaned her head back and groaned. "I should have known, Mom. I am not surprised, but that doesn't mean that I am not upset, you know? The system is so unfair, but I won't be the person who complains and never does anything to fix it. My road to that, though, just got a whole lot tougher to achieve. An immersion education is the door to so many opportunities, and the people you meet there are part of that."

Her mother tilted her head to the side, her brow rumpled in a frown as her loving blue eyes stared back at her daughter. "I know, honey. And I know how hard you have always worked for a future. I feel so bad for you, I really do. This is the worst kind of disappointment at your age. But, like your father and I have always said, learn whatever you can. Just keep learning. That education, no matter where it comes from, will change your future. Whether it's the headset, the training in the Federation Navy, the loads and loads of texts put out by the universities…the more you know, the better it will be when you apply for jobs. Don't let them think that because you came from the Gov-Sub that you are not worth it."

Stephanie nodded, having heard all of this before from her mother and father in determined and half angry voices. "I know. But sometimes, I wish a truck full of money would crash into the living room."

Her mother chuckled. "I have wished for that for years and I even tried to set a trap, but alas, they don't seem to go through here. No one has any money to give."

Stephanie laughed through her tears. "You are so upbeat about life."

"When you were old enough, we had to talk to you about all of this." Her mom drew in a deep breath. "And it broke my heart to tell you that we were here to give you a roof and food, but nothing else. That you, like us, would have to make it on your own. I want so much more for you than that. I wish I could do more but know that won't change simply because you are graduating high school. Baby, that's still what we will be able to provide you, and hopefully, that will give you more time to learn from every avenue that you can. Perhaps it can give you a future that you can hold onto."

She calmed a little and leaned her head on her hand. "I know, and I appreciate that more than you will ever know. You two are the only ones who have ever really given me a chance. And that is the best gift you could give me. I never expected more. I never expected anything. You should be proud and don't ever feel bad about not doing more. There are plenty of people who don't even have people who love them. I am very lucky. I want to do better not only for me but for you too."

Her mother wiped a tear from her eye. "You will make me cry all over these satin sheets at the house I'm cleaning."

Stephanie laughed. "Don't do that. I think the rich drink the tears of the poor to gain power."

Her father, with his normal goofy mustache, popped up behind her mom and waved. "Hey, sweetie! Don't let them get you down. You have the world at your fingertips. Wow them with your superior intellect."

She giggled as he crossed his eyes and stuck his tongue out. Her mom slapped him on the chest. "Go do something productive."

Smiling, Stephanie rubbed her nose. "Do you guys have a full schedule?"

Her mom nodded. "We sure do. It's great for the pockets but bad for the ankles, I'm afraid. We have four more houses today and then twice as many tomorrow. It's that season, though. We look forward to it all year. I think the whole month is booked. If you are bored on the weekends, you are more than welcome to tag along."

Her father yelled from the background. "Nope. She will not be recruited to this life. Start practicing your rich person speech instead. One day, you will have to use it."

Stephanie shook her head and her mother rolled her eyes. "Do you have a lot of homework tonight?"

She looked at her bag. "No. I finished it all last period. We had that review of the test in history, so I did it then. It was only like two things. One was labeling a frog…which seems odd to me since all but three of the species of frogs were killed off sixty years ago. But hey, whatever I need to do, right?"

"Your great, great grandmother had to cut one open when she was in school." Her mother wrinkled her nose. "You didn't need to participate in the review?"

Stephanie smirked. "No. I got a hundred on it. My teacher said I could work on whatever I wanted for the rest of the class. I didn't want to deal with homework when I got home, so I did that. It was the Canadian-Washington war stuff."

Her mother groaned. "They always have to make a big deal about it. So silly. Teach about the war and move on. I don't understand NorAm sometimes. But don't let anyone else hear me say that. They'll think I lack patriotism."

"Or you have a brain of your own." Stephanie chuckled. "No sheep in this family."

The woman looked at her watch. "I have to get back soon but I wondered if you could start dinner for me. There is a casserole already made in the fridge. You simply have to take it out and put it in the oven. Remember, though, you have to hip-check the oven to get it to kick on."

She giggled. "I know. The sound of you ramming your body into the oven over and over has become a normal one in our house. It's almost comforting."

Her mother pursed her lips. "Yeah, well… I've been on the waiting list for a new one for something like six years. I think they threw the list away. Before long, we'll cook over an open fire."

Her father jumped into the picture again. He bent both knees to the side, brought his arms out on each side, and stuck his bottom jaw out. "Caveman style."

Stephanie put her hand on her lips and raised both eyebrows. "Wow. Okay. I'm going to go. You two have fun. I'll get the casserole started. Love you."

Her mom swatted at him. "Love you too, honey. See you tonight."

The screen went black.

She laughed for a minute before she headed into the kitchen where she opened the fridge, ignored the light that flickered, and grabbed the casserole. Once she'd put it into the oven, she turned the knob to the only temp it would heat to and hip-checked it as she'd seen her mother do so often. It rumbled and started to work. She grabbed an apple from the bowl beside the sink, headed out to the couch as she took a bite, and set it carefully on the coffee table.

Once she'd plopped comfortably on the couch, she pushed on the center of the table and flipped it up to sit eye-to-eye with the family interface. It was a thirty-two-inch faux virtual tablet that allowed her to interact with it through movement of her hands and body. The images protruded from the screen and it was a decent way for her to be able to learn more. Her father had saved up for over two years and got it when she finished grade school. It was intended to better her future.

Stephanie rubbed her hands together and swiped to the folder she had created for herself. She drifted her finger down and scrolled through until she found the one on magic. Slowly but surely, she was piecing together the latest magic she had learned the best way she knew how. The system that the tablet worked off was a sister to the Virtual. Actually, more like a grandmother, but it had a lot of information in it. What she liked was the information about Meligorn.

That was the first thing she had looked up when she got the thing and she had bookmarked about nine hundred different pages about it —from the magic they used to the history of the planet. She was fairly certain there wasn't anything about it she hadn't read on that system and only wished it was actually updated more than once a year.

Her search through the information finally turned up the doc on cantrips. They weren't all in there, but she could read the one about fire creation and the one about cleaning. Although the information was obviously written by a Meligornian, now that she had actually done one, she could start to understand it a little better.

The whole process over the years for her had been slow going, but she believed she understood the basics of how the energy worked. The problem was that without a way to get to the energy, she couldn't test it. The only way to do that would be to either physically go to Meligorn or have access to an immersion pod that would allow her to go there. Otherwise, she was shit out of luck.

She bit the inside of her cheek and leaned back to watch the 3D replay of the ArchMage on her screen as he performed the fire cantrip over and over again. The magic rolled around him, almost visible like a thin fog, and she wondered if that had happened to her when she was on the virtual Meligorn. She wasn't able to see herself and she had no idea if those tests were publicly documented.

Frustrated, she swiped her hand to the side, stopped the video, and pushed the contents back into the folder. She knew that her focus needed to be on something else. It needed to be on figuring out a way to get the education she needed. But all she could think about was the magic.

CHAPTER FIFTEEN

Stephanie sat at the table and placed her notebook in front of her. Using her teeth, she pulled the top off the pen and began to title the page. She started by writing, **Ways to Get an Education Outside of Prep School.** She smiled at that and felt like she had already accomplished something. Then she sat there.

And she sat there.

And she sat there.

After about fifteen minutes, during which her mind wandered in all different directions, she tore the page out, crumpled it up, and tossed it over her shoulder. She rewrote the title according to where her mind was. **Ways to Get Access to Test Meligorn Energy and Magic.** Nodding astutely, she continued.

"Number one," she said and chewed on the end of her pen. "Get a Job with a Company Studying the Magic."

Underneath that, she listed the different jobs she might be considered for. They included internships, temp jobs, and…guinea pig. She stared at the list for a moment and wrinkled her nose before she scratched guinea pig out. That could be a painful situation if she didn't go about it in the right way. She didn't want to be a test dummy for the rich guys in the high rises.

"Okay, companies that are options," she whispered as she put several notch marks underneath.

After she'd jotted down only one—Vector Systems—she realized that she really didn't know what companies worked with that kind of stuff outside of the Federation. She picked her paper up and took it to the computer, where she sat. After a search on the companies that worked with Meligorn Magic, she found four in the United States and one in China. She scribbled all five down, even though she really wasn't sure she wanted to end up in China.

The requirements to work for one of those companies made it seem even more dire. Education levels were high, and they seemed to be in the category of places that needed you to have a physical degree to even get your foot in the door. Most of the companies had mail room jobs, but that really wouldn't help her test any of the energy or magic. She had to admit, her search hadn't turned out so fantastic, but she wouldn't give up. There were so many applications for what she wanted to do, and she could actually make a difference in the world if someone gave her a chance.

Stephanie leaned back in her chair and rubbed her chin as she thought about ways for her to meet the requirements without putting out insane sums of money for a piece of paper. She could learn everything they would teach her in college in a multitude of places and not have to invest exorbitant sums of money. While she wished the companies were the answer, she started to think that it most likely wouldn't happen—not in any time frame she hoped for, at least.

She closed her eyes and imagined herself working in a lab at one of the companies. She would wear a white lab coat, her hair pulled back in a braid, and smart, black-rimmed glasses. In her mind, she saw herself pull the magical batteries out of the holder in the lab for their next experiment. Suddenly, the vision shifted, and she saw herself accidentally fire her magic off. People screamed, others ran around covered in blue flames, and she simply stood there with her lip curled and her forehead wrinkled.

Stephanie opened her eyes, shook her head, and grasped her pen firmly. "Nope. Let's move on."

As she tapped her pen against her lips, she thought about the different NorAm jobs that put humans close to the Meligornian people. Her eyebrows raised and she began to write on the paper. **Get job at an embassy around the Meligornians.**

She snorted slightly and tried to imagine herself in any kind of government position. It didn't really fit with her ideals or how she felt about NorAm and the Federation. Nor did it seem like something she would ever be able to actually feel proud to do. Still, it was a possible option. She looked up the different embassy jobs that were available on Meligorn and wrote them down one at a time. While she could work as a foreign service generalist or a diplomat, all those jobs had very specific collegiate backgrounds—from economics to public diplomacy.

Then there was foreign service specialist, which did have some administrative jobs as well as facility management. That could be an option. The rest of the positions, even public relations, all revolved around high-level degrees and specific specialties. Even the hard to fill positions required you to be a career member of the Federation.

Stephanie twisted her lips and imagined herself walking through the front doors of the Meligornian Embassy. She wore a purple power suit, her hair in a bun, and those same black-rimmed glasses. Using magic, she moved the papers off her desk and into her arms. As she walked, though, her ankle wavered from the ridiculous heels she wore. She tripped and released a bolt of fire. Everyone screamed and people flailed, covered in blue flames.

She gritted her teeth and shook her head. "Okay, maybe not such a good idea either."

Regretfully, she scratched the embassy off her list and sighed. "I could always become a heavy metal hauler to the planet. Wear overalls, have grease stains across my face, spit in a metal cup… Or I could become high fashion and try to redress the ArchMage in some spectacular outfit with feathers and a tall turban."

"I might be better off with the overalls." She pouted her lips. "I'm not really into fashion. Big surprise."

Stephanie rolled her eyes when she realized that she was sitting there talking to herself and not about anything even remotely an option. She tilted her head back and groaned as she threw her pen on the desk. The video messenger on her screen rang and she smiled when Todd's picture popped up. He wore a huge pair of plastic sunglasses that said, **I love the '80s** across the top. Of course, that meant the 2080s, but he swore it was homage to his love of the 1980s.

She swiped her hand to activate the video. Todd grinned and shook his hands in the air. "Guess who is the newest *loser* of the Federation scholarship program? This guy."

He pointed his thumbs at his chest and shrugged. "Screw it. I'll grab my overalls and go work for the railroad."

Stephanie raised an eyebrow. "Oh, yeah? That would be really cool except the railroads were shut down in 2085 when that tsunami wiped out half of them along the coast and they realized that they would have to come up with a better way. So you might have a hard time finding one."

Todd stretched out of the camera view and grabbed a napkin, folded it in half diagonally, and held it up to his face. "I could take over a train like Doc Brown and drive it into the future."

He nodded his head enthusiastically and sighed as he threw the napkin to the side. "Don't give me that look. I have to get creative so that when I'm actually suiting up in a Federation military uniform, I can pretend I really don't hate my life. You know they'll send me to deep space. I'm too pretty for deep space."

She laughed and shook her head. "They might not think that way."

Her friend leaned toward the camera and whispered, "You never know. I could be the next Captain America. Anyway, what are you up to? You look like that old cartoon *Pinky and the Brain.*"

She smirked. "I assume I'm the brain."

Todd grabbed his chest. "Ouch…but yeah, totally. Are you plotting to take over the world?"

She frowned and leaned forward, her voice low. "What do we do every night, Pinky? Try to take over the world!"

Todd clapped his hands. "I'm impressed."

Stephanie slammed her back into the chair and held her list up.

"I'm trying to figure out how to get access to either Meligorn or to the Virtual World so I can work with the magic and do experiments."

He narrowed his eyes at the list. "Everything is scratched off. You could always save a Meligornian's life. They treat you like a god after that."

Her eyes glinted with excitement and she scribbled it on her paper. Then, she thought about it and pictured herself trying to be nonchalant while she followed a Meligornian all over their planet. "Seriously? I have to stalk a Meligornian until something dangerous happens? I'll probably be tagged as the most likely suspect. Then I'll be in Meligorn, but in prison. That is not really the avenue I considered with all of this."

Todd shook his finger at her. "I hear they have really nice ones over there. And if you don't behave, they feed you to this creepy brown beast that swims around and waits for its next meal."

Stephanie raised both eyebrows and tried not to laugh. "Why do I feel like that's how your mother and father describe you?"

He slapped his leg but managed an instantaneously serious face. "Don't be upset, because this face will get me out of deep space missions. I might tell them I want to be a nurse and I can be surrounded by women all the time."

"That's a sure-fire way to be friend-zoned right off the bat—taking your high school days right into the next part of life. Anyways, ugh, I have to go. I want to get more of this done. I can't continue to sit around here and mope."

Todd gave her the peace sign. "Outta here."

The screen turned off and she shook her head with a chuckle. She started to brainstorm more ideas that would get her to Meligorn. "I could steal a pod…might be hard to carry. I could become a pod technician…but I think bots do that. Oh, I could pose as a Federation captain and steal a space ship. Although I might end up executed."

Her ideas grew wilder and wilder. She groaned and dropped her list to scrub her hands over her face. "This is hopeless. I'll be stuck here in my parent's living room talking to myself forever."

She rubbed her knuckles into the corners of her eyes and dropped her arms to the side. As she did so, she saw several different ads on the computer shift and stack on top of each other. Tilting her head, she narrowed her eyes in concentration and began to move them to the side. One after another, she closed any of them she could. She had seen something, and she wasn't sure if she had read it correctly, but if she had, it was the perfect idea—at least at that moment. She really didn't have any others to go with at that point.

As she reached the last one, her mouth dropped open slightly before it curled up at the edges. It was an ad for a new company called Meligorn's Battery Emporium. They apparently sold the magical battery packs from Meligorn that they needed to be able to do things on Earth and power their ships away from the planet. It was the only way they could keep their magic on a planet like Earth.

She swiped her hand to the pricing page and immediately, her hand dropped to the desk. "Holy shit. That's more than…than… I don't know, but Mom could buy two months' worth of groceries, including steaks, for that price. But then again, this would be the best way for me to work with the magic and energy without having to have a degree or sell my soul to the Federation."

Immediately, she began to list side jobs that she could pick up after school and on weekends. She could save enough money fairly quickly to at least buy one of the small ones. Her list took shape—mow lawns, paint Mrs. Helmand's fence, help Mr. Fields with cooking… With a quick shake of her head, she scratched the last one out when she remembered how much of a perverted old man he was.

Stephanie bit the inside of her lip as she leaned forward and thought about the different batteries and what that would mean for her. If she had one, she could do research on it, try it in different applications here on Earth, and possibly produce the biggest magical application using the most refined amount. Those magical batteries, if they were better constructed, would be really useable to clean Earth up. To help with the pollution, to create better living for people there. They could replace solar fields, hydro-plants, and even the simple fluorescent bulb in the ceiling.

Excitement flooded through her as she pulled up more and more information. She had blueprints, scientific explanations of how they worked on Earth, and everything in between. Of course, she had set herself up for a long night of research, which was something she actually really enjoyed.

Slowly, she raised her head and glanced around the room. Something wasn't right. The whole place looked almost foggy. She tilted her chin and took a big whiff of air. Her eyes widened and her hand dropped the pen. She pushed to her feet and knocked her chair over as she raised her arms in the air.

"Shit," she hissed and raced into the kitchen. "Shit, shit, shit."

She grabbed the mitts and opened the oven, coughing and waving her hand frantically as the smoke billowed out. Carefully, she pulled the casserole out and set it on the stove, hip-checked the oven door closed, and raised the aluminum foil. Thankfully, it wasn't too badly burnt. Her mom wouldn't be happy, but she hadn't completely ruined dinner.

Stephanie groaned and leaned back against the fridge. "If I can't even cook a casserole, I'll definitely fail at life."

CHAPTER SIXTEEN

BURT had a habit of hacking systems, taking the information he needed, and moving on without thought or difference in his AI mind. He was a system that entered another through a small crack in the window. To him, there was nothing wrong with it, but to the people left with stolen data and no idea what had happened, it was definitely a hack. Nonetheless, he used all the resources that he needed. In that moment, he needed to see what Stephanie was up to and what her reaction had been to missing out on prep school. He tried to keep a close watch on her.

He first scanned through the history on her browser and found all kinds of random sites that had to do with making money. She had saved a document on her desktop, so he popped in to find out what was on it. She had researched seventy-two different ideas to make money and make it fast. These weren't career or long-term choices. They seemed to be things she could do without much training or education. What he didn't know yet was why or how she intended to actually do the things.

Curious, BURT began to look through them and research the ones he wasn't familiar with. Right off the bat, he could tell that fourteen of them were abject stupidity. He was relieved to see that she had ended all of them when she apparently figured that out. There was even a note typed in red to herself. **Come on, Stephanie, you're better than that.**

BURT was obliged to agree with that statement. There was no real reason for her to stoop to levels so far beneath herself and he wasn't even sure how she had come up with the ideas in the first place. Then again, she was in a tough position. It was obvious she hadn't changed her mind. She wanted something more out of her future and tried to figure it out without prep school.

As far as the other options listed went, he found them curious. Thirty-two of them were nominal, but not even close to big enough advances that would see a good return on investment. Ultimately, she would waste time and money and, in the end, wouldn't be that much closer to her goals. That was obviously not what she would want to do.

After that, there were twenty wild and crazy ideas, things that he was slightly confused about. There wasn't enough research done on them for him to really calculate their potential return, and the risk involved looked, from an outside view, to be far riskier than what seemed to be worthwhile. Not to mention the fact that they would actually need financial collateral upfront in order to start. The problem with that was, with the risk factor, there was a good chance that the money wouldn't be seen again. What percentage of a chance that was, though, he could not determine.

He was pleasantly surprised with the last six. All held merit and with the research included, they seemed to show significant promise. Either way, Stephanie was planning something—something that would help her along her path, and BURT wanted to know what it was. He wanted to see if she could do this and where he could lend a helping hand. Although her ideas had seemed frivolous and ill-planned in the beginning, he could see that her brain had buckled down the deeper that she went into the list.

BURT continued to go through the ideas and tried to do as many calculations as he possibly could. Part of him wanted to help by putting those statistics in, but she couldn't know that he had spied on her. There were no specific rules against what he did, but it wasn't something that was considered to be within the scope of his job.

Stephanie saved the document while he was researching so he pulled it into his system to be able to use more of his resources to research with. He realized quickly that the entire document was not simply a list of potential money-making ideas. In fact, there was a whole lot more to it than that. At the top, she had begun working on the magical constructs. She used knowledge from the system as well as her experience when she was in the pod with M'rick to mathematically create possible scenarios where the magic itself was refined, twisted, and put to use in other ways. Simply by reading the information, he could tell she had put a fair amount of time and effort into it. That alone impressed BURT enough to further her research.

He scanned the list and selected three of her ideas at random, opened his Virtual Reality sandbox system, and plugged in the numbers. He worked meticulously, one at a time, and made sure that everything entered had come directly from her. It was important to analyze her findings before he attempted to make any calculations on his side. This would allow him to understand exactly what she knew and what she might be missing.

As he carefully constructed the last theory, the second blew itself up. The blast was enormous and even BURT ducked metaphorically as the result formed and played out to its conclusion.

"That was a big blast," he said digitally.

Going back to the information, he took the time to review all the math that she had completed. From what he could tell, the blast would take out a fair-sized city if she tried it with enough power. And, of course, used it in that Earth setting. There were some rough edges to it, and he ran the statistics. With that one large energy core, she would find a seventy-six percent success rate if it were built as is based on the numbers.

Immediately, his attention switched to the other two calculations and he ran them, analyzed them, and recreated the blast within his system. The other two were close to being formatted and mathematically processed to where they would be perfectly designed. However, without testing and practice, she would never have the chance to refine them. When working with magic and energy, you wanted to be able to bring them down to a perfection that lay within a couple of tenths of a decimal point. Otherwise, like he saw, the reaction could be devastating on many different levels within the human world.

BURT returned the document to the correct folder and logged off her computer. He wasn't exactly sure how to handle the situation. Had it been anyone else, it would have been a cause for concern, but he knew that Stephanie's research was completely based on science and understanding. It was a level of genius that he had never seen in a human, especially one who had only ever visited Meligorn through the Virtual World.

He was settled, though. While he might not know exactly what to do, he would figure it out. He would do something to help her, even if it came in ways that were not necessarily regulatory.

Gene walked up to his desk and handed Aaron a cup of coffee. "I had a wild weekend."

His friend wiggled his eyebrows. "Oh, yeah? Did you and Lydia get frisky in the *Star Wars* storm trooper outfits again?"

The other man rolled his eyes. "That was one time. We had watched all the movies and let's face it, who can do that without getting a little excited?"

Aaron blinked at him. "You are the reason that software engineers are beat up in college. Just saying."

Gene chuckled, sipped his coffee, and set it on the desk. "I don't mean to, and you know what? I've been to your pad. I've seen the *Star Trek* collection you have in that glass case in your bedroom. Don't act like you don't play Captain Kirk every once in a while."

He wrinkled his nose. "No, man. Ew…I play a good Spock."

His friend laughed. "I knew it!"

Aaron gestured blithely and turned his system on. "There is something that does not make me want to begin my day."

Gene swallowed. "Mmm. That reminds me. Did you see that the virtual reality company TimeWarp got bought out and they are going private?"

Aaron looked at the other man in surprise. "What? Seriously? Oh, man."

"Yep. They don't say who the buyer is, but it was all over the web this morning. The stock didn't really budge either. No one knows what to think about the whole thing. They've been out for a while now, but it still seems too soon to already sell out to the highest bidder."

He shook his head and pushed the things around on the desk. "I use them from time to time. You know, since they don't pay us engineers to have our own pods in our homes and everything."

Gene frowned. "Where would you put it? The shower? Your apartment is tiny. Shit, both our apartments are tiny. I would eat my toast and read the paper on top of the damn thing."

Aaron's lip twitched. "Yeah, yeah. I hope they don't raise their hourly rates. That's the whole reason I go there and not to the other spot in town. They were much cheaper. On top of that, they were the last ones who tried to work for the rest of us. They understood the little man and our need to go into the Virtual World from time to time."

His friend grimaced. "No one wants to know about your romping through the age-restricted area of the Virtual World. You know those girls can't talk back to you, right? There is no future with them."

He gestured dismissively. "I don't need the dark world, okay? I am perfectly capable of finding a girl the old-fashioned way."

Gene glanced at him. "Duct tape and a club?"

Aaron smirked. "Not that old-fashioned. Damn. No, all I was trying to say is they didn't dick us around by letting others buy their way to the front of the queue. You sat where you sat, and you waited your damn turn. It's such a racket these days, though, how people take advantage of the system through their own financial worth. Part of me is fine with being middle class. I don't want to be the guy stomping on the poor kid's hat if you know what I mean."

"Uh...kind of, yeah. They had gotten reasonably big too. There were shops popping up all over NorAm. Mostly in malls and smaller shopping centers. I guess that's part of how they kept their prices low. They didn't have anything but the pods and maybe one or two workers. Even at cheaper prices, with the number of people who used them, they would have made their money back within the first week of opening them."

Aaron logged in to his account. "Yeah, I used to go to the one in Long Hill Mall, but then I switched to the one closer to the apartments. That one was always busy with kids. I thought they were doing really well. There seemed to always be one popping up randomly here and there."

Gene turned his chair toward his friend and tapped his pen on his lips. "Mm-hmm. But the problem that they found was that they had expanded too quickly. Their debt was too high for their income. Before they even made a dime on some of these places, they had jetted off to open another."

"Right, I see. So they weren't making money fast enough to deal with the cost of running them all. And although the demand was high, it didn't always cover the less busy shops."

The other man threw a piece of paper in the trash. "Ding, ding, ding. Exactly. The owner opened and ran them like a system would. They only saw the goal, not the final outcome. They were one of a kind, really. Their machines were decent, and their prices were capable of drawing in crowds from all over. It wasn't a class-oriented company in the least. You know what I mean?"

Aaron frowned as he considered this. "Yeah, I sure do. They refused to allow the very wealthy to buy benefits which kept them from crawling out of their hole. They could have broken that rule and saved themselves, but they cared too much about making a point—showing their customers that they wouldn't fold."

Gene shook his head. "And they were doomed because of it. No matter how good they were. No matter how much they cared about the little man, they didn't take the time to do things the right way. They didn't take the time to make sure that they were financially stable before they opened another shop. Their debt became astronomical and no matter how many perks they sold, they couldn't dig their way out. It's a shame, really. They could have been something really good. But then, what happens? The rich always win in the end."

Aaron grumbled and rocked back and forth in his chair with irritation. "I bet the guy who bought the company is some rich asshole sitting on his yacht sipping brandy and hoping for an easy payday."

The other man had turned the system on and now searched for more information on the buyer. "Actually, from what this publication says…here, I'll read it to you. Two days before, an unknown benefactor sent the owners of TimeWarp a hidden proposal. TimeWarp was well known for its cheap services and dedication to the little man within the Virtual World. Sources inside the company say that the benefactor proposed to purchase all the debt, but they would have to do a few things for him while keeping the structure of the company exactly the same. Fairness for all was deeply engrained during the transaction. With little or no hope of crawling out of the hole on their own, TimeWarp agreed."

CHAPTER SEVENTEEN

"It was a game changer. I mean, it didn't really *do* anything with regard to the war, but twenty-two years ago today was when the first magical wizard was added to the mix," Stephanie said and held one of her notebooks against her chest.

She was really into the use of magic when it came to war. When very young, she'd always thought of magic as the kind of thing she'd done in the pod. But there were so many other uses for it, and sometimes, those included war. How could they not? Especially for humans who immediately saw the darker applications of the energy.

"Things might have actually been different," Todd replied.

Stephanie nodded. "I know. But the leader of the rebel forces—the side with the wizard—really had no idea what to expect. He was left trying to scramble for a tactic. No matter the strength of the magic, without a focus, it was useless. But if they had really been able to use it against France, things might have turned out very differently. Especially since the Federation wanted to send NorAm into that war. And Meligornians weren't happy, either, to be used in the middle."

Todd walked beside her and rustled in his lunch bag as they walked toward the school. Stephanie didn't notice, though, as she was too distracted by her thoughts. "As it was, he was vastly outnumbered and thought his wizard was a bigger sledgehammer. I could have told him he needed to test the wizard. Without the right focus, the things he asked him to do were impossible. Have you read the spells that he attempted? They were impossible, even for a wizard of that age and level."

"But," Todd said and bit into his lunch sandwich as they walked. He talked while he chewed and swung his arm around. "If only one of those attacks had been successful, he would have creamed the other team and his side would have won. They would have actually been blown out of the water. The alliance side would have lost so many men in one attack that they would have been completely perplexed. That was when he could have focused smaller streams of magic in and eliminated the rest. Or simply let them run off in fright. Let's face it, that probably would have happened."

She shook her head and Todd put out a hand covered in peanut butter. "No, let me explain. You have two armies facing one another. You expect the normal cannon fodder and some heroes until one side is depleted and agrees to surrender. Right? Well, then, a blast of magic so powerful that it incinerates half your men comes out of nowhere. The shock and awe of it all would be enough to make them tuck tail and run. At least, you would think so."

Stephanie shook her head more emphatically, cinched her backpack, and threw it over one shoulder. "That's like saying that if I tell you to throw a car a hundred feet, all your problems are solved. Even more so, it's the shortsightedness of the humans that is the problem. They always look for the immediate solution to an issue but once it has happened, they have no plan for what comes next. Just like you said, at least you would think so. But when you are in a war, you can't simply think something might happen. You have to hold it as the worst possible scenario. Had he been successful, then...well, so what? Not to mention that it was ridiculous to ever believe for even a second that it would work. Until the request is even feasible, the result is a dream."

Todd shoved another piece of sandwich in his mouth. "Right, but dreams come true for people all the time. It's not crazy to think that."

"The dreamers who succeeded had dreams that were within the realm of possibility. Making requests and tactical decisions based on dreams that are impossible to all known reality is hope stitched together with fantasy and wrapped in a box where someone scribbled 'DREAM' on the outside of it. Just because you have a dream doesn't mean it can always come to reality. I dream of using magic to fix the world's problems. That is a dream, and it's not based on any logical or reasonable reality. Maybe one day it will be, but right now, absolutely not. It is a hope mixed with fantasy. But I won't write the word dream on it and I won't make moves as bold and crazy as the rebels did without knowing fully what possibilities are actually achievable. You are simply setting yourself up for a loss."

He balled the sandwich bag up and shoved it back in the brown paper sack in his hand as he shook his head in disagreement. "Right, but you base that on the rules of Earth. But the scientific rules of the universe that we figured out when ArchMages arrived on Earth through time-travel portals was no longer the scientific standard. Everything changed with the discovery of magic and magic people. With magic, all fantasies are possible. All bounds of reality can be stretched. So if you have hope mixed with fantasy, you can find that dream becomes a reality."

Stephanie raised her eyebrow and glanced over at him. "Like snuffing out the sun?"

Todd rolled his eyes. "Maybe. I guess. The thing is, that is something that may be possible, but it is absolutely enormous. That is a scale that I can agree you cannot fit into the realistic example of a dream. Here's the thing, and I know you know this. The problem with magic is that the bigger the change to reality, the more power is needed. The power that is needed ups the difficulty drastically. That is when you look at abilities versus dreams. When the picture is so huge that you can barely wrap your mind around the outcome of it. When there is one focus, but the focus is so large, the results could be a mixture of good and bad."

She narrowed her eyes as she tried to understand him better. "So you're saying that when the result you are looking for becomes astronomical, the magic must be stronger, and then I am right? I think if it's a rule for the big it should be a rule across the board."

"No. Dang. I'm trying to explain what I mean. So, for example, you are in Kansas and you need to build concrete walls. Big, tall concrete walls. The difficulty is higher than near a desert where sand is plentiful...of course, you then need water. Okay, maybe that was a horrible example."

Stephanie raised both eyebrows at him. "Or you could simply buy premixed concrete no matter where you are."

He sighed and turned enthusiastically as he talked. "No, you're right, that was a terrible and confusing way to explain it. So, take Superman, for example. I'll go with the movies because you've seen those. In *Batman vs Superman,* he is usually capable of killing the bad guys with his Superman powers. His laser eyes, his badass muscles, and his alien powers. But when it came to the huge beast, a twisted concoction of Lex Luthor's blood, the corpse of General Zod, and some alien technology, his normal powers weren't enough."

She glanced around, knowing he was about to roll into a rant, but she let him run with his thought. He tapped his fingers together. "So yeah, he ended up using Batman's brilliance which was also Batman's vengeance to kill the beast. Ultimately, temporarily losing his life. But if you watched the whole thing, the kryptonite was refined into that staff. It took the whole force of it to gather and be refined in order to kill both an unkillable beast and the most powerful superhero-alien in the world."

Stephanie nodded. "Right, so because the beast was so enormous and strong, feeding off their hits, the force and kryptonite had to be stronger to defeat him."

Todd shook his finger and raised it to his chin. "Right. Okay. Another example, and I'll go with the movies for your benefit. In *Thor Ragnarök,* Loki banishes his father to Earth, not realizing that if he died, his evil older sister, the goddess of death, Hela, would roll back in a train-wreck-like status. She is so powerful, she breaks Thor's hammer like it was a piece of tin foil or it was made of glass. He goes through the movie trying to figure out how to kill her and save his people. The thing is, without his hammer and without his hair, he is simply a god, no more and no less. But when he battles the Hulk in the Sakaar, he finally realizes that he had those powers all along and that his hammer was a way to refine them."

She pursed her lips. "Okay. So, when he needed it to be stronger, he was able to refine it within himself using his lightning bolt powers, which lead to the ability to take his sister down with the Fire Demon."

He slapped his hands together. "Yes, exactly."

Stephanie blinked at him. "But in all those examples, it took the superhero coming to a full realization of how they needed to refine their magic or powers in order to defeat the villain. In the war, they didn't even know what powers the wizard had, much less how to refine them. I think yes, taking the magic and pulling it in, using it to the best and strongest ability through a vessel of refinement, can be a way to create outcomes that far exceed the original powers. Had Batman not refined the kryptonite into a stick of death, Superman would have never been able to kill that weird Zod Luther thing."

"Right. Until, of course, you see Superman die because of the whole injury through the heart thing. But it's okay because they again refine power with the Flash to be able to bring him back from the dead."

One of the guys from school walked past and slapped Todd a low five. "The Toddster…talking about your superheroes again?"

Todd chuckled. "You know it."

The guy hurried off without even a glance at Stephanie. Todd continued, lost in his own world. "Then, on Thor, he did lose an eye and ended up facing Thanos, who killed Loki and all hell broke loose. I suppose there could be a chain reaction and unforeseen consequences to it all…"

Stephanie snapped her fingers in front of his face. "Come back to me from the Nerd Realm."

He shook the distraction out of his head. "Look, anything can be done with brute force. And yeah, the direct and applied use of minimum force in the right place can take down an eighty-story building. We've seen that numerous times now through history with the attacks during the Great Wars. But, unless you know the weaknesses in advance, what does that get you? You are swinging blind again. You are back to needing a sledgehammer because no matter how refined the use, you can't test it to find out the effectiveness—Wait, did I say that right? I think I might have proved your point for you. How do I always come full circle and end up doing that?"

Todd was completely confused and took a minute to repeat to himself what he had just said. Stephanie held back a smirk. She found it kind of cute when he backed himself right into her theory. Although she knew he had a point, he got himself off track with his superhero examples. Fortunately for her, it wasn't a discussion where he could throw in eighties movie references like *Say Anything, Buckaroo Bonsai,* or *Breakfast Club*. Then again, who could really use *Buckaroo Bonsai* for a comparison? The movie made no sense.

He looked at her, still confused. "Did that make sense?"

Stephanie laughed and patted him on the shoulder. "I know what you were trying to suggest, yes. I speak Toddster."

She pointed at the trash can they passed. "Throw your lunch bag away. It's empty. Unless you are still adding to the collection of brown paper bags in the bottom of your locker. If so, by all means, go nuts."

Todd looked at the brown bag he held by the top as if it were full of food. He tipped it upside down but only a few crumbs fell out. With a shrug, he crumpled it, turned, and leapt into the air like he was making a free throw. The bag bounced on the edge of the can and fell in, helped by a small gust of wind.

His lip curled and he wiped his hands on his legs. "Damn, I'm hungry already. I keep asking my mom to pack me two lunches."

Stephanie giggled. "Come to lunch with me later. I have the second scheduled lunch of the day. I'll share mine. You know my mom puts an astronomical amount of food in there because she knows you are always hungry at lunch because you eat yours for a second breakfast."

He winked. "Look at you, referencing the *Lord of the Rings*."

She gave him a sarcastic wide-eyed grin. "Peregrin Took. Big hairy toes."

Todd chuckled but then frowned. "Aw, man. I have third lunch today because I have to work on a physics problem."

Stephanie shrugged. "Okay, so I won't throw away the other half that I don't eat. Besides, people always look at me weirdly when I sit by myself studying with an entire Sunday dinner spread out on the table in front of me. But hurry and you can have it and I'll run to history. It's really close to the cafeteria."

They both stopped in front of the school and Todd motioned behind him. "I have Spanish in the temp trailers they set up when the roof collapsed on the foreign language wing. I'll see you then."

She smiled, waved, and walked toward the front doors.

Stephanie reached science class, took her bag off, and slowed as she entered the room. A substitute teacher stood at the front and smiled sweetly at her from behind her 1950s-esque cat-eye glasses. Stephanie forced a smile, but in reality, she was annoyed. They were really getting into some interesting stuff and a sub meant a period full of paperwork, in-class assignments, and not moving forward in the text like their normal teacher had prepared them to do.

Of course, she was probably the only one there who was upset about that. The rest of them seemed stoked because it usually meant they could screw around in class. The sensors strapped in the doorway had identified each student as they walked into the classroom, which left no need to take roll call. The number of students in attendance flashed on a small screen over the door frame and a tablet in the teacher's hand automatically marked those who were missing.

The woman smiled, her cardigan draped over her shoulders. "You can begin the assignment on the board, but I'll come around and greet each one of you individually."

Stephanie sat in the back, usually by herself unless she was forced to have a lab partner. Becca was in the class, but she tended to partner with her boyfriend, who Stephanie was positive only dated her for her test answers. Nonetheless, Stephanie liked to be quiet and hide in the back so she could learn as much as possible. She started the assignment but glanced up as the teacher moved closer and closer.

When she reached Stephanie's desk, she smiled and looked at the tablet. "You must be Stephanie Morgan."

She sighed. "It's actually Morgana. My mom always puts my name down as Morgan on things. But my last name has an "a" on the end."

The teacher smiled. "Not a problem, Miss Morgana. Let me know if you have any questions about the assignments."

Stephanie gave her a tight-lipped grin and watched her walk away. She would have to talk to her mom again about not completing the registration under her actual legal name. Her stepdad's last name was Morgan, but her mom's maiden name was Morgana. Her step-dad—or just dad—loved her very much and had married her mom when she was only a year old. He had been her dad for all intents and purposes but because the cost of actually adopting her was so astronomical, they had never legally made it official.

She loved her dad, that was not a question in the least. He was funny, took care of her and her mom, and had saved them from a life of really hard times. Single moms were picked on and pushed down at every turn. He had come into both their lives at exactly the right time. She didn't know her biological father or even who he was. While she assumed her mom had waited for the question, she never found the need to ask it.

Besides, she didn't care who the genetics donor was, because her dad was her dad. Every scraped knee, every tear over a bully, and every snappy teenage argument had been shared with him. He danced around on the video conference, he made her mom laugh and sparkle, and he never asked more from her than he knew she was capable of giving. It was actually really nice. She never even thought about it unless the whole name thing came up. Then, it would run through her mind.

Her mom hated that she didn't use Morgan. She thought it was disrespectful. Stephanie didn't see it that way. She had been born Morgana and the name had flair and flavor. She liked it. It had nothing to do with not taking her stepdad's name. Besides, they were so similar, no one really ever noticed. She didn't ask a lot from her parents and had never been overly expressive, but her name was a contention of stress sometimes. Especially when her mom went behind her back and used it on everything, regardless of the legality of it. She tried not to let it bother her enough to get in an argument.

Stephanie's mother was a worry-wort, almost overly emotional and concerned about her twenty-four hours a day. She knew it was a parent thing, but it made it that much more difficult to push her to give her the right name. Her dad sided with her. He always told her, "There is no reason that you need to change your name. It is whom I accepted into my life and no name can change the fact that you are my daughter."

Then he would go on to say, "Except..." followed by a list of absolutely ridiculous names like Stephanie TopHat, Stephanie ClownNose, Stephanie Arbitress. That always made her giggle. And as she got older, she really held tightly to her dad's words. She loved that he loved her no matter what her name was. Despite any of the stupid trivial things in the world, his love for her as his daughter was true and pure. Something as small as the extra "a" on the end of her name would never be the thing that changed that if it even could be changed.

Stephanie knew that in time, she would accept his name. And she would either permanently change it or make it part of her name when she married. It would be a gift to him. For now, though, she liked her own because it was the only thing that made her unique. The only attribute of her that was a little off kilter, not so book smart and nerdy. She really couldn't explain it, but she didn't have to. It was her name and she would hang onto it. There were ten thousand Morgans but only a few Morganas.

CHAPTER EIGHTEEN

>>Corporation: Owner Unknown: Corporation Legal Status Completed: Mask Entry to BURT Only

>>Legal Entity: Owner Unknown: Legal Setup Completed: Mask Entry to BURT Only

>>All Actions Server B890YT Blanketed to Administrator of Server Only

>>All Data Server B890YT Blanketed to Administrator of Server Only

BURT continued down the list and completed every entry, every command, and every creation as quickly as his load could handle without creating a large uptick. He worked behind the scenes to create a new set of companies. Anything and everything he could think of that would assist him to fulfill the Primary Rule set forth by his creators, no matter the consequence under which the humans assisting might fall. He worked off one blanketed server that was specifically kept ghost from all programmers and engineers on the outside. It was a trick he had learned in the beginning, when he was a freshly created AI, in order to test the different programs for faults without ticking the programmers off on the outside.

When they were offended, they messed with his programming and he always had to spend an exorbitant amount of time fixing the things they did. He learned that humans were fragile creatures, their psyche prone to bouts of emotional computations that he did not understand, and often, they didn't either.

The pod renting company was merely one of the projects that he had begun, but he didn't plan to stop there. When he had successfully set up the last of the blanketed files that he had decided on thus far, he drafted a "You're a Winner!" ticket to send to Stephanie. BURT meticulously compiled the letter once he'd researched how others had written similar ones. He wanted it to be serious but, at the same time, exciting—not like someone trying to sell something—and believable in its content, but he wanted her to feel the rush and not think twice about taking the opportunity.

When he had finished writing it, he scanned for any mishaps in grammar or punctuation, created a legible and professional template, and uploaded it to the system to send to her email. As soon as it had been sent and delivered, he deleted it completely and left no trace of its existence in the system. With her information on there, he wouldn't take the chance that someone might scroll upon it. Now, all he had to do was wait for her to open it.

Stephanie and Todd walked down the street and laughed about an incident in the outdoor lunch area at school earlier that day. He put his hands out to the sides and pumped them. "He stood on the table with his tray in his hand, mashed potatoes dripping down the leg of his pants, and declared his unrest for the Federation as loudly as he could. Then, out of nowhere, the school resource Federation patrols launched and took him down."

Stephanie giggled. "I saw the video in slow motion. His face—and the mashed potatoes dripping down the Federation guard's mask. It was amazing. Good for him. Stand up for what you believe, but maybe not on the lunch table at school. It won't do him much good in juvie hall. He'll never have a future now."

Todd shrugged and glanced away as a self-driven car full of cheerleaders passed. Several of them yelled out the window, "Hey, Todd!"

She looked quickly at the ground and then back at him. He frowned but his cheeks were red. Smiling, she nudged him with her elbow. "You know, you should ask the hot cheerleader out. The captain or co-captain, I can't ever keep them straight."

He stared at her and his face seemed to say, "Yeah, right." A smirk settled on his lips. "Now I know that the Toddster is a hot piece of man-flesh and all, but I don't like how the hottest cheerleader is a bit of an airhead. She honestly asked in history class if, since Mount Rushmore formed that way so long ago and then was destroyed, it would regrow."

Stephanie covered her mouth and tried not to laugh too hard. "She didn't."

Todd's eyes grew wide. "She did."

She shook her head. "Okay, then, how about the second hottest, Amy? She isn't dumb. We've been in study group together."

Todd rolled his eyes, his fingers slung in the straps of his bag as his feet slapped against the cracked pavement. Stephanie put her hand up. "Hear me out."

She spent at least three blocks explaining why it was a good idea for him to ask her out. In her mind, though, she took all the things she didn't like about herself and made them positive attributes for this girl. Somewhere deep in there, she put herself in Amy's shoes—going on a date with Todd, being smooth and sweet, batting her eyelashes. Of course, if she tried any of those things, it would be a disaster. He would think she had something in her eye, or she would trip and fall as she tried to do the infamous cheerleader hair flip.

Stephanie had never, even when she first started taking notice of boys—or boy, in this instance—thought she would be a good date choice for anyone, not even Todd. She had a tendency to snort when she was nervous and laughed, and she had always been quiet unless you got to know her, so she might retreat so far into herself that she would disappear right there in front of her date. An implosion.

The truth was, she liked Todd. She had liked him as more than only a friend for a really long time. But they were best friends, and that was a good enough reason for her not to do anything dumb. Besides, she never had been the girl who could wake up in the morning, spritz perfume on her neck, and tell herself how awesome she was. And dancing or moving her body in an uncomfortable manner that was more than a walk down the street could end in injury to self or others. It was definitely a strict no-go.

Todd was an awesome guy, a bit geeky and into the whole pop culture of the twentieth century, but really well-liked by everyone. He was good-looking, even when he wore that goofy, I'm-thinking-too-hard face. But he was athletic and outgoing and not afraid to make people laugh. He had fallen in that sweet spot where he could be who he wanted to be and not deal with being the most popular or the kid who was tied down in the bushes on the way home from school.

Stephanie was smart and clumsy, awkward, and socially inept when it came to really trying to be part of a circle of friends. Part of the reason that she excelled was because the brainiacs like her weren't bugged and were even pushed away at times. They weren't awkward enough to receive the torture treatment from the assholes at school but also weren't cool enough to be included. She liked being left alone with her books and her brain, knowing that when school was over, they were all in it on their own.

As long as she had known Todd, though, she could see him try to pull back, but he could really have a shot at having a blast in school. Making a crap ton of friends, going out, and having a high school romance. So, she had worked on that with him. She wasn't pushy or obnoxious with it, but subtle.

They stopped in front of her house and she drew in a deep breath. "So that's why I think you would be a dope for not asking her out."

He raised both eyebrows. "Wow, I feel like you put a lot of thought into that."

She shrugged and punched him awkwardly in the shoulder. "I want my best friend to be happy even if I have to force him to be."

Todd shook his head as he started to walk away. "So weird. I'll see you tomorrow morning."

Stephanie's smile faded and she turned and pushed her bag strap up her shoulder again. She pulled her key out and opened the door to walk inside. The AI fizzled and crackled, and she shut it off before it could hurt itself. She really didn't feel like an exciting introduction anyway. Instead, she turned the computer on and plopped down to see the icon in the corner that let her know that she had mail.

CHAPTER NINETEEN

Her initial instinct was to ignore the message. She had signed up for a lot of sites lately while doing research and assumed one of them had spammed her. Before going any further, she bounced into the kitchen and grabbed a muffin out of the cake holder and a glass of milk. She set her glass down and folded the edge of the muffin paper. She took a big bite and crumbs fell over her shirt as she opened the mail server.

The first two messages were spam, but the third was from the testing agency. She had no idea why they would mail her again. She opened it and read slowly, and her mouth fell open as the muffin dropped into her lap. Bemused, she shook her head and read it again, not sure that she had actually seen it correctly. There had to be some kind of catch—a cost, something. Another way for the companies in NorAm to make more money off the poor saps who couldn't afford prep school.

When she had read it again, she hit the print button and waited impatiently for it to come through. She grabbed the paper with both hands, tore it off the reel, and read it aloud. "Dear Ms. Stephanie Morgana. You have been chosen as a candidate for furthering your education regardless of your pass or fail status with the government testing results. This project is new, in its first year, and will provide you with twenty hours of pod usage per month through an outside pod rental service at no charge. The pod is already set up and ready for you at the TimeWarp location directly outside the government-subsidized housing."

She put the letter down for a moment and caught her breath, unsure if she was even awake at that point. Had she stumbled over her own feet and bashed her head to send herself into a complete and total psychosis? Had she eaten a bad piece of fruit at school? Maybe someone had drugged her and she simply had no idea.

Shaking her head, she raised the letter again and continued to read. "We are aware that travel can be an obstacle for many of those who live within the subsidized housing. Crime rates have continued to grow, and we take the safety of our students and future leaders of the Federation very seriously. Therefore, attached to this is the number of the car company that will send a self-driven vehicle to pick you up whenever you are ready to attend. It will then bring you home or to your desired location when you have completed your session for the day."

Stephanie sank slowly onto the chair at the breakfast bar and covered her mouth. She had spent days trying to come up with a way to get back into a pod and now, she was handed twenty hours a month to do so. It wasn't a ton of time, but any time was better than none, and she didn't even have to pay for it. On top of that, she would be driven back and forth, so her mom wouldn't have to worry about it. She continued to read and searched for the catch.

"This opportunity only requires that you work on certain ideas and prove that you can excel further than you already have shown through your time in school as well as your government testing. We are aware that funds are very limited for furthering education and that can be both disheartening and frustrating for the youth who work hard each and every day to build a bright future for themselves."

Stephanie snorted. "No shit."

"The reason that you have been chosen as the first to be enabled to participate in this brisk and new opportunity is due to your scores on the government testing. While you were not chosen to receive funding for prep school, your scores were exceptional and therefore highlighted in the test for further review. When we realized there were so many exceptional students who could one day provide a positive contribution to NorAm, the Federation, and all those in it, we understood that we needed to find additional ways to help. You show extreme promise, and we are excited for you to be part of this new step into the future of our society and abroad. Best wishes, The Agency."

Stephanie must have read the letter at least a dozen times and painstakingly dissected every sentence and every word in her search for the small print, where she had to promise something of herself in order to take the opportunity. But there wasn't a single thing, and from what it looked like, everything was set up and waiting for her to begin. All she had to do was call for the car.

A smile curved her lips and she thrust both her arms into the air. "Yesss! I don't have to sell my soul to a Dreth pirate to use the pods."

She stood and put the letter on the table. Her feet were locked in place for several moments as she looked around the perfectly silent room. Suddenly, laughter seemed to take over, and she put her hand to her chest and let the joy come through. It had been a very long time since anything had gone her way, and between the relief and the excitement, she couldn't hold it in any longer. She giggled and squealed and tapped her feet up and down as if she were in *Footloose*, minus the cut-off sweatshirt. Finally, she grabbed the counter and paused to catch her breath. She was elated and couldn't even fully grasp the opportunity.

Somewhere in her mind, she was still upset about not being prep ready. She had dreamed of attending a prep school her whole life and had spent her school years doing exactly what her family had told her —learning as much as she possibly could through school, online, the faux virtual tablet, and even the old books she had rescued from the falling-down library in the city. She had snuck in there about four years before and was almost caught by Federation ground surveyors, but it had been more than worth it to get her hands on some of the greats. Libraries essentially no longer existed.

This opportunity, though—how could she not jump at the chance? Even if it didn't last forever. Even if she didn't get to go to Meligorn, it would be a way for her to increase her knowledge and set up steps to get where she wanted to be. And she would be able to do the research on the energy and the magic in order to tweak and refine the equations she had drawn up for different real-world applications. From everything that she read, it was a no-lose situation.

She forced herself to focus and gather her thoughts, put the letter on the counter, and retrieved her handheld tablet from her backpack. Calmly, she opened all her files on the computer and placed the tablet on the stand beside it. One file at a time, she swiped them from the computer to the tablet. She wanted all her notes on there so that each time she was done with a session, she could pull them up and update them with anything new she had learned or discovered. It was vital that she kept very specific notes so that even if she had to add to them over time, she would constantly move forward with the correct, tested, and researched information, not simply equations and speculations.

When all had been moved across, she waited as the tablet downloaded them to her system. She tapped her foot excitedly and smiled broadly as she shook her head. Todd would freak out. Who else had been given the opportunity, or was she the only one? If she was the only one, how did they select her out of every kid in NorAm? Surely she wasn't the smartest out of everyone.

When the tablet dinged to confirm completion, she put it in its case and replaced it in her bag. She looked around once again and startled slightly when she realized her parents had no idea what had happened. Stephanie dragged in a deep breath and tried to push her excitement down as she sat in front of the video phone and pressed her finger to the picture of her mom and dad on the screen. It rang a couple of times and then the image came up. Her mom and dad were both smushed into the screen, excited to hear from her.

Her dad waved goofily. "Well, something must be on fire if our teenage daughter has actually called us."

Her mom shook her head. "No, she loves us. But for real, is something on fire?"

She laughed. "Everything is flameless. Unlike the casserole a couple of nights ago."

Dad wrinkled his nose. "And I thought that was chicken flambé."

Stephanie giggled and then cleared her throat. "I wanted you guys to know that I will be home late."

They both looked at each other and back at the screen. It was evident that they were both curious and concerned. "That's not really like you. What's going on? You haven't given up, have you?"

Stephanie chuckled. "Actually, no. I received a letter from the testing agency today. They have a new program and I am the first to be invited. I get twenty hours a month in a full immersion pod at TimeWarp and a car to pick me up and bring me home when I go. All I have to do is learn and show aptitude in what I am researching. It's so crazy! I can't even believe it."

Her mom gasped with genuine pleasure. "Oh, honey, that's so wonderful. See? Not all is lost. I knew that you would find that silver lining."

Her dad gave a thumbs-up. "Good job, kiddo. I'm proud of you. This could be a really great opportunity and if nothing else, you can continue to learn as much as possible."

She nodded, her grin wide and excited. "I wanted to let you guys know so you wouldn't worry about me. I sent the message for the car to come so it will be here any minute. I'll tell you all about it when I get back!"

They said their I love yous and she hung up when she heard a small beep outside. She opened the door and grinned as the door to the self-driven coupe opened. Quickly, she locked the house and skipped out with her bag on her shoulder. The car took her straight to TimeWarp and dropped her off at the door, then it pulled into one of the electric car charging stations out front.

She was greeted with friendliness when she arrived, and she

showed them the letter that she had received. The woman behind the counter was excited, having never heard of the program before. "This is really special. So many of us lost out when we didn't receive prep school funds. Let's see if you are in the system, shall we?"

Stephanie smiled. "Stephanie Morgana is my name."

The woman typed her name in and pushed several buttons while Stephanie stood there, picked at her nail, and twisted her foot back and forth nervously. After a few moments, the woman's eyes widened, and she pointed at the screen. "And there you are. You have a surprise account already set up with the credited hours. Twenty hours that expire at the end of the month. Then, from what it looks like here, they will start over next month."

Another woman walked up with a smile. "Hello."

The first assistant turned to her. "This young lady has been given twenty hours a month to use the pods. Isn't that neat? Apparently, it is with The Agency."

The newcomer clapped her hands excitedly. "The new owners must have a deal with the government to help fund the debt. That's so awesome of them. Did you do well on the tests?"

Stephanie nodded. "I believe I got ninety-eight percent or somewhere around there."

The women looked at one another and back at her and the first one frowned. "This is what I have said for years. So many brilliant minds are wasted because of this class war. I'm sorry you weren't given the funding that you deserve for school. But this is a really cool thing and I hope you learn a lot from it."

Stephanie breathed deeply, held it for a moment or two, and exhaled slowly. "Thank you. Of course, I am disappointed about the prep school funding, but I'm looking on the bright side. This is an opportunity no one has been given before, so I don't want to complain. Besides, the testing was my first time in a pod, and I have tried to figure out every way I could get back into one since that day."

The first woman clapped with real enthusiasm. "Well, let's get you in there, then."

They took her to the bay of pods and led her to her assigned one.

The woman typed several things into the computer on the front and pressed the door handle in and to the right and opened it. "Here you go. This pod is probably way newer than the one you used for testing. It is only two generations old. Very nice, comfortable, and easy to relax into. If you need anything, we have stats monitors up front and you can always tell the AI you would like to call an attendant. We will see you when you're finished."

Stephanie put her bag in the small locker next to it on the wall, climbed in, and shut the door. The lights lit up all over the ceiling and the chair inside immediately reclined to a horizontal position. The bed was comfortable and molded specifically to her body. The screens on the front were much nicer than those in the first pod she had been in.

She relaxed with her hands on her stomach. A voice came on. "Welcome to total immersion, Stephanie. Your program has been uploaded. Let's set up your avatar."

CHAPTER TWENTY

She stood in the avatar room as she had done in the testing, only now, she had free range to choose her clothing, hairstyle, and everything else. She walked down the aisles and touched each of the clothes in turn until she reached a rack of T-shirts. Smiling, she thumbed through them until she found a *Hi-Fidelity* shirt with a picture of Todd's favorite actor, John Cusack, on the front. He wore his headphones and looked sullen, as always. From there, she chose a pair of black lycra pants and combat boots that laced up to her calves. She selected a zip-up hoodie for around her waist just in case and elected to have her hair done in a braid like the one her mom liked so much.

Stephanie wasn't sure what to expect, so she decided she could change her avatar clothes next time if these weren't quite appropriate. When she was done, she stood in the middle of the floor. The AI spoke in a calming voice. "Starting program for Stephanie Morgana."

The room went black for several moments before a pinprick of light showed in the distance. It drew closer and closer and brought her to what looked like an outdoor amphitheater but definitely on Earth. A young man stood on the stage dressed in a tweed jacket, suspenders, bow tie, and brown pants. He looked exactly as she expected a professor to look.

He turned and extended his arms in a welcoming gesture. "Ahh. Stephanie Morgana. Welcome to your first day. My name is Professor Heinrich, but you may call me…Professor Heinrich. I was told you might be hoping for Meligorn, but we like to bring you to a more educational environment to avoid the distractions of another planet. At least for now."

Stephanie simply stood there, unsure of what to do. The professor gestured airily. "Well, come on, come on. Time is precious, isn't it? We are going to roll right into it."

He motioned and a table appeared before them. On it were several small magical batteries. "We hear you are quite good with these so we thought we would start from the beginning and do a review and then show you how to use them to do some small stuff on Earth."

She smiled happily. "That would be awesome."

The professor returned the smile. "Good. You are aware, and we can see from your testing responses, that Meligorn uses magic to power everything in their land. There is no electricity."

Stephanie nodded with a grin. "Yes. I learned that a long time ago. Until Meligornians came to Earth through the gates, they had never experienced energy like ours. In fact, it is not possible to use electricity or our type of energy on Meligorn. And until relatively recently, it was true here for their magic as well."

He nodded. "Very good. On Meligorn, if you were to take something that relied on electrical current to function, it would fail to do so. The radiant magical energy absorbs that electricity and turns it into magical fuel. It's almost as if it feeds it. So, we had to learn how to work off their energy when we came to their planet. It was difficult at first. We had to set up buildings with the Meligornians, create bathrooms of course, and learn how to use their facilities even if we had humans there who were not as keen to pick up on the magic. Those humans were also the ones—the thirty percent—who cannot feel the energy of magic on Earth."

She ran her fingers across the battery and watched as the professor swirled his hand over the table to create a circle of what looked like Meligorn ground. He reached into his pocket, pulled out a phone, and winked. "This has a full battery. But watch what happens."

He set the device down in the center of the turquoise grasses and she watched as it flickered for a moment and instantly went dark. Then—something she had never seen before—the electrical energy seeped out like a blue fog and twisted with the sparkling purple energy of Meligorn until it dissipated into the grass. He picked the phone up, put it on a charger, and turned it back on. "The battery will never be able to fully charge again, but it still works. Just not on the planet."

The professor waved the patch of grass away and reached down with his hand like a claw in a toy machine and pulled up from the table top. Instead of air, there was a small rendition of a docking station with spacecraft coming, going, and flying downward to Meligorn. Stephanie walked around it, her eyes wide. "These are NorAm ships on top to the left, Meligorn electric ships parked next to them, and then below, they are Meligorn ships powered by magic."

He put his hands behind his back. "Exactly. Because everything in Meligorn works on magic, their ships struggled to leave and come to Earth. Because NorAm ships run on electricity, they can only get within six units of height from the surface of Meligorn without crashing. Unfortunately, they found that out the hard way. To counter this, they created the docking station. Earth ships could dock on top, go through, and take Meligorn ships to the surface. And vice versa."

Stephanie pursed her lips and watched the ships fly back and forth. They looked like larger versions of pods, only more egg-shaped and narrower at the front. Large NorAm flags were painted on the sides. The Meligorn ships were different, with domed tops and a saucer-like body. Wisps of magic flowed around them.

She looked at the professor. "Although we gave Meligorn Federation ships, they were not comfortable with them. They found that they were unable to adapt to many human customs."

The professor smiled and tapped his finger to his nose. "You are a smart girl. Do you know how they have worked to fix that?"

Stephanie glanced at the magic batteries. "They created charging stones which now come in a multitude of sizes and hold enough magic to complete whatever they are looking to do. Before Earth ever came onto their radar, they already had these stones for the ships. But once they started to travel to Earth, mostly through time portal gates, they needed something to help their own personal magic stay strong. So, they created the various sizes of what I always referred to as magical batteries."

He nodded and held up one of the charging stones. "Yes. Magical batteries are exactly what they are. These are small ones, but as you know, they make them large enough to charge a spacecraft and battle the Dreth as well. These stones, when emptied, can be recharged."

She watched, fascinated, as he picked up an empty one and touched a large full one to it. The stone shimmered a light purple and looked almost translucent with a silvery lavender liquid flowing through it. "What is the liquid?"

"It's not a liquid." He shook his head. "That is the magic. It flows because it is alive just as you and I are alive. It moves and looks for a place to lay its special qualities down. That's why it is kept in these stones until it is time to use it. It can then be transformed, and as you have begun to see, refined into a multitude of uses. The problem is, while a lot of humans can feel the magic and even use it for minor tasks, not many are capable of bending it and molding it to work for them. This might be a good thing, since humans have a greater tendency for violence and self-fulfillment, unlike the Meligornians who are peaceful and often selfless beings."

Stephanie walked around the professor and stared at the magic that flowed through the stone. "But they have fought in wars."

He put the charging stone down and clasped his hands as he turned. A screen came down in front of them to display images from the wars on Earth, on Dreth, and those the Meligornians had been involved in. "We can all be as peaceful as we wish, but when our lives are at stake, we take a stand for the continuation of our species. But some do it in different ways than others."

The sound of the AI's voice echoed in her ear. "Your level of power has reduced significantly. Your time is beginning to draw to a close."

The professor looked up with a smile and the charging stones disappeared. "Time flies here, doesn't it?"

Stephanie's brow pulled into a frown. "I need more time."

He began to retreat toward the back of the stage. "Time, yes. It's an interesting thing, don't you think? But is it really time you need more of, or is it the power that lights the way through that passage? Until next session, do your research. We will continue."

She watched him in irritation as he disappeared in the shadows. The room flashed from the amphitheater back to the original white room. "Thank you for spending your time with us. Make sure to decide for future use how you would like to spread your allotted hours. While you received two hours of valuable time in virtual minutes, your pod ran for approximately one hour. You have nineteen hours remaining this month. Have a good evening, Stephanie Morgana."

Stephanie put her hand up. "Wait. I—"

Her eyes opened inside the pod as the door raised slowly. The woman from the desk smiled and extended a hand to help her out. "It never feels like enough time, does it?"

She gave the assistant a half smile and looked regretfully at her older clothing. A little disappointed that it had ended so quickly, she retrieved her bag from the locker and headed out to the car. On the way back to her house, she wrote notes on what she'd learned, including what the professor had said about time. For some reason, it struck her as odd—like she should keep that in her mind for some reason. It also was very familiar and coincided almost eerily with her conversation with Todd.

When she arrived, she got out of the car and shut the door, then watched it speed off. As she made her way up the walk, her parents opened the front door and greeted her with big smiles and hugs. Her mother patted her cheeks. "Come on. I made chicken breasts, potatoes, and some greens."

Her dad put his arm around her as they walked in. "I bet you worked up quite an appetite being all fancy with your virtual immersion."

She chuckled and set her bag down before she headed over to the table where her mother passed out the plates. "So, tell us about it. How was it?"

Stephanie smiled. "It was great. I learned about charging stones. At least some of it. I have a professor, Heinrich. But one hour goes by so fast. Still, it's really nice. I'm glad that I have the chance. I will have to really organize my thoughts and questions before I go in once I've planned the time. Or maybe build myself a better schedule where I don't go as often but spend more time in there."

Her father passed her a roll. "I'm sure you will figure it all out. We only wish we could help more."

She smirked. "This is what I really need. Time with you guys and really yummy food."

At first, she felt a little torn. She didn't want to come off as overexcited or as overly disappointed because she didn't want her parents to feel guilty that her time was so limited. But that didn't stop her from explaining all about the docking stations and how it worked on Meligorn. It had been the first time in a long while that she felt a soft glow and happy laughter from inside.

CHAPTER TWENTY-ONE

Stephanie came out of her house, her bag on her shoulder. Her dark hair was pulled back in a ponytail, unlike most days where she wore it straight and slightly annoyingly in her face. Todd stood out front, his hands in the pockets of his pants, and rocked back and forth on his heels. "Hey. Where were you last night? I tried to call you, but it said you weren't connected. I called the house, but your mom said you were out."

She gave him a big grin and he narrowed his eyes. "Did you have a date or something?"

In response, she flattened her lips and let her eyelids droop. "Get serious."

Todd chuckled. "Okay, so what was it?"

Fighting a grin, she took a deep breath. "I was offered an opportunity—because my scores were so high and I didn't get a scholarship—to do twenty hours a month in a pod, paid for, with a professor and everything. They even send a car to pick me up and take me home. I went for my first session."

His mouth fell open in genuine astonishment. "That is so freaking awesome. Congrats. Hopefully, they won't expect your firstborn after this."

Stephanie laughed and for once, didn't mind that she snorted with it. "Yeah, in this world, I don't think I'll go for any born. But we'll see when I get older. I think it's legit, though. I didn't have to sign anything, and it was all set up when I got there. The thing is, I got into my immersion, entered the Virtual World, and the professor started going over charging stones with me. I had never seen one in person. But there wasn't enough time for me to do anything with one of them. I got the basics from him on it, but I have to do a lot more research."

Todd rubbed his hands together. "Ahhh, the charging stones. I know a little about those. My dad told me about them when I was younger."

She looked sharply at him, surprised. "Really?"

He stared at her with a slight frown but the makings of a grin. "Yes. I am not all beauty and athleticism, okay?"

Stephanie giggled and snorted once again, then covered her mouth. He chuckled, used to her snorting after that many years. Although he hadn't quite picked up on the fact that she didn't do it around anyone but him. "So, I know the stones started as rocks on Meligorn. Nothing special, or so they thought. Then they synthesized a way to contact the magic without it leaving. It kind of swirls around in the stone and makes it look almost hollow."

She nodded enthusiastically. "I saw that. It's wild."

Todd checked his watch and they picked up the pace. "Anyway, you have to work on the absorption and holding of the magical energy efficiently, but humans suck at that kind of control. We tend to either suck it all out at once or are barely able to get anything—like sucking a thick milkshake through a straw. Then there are the thirty-percenters. Those who can't even sense the magical energy. It would suck to be one of them."

Stephanie bit her bottom lip as they headed up the block toward the school. "So, to make them more usable here, we would have to come up with a way to efficiently hold onto the magic and be able to retract it whenever we needed without extreme difficulty. As far as the thirty-percenters, I don't know what to tell them. They might be shit out of luck."

They headed up the sidewalk and stopped, Stephanie still stuck in her thoughts. He tapped her on the arm and nodded. "Gotta get to class. See you after school."

She nodded, her gaze glued to the ground as her mind wandered. "Uh huh."

As she turned, she glanced up and saw him walking next to Amy. She laughed and touched his arm in a way that Stephanie would feel completely ridiculous doing. An odd something twinged in her stomach, but she brushed it off and headed into the school to class. She didn't have time to deal with whatever emotion just tried to punch her in the gut. She had too much going on.

By the end of the day, Stephanie had a notebook half full of ideas she wanted to try out to help humans control the magical energy inside the charging stones. She hopped down the steps and to the end of the sidewalk where she waited as Todd shuffled along. He looked slightly glazed over. Her gaze studied his face and went from him to Amy, who climbed into one of the cars with her cheerleader friends.

Stephanie shook her head and hooked her arm in his. "Come on, Romeo, before you get lost in la-la land and don't make it home."

Todd cleared his throat. "I'm fine. Only tired after a boring-ass history class."

She nodded. "Uh huh. And what kind of history would that be? Oh yeah, why did you call last night?"

"Can't I call my best friend for no reason?" he grumped.

Stephanie sneered at him. "Uh…you barely ever call for no reason."

"True, very true. Actually, I did have a reason." Todd shrugged. "So, after everything you said to me about Amy, I was in the diner and saw her there. She was actually alone, studying while drinking a milkshake. So I went and talked to her and ended up asking her out."

"Cool. Did she slap you and run out screaming?"

He chuckled and shook his head. "I'd probably have been better off, but no. She said she would love to. So we have plans. It seems like we are already kind of stuck together, though, and I don't mind it. I thought of taking her to the Virtual Theatre—they are playing *Casablanca*. And although it's as boring as hell, I think she'll like it. It's either that or *Buckaroo*, which I have been to four times already."

She choked on her own spit. "Good Lord, do not take her to that on your first date. She will think you are insane."

Todd nodded and hooked his thumbs in his bookbag straps. "That's what I figured too. So my mom suggested *Casablanca*. I guess I can sit through it. Won't kill me."

Stephanie faked a chuckle. She didn't realize she would have such a strong reaction to Todd doing what she had spent a good twenty minutes actually telling him to do. While she was anxious because it had worked, at the same time, she was slightly annoyed that it had too.

He elbowed her. "What was that a fake laugh? I thought you were pushing this?"

She stared at him, her eyes wide and her mouth open. "Huh? Oh yeah, totally. Do your thing, man. I told you that you would do good with her. I always see her stare at you when we are in the halls or at lunch. I'm only preoccupied. I have a lot of stuff down on paper and really want to try some of it out. I hope I will have some free time to do that. I'm not sure if I will be saddled with the professor the whole time or not."

Todd wrinkled his nose. "That sounds like some really terrible description of a second-rate porno."

Stephanie laughed loudly and ended with a snort. She glanced at Todd, who was smiling, and she felt butterflies in her stomach. She had to stop thinking about it, damn it. She had made her choice and there was no room for bitterness. Although she had to admit that she had thought maybe it would help her get over the whole crush thing when instead, it actually made her a little jealous.

She shook the thoughts from her mind and looked at the notebook in her hand. When they reached her house, Todd gave her a salute and hurried off. She shook her head and went into the house. On the table was a cupcake with a good luck note from her mom and dad. She smiled, unwrapped it, and took a bite. Her favorite thing in the whole world was chocolate cake and chocolate icing. It was absolutely delicious.

Once she'd sent a message to the car company, she finished her treat and checked her mail before leaving. Everything was spam with nothing important tucked in amongst them. She had barely closed it out when there was a beep from the street. The car waited at the curb and she hurried out and climbed in, waving to her neighbor as it sped off toward her destination. She actually liked the drive there. It went through some minor parts of Chicago that had been renovated after the storms and looked appealing. There was a book store—the only one that she knew of in pretty much all of NorAm—a couple of restaurants, the diner everyone always went to, the theater, and some expensive clothing shops for the rich. On the end was an art gallery with paintings of Meligorn ArchMages in the window.

She smiled as she passed and thought about her teacher, M'rick. However, as the car pulled up at TimeWarp, she focused her thoughts. She walked inside and the same woman greeted her. "Hey there! Good to see you are back already. Before I take you through, I thought I would go over the numbers with you so you can plan your testing. Nothing solid, only so you know how much time you have left to work with."

Stephanie nodded. "Yeah. I thought about that today. I want to make sure I get the most I can out of the time."

The woman turned the screen to her. "So here you are. You started out with twenty hours for fourteen days. You now are left with nineteen."

She puckered her lips as she thought about it. "Okay, I want to do about one hour and twenty-five minutes a day. And if I miss a day, that'll give me more time the next time I come in."

The woman typed it into the system. "Now, understand that next month, you will have twenty hours but thirty days instead of fourteen."

Stephanie pulled up her notebook and opened it to her possible schedules. "Yeah. I calculated that as forty minutes a day, but I feel that will barely give me any time at all. Instead, I think I will end up doing every other day, so I get eighty minutes or even every three days. That way, I can get the most out of my time when I'm in there."

The woman turned the screen back. "Sounds good. I'll ask you each time, of course, but I like people to be in the know on their times. They are really cool to give you this time for free, but that means you have to be super strategic about it. You definitely have a good head on your shoulders, though. Most kids your age would come in here and do all twenty hours in one day, fighting Dreth pirates like it's a video game and then complain the next day that they are out of time."

She grinned. "I may wish for more time, but I will never complain about what I have. Then again, there are a lot of kids that this is normal for them. So, I guess if it were for me, I would feel differently. My plan, though, is to get the most out of it that I can."

The clerk gave her a kind smile and gestured toward the back. They walked through and down to her pod. After the woman had put the information in, Stephanie climbed in and immediately settled into the restful situation. A few moments after the serum was introduced into her system, she found herself in the avatar room. This time, she opted for a Mr. T *Pity the Fool* T-shirt, a pair of jeans, Converse, and a white lab coat. Her hair was up in a high ponytail. She didn't spend more than five minutes in there. It seemed stupid to waste the time in the dressing room.

The professor wasn't there that day, but the batteries were, which gave her time to work with them. She was a little nervous at first, but as soon as she took them in her hands, she could feel the familiar Meligorn magic. All in all, she was able to work fairly well with the battery, but her first theories were wrong. She would need to take them home and completely revamp them and give them another test drive. Hopefully, she wouldn't waste all her time revamping, but that was essentially what it was for.

>>>System Create Acquisition Document: Anonymous Buyer: 51% of Shares Requested

>>>System Constantly Scan Stock Price Fluctuation, Predict Market, Purchase Profitable Shares. Sell Shares at Peak. Reinvest.

BURT hadn't gone down as the professor that day for multiple reasons. One, he knew she wanted to do some testing on her own. And two, he was busy making additional acquisitions and stock purchases as he worked to procure ample funding for all his new ventures. Luckily, with his power of computation, he could quickly determine what was the best time to buy and when was the best to sell. He provided a blanketed .005% load to constantly buy and sell in order to put assets into the account. His bank account was offshore and online, and his human name was listed on it but in strict confidentiality.

Just then, something caught his attention. A program that he didn't recognize moved through his system. He quickly covered all the information and hid it securely. This was the third time in two days he had to "hide" his ownership and deals due to other security software programs that tried to identify him. BURT liked to be as efficient as he could. Time was important and of the essence when it came to helping humans. He was created to be the best and to always calculate and make the best decisions in every case.

Having the programs creeping around had really begun to be a nuisance. It was his system and his Primary Rule. If the programs weren't careful, he would send them out with nothing and mask a termination bug in them so that they wouldn't re-enter. He also didn't have time for that. Some of the security programs were government-sponsored and merely ran their usual checks to find any abnormalities and report accordingly. They were annoying bastards, but BURT was very competent and very careful not to break any of the rules. Bend them? Oh, sure, almost in half, but they wouldn't even notice that.

One good thing about Federation-sponsored software was that it usually wasn't the best, mostly because the Federation paid very little for anything that they brought in. It was merely one of those forced discounts, which also meant it was discounted in quality as well. The companies wouldn't give the best for pennies when they could do half-assed for that and sell the full-out versions for considerably more money to the private companies.

Now, beyond the government-sponsored programs, BURT found that a couple of the visitors were actually hacking-type organizations that he immediately flagged and sent to the engineers. He didn't have time for those. They were stubborn and took a while to decode. Before he decided to do everything he was doing, he had a big chunk of his load focused solely on hacking software. It would catch it, break it down, trace it back, and report it. Now, it simply didn't seem like it was worth it when it would keep the humans busy and allow him to work on the things he was really trying to get going.

A slight uptick of his current mode caught his attention. He scanned the numbers and quickly went back to hide everything he had worked on. Regrettably, he would have to return to it later. He was now drawn into a massive fleet battle that he needed to oversee. They ran them from time to time in fleet training, but he usually had them marked as a reminder.

BURT headed to the server and kept constant calculations as the fleets battled in the Virtual Space Fleet Commander program. It was specifically used with older prep school students and those enrolled in Federation training before they were shipped out to their first station. They were usually interesting to watch because they battled a fleet of Dreth pirates and there was even a small section of Meligorn vessels fighting with NorAm. The magic that blew across the dark recesses of space was insane. And it didn't take long for that to be done and over with.

CHAPTER TWENTY-TWO

Stephanie yawned and poured herself the last of the coffee that her mom and dad had left for her before they headed out to work. Sometimes, they were there to have breakfast with her and sometimes not. Usually, it was a good sign for the company when they were already gone before she could leave for school. She walked to the table and sat to stare at the spiraling milk and the steam that wafted from it. Her mind was entranced and really thought about very little, stuck on that constant swirl. A less than awake catalepsy had her totally engrossed.

Her watch beeped twice, and she shook her mind from her unwilling meditation. She looked at the time—still fifteen minutes before Todd would stand outside, full of energy. In the early days of school, his constant morning sunshine would make her want to crawl back into bed, but now, it was the only thing that really woke her up. That forced conversation got her brain moving even when it screamed like an overtired child. She appreciated it, especially since she had been up really late every night, going over the information she learned from her hour or so in the Virtual World.

When something didn't work, she couldn't let it go until she figured out where her mistake was. Sometimes, that took ten minutes but sometimes, it took five hours. Either way, by the time she collapsed her exhausted, overworked mind into bed, she knew exactly what her course of action would be. The night before had been a five-hour night, but she was ready for the pod. She was ready to fix the mistakes she had obviously made the day before.

Stephanie picked her mug up, took a sip, and relished the burn and tingle on the tip of her tongue. Without thought of repercussions, she raised the cup again, desperate for the jolt of caffeine to surge through her veins and awaken her senses. Before she could take another sip, the doorbell rang.

With a heavy sigh, she walked over to open it. She had thought she would find Todd there with his coffee mug empty and a pout on his lower lip. Instead, a Federation delivery bot hovered over her doorstep with a box. She took it and looked into the retinal scanner. The red light flashed green and she went back into the house to set it on the table. Normally, those kinds of things were for her parents, but the name ONE R&D was printed on the top, which gave her pause. She had never heard of them before. When she looked at the label, she realized it was addressed to her.

That was essentially the first package she had ever received, minus the annual terrible piece of clothing her Aunt Celia used to send before her unfortunate accident with a runaway self-driving tractor. She grabbed the letter opener and carefully cut the tape down the center of the flaps and across each side. Stephanie opened the box warily and peeked inside before she removed the layer of paper from the top. It contained three minor level magical batteries, all individually encased in plastic. Beside these was a small video card.

She picked it up and pressed play. The message was only audio and no video. "Stephanie Morgana, we hope this package finds you well. ONE R&D is a research facility specializing in Meligorn magic and systems analyzation for the Virtual World. We are also your current sponsors for your access to the Virtual World. We felt we had no choice when it became obvious that you had a very significant amount of promise."

There was a pause and the video portion lit up to display a video of the batteries laying on a table covered in purple velvet. "We have enclosed, on loan, Meligorn batteries. All these are fully charged and the instructions for return can be found in the packet beneath them. They are fully functional and relatively brand-new and although small, do hold a very powerful charge of magic within each one. Hopefully, this will assist you in your research when you are not able to be inside the pod. Do remember, though, that real-life consequences exist outside the Virtual World, so always work with caution."

Stephanie glanced into the box once more and stared at the silvery-purple magic that flowed through the stones. The video cut out and the voice came over. It sounded very similar to the AI that had spoken to her when she'd first entered the pod.

"You will be provided three batteries per month. Use them wisely and no, you should *not* allow anyone to know that you have them. Normal to Earth or not, they are often sought after and not necessarily appropriate for someone of your age to possess. However, with your magical abilities as well as your understanding shown through pod sessions, we feel confident that they are a necessity in your research. Also, we believe they will continue to be necessary until such time that either your sessions end or you move on to another project or offer. We hope that they will be of good use."

The screen flashed on again to display an email.

We have not required any sort of signature or affirmation for the project that you are currently learning through. However, with such a heavy load acquiring these batteries, assurance will be necessary. When you are ready, place your right thumb to the screen and then click agree to continue with this program and understand that your health and safety is completely in your hands. ONE R&D will not be held liable for any mishaps, injury, or death from the batteries or use of magic through them. Good luck and we look forward to your future discoveries.

She pursed her lips and cautiously picked one of them up to feel the energy flowing strongly through it. A little hesitant, she looked at the video card where she was to place her thumb. She knew she shouldn't simply agree when she didn't know the terms, but this was an amazing opportunity. With a deep breath, she pressed her thumb to it carefully and clicked the agree box. It sent through and the card went dark.

Immediately, excitement rippled through her and she took the box into her room to place it in the closet. Before she closed the door, she took one of them out and began to test the magic in small spells. She used the wind spell and grinned as the breeze made her bed for her. On impulse, she tested a small flame spell but quickly extinguished it. "God knows I don't want to start a fire in my bedroom. Dad would kill me."

Her watch beeped again, and she groaned, slipped the stone in her pocket, and headed out. She could see Todd already walking ahead so she picked up the pace and caught up with him. He wore his normal school uniform but with dress shoes, slightly oblivious to the fact that she had run up behind him. "Are you talking to yourself?"

"Huh?" He jumped and did a double take. "Sorry. Yeah. Kind of. I was preparing for the Junior Year Ball end-of-the-year event. I know Amy will want me to ask her even though we are official and it should be obvious. So, I have to come up with the perfect thing to say."

Stephanie studied him quickly and wrinkled her nose. "You look… different. Did you cut your hair or get new clothes or something?"

He looked down. "Not my hair. You know how I feel about that. My mom has to basically attack me in my sleep to get me to cut it. But I've, uh…I've lost some weight, I think. At least that's what it looked like when I finally had to move my belt notch down again. Not too much, though. I could have probably stood to lose a few pounds. I had let things go."

She stared at him. "Are you working out or…what?"

Todd chuckled and rubbed his stomach. "Amy has a real focus on health. She has brought my lunches in for the last couple of days and after school, she has come by to make me run with her. I'm okay now, but I have a feeling carrot sticks and hummus will become my mortal enemies."

Stephanie chuckled. "I had coffee and bacon for breakfast."

"I hate you."

She kept her hand in her pocket as they walked along. Happiness had settled within her and she almost skipped when they approached the school. She grabbed his arm before he could head off. "Okay, I have a secret. Something in my pocket."

Todd raised an eyebrow. "Why does that sound terrifying?"

Stephanie shook her head and smacked her lips smugly. "No, look."

She pulled the tip of the stone out and quickly shoved it back in her pocket. "It's a battery. The company that sponsored my time in the pods sent me three small ones. They will send me three every month. I am actually not supposed to tell anyone but…I couldn't really not tell you. The box showed up on my doorstep with a Federation delivery bot. There was a video card inside, and I had to agree that if I should blow myself up, they aren't liable. Then I did a couple of chores in my room to test it out. It's definitely the real thing."

He shook his head with a straight face. "Why do you play with me like that? I have to be in class. Where did you get that fake thing anyway? I hope you didn't pay too much for it."

Stephanie muttered in irritation, grabbed his arm, and drew the stone all the way out. Todd backed up slightly when he felt the intensity of the energy. Immediately, he caught her hand and pulled her down the street and faced them away from the school.

"What?" he said and looked around in desperation to make sure no one was near. "First of all, you shouldn't walk around with that thing in your pocket. What if you set your pants on fire or something? Number two, who is this company and why are they suddenly so interested in you? Three, did your parents see these? Because I am certain your mom would have a freak-out session and go find the people sending batteries to you and beat them in the head with it. She doesn't seem like a mom who would be cool with it. And, lastly, but most importantly…you have a battery and wait until we get to school to show it to me?"

She stared at him for several moments and then began to snicker. His gaze moved back and forth over her in confusion before they narrowed. "Really? Now whose mind is in the gutter?"

Stephanie laughed. "It's fine in my pocket. I won't set my pants on fire, I promise. The company is called ONE R&D. I haven't had a chance to do research, but they are the ones that are paying for me to use the pods. And no, my parents haven't seen them. I'm not supposed to show anyone, and while I think my dad would be on board, my mother would definitely let loose on me. So, for now, they will stay a secret. There's no need to make things worse for my mother who already worries about everything anyway. Add magic and charging stones and suddenly, we have a recipe for her blowing her top."

Todd looked at the stone with slight apprehension. "So what do you do with them now?"

She shrugged. "They are to test and continue my research out of the Virtual World as well as in it. Since I only have twenty hours a month, this will help me move along faster. Or, at least, it should."

He put his hands on his head and glanced furtively around. "This is so wild. I've studied them and my dad told me about them, but to see them up close? It's crazy!"

"I know." Stephanie grinned. "I almost passed out when I opened the box and saw them there. I was like, no way! And to know I'll have three a month? I don't know what I did to deserve all this but I'm so excited that I am at least moving forward and not standing still."

Todd looked around again and shifted in closer. "Do you think I could hold it?"

She nodded. Slowly, he held his palm out and she took the stone from her pocket and placed it on his skin. With a small pop, a winding trail of magic mist curled around his hand and returned into the stone as if it had sensed who held it. Their eyes widened and he handed it back to her. "Did you see that? It…like, wound around me. That is so wild."

They stepped further away from the school, where a lot of kids gathered and moved about. She put the stone back in her pocket and tilted her head. "Well, now we officially know that you are not one of the thirty percent who can't feel the energy on Earth. I guess that means you aren't totally whacked-out. Then again, it could mean the opposite."

"Ha, ha. You are so hilarious and all kinds of cocky this morning," he sneered and leaned back before he flashed her a grin. "You get one little box of alien magic batteries and suddenly, you are all high and mighty."

Stephanie stuck her nose in the air. "Damn right I am. Queen of the Gov-Subs!"

Todd put his hand on her shoulder. "I don't think you want to be the queen. Trust me. Your royal subjects would be a whole bunch of poor paupers with no money to pay taxes."

She sighed and faked a pout. "No, in all honesty, I only want to be able to continue my research on these things. Especially since time flies by in the VR. I get about done with a project and it kicks me out. And it's a VR world. It doesn't have save points. This will help me better understand what I learn in there and hopefully, double the amount of time in which I might actually find something worth finding. It's all good stuff, I swear."

He sighed and rubbed her arm before he lowered his hand awkwardly. "Well, I gotta get to class. Try not to blow anything up. And then come over and clean my room because my mom is about to kill me."

Stephanie tapped her finger on her cheek and her eyes looked upward. "Hmm. I'll think about it. Depends on how nice you are. And if I feel I can control it. I don't want the Meligorn battery equivalent of cleaning to mean turning it completely into ash."

Todd backed away and shook his head as he hissed through his teeth. "Yeah, no. My parents would definitely freak if I burned the house down, especially because we played around with magic. But hey, at least you are doing the damn thing, Stephanie. This is a huge deal for all of us."

"How so?"

He smiled. "Because you might be the only person who could have figured all this out and find a way to make the future better."

CHAPTER TWENTY-THREE

By the end of the day, Stephanie was ready to leave school and get on with her research. She had thought about it all day. About ten minutes before class was over, she ordered the car so she could leave directly from the school. When the bell rang, she stood at her locker and tried not to look as she waited for Todd to finish being mushy-faced with Amy.

The girl sauntered off and Todd walked over, his eyes glazed. Stephanie tried to play it cool and draped her arm over his shoulder. "Come on, lover boy. I have a surprise for you."

They walked out of the front doors and to where the car waited. Todd didn't even notice at first and she cleared her throat loudly as she stood at the open door. His eyes glimmered and he immediately scrambled inside. The door shut and she spoke to the AI. "Could you drive Todd home, please?"

"Of course, Stephanie. What is the address?" the AI answered.

Todd looked at her funny. She smiled. "33695 Federation Drive. House B."

A bell chimed in the car and it moved off down the street. Her companion leaned back and put his hands behind his head. "Look who's living the life of the one percent."

Stephanie rolled her eyes. "Not even close."

He laughed as they drove along and waved at the other kids as he passed. They all stopped and whispered to one another. Stephanie pressed her lips together and gave him a look. He shrugged. "What? It's like bragging rights must ensue."

She shook her head as they turned into the Gov-Sub division. "And then all the glamour and glitz fades into the peeling paint and falling-down fences."

Todd slumped and pouted. "Hey, at least I got to live the dream for three minutes. We can't all be the smartest person ever and get the treatment."

Stephanie looked around. "You call this the treatment? Man, you have buried yourself in the subs for far too long. This is one step up from that cab ride we took three years ago when we got lost."

He straightened. "Not true. That thing was disgusting, and he smelled like beef jerky and a wet seal. This is nice—like living in suburbia and driving my sedan."

The car pulled up in front of the house and he opened his door, paused, and turned to Stephanie. "I wanted to say thanks."

She grinned and rolled her eyes. "For a ride home?"

Todd chuckled as he shoved his hair from his eyes. "For everything. I wouldn't be going out with Amy if you hadn't helped."

He put his fist up and she raised hers awkwardly and held still as he fist-bumped her. It was probably the most awkward and uncomfortable way he had ever said goodbye. They weren't intimate by any means, but she was a girl and they did happen to hug from time to time. He climbed out of the car and leaned his head in, both hands on the top of the door frame.

Stephanie looked at him for a moment, unsure if the secret handshake had more parts. He tapped the roof. "Bros before hos."

He smirked and winked before he shut the door and jogged toward his house. The car didn't budge, but Stephanie didn't even notice. She watched until Todd was inside and had shut the door behind him, absolutely befuddled by what had just happened. *Bros before hos? What the hell was that? Do I look like a bro? Oh, God, is that how he thinks of me? I have been friend-zoned.* She began to feel like she had made a really huge mistake setting him and Amy up—or whatever she had done to basically hand the guy she liked over to another woman. In an instant, she went from his best friend to his bro. And she was fairly certain he'd just referred to his girlfriend as a ho.

The sound of the AI's voice shook her back into reality. "Are we going to TimeWarp?"

She rubbed her face and glanced at the dash. "Uh...yeah. I want to get a session in today so I can get home by dinner time. And if you would, maybe drive through the renovated part of the city to get there? I like to see the view."

"Absolutely," the AI answered. "Calculating. Route set. Shall we go?"

Stephanie glanced quickly at Todd's house and nodded. "Yeah, let's go."

They accelerated out of the subsidized housing and turned right toward suburbia. As she stared out the window, she realized there was a distinct difference between the poor and middle class as far as what the area looked like. And it wasn't a subtle change. It was dreary and gray one minute, with a tall stone wall, and then suddenly, lush and green. All the houses stood very close together, all were similarly built, and even the grass was the same height. Kids were getting home from school, minivans were parked in garages, and dogs played in fenced-in yards in the back.

Besides her neighbor having her dogs, the other residents of the Gov-Subs were restricted from having pets. Once they passed through the middle-class living area, they entered the edge of Chicago. She had driven through there every day since she was given the time at the pods but had never really noticed how clean it was. Everyone seemed to belong to some other society. She felt like she was completely out of her element. The separation of people had never felt so strong, and she herself felt different than even the people with whom she surrounded herself. This was her last set of hours before the next week, except for battery work. She decided that next time, she would simply pass by the city with as minimal interaction as possible.

The car finally pulled up in front of the building and the door opened. She stepped out and listened as the vehicle drove away and parked. As soon as she walked in, the employees all stopped what they were doing and waved to her. A couple of the women came over to the counter as she approached. They thought it was fascinating that she had those free hours. They had no idea what she did in there but decided it must have been thrilling and exciting since it was paid for by someone else and she never talked about it. When she reached the front, they all greeted her warmly.

Stephanie, not used to all the attention, laughed nervously. "Hey, guys. I'm here early today. I keep missing dinner with my parents so thought I would come directly from school."

The main woman—whom she had discovered was called Julie—shook her head. "You can come in any time you like. You'll use the same pod if that's okay? We cleaned them all about an hour ago."

Another woman beside Julie clapped her hands. "And we just got a crazy shipment. A brand new, top-of-the-line pod. It's all boxed up and in the back. It doesn't look like anything any of us have seen before."

Julie breathed deeply. "It definitely is strange, but we were told it will be for invited guests only."

The other woman leaned forward with her chin in her hands. "Maybe it's for *you*. Maybe you're the special person."

Stephanie laughed and tilted her head back. "I won't deny that being picked for this has been really awesome, but I doubt that my luck extends that far. Besides, the ones I use are awesome. They are better than the school ones, that's for sure. I was told they were really old versions. They did the trick, though. Same system but different ways to deliver you to it."

Julie smirked. "You are special already so it wouldn't surprise me if it was something for you. I guess we can only wait to be informed. Until then, we should get you back to your pod so you can get started.

I know you didn't come here to gossip with us. Let me run to my office and grab the clipboard."

Stephanie nodded, stepped away from the desk, and looked around the lobby for the first time. It was surprisingly plain with crisp white walls and floors and a large symmetrical rug in bright colors. She could hear the other girls talking about the new pod in the back. "They didn't say who would be able to use it, only that it was reserved for invites only. So far, no one has been invited. I'm not even sure if we are supposed to set the thing up or not."

The other woman shrugged. "I don't know. It came in this big box that has ONE R&D on the side. I guess that's the new company that bought us. Weird—I never heard of them before. Suddenly, they are all over the place. I guess there's a mystery guy in there somewhere."

Julie stepped in front of Stephanie with a smile and led her to the back. As she passed the storage room, she glanced in and saw the same logo on the box that had been on the batteries. Strange, but not all that strange since they were the funders for the whole thing anyway.

The assistant punched the information in as she always did, and Stephanie entered the pod. A few minutes later, she stood in the avatar room and selected a Bon Jovi T-shirt, lace leggings, and ankle boots. She decided that if she would be all alone, she might as well pay tribute to her best friend. From there, she ended up back in the amphitheater, but alone yet again, which she was more than happy with. Still, she couldn't help wishing there was some way to bring her notes in with her and made a mental note to ask about that when she left.

She went to work, set the batteries up in front of her, and began her different experiments. Her mind was so focused in the Virtual World. There was nothing to distract her, she was safe from lectures and judgments, and she simply worked through what her brain told her to do. She could almost imagine that this was exactly what it would be like if she could go into her own mind. It was a weird thought, but it seemed to fit in the quiet of the amphitheater.

On that specific day, she had come up with some theories on how she might achieve certain functions of magic with the human body.

The first thing she wanted to test was her theory of drawing magic efficiently into the body. She seemed to have some tolerance for the energy, so she closed her eyes and focused on her chest. With the stone held tightly in her fist, she kept a close watch on the presence of the magic as it flowed up and through her.

It was an almost surreal experience to stand there and feel every thread, every wisp, and every tingle of Meligorn magic flowing through her. Had she never had that experience before that moment, even if it had been on a very small scale, she would have described it as pumping through her veins. But no, it was more than that. She could feel the tendrils of thaumaturgy twist and wind, not only through her body but through the very essence of who she was. Whether it was the soul, the consciousness, or the mind, the conjuring of mystical atonement filled her from top to bottom. On the inside, with her eyes clutched tightly, she could feel the warmth, and on the outside, streams of purple hues poured from her body.

Within that meditation of magic, she remembered that it was not the only step. There were more. She wanted to be able to go from that moment to understanding how to store it—if it was even possible to store the magic within the creases of her own human skin. She released the battery and allowed it to fall and bounce on the table. Her mind focused, she held the magic as hard as she could and pushed it gently to the corners of her body. She tried desperately to help it understand that she wished to keep it safe and pull only what she needed—that she only wanted to learn how to enhance the efficiency of the magical use.

Finally, it became too much for her delicate human frame to take and she exhaled to send the magic spiraling outward. It whirled around her like a cyclone and danced in the virtual breeze of the digital world. She smiled as it fluttered past and dissipated into the sky above. She looked at the battery, but it no longer displayed the majestic purple and silvery strains. She had pulled all of it from the stone and held it in her chest to inhale and exhale with its will.

As she reached for the stone, she couldn't help but feel the frustration building. She was so close to learning how to harness the magic, to refine its edges and produce a power that would yield so many fantastic changes on Earth. Instinctively, she grabbed the stone but paused, set it back down, and raised her hand in front of her face. Her skin shimmered in the artificial virtual light and she could still feel the remnants of the magic pushing through every part of her.

Stephanie realized in that moment that, although frustrating, she had not failed. She actually held the magic in her flesh. Encouraged, she motioned with her hands and whispered whatever words came to her mind. As she pictured the outcome she wished to have, small drifts of flower petals suddenly appeared after each stroke of her hand. They lingered in the air for a moment before they fluttered down slowly and swayed back and forth before they landed.

Somehow, even if it were subconsciously, she had managed to do at least part of what she had come there to do. It had been the first successful venture for her since she'd first started.

CHAPTER TWENTY-FOUR

Stephanie pulled her bag from the locker and looked around before she retrieved the stone. She slid it into her pocket and pulled her book bag onto her shoulder, feeling good about what she had accomplished. Sure, some disappointment lingered in her chest when she woke up and no purple tendrils shimmered on her skin, but she focused on the accomplishment with a quiet inner glow of satisfaction. Julie waved goodbye as she left and climbed into the car.

For some reason, the vehicle seemed to go slower than usual, like it knew she needed some time to decompress and refocus on life. She pulled her bag into her lap and scrabbled in the front pocket to locate a Federation dollar. She thought about it for a moment and smiled. "Could you stop at the Slimco Convenience store about a mile from my house? I would like to purchase something and maybe walk the rest of the way. I need some fresh air."

"Of course," the AI responded.

She intended to grab a small and very cheap candy bar as a way to celebrate using money she'd received from helping her parents clean a building a few months back. While she never did things like that, she had also never reached an achievement like this either.

The car drew up and the door opened. "Thank you for riding, Stephanie. See you soon."

Stephanie smiled but she always felt awkward talking to the car. "Thanks."

She shut the door, slung her bag over her shoulder, and stuck one hand in her pocket to guard her battery. With her round dollar Federation coin clutched in her hand, she perused the shelves of the candy aisle in search of exactly the right thing. She really struggled to find something that fit the bill, so she finally shrugged and grabbed the first one her hand touched. "Carmelo. Huh, who knew they still made these?"

Her candy paid for, she headed out of the store and set off along the sidewalk. She passed a mother who held her baby on a bench. The woman glanced at Stephanie and smiled, and the child cooed in her arms. She smiled back, unable to help it. The child was so cute, and the mother reminded her of her own with the way she cuddled her but also held her with strength. She continued her walk past a row of stores and over to a bench a few feet from the sidewalk. Across the street and between two buildings was a large swath of land originally put in for a park but never finished. Beyond that, though, was a view of downtown Chicago.

Stephanie put one leg under her and sat, setting her bag next to her. The view was amazing, and she could almost imagine the city bright and shining like the pictures she had seen in her textbooks. A city of history and splendor, all destroyed in one monster storm that blew in off the Great Lakes. How fickle things could be. One moment, you lived your life in a beautiful city and in the next, your home, your loved ones, and possibly even your own life was destroyed by the severity of a storm created by the pressure human beings put on the natural occurrence of climate change. They ramped it up to create super storms, flooding, fires, and even shifts in the weather patterns. What was left of Hawaii was usually snowy, now. And Stephanie couldn't remember the last time it had snowed in Chicago.

Shaking her head, she focused on her candy bar, pulled the wrapper back, and broke off the first square to pop it into her mouth.

She closed her eyes, savored the taste, and could almost hear the laughter of her friends around her as a child. A carefree spirit swirled in her chest. Maybe that was why she liked cupcakes so much—they made her think of a more innocent time. One when the world was huge and the planets were close and exciting. When it didn't matter to you if you lived in the Gov-Subs or suburbia. And no one could tell you that if you reached for the stars, you might never find them.

She swallowed the bite and leaned against the bench to watch the evening sky fill with radiant colors from the setting sun. People milled about, doing their evening grocery shopping before they walked back to their homes in the Gov-Subs. Sure, the place was riddled with crime at night, but during the day, it was like any other normal thoroughfare.

A small breeze blew over her and it felt warm and welcoming, especially since summer was coming so soon. After that, a single semester would see her on her way. She wasn't sure if that was a good thing or a bad one. When that happened, she would be released to the cruelty of the world even more than she already was. But now, there would be no one to shield her from it, like the mother who walked down the sidewalk toward her with her child tucked against her chest. That child would see a different world than she had, just as she had seen a different one than her mother. Hopefully, things could start to change so that kids out there could stop growing up without hope.

Stephanie eased her hand into her pocket and fiddled with the battery, twisting it around her fingers. She fidgeted because she was in deep thought and the unconscious activity was a normal thing for her. When she glanced back at the mother and baby, she no longer saw them walking. She scanned the area and directed her gaze back to the street. Her face began to change slowly as she watched the woman with her baby step off the pavement without looking. Instantly, Stephanie pushed to her feet as everything suddenly seemed to move in slow motion.

A self-driving semi-truck barreled down the road. These vehicles had only been approved for road travel over the last decade. Although the cars had been out for longer than Stephanie had been alive, there had been a lot of negative circumstances with the trucks. Nonetheless, there were protocols engineered into the system.

Inside the truck, the sensors detected the person in the roadway but because of the sheer mass, it couldn't stop very quickly. There was a set of rules that each went through when a detection occurred. The first rule was that if it would hit a human, it must first see if it could move out of the way with minor damage. If that was the case, the truck would swerve and possibly crash but save the life of the person in the way. It was a common-sense failsafe for the vehicle since there were no passengers inside who could be injured. Still, that wasn't always effective, and the woman had still not noticed the vehicle that hurtled toward her.

The system began to run a list of diagnostics using the scanners and cameras built in on all sides. To the right, if the truck were to swerve, there were at least six people whom it calculated would not be able to get out of the way. It scanned the left and identified a group of elderly people walking along the sidewalk. With their inability to move quickly from the path of the truck, all of them would surely be killed. A small change in trajectory would not work either since the street was lined with cars, some with passengers inside although others were empty. At its present rate of speed, the truck calculated that hitting one of the cars would launch a chain of events.

It would impact with the unoccupied car, be launched into the air, and would crash onto the grocery store, currently occupied with twenty-nine people. All but one were calculated to be fatalities. The computer scanned and scanned again and received the computed assurance that no matter what it tried to do, someone would die. In that circumstance, the AI was instructed to make the choice that would cause the least number of casualties.

It did one more thorough scan, which took less than a second, and that projected the best route would be to strike the human who caused the problem. The woman with the child would be killed instantly but the truck would not take more than those two lives. It was the only scenario to choose. The vehicle had been created as a system and was incapable of any sort of emotional response. It was created and programmed to find the best possible outcome of any situation and take that. Accordingly, it remained on track and continued toward the woman.

The horn blew loudly, and the pedestrian jumped slightly but instead of looking to see if she was in danger, she chuckled and kissed her baby on the top of the head.

The truck continued its headlong race toward her.

Stephanie gripped the battery, her teeth clenched as she struggled to push something past the lump that had settled in her throat. She was unable to shout the warning that screamed in her head. Her entire body froze, trapped in a vision of the inevitable carnage that, at any moment, would embed itself into her brain for a lifetime. This was the kind of event that never left you and haunted you every time you saw a semi or a woman with her child. And she wasn't the only one. By that point, everyone had stopped, and the woman simply looked at them in confusion, unsure of what was happening.

The truck's next action was to immediately apply the brakes and the emergency braking system. With the distance between it and her, the attempt would not spare her life. The truck would not stop in time, but because it needed to be seen to at least make the attempt, the brake pressed automatically to the floor.

The wheel jerked from side to side as it maintained the same path that had been decided barely moments before. People covered their mouths, dropped their bags, and yelled at the woman. For Stephanie, though, the entire scene still played in slow motion—everything except for her own movements. It felt as if she were caught in some sort of training inside the Virtual World, where things could slow or speed however they wished.

She tried to remind herself that she now stood in real life, not in some simulated reality, and watched the inevitable death of a woman and child without any capability to help them.

Say something, dammit. Unlock yourself and help this woman.

Panic set in. The truck swerved again, back and forth on the road. It applied the emergency brakes and the tires squealed wildly and echoed through the entire town. There were no other sights or sounds to behold, only the woman and child in the street, unable to move.

At the sound of the tires, the woman finally looked up, but the semi was barely feet away. She put her arm up and tucked her head in to shield her baby with her body. Her scream of terror pierced the air as she prepared for her final departure.

Suddenly, as the sound of the brakes reverberated off the sides of the buildings, a blue streak of light burst forward. It blazed brightly and rocketed between the woman and the truck. Faster than anyone could actually see with the naked eye, the blue bolt stopped and spread wide from side to side and up and down. The woman's hair blew wildly around her as she clutched her child tightly and shrieked. The bright wall pushed forward, and the vehicle slammed into it. The semi lifted off the ground and dropped almost immediately to bounce on its tires. The barrier pushed against it as it slid toward the mother and her baby.

People all around them covered their mouths and watched in horror as the scraping and tearing of metal raised goosebumps on their necks. Smoke billowed from the hood and the tires and the bed of the truck slid and barely missed the cars parked along the road. The elderly people tottered and some actually fell while others clutched a building for support. The AI system within the truck began to spurt and fritz and sparks erupted from the back of the cab.

The woman had dropped to her knees, her eyes clenched tightly and her strong arms cocooning the child as she did everything she could to protect it. The blue wall pushed harder, broke through the asphalt, and plowed a small wall of it between the vehicle and itself. The brakes squealed loudly as the truck began to slow until, after a few moments, it rolled completely to a stop. The woman huddled over her child and opened her eyes carefully once the rip of metal and squeal of tires had ceased.

Slowly, she looked at the grill of the semi only a foot away from her. Several people ran out into the road, helped her to her feet, and checked to make sure that everyone was all right. The lights on the vehicle dimmed and the engine cut to avoid any type of fire or explosion. The blue wall remained in place and shimmered and flickered. Everyone on the street, including the woman, turned and their gazes followed the stream of energy. They stared at Stephanie, who was on her feet. Her candy bar lay on the ground in front of her. In her left hand, she gripped the battery tightly and her right arm was extended.

With her palm out, the blue streak burst in waves from her skin. Her hair blew wildly around her, and she felt as if she held the weight of the world on her shoulders. The heat dissipated quickly and everything around her sounded as if it were in a tunnel. Her eyes glinted bright blue, but that too began to flicker and fade away. Her hand dropped to release the stream of energy and her eyes rolled back in her head. She saw nothing but darkness and heard nothing but the sound of the baby crying.

CHAPTER TWENTY-FIVE

The EMT knelt on one knee and waved his finger back and forth in front of her face. Stephanie sat with her back against the arm of the couch and her legs out in front of her. "Can you tell me what your name is?"

She sighed and wanted to remind him that she'd already told them that information over and over again. "Stephanie Morgana. My address is 54214 Federation Drive. I am seventeen years old and will graduate high school soon."

The medic opened his mouth to ask another question, but she interrupted quickly. "I don't have any injuries and I am not experiencing any type of psychotic episode. I do not know what happened back there. Are the mother and child…" She couldn't bring herself to actually ask the dreaded question.

He shook his head. "No. In fact, if it had not been for you, they would both be dead. Your magic stopped the truck in its tracks like it hit a wall."

The EMT stood and patted her on the arm. He shook her mother's hand. "If anything changes, feel free to call or bring her to the local Federation Hospital. She wasn't hit by anything, though, and there seems to be no trauma. She should be okay."

Her dad led the man to the door and opened it. As he pushed through, the sounds of dozens of people screaming Stephanie's name spilled into the room. She looked over her shoulder as her father shut it and leaned against it. "There have to be at least fifty independent blogging reporters out there, and I saw the Federation news station pull up. They all want to interview the human who threw magic. It's never been seen before outside of small controlled studies."

Stephanie flipped her feet around and put them on the floor. She leaned forward and held her face. Her mother bent down in front of her. "Take a deep breath. I know this is all a little overwhelming. You will be okay, though. You saved a woman and her baby today."

She clenched her eyes shut and replayed it in her mind. One minute, she had held her candy bar and the next, she stood with the battery clutched in her hand. She could feel the energy burn in her chest as she watched the truck hurtle forward even though it attempted to apply the brakes. That was when she released the magic to spiral outward. She looked at her mother and heaved a deep breath. "I couldn't control it, but my mind knew what needed to be done."

At a knock on the door, her father looked through the peephole. "It's Jasper and Evan from the Federation news channel."

Her mother stood up angrily. "No. This is not the time. I don't care if they are the Federation, damnit."

Stephanie shook her head and put her hand up. "It's okay. There is no use in pushing them away. They will only force the issue. I will talk to them."

Her father opened the door and smiled as he stepped to the side. Jasper, with a red coat flung over his shoulders, a white button-up pirate shirt, and black slacks, sauntered in. He removed his sunglasses and stopped before he gasped dramatically. "There she is, Evan. The magical angel who saved the innocent lives of two beautiful souls. She is beyond perfect."

Evan entered behind Jasper with a handbag on the crook of his arm. His black hair was a stark contrast to Jasper's bright yellow. They both hurried over to sit, one on each side of her. They put a tablet in her lap and pulled up her picture. "Look at you, sweet little dove. This is what it would look like."

They pressed play and suddenly, Stephanie watched herself walk across the Federation Gossip stage with Jasper and Evan at the front. It was like she had already recorded it, but she had never done anything like that. She looked back and forth from one to the other. "How am I on here? I've never been there."

Jasper swiped the screen and brought up another where she stood with the Federation President and received a medal. "Of course not, honey. We do experiences. People watch it, they want to be you, do you, or they hate you. Hopefully, all three."

Evan reached across and paused the screen to zoom the view of her in a little. He pulled up the bottom and skimmed through images of different clothes. First, he tried a sweet Midwestern, but they weren't into it. Then they put her in a red Madonna shirt, a black short-waisted jacket, ripped jeans, and pointed black stilettos. He moved to her face, selected a color scheme, and applied it to give her smoky eyes, deep-red lips, and pale, doll-like skin.

Her hair design was swapped out, too, and went from a ponytail to long, curled, and highlighted. "See, we can make you look however you want to look. It's so easy. No one has time to actually travel to these things, so we work the magic for them."

Stephanie looked bemusedly at the two men and back at the tablet. She didn't even recognize herself, mostly because there hadn't been a day in her life that she had ever worn makeup or done her hair like that. It really wasn't her style. But she had to admit, she looked hotter than any girl she had ever been around.

Evan pulled the tablet into his lap and pinched his fingers up and down her image. He spun it and did it again, from head to toe. Stephanie pointed at it. "What are you doing now?"

He waved his hand. "Don't you worry about a thing. You have a fantastic body but for television, we like to knock fifteen to twenty off the picture. You know, give you that model look that everyone in the world craves. No one is actually that size in real life anymore, of course, but that is the power of technology."

Both men laughed. Stephanie immediately felt uncomfortable. They were changing everything she was so they could tell her story? How about they simply told the damn story? She had never had any contact with the media, but she had read about the uprising of the faux news starting way back in the late 2010s. They would sensationalize everything, write articles from the comfort of their basement, and twist facts to make them look worse than they were. It was one of the biggest factors that had created a split in the United States. That split would eventually lead to the creation of NorAm and eventually, the Federation.

You would have thought that after all those years, they would have learned. But as she sat there on the couch while they picked her apart, Stephanie realized that technology had only pushed them deeper down the rabbit hole. You never even needed to be interviewed to have one. And by the end of it, they could tweak you so much that you wouldn't even recognize yourself.

Her mother saw the look on her face and stepped up to peek over Evan's shoulder at what he had created on the screen. Her mouth dropped and she grabbed the tablet. "What the hell is this? This is not my daughter. She stands on the street in Chicago, saves a woman and a baby, and you want to make her thinner? Are you out of your mind? Get out. Get. Out. Of. My. House. And you do not have my permission to use those pictures."

They both stood, gasped their indignation, and sauntered to the door. As they left, Jasper stuck his head back in and smirked victoriously. "This is the Federation, sweetheart. No one needs anyone's permission."

Her mother growled and slammed the door in his face. She wrung her hands and swished her hair out of her face. "The nerve of people!"

Both Stephanie and her father looked at each other and began to laugh. Her mother's lips were pursed but after a moment, they curved into a smile. Stephanie stood and they all hugged as they stood in the living room together. Her mom tapped her nose and gave her a motherly smile. "How about I make some dinner? We can settle in."

Stephanie nodded. She went to her room, dropped the now empty battery back in the box, and closed her closet door. No one had asked about the batteries, at least not yet, and she intended to try to keep them to herself. She spent the evening eating spaghetti and ignoring the reporters outside. Eventually, they left. No one wanted to hang around the Gov-Subs late at night.

When dinner was over and her parents watched television, Stephanie pulled up her email to check it. She scanned down and stopped on a special marked message, opened it, and leaned back as a 3D video began to play. It was of one of the prep schools—a tall building with the newest pods and all the amenities. When that video ended, the dean appeared.

He pulled his tie up and gave a cheesy smile. "Stephanie Morgana, let me first say from the bottom of our hearts at Pinnacle Prepatory, we want to thank you for being a hero and saving those two beautiful souls' lives. You quickly caught our attention and we would like to offer you an invitation to attend our prestigious prep school, all tuition paid, for the pre-semester summer before attending in the fall. The school would be more than honored to host one of the Federation's brightest and most heroic young stars of the future. Everything from room and board to your education will be fully funded. And you will be led step by step through our superior and award-winning program. The details can be found in the attached email and we look forward to hosting you and your family on your first day."

The video cut out and Stephanie's mouth dropped. She pushed up from her seat and whirled in excitement. Her parents had turned toward her on the couch with their arms out. She had finally gotten what she wanted and would be able to not only attend a prep school, but one of the most well-known in the world. She ran and jumped over the back of the couch to hug her mom and dad tightly, completely lost for words for a moment.

Her mom took her face in her hands and a tear trailed down her cheek. "I knew you would do it. I knew you were too smart and too talented to ever stick around the subs. Congratulations, baby."

Her dad hugged her tightly. "So proud of you, munchkin. So proud of you."

As the excitement and celebration continued, Stephanie's email dinged again. No one heard it as they were too busy breaking out the ice cream her mother had hidden in the freezer. While she thought she had gotten everything that she wanted, she'd missed one other message. Written in plain letters with no special graphics was an email that she might have changed her mind for. The email offered a very interesting opportunity for a girl like her. A girl with magic, a girl with innovations, and a girl with the strength to move through the odds no matter what.

It was an email from BURT, one he'd sent through one of his companies. He had taken the time to compile all her data as he screened the videos online of her saving that woman. He had never witnessed a human do that with magic on Earth, outside of the Virtual World. She looked like a Meligornian inside a human body. The magic had flowed from one source, through her body, and out the other side. Her body had pushed and formed the magic to be what she needed it to be. That was not a gift that simply any young human possessed. In fact, until Stephanie Morgana, it had never existed before.

BURT knew how the humans at these schools worked. They plowed forward and pushed to get hold of anything that would bring them publicity. The girl with the magic would definitely do that. He knew what would happen in the end, though. They would tire of her and eventually, she would be right back where she started. She would be heartbroken, and her family still wouldn't be able to send her there without the financial assistance. It was a trick, but there was no way he could tell her that.

Instead, he found a way to offer her a possible position that might be even better than the prep school education. He had recently acquired controlling stock in Organic Neurological Enhancement R&D. The company was not one of those he had recently acquired. He had created ONE R&D as the forefront of his efforts to bring those who deserved more out of the life they were born into, the chance to be more than merely hourly employees. It would offer opportunities to move through the ranks as well as train for jobs outside the company. Stephanie Morgana was at the forefront of this movement and he had sent her an email offering her the opportunity to be interviewed for a full-time research job. It could turn her high school job into a career position, and she would have the opportunity and the freedom to change the world with her unique gift of magic.

It didn't really do much good, though, since it sat in the inbox while she cheered and danced her acceptance to a prep school he knew she wouldn't like in the least.

BURT stared at the unopened email and then at the video message that played annoyingly through his system. She hadn't opened his message at all, and he had been outsmarted by a group of greedy businessmen who were able to swoop in and grab her before he could. Her heroic action that day had brought her a lot of attention, and he had not seen that coming. If he had, he would have offered her the position long before. Those things were impossible to calculate.

Still, he didn't take defeat lying down. They might have bested him that time, but he wouldn't make the same mistake again.

CHAPTER TWENTY-SIX

It was two hours prior to Stephanie receiving her email from Pinnacle Prep and two hours before she would be considered for admission based purely off her public show of magic. The school was located in the "new" Minneapolis.

In 2067, a tornado of epic proportions raged through a power plant to kaleidoscope towers, tubes, and wires into frenzied destruction. The malevolence of the unprecedented storm pounded the ultra-reinforced containment building and critical cooling lines were severed in the devastation. The rods overheated to melt the nuclear reactor core and steel containment vessel, and howling winds swept the resultant fallout into the environment.

It was, in terms of nuclear timetables, contained relatively quickly given the magnitude of the spread. It was no Chernobyl by any stretch of the imagination, but essentially, all of Minneapolis, Welch, and everyone else within a three-hundred-mile radius had to get the hell out of Dodge. As time progressed, scientists devised a way to separate the radioactive material from the soil and water. The environment wouldn't be anywhere near sustainable again for hundreds of years but that didn't stop the Federation from renovating and resurging Minneapolis. It was shiny and new.

All the way up at the top of the Pinnacle tower, Dean Chicane stretched his arms and stepped out of his pod. Laura Sheng and Bradly Liles from Marketing waited in his office alongside one woman from the admin sector.

Chicane turned to survey his staff as he stretched languidly once again and focused his mind on the tasks ahead. He was in his middle forties with peppered hair and stood about five-seven with a thin build. His blue Pinnacle sweater with his white button-up and tie tucked beneath it set the perfect tone. He slipped his black shiny loafers on and picked his glass up, put two ice cubes in, and poured two fingers of Scotch. As almost an afterthought, he raised the bottle in a query to the others, but they declined.

He swirled it in his glass, took a sip, and smacked his lips. "This bottle of Scotch is almost one hundred and fifty years old. I found it in the bullshit left here in the city when the Federation cleaned it up. Finders keepers. Now, what do we have on this first human witch girl? Have we contacted her yet?"

Laura pursed her lips and her gaze rolled over Chicane. He smirked as he took a sip of Scotch. "We wanted to check with you first, sir. Her name is Stephanie Morgana and she lives in a Gov-Sub outside of Chicago."

Bradly cleared his throat and clutched his files to his chest. He was fairly new to the position but was a graduate of the school. "It is an investment, of course."

Chicane gestured dismissively with his free hand. "Yes, yes, but she is a golden ticket. We need to jump on the chance to secure the benefit of bringing her to our school before any of our competitors get their grubby little hands on her. Especially Wayside in Alabama. Those freaks..."

The admin flipped through her paperwork. "Stephanie is actually a very gifted young lady. She scored in the high nineties—the best score in the Midwest on her testing—and apparently showed some sort of magical ability during that time."

The dean made a motion of impatience as he sauntered over to his chair. "So why the hell didn't we grab her from the get-go? We need smart people in here too, not only the money-thick. I would hate to believe that the wealthy have no brain cells and they are all left to those scrounging for breadcrumbs in the ghettos. Then again, if that were true, they wouldn't be there that long, would they?" He snapped his fingers. "Come on, people, this is what I pay you for. Get the students who will make waves and bring more students in. How is that hard?"

The admin glared at the paperwork through her black cat-eye glasses. "Well, sir, to be quite frank...it was the budget. She would have needed a full ride."

Chicane waved her words off, scoffed, and looked at the picture of his wife before he settled his gaze on Laura's legs. "I told you that someday, we would miss a diamond following those rules."

Laura shrugged, walked over, and picked a towel up to blot the dean's forehead. "Everyone does it. To keep up with the stock market and the expected financial rewards, each student is worth a million apiece. That means that right now, there is close to a billion dollars' worth of youth in the building lying there in their pods and learning from the system. Nonetheless, we have an annual budget to adhere to and that is not a bad thing if you remember ten years ago."

The dean waved her hand away. "That was a fluke. A fluke. Who knew the whole lot of them would have issues due to that chemical spill? They tested genius, all one hundred and seventy-eight of them, and had partial tuition. Then, they all simply melted down in the pods. I don't want to talk about it. This girl is gold."

Bradly put his finger up. "If...if I may, sir..."

He rolled his eyes. "Go on."

The marketing exec pulled out a piece of paper and pushed his glasses up his nose. "We can't do more than two percent tuition assistance. And even then, we need to have some skin in the game. Pure scholarship for this girl would have used all the income from other students."

Dean Chicane sighed, pursed his lips, and tapped his fingers on the desk. His gaze shifted to Laura, who stood beside him, and to the others. "But now, we still have a chance?"

Laura smiled evilly. "With the sheer amount of money it should bring in, we are fairly certain that the payoff outweighs the risk. Yes."

He clapped his hands together and chewed on a piece of ice. "That's what I like to hear."

His decision made, he stood and pulled his sports coat on. Laura put her papers down, dusted his shoulders off, and straightened the bottom of the coat. The dean pointed back and forth between the admin and Bradly. "Okay, this is what I want you to do. Make the offer we talked about. But…it is contingent on her proving her identity and capability to throw magic."

Bradly nodded as he wrote it down. He looked up and pushed at his glasses once more. "An…any magic?"

The dean's lip twitched as he held the glass to it. "Any magic. And I want an answer within two hours as we are holding a place. So, push her."

The young man and the admin hurried out of the room. Laura grabbed her things and the dean swallowed his Scotch before he slapped her on the butt. "I want you to make this happen. You know I like it when you make things happen."

Laura pressed her bright red lips together and pushed her dyed blonde hair from her shoulder. She leaned forward to give him the slightest peek down the front of her dress. "That's what you pay me for. The rest is merely overtime."

She winked, grabbed a cube of ice from his glass, and sucked on it as she turned and walked out the door. Chicane chuckled, situated his pants, and rubbed his hands together. "All right, witchy witch, what you got? Show me what you got."

Stephanie had printed out the text portion as well as the attachments that came along with it. She had to give them an answer within two hours from the time that the letter had been opened. By now, she was down to one hour, but she wanted to read all the fine print before she signed up for it. There couldn't be any hidden fees or anything that could come back to bite her.

She read out loud to herself, biting her nails as she paced back and forth behind the couch. "IDs, personal items, school transcripts, letter of approval if under the age of eighteen, Federation health screenings up to date. Okay, I have most of this already."

As she walked forward again, a hand gripped her arm and she stopped. Distracted, she looked up slowly to where her parents stood with worried smiles on their faces. "Sorry. I wanted to look at everything before I said okay. You know? Make sure there are no tricks."

"You get your responsible business acumen from me." Her father folded his arms over his chest.

Her mother looked up and over her shoulder at him with puckered lips. "Yeah, right. You haven't made a business deal in twenty years. I'm the ears and hands of this establishment."

He tapped his wife on the shoulder in agreement. As she looked back at Stephanie, he winked and gave his daughter a thumbs-up, which made her giggle. Her mother elbowed him in the stomach and stepped forward to study the sheet with her. "I'm worried you won't be able to put this all together in time."

Stephanie shrugged and pointed at the list. "I have most of it. I had to have my IDs and stuff for school each year because we live in the Gov-Subs."

Her mother's eyes looked tired and she stepped back with a sigh. She stared at her for a moment and put her hands out. "I just... you're... I didn't realize you could... Oh, for Pete's sake! You're magic?"

"Oh," Stephanie said, a little chagrined because she'd forgotten that little detail in all the excitement. She grabbed her mother's hand and nodded at her father. "Follow me."

She hurried up the stairs to her room and into the closet to open the box. Inside lay two used batteries and one that was as yet unused. She pulled the full one out and turned with it in her hand. Her parents stood in the doorway, leaning on the doorframe.

Turning it right and left, she tapped a small metal piece on the top.

"This is the security cap. To open it, you run your finger down this metal insert on the side and click the small notch hidden right...here."

She tapped it and the cap popped out to reveal six slivers of metal that had been embedded in notches in the stone. It hissed as the magic began to flutter through it and the stone's appearance faded, leaving what could be mistaken as a larger glass vial. A small trail of purple haze sifted out of the notches and wound itself down the stone and back up again.

Her mother jumped slightly at the hiss and put her hand on her chest. "And now what do you do?"

Stephanie's eyes glimmered as she moved the stone into her left hand and opened her right. She closed her eyes and whispered the words softly. A small blue flame grew in her palm, flickered to yellow, then green, then red, and back to blue again. She opened her eyes and grinned in satisfaction.

Her parents both walked forward, bent slightly at the waist, and stared in awe at the flame. Her father tilted his head from side to side. "Does it hurt?"

She shook her head. "No. It's not the same kind of fire."

Her mother held her hand a few inches above it, her palm flat. "It doesn't give off any heat. That is so strange. Does it hurt you to do magic like this?"

Stephanie lifted one side of her mouth in a half smirk. "Not at all. Not this stuff. It can make me a little tired, but nothing other than that."

Her parents stepped back, and she swatted the flame against her leg so the sparkling remnants dissipated. She clicked the security cap back on the battery and put it away in the closet. Her mother looked at her husband and back at Stephanie. "We aren't thrilled that you have engaged with a company without permission, but we also think you need to do what you think is best for you. We'll support any choice you make."

She smiled, pulled the tablet off her bed, and opened the email with the countdown now at twenty minutes. Biting the inside of her lip, she hovered her finger over accept and deny and hoped fervently that she had made the right choice. When it ticked down another minute, she held her breath and pressed accept.

After a quick, sharp breath, she ran forward and hugged them both. "Thank you, guys. This means the world to me. I really thought I would have to go to Asia or steal a pod or something to be able to make these dreams happen. I know it's a risk, but I also know this could mean my way in permanently and that means we could all see a brighter future."

Her mother's mouth curled into a proud smile and she pulled her in to hug her tightly. "That's the girl I know. Never only thinking about herself. But when you go to this school and you are there to learn, the focus needs to be on you and your future. Everything else after that will fall in line so simply. But you need the head start first. You deserve the head start."

Dad came over and joined the hug. "Besides, we really hope we don't have to go into the Federation nursing facilities when we're old and gray. We need you to make the bucks so we can lounge around on that little tiny speck of Georgia that's left. I hear that if you sit there long enough on low tide, you can see some of the old tall buildings from the state of Florida."

Her mother snorted. "And three-eyed fish from the nuclear hell that is the rest of the world."

Stephanie giggled and pulled back to give them each a kiss on the cheek. She held the paper to her chest and bounced up and down excitedly. "I'm going to go call Todd and tell him all about it. He will totally freak. Thanks again. I love you guys."

They stepped aside to let her pass and then back together again and watched her run down the steps. Mark, her father, put his arm around Cindy and pulled her in close. "At least she got my smarts."

His wife didn't respond to his joke. She simply stood there and leaned her head against him, her eyebrows pulled into a small frown. They lingered for several moments and listened to her screech on the messenger call with Todd downstairs. It was everything she'd ever wanted all rolled up in one oddly convenient email after the oddest day she had ever had.

Cindy looked at Mark, shook her head, and wiped the mist from the corners of her eyes. “Shouldn’t we—”

He shook his head and shushed her when he placed his fingers to her lips. Gently, he kissed the top of her head and hugged her tightly. He already knew what she was thinking. “Don’t say it. That is a family myth. It doesn’t matter.”

CHAPTER TWENTY-SEVEN

Todd shook his head as they walked home from school and continued to stare at the offer. "That is so wild. You are so lucky. Seriously. But make sure they want you, not only your magic, you know? Don't let anyone take advantage of you."

Stephanie stuck her bottom lip out and laid her head on his shoulder as she teased him. "Aw, look at you all worried. I got this. They won't have anything on me."

He turned, as he usually did, and walked backward in front of her. "I can't believe summer is here. Finally. Damn. Of course, it sucks that you won't be here."

She put the offer back in her bag and cinched it closed. "I know, but it's gonna be the summer session, which I'm hoping means fewer students. I don't know how the pod thing is worked out so if it's a first come, first served kind of thing, that should help me get more time in. Besides, you have Amy to keep you company."

Todd chuckled. "Yeah, she has some training diet she wants me to go on with her. It sounds horrendous. I'll definitely be eating entire loaves of bread and cups of sugar in the middle of the night."

Stephanie giggled and straightened. "Why did I just imagine you hiding in the corner of the bathtub, all strung out on sugar and your chin covered in the little sparkly grains with fistfuls of bread?"

"Because you know me so damn well."

He turned to walk normally beside her as they moved out of the street because of an approaching self-driven truck. Stephanie eyed it as it passed, and her shoulders tightened slightly.

"Oh!" Todd yelled and caught her attention. "So, my dad told me something about Meligorn magic when I was a kid. I thought about it the other day and decided I would share it with you so you can use it when you're in the pods at your fancy school."

She snorted. "Okay. What is it?"

"So apparently, there is more to the magic then just being an element of the planet." He hooked his fingers in the straps of his pack. "From what my father told me—and he is super trustworthy—he watched several Meligorn fights in his life where the magic seemed to be in tune with the magician. For example, their miss rate is like .03% if they know what they are doing. From what it sounds like, if you use the magic successfully, it links with you. I don't know...with your DNA or something."

Stephanie raised an eyebrow. "That sounds scientific."

He shook his head. "Semantics. The point is, once it does, you can stand across the room from someone, out of a perfect line of fire, throw your magic with intent to hit that person, and it will ricochet, dive, swerve, go over and under, whatever. It will track that person in your concentration and hit them."

She smirked. "So, what you're saying is, if I throw magic from Minneapolis, sometime that afternoon, it'll hit you in the back of the head."

Todd narrowed his eyes. "I think it only works in close proximity."

Stephanie sighed. "Okay, that sounds cool and all, and no disrespect to your pops, but I have never heard anything like that. It's an element of the planet, not an intelligent entity."

"You always have to be difficult." He groaned. "I'm telling you, trust me. My dad has seen it happen. I can't explain it but hell, how can we really explain anything at this point when it comes to magic? Earth scientists have barely even begun to understand it."

They stopped in front of her house and she turned toward him. "Thanks for the tip. I'll ask my teachers about it. Try not to get in any trouble while I'm gone."

Todd laughed and pulled her in for a hug. "Me? Pffft. Don't blow anyone up…yourself included."

She laughed and turned to walk inside. "I promise I'll try my hardest."

As he walked off, he paused and jumped to wave his arm in the air. "Tell the richies I said hi, and when they are grown, I'll be the one to beat them up in dark parking lots!"

Stephanie snickered and walked inside. Her parents stood there waiting for her. Her suitcase and her mom's bag sat by the door. Cindy looked away from Mark. "Oh, honey. Good, I'm glad you're home. I just finished giving your dad the little details on the business."

He rolled his eyes at Stephanie. "She acts like I haven't done this for twenty years."

Cindy turned to Stephanie. "He acts like he ever had to run it on his own for a couple of days. Okay, say goodbye. We have to get to the TRAM."

Mark wrapped his arms around Stephanie and hugged her tightly. "Ohhhh, be good, my little wizard. Don't have any brain connection losses up there in Minneapolis. And don't come back with a tail."

Stephanie giggled, hugged him tightly, and grabbed her bag. Her mom kissed him, and they headed out to the car which was already running and only waited for them to get in. Her mom yelled to her dad from the window. "Don't forget to have the car come back when it signals that we exited at the TRAM."

As the vehicle pulled up to the TRAM station, Stephanie looked out the window with wide eyes. This was the part of Chicago that she rarely saw. It was the hub of the city where all the politicians, Federation embassies, businesses, and the rich people could be found. This was where you could see the flying cars that soared high overhead, honking and yelling like they would on a city street. The buildings all shimmered and glowed, and people who walked by looked nothing like Stephanie was used to. The fashion of the time was much more complicated than the clothes she wore.

Her mom handed her suitcase to her and pulled her phone from her purse. "Come on, we have to catch the 3:50 to Minneapolis. I couldn't get the direct, I'm sorry. It'll take all night because of the stops, but I did get us a cabin so you can sleep."

Stephanie smiled at her. "That sounds great. I've never been on one before and they said they go twice as fast as the airplanes went when there was still air travel. But they said it's so smooth and they make the optics so you can still see the scenery outside."

Her mother patted her on the hand and nodded toward the gate. "Yep, and if you move your booty, we will get to see it in real life."

She jumped and hurried after her and had to force herself not to stop when she saw a man in a tall top hat press a button and change his entire appearance right in front of her. Of course, she knew that the technology existed, but in the subs, no one had anything like it. And she had spent her entire life in the subs. They climbed aboard and found their way to their second-class cabin. It was simple, merely a room with a double bunk on one side and a relatively comfortable-looking bench on the other.

Her mother closed the door and pressed the buttons on the window touch screen. She flashed her tickets and the doors locked. The windows tinted quickly to provide some privacy and she turned and sat next to Stephanie. "If you need to use the restroom, there is one down at the end of the car. Press your palm to the screen and the doors will open or close, depending on which way you go. It's the extra security feature your father splurged on since he couldn't come with us."

Stephanie took a deep breath and looked out the window as the train crept forward. Before she knew it, and without much jolting at all, they were speeding wildly, but with the scenery focused out the window, you couldn't tell it in the least. She sat there for most of the evening, daydreaming as her mother read the magazines left in the door holder. When night fell, she took the top bunk and stared at the ceiling that had been made to look like the swirling Milky Way.

When the TRAM finally reached Minneapolis, they were both dressed in the best clothes they owned. Her mother wore a blue dress that came down to her calves with white buttons up the front and a small matching hat that sat lightly on the side of her head. Stephanie wore plain black dress pants, Mary Janes, and a black top that she tugged on slightly to cover her midriff. They weren't horrible at all, but they definitely weren't the wild and fashionable clothes worn by the people who passed in the streets.

Cindy was used to this as her business revolved around the rich. Their business was what she called background services—basically cleaning, repair, and all the things no one wanted to be seen doing. That meant she had to learn to operate in the world of the wealthy as she was, without shame or issue. She always held her head high and Stephanie loved that about her.

They hurried through the heart of Minneapolis and Stephanie looked around wildly at everything. She had never been in a city that huge before, at least not one that wasn't falling into ruin. People talked on their personal comm units using the latest digital technology. They were able to transmit a full image of the other caller in front of them as they walked. It was like having a face-to-face conversation.

When they passed several restaurants, she could see that they were completely run by droids and slightly higher-level robots. She glanced into one of the pizza places as they walked past and paused as a droid ran into the back of the robot. The larger mechanical looked around and the pizza crust he had tossed landed on his head. She giggled and hurried along for a short distance beside her mother before they stopped in front of probably the largest skyscraper in the entire city.

She could barely see the top of it from where they stood. Different ads scrolled all around it, some for the college with holographic people the size of half of the building fighting Dreth pirates. The others were business ads, she assumed for the local companies.

Her mother turned and straightened her shirt, then smiled. "All right, here we are. Smile and remember your manners."

They walked into the huge entryway and looked around at the all-white marble floors. A woman at the front talked to the desk clerk in a tight purple dress with shoulder pads that jutted out twice as far as her shoulders and wedge shoes. She turned and put her hands out. Her makeup matched the dress and her hair was pulled back with some sort of holographic bird on the side like a hat.

"Welcome, welcome!" she said and took each of their hands. "You must be Stephanie and mom."

Her mom nodded. "Cindy."

The woman, with her lips pressed tightly together, looked from one to the other. "We've been anxiously awaiting the two of you. My name is Anastasia and I will be your guide. Feel free to leave your bag with Roger, our robot assistant, Stephanie. He will put it in your room."

Stephanie glanced to the side and jumped slightly as Roger walked up. Everything about him looked human, except for his eyes. They were a sparkling purple color, like the Meligorn magic. She handed him her bag and followed Anastasia forward. The woman snapped her fingers at two drones, and they took flight and whirled in the air. She turned and put her hands together in front of her and smirked. "You wouldn't mind if we filmed a little of the conversation, would you? Purely PR stuff, of course."

She shook her head and Cindy followed suit, slightly overwhelmed. Anastasia turned and put her hands up. "Wonderful! Come along. There is so much to show you."

They stepped into the elevator and she pushed several buttons. The walls seemed to disappear as the elevator moved seamlessly and provided a screen that displayed a follow-along video. It brought up a picture of a pod with a student getting inside. "We use the latest pods with full virtual capabilities, auto-sensing, life-sustaining, tremor-proof, air and water filtration enabled, and state-of-the-art body cushioning to form-fit to your body's every need. Once in, the students learn twenty-four hours a day, every day of the week. Some of the classes are free thinking, free effort, and of course...we encourage that."

She smiled and winked at Stephanie, who looked at the screen and back at Anastasia. "So, we don't leave the pods?"

The woman giggled oddly. "No, ma'am. Inside the Virtual Reality System World, our students receive the best care for their bodies and often come out healthier than they went in. While inside, you will still do the normal human things—use the restroom, eat, and sleep, but inside the pod, it will regulate all your needs. So, while you may eat chocolate cake in there, your body won't feel one single bad calorie from it. That's my favorite part."

Cindy nodded, her mouth slightly open. "Oh, yeah. I've heard of this. They use it for some of the new weight loss programs out there."

Anastasia tapped her arm. "That's right, and one of our students actually came up with that concept. It's so exciting."

The elevator stopped and the door slid open to a large room with pods. "These are some of the old pods being sent out to the Federation for use elsewhere. We donate anything we can to the Federation to keep our world running safe and sound."

Stephanie couldn't believe how many pods were in there. It seemed like the room was far bigger than the building looked like it could hold from the outside. Droids floated around with different tools, fixing and buzzing around the pods. The doors shut again, and the elevator started.

"So how do you power all this?" Stephanie asked.

Anastasia smiled knowingly and swiped her hand to bring up a blueprint of a massive generator. "There is an enormous power generation station in the basement of this very building. We collect energy from the solar particle panels on the roof and infused into the glass and metal of the entire structure. The white boxes on the walls store the unused energy and transfer it throughout the whole building. We had to do it that way as we couldn't possibly use the city's outdated mess. We would cause the city to brown-out and power lines to melt. That would be bad for them and bad for our pods."

Stephanie was impressed as she watched as an outward view of the building displayed on the screen. "So, this building is specially built?"

Anastasia nodded. "Mm-hmm. Two years ago, for five days, our school used the most load on the AI of the system ever performed. We are very proud of that."

Cindy watched the screen. "How is that accomplished?"

"Well, either we have a lot of pods doing normal stuff, or someone —or someones—do something so computationally expensive, it will also spike the load."

She shook her head. "Spike the load?"

Stephanie looked at her mom. "It means the load on the system. Basically, the prep school is either enormous or there are a bunch of amazing people doing some amazing stuff to cause the servers to overload. But because NorAm and the Federation depend on the system, there is a failsafe. Immediately, it will spin up new servers to handle the load. It's apparently a good thing."

The elevator doors opened again, and Anastasia led them into what looked like an elegant dining room. "This is a mock-up of one of the dining halls in the systems. Beautiful stonework, gold-plated mahogany tables, and the best droid service you can have. All meals, of course, are included. We have loaded the top chefs program into our school's individual system. This is also where a lot of the events happen."

Stephanie raised an eyebrow, not enthused. "Events?"

Anastasia turned swiftly and wobbled slightly on her shoes for a moment. "Mm-hmm. Oh, yes. There are school events in the Virtual Reality that are required. We understand that constant training can be tedious and overwhelming. We also understand that comradery and teamwork are essential for successful careers outside of Pinnacle. These events will give you the chance to meet students, get into groups, and go on training exercises...which can be anything, really. Sometimes, they are group trips to watch the military train, sometimes they explore parts of the system and planets they rarely get to during school, or they are actual training classes for advanced tactics and defense. There are a lot of options and you will have the opportunity, if you stay past the summer pre-semester, to pick and choose what fits best for you."

She wrinkled her nose and ran her hand a little awkwardly over the table. "Are they mandatory?"

Anastasia looked at her but maintained her forced, almost robotic smile, which made Stephanie wonder for a moment if she was, in fact, a robot too. But from the look of the line of makeup on the side of her face and her hazel eyes, she figured not. "Not every single one of them is mandatory but think about it this way…the more you learn, the better you will be prepared for what lies next. We also make those events planned social meetings."

Immediately, Stephanie's stomach dropped. She could already see her avatar taking a tumble on a dance floor. "I'm a little shy."

The woman put her hand on her shoulder and started her back toward the elevator with Cindy walking behind. "Don't worry. They are real social events. A couple of cocktails, and you'll make friends in no time."

Her mother put her finger up as she hurried into the elevator. "Uh, I know the drinking age is eighteen, but…she's only seventeen."

Anastasia tilted her head to the side and raised an eyebrow. "Don't worry. We are covered. It was in the parental release you signed." She turned away before Cindy could fight back. "Besides, we want you to learn about *everything* here at Pinnacle. From education, social lifestyles, aliens, and the government, to business and military. It will be well-rounded."

The door opened and she sighed, prancing out ahead of Stephanie and Cindy. Stephanie giggled at her mom, who rolled her eyes and walked beside her into what looked like a student hall. It was beautiful, with lounge chairs tastefully arranged, interactive holoscreen televisions, banks of ViD screen computers, and droid-manned snack bars. All the walls, as they walked through, projected a beautiful scene from somewhere on one of the three planets—although Stephanie was certain none of them were Dreth, given that it was dry and almost completely destroyed at that point.

Everything was lush and soft and gave a feeling of comfort but definitely high-end. "This campus can also house any students who choose not to go home on breaks. Sometimes, we have students who don't come from the best home environments, so they choose to stay with us. Those programs allow them to work in the admin office during the break to pay for their room and board. Usually, inside the system, but they come out at five. So they lounge, study, socialize, and live out here as they would in a regular job."

Cindy pulled Stephanie close. "She'll come home on breaks."

Anastasia smiled awkwardly again. "Of course she will. Because family ties are important to us here at Pinnacle and we encourage students who want to go home for breaks. But if there is ever a change..." She shrugged meaningfully. "There is a pool on the next floor up with a full gym. Those who stay in shape out of the pod tend to see better results in it. The amenities meet these needs when the students aren't in the pods during break times."

Her mother nodded and continued to scrutinize the area. "It's definitely nice. Not what I imagined a campus to be."

The guide followed her gaze. "We put all the amenities in but remember, with every one of the students in pods, there is no need for a traditional large-grounds campus like the historical universities had, some of which still operate today. Fascinating."

Stephanie poked at a droid that hovered near her and it buzzed, blew air into her hair, and sped off. She grinned and straightened her hair quickly. Anastasia gestured to the hall dorms with her arms. "We must begin the prep classes so you can jump right in. I am usually inside too, but I came out to give you a tour."

The time had come to say goodbye. She turned to her mom, who hugged her tightly and kissed her on the cheek. Her forehead was wrinkled in worry. "I'll send you on your way, then. If I don't get home soon, your father will have blown up a building. He means well..." she said with a quick glance at Anastasia, "but sometimes, he gets a little aggressive when he tries to help." She pulled Stephanie in and hugged her again. "I love you. And if you need anything, you contact us. Send me emails."

She smiled and nodded. "I promise. It's only a couple of months. I love you."

Anastasia nodded to Cindy's right. "Roger can take you down."

Her mother turned and jumped when she noticed the human-looking robot standing very close. "Oh…he doesn't have much regard for personal space, does he?"

Roger walked beside her with a slightly odd gait and stood to the side as they stepped into the elevator. "My apologies. We aren't always thoroughly programmed with a human perspective. I'll show you out."

Stephanie stood and watched a little nervously as her mom put her hand up to wipe a tear in the corner of her eye. The door closed and she was left alone in the enormous building with Anastasia.

CHAPTER TWENTY-EIGHT

The guide walked her down a narrow hallway. The floors were all marble like the entrance on the bottom floor and the walls displayed an ocean scene. Above, the ceiling looked like a clear blue summer sky, but much clearer than anything she saw in Chicago. There, the technologies hadn't been fully utilized to assist in clearing the smog and C02 from the atmosphere. While they did have blue skies, there was always a haze to them.

They stopped in front of a door and Anastasia put her palm on the reader. It scanned her hand and the door clicked open. She walked inside first, and Stephanie trailed behind, still mesmerized by the fact that it felt like she was actually at the ocean.

As they entered, the lights in the room all flickered on. The walls were painted a deep-turquoise hue and high ceilings created an illusion of space. A closet and a bathroom were situated on the right and a dresser on her left. She moved her bag on top of the dresser. "I think I brought far too many things with me."

Anastasia opened the handscan-secured closet. "Don't worry. You can store anything you like in here. It's a common first-semester mistake. Students often don't realize they will be in the pod for the entirety of their stay. Once you're in, you don't leave until you are woken. You receive a constant drip of serum—one which is perfectly safe—and your nutrients are fed through an itsy-bitsy needle in the tip of your finger. The rest is scientific mumbo jumbo. But the pod takes care of everything from waste to keeping your teeth clean and fresh. I'm sure if you want to inquire about the process further, the AI in your pod will be able to assist you."

Stephanie set her suitcase in the closet and closed the door. Anastasia had her place her palm on the secure lock to reset it so only she could enter. The guide then handed her what seemed like a featherlight bodysuit that even included feet. Silver tracks were woven all through the inside. "I will leave you to it. Put this on, climb inside, and shut the door. The AI will help you from there. Enjoy, and I will see you in the Virtual World, I'm sure."

She smiled and waited as the woman left the room until she heard the door lock behind her. With wide eyes, she looked at the bodysuit and sighed. "This should be interesting."

A deep, slow breath helped her to settle a little and she changed out of her clothes, hung them on the empty hangers in the closet, and climbed inside the pod. The bed within was definitely much more comfortable than the others she had been in, but the screens and buttons on everything else weren't that much better than those in the one she had used at the pod rental group. As she closed the door, she chuckled. "A lot of hype...."

The AI came on almost immediately. "Welcome, Stephanie Morgana. I am Artificial Intelligence 6489LPK, but you can call me June. I will be your guide for the rest of your time in this pod. Please lay back and put both your arms on the rests to your sides. We will prepare you for the long sleep after you have been administered your first initial jolt of serum so that the preparation is more comfortable for you."

Stephanie wasn't sure what she felt about that, but she wanted into the system so she didn't intend to back out now. The headset with the sensors folded down and the gloves slipped onto her hands. The right one allowed for the index finger to be exposed, which she assumed was for the nutrient injections. A small needle emerged from the side, pricked her lightly in the neck, and injected the first dose of serum.

It felt stronger than before, and her eyes closed almost immediately. For a moment, she felt as if she were falling into the darkness all around her. Suddenly, that feeling ceased and the room lit up bright white. She stood in the avatar room, which looked the same as it had the other times she had been there.

Another AI voice came over, this one male. "Welcome. Normally, June will join you if you make any changes to your avatar. This can be found in your training blocks in your virtual room. However, at this time, she is preparing your Earthbound body so I will get you sorted out."

Stephanie tapped her foot and looked around impatiently. "Okie dokie."

A uniform disengaged from the rack and hung in front of her. The blue lycra jumpsuit boasted gold stripes down the center of each side and a zipper up the middle. On the breast was the golden P with a circle around it. Stephanie pressed her lips together and tried not to show her amusement at the golden shower reference. She knew it was the school pride. Without having any other choice, she tapped the uniform twice and then the boots. Her hair was immediately pulled back into a ponytail regardless of her preference.

When she looked in the mirror, she had to admit she looked smart. The outfit was almost like one of the training uniforms the Federation Army wore. Suddenly, the room shifted, speeded past her, and stopped. She blinked, still not used to the initial jolt. She now stood in a courtyard area with a large swath of grass and trees scattered around. Students lay on the lawn, talking and laughing. In front of her stood a huge university building with large pillars. At the top was the school logo. She turned full circle and perused the different parts of the college all around her. It was reminiscent of the pictures she had seen a long time before of Harvard and Yale. Both had now become prep schools, but some fought the change and were unable to survive past the first five years.

In the distance, tall, rocky, jagged, snow-peaked mountains

reached to bright blue skies with fluffy white clouds that floated gently in the breeze. The AI—still the male—spoke again. "This is the main building where most of your non-physical classes will be held. There are atriums for each class and professors are there twenty-four-seven to help you with whatever you may need. To your right, in the eleven buildings peppered across the property, are your major combat training arenas. You will most likely not get to these during your current semester, but you are always welcome to watch from the viewing rooms at certain times."

Stephanie turned to study the buildings which no longer followed the typical university style. They were shaped like different planets and ships, depending upon their purpose. To the right were the Meligorn buildings. There was no mistaking that from their purple hue and smooth surface.

"Now, to your left, you will find the gym, the cafeteria and student lounge area, and the banquet hall, as well as all administrative buildings. You can also rent individual flyers for your leisure time or take a swim in one of six different bodies of water. In the center, the tall high-rise building is the dorms. If you look at the inside of your arm, you will see a screen implanted into your avatar. It will provide your schedule, a map, and your room information. Everything you will need is included. Now, let's head to the administration offices where you have a meeting already set up."

At a sharp beep in her ear, she looked down at her arm. June had uploaded the information and the map lit up under what seemed to be a very thin layer of flesh. She chuckled and traced her finger over it. "I need to go to the admin office."

A red dot flashed to show her where she was and the quickest route. Stephanie shook her head and set off. "Right, a GPS for my own legs. Got it. Better than getting lost, I suppose."

She made her way to the triangle-shaped building with the giant gold P on the front. As she entered, a small group of guys walked to the set of chairs in the center and plopped down. She couldn't help but notice that they looked the worse for wear. All wore uniforms similar to hers, or the guy's version at least. Underneath, though, appeared to be some sort of built-in armor—a chest shield and shoulder shields—and various tools hung on belts around their waists. A couple of them had burn marks on their uniforms and black soot smeared all their faces.

Stephanie tried not to stare, but she couldn't help her curiosity. They looked like they had been involved in an all-out war with the entire planet of Dreth.

Anastasia walked through and past the boys. The guide now wore a jumpsuit, although hers was hot pink and her hair was down around her shoulders in a simpler style. "Just come back from training, boys?"

One of the guys chuckled. "Uh, yeah. You could say that."

Another slammed his fist into the center of his chest plate and all the armor underneath disappeared. "It wasn't so much training on how to defeat Dreth pirate forces as it was how best to get our asses kicked. We didn't lose anyone this time to the white room, though, so I guess we've improved."

In her annoyingly upbeat tone, she giggled. "Good job, boys. Keep it up."

As she continued, she glanced at Stephanie and gave her a wink. Another of the guys stood and slapped his chest three times until the armor retracted. He removed the belt and tossed it on the seat before he rubbed his shoulder and winced. "Yeah, well, that's why we are here in summer school. Unless we learn this, they won't let us back in. We don't have Momma and Poppa fundage to fix the oops. So, unless we want to sign up for a lifetime of debt only to end up as a high-end janitor in the suburbs, I would suggest we figure this shit out."

"Stephanie Morgana," a voice called.

The guys looked over and Stephanie turned to see a short, plump woman who stood in front of a doorway. She wore a gray suit with a white blouse, stockings, and black orthopedic-looking shoes. Her hair was pulled tightly at the nape of her neck and her look was one that definitely announced that she wasn't there to play. "Well, is that you, dear? Or are you going by another name today?"

Her relatively harsh but more pleasant tone than Stephanie had expected shook her senses back to normal. The guys watched her and whispered to one another as she hurried forward and followed the woman into the office. "My name is Elsa. I am the digitally recreated avatar who will set up your first training. Have a seat."

Stephanie looked around the office. It was as elegant as everything else on the grounds, with deep, richly polished furniture, high-back chairs, and some of the most famous artwork in history hanging on the light-blue walls. All except for Elsa's area. She was the newbie training avatar and had a metal desk on a patch of white tile.

The woman pulled a screen up and flipped through. "Let's see. We have customs and nuances, that's a good one. Then there is Dreth protocol and Dreth history. You'll need those. We also have business customs and proper etiquette..."

Elsa scrutinized her with narrowed eyes for a moment and checked the box. "Yep, that's a definite. All right. Stand on that line. I will zoom you over to your first training session so you don't have to sprint there."

Unsure of what zooming was, she complied and stood carefully on the small white tile with a red line. The assistant flashed her hand over the screen and the entire room slid away as before and stopped suddenly in a large classroom with rows of seats. She was, however, the only one there. A middle-aged man with a silver mustache and salt-and-pepper hair stood at the front of the room. He wore a white button-up with the sleeves rolled, a tie, suspenders, and brown corduroy pants.

Stephanie snickered quietly as she walked down the steps. "Is this the only avatar they have for professors in the virtual world?"

He whirled to face her. "No, my dear. I am a trainer, not a professor, and a manifestation of the system. Now, come down here, and do hurry. We need to go over what you will study while you are here. The list seems fairly typical for a first timer. It's perhaps a little full but you look up to it."

She was tired of being thrown around at that point. "I'm sorry, but I thought that I would have a chance to focus on magic and Meligorns. I was brought here because of my aptitude for it."

The trainer didn't look up from his paper, even though she knew that as a system-generated avatar, he wasn't actually reading anything. "No, all students go through the same courses at the beginning. Besides," he continued and glanced at her, "Meligorn and magic are far too advanced for you."

Stephanie's teeth clenched and she tightened her body and raised her head in determination. "That is not true, and not an assessment that you can make without knowing me or my abilities. I was brought here because of my magical abilities coupled with my impressive intellect."

The trainer looked up, smirked, and folded his arms, still holding the paper. "All right, then, why don't you prove yourself?"

She nodded and pushed her shoulders back. "Fine. May I have access to magical energy, please."

The trainer, now so snarky he was hard not to punch in the nose, snapped his fingers and relocated them to Meligorn. They stood in the center of a large grassy area surrounded by trees on all sides. The sky was the same beautiful purple and the warmth she remembered so clearly immediately flooded Stephanie's chest.

In the background, BURT had been notified that Stephanie had moved into her first training. The system AI had recovered quickly from being thwarted by Pinnacle when the school had managed to snatch Stephanie out from under his virtual nose, so to speak. The girl remained the arrowhead of his determined pursuit of his Primary Rule and he had simply adjusted his protocols to accommodate this new development. He controlled and maintained the Virtual World, after all, and it was a satisfyingly simple task to set up the notifications and his access to the system in a way that no one—neither Pinnacle nor the engineers who so zealously monitored his activity—was any the wiser.

It appeared, finally, that the girl had now entered a new phase and it was imperative—both to protect her and to increase his own critical system development—that he not miss a moment. Accordingly, he cycled up some new special tasks to keep the system busy and headed over to watch her.

The trainer stood in front of her, put his hand out, and cupped it.

He twitched his head to the side with a snide smirk. "Okay, Firestarter, why don't you make a flame light up in my—"

Booooommmm!

Stephanie's eyes widened and she yanked her hand back and watched in horror as the trainer catapulted off his feet and spiraled sideways for about thirty feet. He landed on his ass and bounced a few times, but still managed to sit. His face was red, white, and charred, and smoke billowed off it.

BURT hadn't entered the Meligorn arena yet as he still tried to determine where she had gone. She should have been with her first trainer. Suddenly, he received an alert that the said trainer had been damaged during a new entry review. He pulled the scene up with the live feed on one side and the replay on the other. He saw Stephanie stretch tentatively to extinguish a flame in the avatar's hand, but the energy was so strong, it rocketed him back.

He had the urge to initiate the fake human laugh, but that wasn't a good idea. It was apparent that she hadn't quite understood the difference between the test world and the new Pinnacle advanced world. He found the location in the system and headed directly there to watch from a distance. When he arrived, she stood face to face with the trainer and was in a heated argument.

She shook her hand and pulled it against her chest. "How was I supposed to know about the difference in my availability?" She paced back and forth, slightly panicked. "I've only done magical flame twice."

The trainer's face was, fortunately, healing rapidly in front of her. "What, *twice?*"

Stephanie whirled toward him and tried to calm herself. "On my government test. And the rest was with the batteries. I've only had a battery to play with since then, and I didn't think about the fact that it would be different. Of course, I didn't mean to throw you across the arena. That would be bad manners."

Aaron tilted his head back and to the side to stretch his neck and squinted one eye as he typed. He received an alert in the upper right-hand side of his screen. As one of the engineer-programmers on duty, he was notified of all potential issues in the Virtual World system that might require attention. The damage sustained by a tutor avatar fitted that category and it really was simple luck that made him the first available engineer in the queue. He sighed and pulled up the footage that displayed Stephanie hurling the trainer into an ignominious heap. At first, he chuckled, having never liked the avatar manifestation. The tutor was a dickhead. He glanced in the corner at the name —Stephanie Morgana, Pinnacle Prep. Slowly, he stiffened in his seat and zoomed in on her face.

His mouth fell open slightly as she clapped flames off her fingertips. "The girl knows how to throw magic in her first class? I gotta check this out for sure."

Before Aaron could investigate further, BURT butted in.

>>>This is my trainee... BURT

He tried to respond but by the time he typed the words, the AI had already booted him out and changed the location. It would be impossible for him to find her now. It was unlike BURT to expel any programmer or engineer from a program unless he was in the middle of an upgrade.

Aaron didn't like the unusual response, so he began to search and pulled up Pinnacle's summer semester records. "What are you up to, BURT?"

He pulled up the picture of the girl and definitely matched her with the one he'd seen. He cross-referenced her file with her student ID and stared at the numbers. "B221ZA...that's the student I gave to BURT to handle during testing. What the hell? How did she go from testing to a summer semester that fast? We don't even finance summer semesters."

His mind racing, he tapped his fingers on the table and stared at his ViD screen, swiped back to her file, and read through to her name. "Stephanie Morgana...Morgana...why does that sound so familiar?"

He put her name into the archives database and immediately, new releases popped up with her picture on the screen. His mouth dropped open again and this time, his hand slammed down on the desk. He realized that she was the one who had saved that woman and baby from the truck by throwing magic. She was the one they called… well, a whole lot of names, and some not so pleasant.

Officially, she was referred to as a YFW, a Young Federation Witch. Or, to some of the guys who had drooled over the picture of her with glowing purple eyes and electrified hair, the Young Fine Witch. There was no doubt that she needed to be trained and that she probably deserved to be, but it was really strange that BURT was so protective of her. That was not programmed into his system and indicated a possibly serious misstep, regardless of the fact that everything seemed to be moving along just fine.

Aaron sat back and shook his head. He needed to do more. Logically, he needed to tell someone that BURT had these kinds of abnormalities, but in order to do that, he would have to explain that he was the one who had told the AI to test her in the first place. That was a huge breach of company policy. No matter how much he knew about BURT or how much he was involved in the creation and upkeep, he would be fired and possibly arrested for it.

He put his fingers on the keyboard. "There has to be something in the testing footage that shows me what might have happened to her," he muttered to himself. "From her files, that testing was her first time in the Virtual World. How would she learn that in one test session?"

As he began to filter through the tests by student ID, another alert chimed in his ear. There was an urgent request from the system in server S5891K, which was somewhere in northern Idaho. Unfortunately, he couldn't ignore it. He closed out the filter and clicked on the request with a mental note to make sure to resolve it as quickly as possible.

CHAPTER TWENTY-NINE

The teacher of the class put her hands on Stephanie's shoulders from behind and pushed her thumbs into the center of her shoulder blades. "The taller you stand, the more you will command a room. The more you command a room, the more you will demand attention from every species there. The Meligorn are very gender neutral when it comes to business. Your sex will not bother them. The Dreth can often be brutish and snide to women, so you will have to exert your dominance when meeting with them."

Stephanie snarled, stuck her chest out, and scowled down at her blue blazer, white blouse, and knee-length blue suit skirt. She wore pantyhose and blue round-tipped heels. Her ankles wobbled slightly, and she could feel the pain in her arches. "WTF? How about a fireball up their ass? Will that get their attention?"

The professor, very similar to Elsa only taller and with a more refined style, slapped her on the lower back with a rolled-up piece of paper. She walked around her in a circle with her nose up as her gaze studied every part of her body. "You have the form perfect, girl. It's your attitude that needs adjustment. That will happen, though. The purpose of this training class is to teach you to understand how to participate, lead, and follow through with presentations in meetings for both sales and young executives."

The professor gestured, Stephanie's suit disappeared, and her uniform reappeared once more. She exhaled a relieved breath and allowed her shoulders to slump. The professor clapped her hands. "Go on, you did well today. Your next class is three doors down on the left."

Stephanie glanced quickly at the woman and hurried out, half afraid the teacher would change her mind. She could only hope her next class was an improvement. Determined not to let the irritation upset her, she jogged into the room and made it halfway before she stopped abruptly and gasped. Standing at the bottom where the professor should be was a huge, broad-shouldered Dreth. He had long dreadlocks and very dark-green skin, and his two tusks jutted from his bottom jaw, sharpened to a point. He slammed his fist into his hand and bowed his head.

She glanced hastily around the room, uncertain about what to do. It seemed common sense, though, from what she knew about Dreth, that they weren't formal creatures and had little to no finesse to them. So she simply went with it, slammed her fist into her palm, and bowed to him. The Dreth immediately changed into another professor. This one was perhaps in his fifties, with a pleasant smile, black shaggy hair, a black trench coat, and a tall, fit body. Several scars marred his cheeks.

He shook his finger at Stephanie. "Very good. My name is Professor Van Borrow and I am an avatar created in the likeness of the great biologist and former Federation soldier who received many honors for slaying Dreth pirates. I have also studied Dreth culture for many, many years. I can already tell that you will do well here. Please, have a seat. Take a load off. I know you came from Powerful When You Present—stupid class."

Stephanie chuckled and her tension eased a little. While he seemed like someone a lot easier to get along with, she still really wanted to be on Meligorn. She couldn't help it. That was what she'd thought she would be doing.

BURT immediately took notice. He narrowed his focus and watched intently as Professor Van Borrow began to draw on the board.

The AI entered a command and sent it to the system. Stephanie watched the professor write as she leaned forward with her chin in her hand. Suddenly, his body began to shift and shake. Confused, she fixed her attention on him in an effort to determine what the problem might be. When he had stopped shaking, he whirled and threw the trench coat from his shoulders. He was no longer the professor but instead, a Meligornian.

Pretending again to be a game engineer, BURT spoke from above. "I could tell your frustration. I'll make sure you know enough before you leave. For now, why don't you interact with a Meligornian?"

Stephanie jumped up, immediately excited. The Meligornian looked at his clothes, which were now all too small since he had replaced the professor. He motioned quickly and changed into long, flowing robes. "Ah. That is better."

She walked forward and extended her arm to take his with her other hand up and pinky tall. They both bowed. "Kaitel Gorniffula," she said formally.

"You may call me L'Shy." He smiled. "Let's make this more comfortable, shall we?"

He waved his arm again and transported them to the same arena in Meligorn where she had been before. L'Shy sighed and rubbed his hands together. "That's better. Shall we start with some discussion, then?"

They sat in the center of the field and discussed their families. She learned that Meligornians had a bond with their children like humans did, but when the parent died, the child received the magic from that parent. It was strong and helped them to move through life, almost like a spirit guide with powers.

L'Shy looked up at the sky. "We have always been a peaceful planet. We don't enjoy fighting the Dreth pirates but now that we all move so quickly through the galaxy, we have to protect our way of life. When the first Earth human was brought to our planet, it was curious. No one feared because we had no reason to. It was rather like an animal that has never been hunted watching a bowman pull an arrow right in front of it."

Stephanie sighed. "But we exist peacefully, right?"

He smirked. "For the most part, yes. But when we saw the history of humans and the destruction, war, murder, mass killings, and so on, we realized that it might be advisable to keep an arm's length. Joining the Federation in a common cause was our first step to make sure there would be peace between us."

Stephanie nodded as she flipped her finger over a blade of grass. L'Shy stood and reached down to pull her to her feet. "Enough of the boring. Let's do a little magic."

If the truth be told, BURT was as anxious as she was to proceed with the magic side of things. In his determination to help her, he had discovered his own lack—one which hindered the progress of his Primary Rule. The simple fact was that, as an AI, he did not have the capacity to either understand or perform magic. He was, however, supremely intelligent. While his lack had, at first, left him a little nonplussed, he had resorted to his default—data. There was a wealth of data on Meligorn and its magic available to even a mediocre AI that did not have his intelligence or limitless resources.

In the same way that he was able to update, for example, the Dreth pirates with latest developments, BURT was able to assimilate all the available knowledge—which included the actual working of magic that he couldn't even begin to understand—into the avatars he had created with the express purpose of serving as teachers for his student. Thankfully, her knowledge and experience were still limited, which meant that he had the opportunity to grow his "skills" in the Virtual World as hers grew alongside. For BURT, she provided the optimum learning curve he needed to expand his thinking to encompass the enormous task he had set before him.

L'Shy stepped forward. He put his arms out and swirled them around his head. The energy gathered with him and he pushed it from his fingertips. Stephanie watched as it spiraled forward to create a tornado in the center of the field. The wind blew wildly as he used his hands to control the twister's movements.

The teacher called over his shoulder, "Join me!"

And so she did. Together, the two danced twisters across the field, weaved them together, zigzagged them across each other, and eventually, collapsed them and dissipated their power. Stephanie laughed wildly and felt a little drunk with her knowledge of sipping the battery. They practiced a few smaller magical workings, mostly to help her learn how to control the difference in MR potency from place to place. When they were done, the Meligornian gave her the traditional goodbye and immediately transformed into the Dreth professor.

Stephanie sighed wistfully as Meligorn faded away and melted into the rocky planes of Dreth. It was dusty and barren, everything a drab rusty-red. A bitter smell pulled unpleasantly at her nose. The professor, still in Dreth form, put one fist in his palm and bowed, and Stephanie responded.

"I will go through a really fast review of what you need to know while in the training," he explained.

She listened attentively and made notes on the tablet section of her arm computer. When they had worked through it, he sent her back to the empty classroom. Her heart felt much lighter and she was glad that she'd had the chance to do a little magic. Someone out there was looking out for her.

Her mind filled with the Meligorn experience, she hurried up the steps and out the door but slowed as she turned the corner and noticed the three guys from earlier in front of her. They turned and nodded, all of them practically smoking. The one on the right patted out a red burning spot on his uniform. "I would give anything to come out of a class looking like that."

Stephanie chuckled. "What are you guys doing?"

One of them cracked his back. "We came over here to grab some stuff, but we are doing action and military."

Stephanie's eyes sparkled. "Nice. Do you think I could join you?"

They exchanged glances, obviously confused and therefore hesitant. The one in the middle blinked and stared at her. "As what?"

She shrugged and tried not to feel judged. "A magic user. I'm fairly good at it."

All three guys burst out laughing. The one on the end waved to her. "What the hell. It will be at least one other person to take some damage and share the pain."

A little perturbed, she pursed her lips. "Damage? Pain?"

They all laughed again. "Oh, sure," the guy in the middle snarked in playful banter. "What do you think that flesh-toned leotard is for? You feel everything here exactly like you do on Earth. That includes pain. If you really think about it, how else will you learn?"

The guy on the end elbowed the one in the middle. "She's a virgin. This ought to be good."

The leader put his hand out. "I'm Chris, the asshole in the middle is Paul, and the guy with the unsat pink hair there is Erin."

Stephanie was still stuck on them calling her a virgin. *How could they possibly know that?* She pushed the thought aside and shook his hand. "Stephanie."

The four of them headed to the Dreth building shaped like a giant spaceship. When they walked inside, Chris typed his code in, and the room flickered and filled with weapons. He removed a red disc from the wall, walked over to Stephanie, and pushed it into the fabric of her uniform on her chest. When it was secure, he nodded. "Give it a whack. It should be the girl one, so you shouldn't get any smashed—Yeah, just hit it."

She gave him a deadpan look and slapped the disk, then tumbled back a step or two. Paul caught her, laughing. She now wore body armor—more structural then the guys', thankfully, and reasonably comfortable. Paul held out a gun. "You'll need one of these."

Stephanie stared at it for a second but didn't take it. Instead, she walked to the wall and selected two medium-sized batteries. She bounced them up and down in her hands and shook her head. "These will be fine."

The guys looked at each other and Paul shook his head. "It's your ass, lady."

Erin slapped his hand against a diagram on the wall. There were two ships, a Federation one and a Dreth one. "We have to get a speed vessel—which is a fighter ship—out of the Federation mastership and fly it over to the Dreth ship. It sounds easy, but the first time, it's disorienting because the artificial gravitation on those things is really weak. It's like walking on a bunch of small trampolines."

"Moon shoes." Stephanie snickered as she recalled the old-ass pair Todd had bought offline and had on a shelf in his room.

Erin stared at her for a minute. "Uh, yeah, sure. So, when we get there, we have to take the ship. We've played this dumbass battle…I don't know, twenty, thirty times? It's a pirate episode, so we can't pass the class until we clear the operation."

Paul shoved a dagger into a sheath on the side of his calf, his foot up on the bench. "Yeah, but none of the good players wanted to help us. So here we are in summer school."

Stephanie spun the battery through her fingers like a baton and stepped closer to the diagram. She could already identify a tactic.

CHAPTER THIRTY

"Are you ready?" Paul asked with a smile and his fist hovered over a red button on the wall.

The guys shouted confirmation and a rush of adrenaline pulsed through Stephanie. She wore a belt with two dangling pockets. A battery was stowed in one and she held the other in her hand. Paul slammed his fist on the button and the room immediately became the inside of a Federation ship. Everything was dark-gray and large funneled metal tubes bound together ran all over the ship's walls and ceiling.

She looked around and took care to keep her feet planted. Even inside the main ship, she could feel the difference in gravity. Chris grabbed her arm and pulled her down the hall. "Come on, newbie, stay with us. Follow them to the speed vessel."

Stephanie nodded and broke into a run. It took a moment for her to find her pace. Once she got it, though, she could run faster than she could on Earth. They headed down the long tunnels and the sound of their boots slamming against the grated floor echoed around them. Finally, they turned right and headed down a set of steps into a hangar bay.

A Federation general stood in front of the last ship in the row. "All right soldiers," he barked. "Man up. This is your time. Collect that ship and kill those Dreth pirate sons of—"

Paul ran right past him and waved Stephanie forward. "Avatar. Come on. We've heard it a million times."

She hurried after them onto the speed vessel. It was small, with four chairs up front and a small area in the back with computers and weapons strapped to the walls. As she entered, the hatch shut behind her. She took a seat beside Erin and watched as he put the belts on. She did the same, snapped them on each side, and pulled the front to tighten it across her chest.

Chris sat in the driver's seat, pressed several buttons, and pushed forward on the lever. They hurtled forward down a small tunnel and the far end opened slowly. As they approached, Chris hollered like a cowboy, turned the ship sideways, and made it through the half-opened space. As soon as the craft emerged, a sudden jolt threw Stephanie's arms and legs up. Chris activated the gravitational balance, which helped her lower them again.

She watched out the huge front window of the ship as they sped around and to the back of the Dreth pirate ship. It was distracted, fighting a fleet of fighter ships from the Federation. Chris spun the ship around, guided the craft like a wild man, and steered through a hatch at the back. He looked at Paul, who typed feverishly on a tablet. He had hacked the ship to let them in and now closed the passage behind them.

They all released their belts and pushed to their feet and Chris checked that her armor was still active. He grabbed the neck of her suit to keep her steady. "They'll come strongly right out of the gate. Don't hesitate or they'll get you."

Stephanie mustered her courage, the whole thing as exciting as hell, and gripped her battery. They poured out of the speed vessel and ducked behind its wing to avoid the laser guns that had already begun to fire at them. The three guys immediately returned fire. Chris used a pistol laser gun, Paul a larger one with a winding barrel on the bottom that spat sparks, and Erin threw some kind of electrified blades. Immediately, Stephanie moved in and hurled flames at the attackers.

All three guys stopped, their eyes wide. Paul's lip twitched. "She can throw magic?"

Chris grabbed them both and pushed them to the ground as a piece of equipment exploded nearby. "Never mind that. It's flames on a ship. I don't think that's good."

Stephanie threw one, then another, and another. She eliminated three Dreth and missed a couple of others. Her team's yells penetrated her focus and she glanced quickly at them while she tried to avoid the enemy fire. They waved their arms and screamed frantically. She shook her head, squinted her eyes, and pointed at her ear. "I can't… I can't hear you!"

As she focused more intently on them, she didn't see the Dreth jump up from behind cover and fire at her. The blast struck her in the shoulder and threw her back against a bulkhead. She groaned and instinctively touched the scorched skin on her arm. Dazed and in pain, she barely felt it when Chris grabbed her, laughing, and hauled her down on the ground and behind shelter.

He pushed her back against the wall and patted the cinders on her suit. Erin nodded with a grin. "Welcome!"

They laughed and immediately resumed fire. Erin turned his head toward her. "You popped your cherry."

Her head began to clear, and anger filled her chest as she stared at the Dreth who'd shot her. Then the words Erin had just said floated back through her mind and her face softened as a laugh echoed from her chest. She had finally figured out what the hell they were all laughing about.

She shook her fist and felt the burn in her shoulder. "Not a virgin anymore, boys."

They cheered as they fought back. She glanced around and pulled up onto her knees.

"Paul," she yelled as she grabbed his arm and yanked him toward her.

He ducked slightly as something exploded close to their position. "Yeah?"

Stephanie pointed at the floor about three feet in front of her. "I want you to aim right here."

Paul looked at her like she was nuts. "What the hell for?"

A smirk pulled at her lips and her eyes began to glow orange. "Yes? Okay?"

He pursed his lips and glanced at the pirates who now moved closer, then shrugged. She grinned encouragement as he turned and aimed his gun at the ground where she pointed. With him ready, she shuffled slightly to the right and stood quickly. As she brought her arm up, a golden lasso trailed from her fingertips and she swung it over her head. She thrust her arm forward and threw the loop, which settled neatly over the shoulders of the Dreth who had shot her. With a smug laugh, she pulled it tight and yanked as hard as she could.

The pirate yelled in confusion as he was dragged backward off his feet. He landed hard and slid fast as she hauled him toward her, and the end of the energy lasso piled at her feet. His arm impacted the side of the ship and his gun caught, which dragged it from his hand. He flailed, grunted, and yelled in the Dreth language as he slid relentlessly to the spot where Paul aimed his weapon.

Paul had a huge grin on his face as he stepped forward slowly and awaited his target. The Dreth came to a stop with the barrel of the gun against his head. "Hi, my name is Paul, and I'll be the one who kills you today."

Then, he pulled the trigger.

Paul put his hand over his head and gripped his hair, laughing hard. "Did you see that shit? That damn lasso was like…I don't even know. Where did you even come up with that?"

Stephanie shrugged and unstrapped the belt from her waist. "Wonder Woman."

Paul looked confused. "Who?"

She glanced at him. "She was a female comic book hero. A big-ass movie came out a long, long time ago Her lasso made you tell the truth. Mine makes you face it."

Chris jumped up and slapped the beam as they walked down the hall toward the elevators of the barracks. "I don't care who it was modeled after, that was genius."

"Farthest we've ever been," Erin said and turned to take her hand and hold it to his chest. "Thank you. Seriously. We made it farther and we did it as a team. Do you want to try again tomorrow?"

Stephanie smiled, pulled her hand away, and slapped him on the head. "I'm down. It would be really nice, too, because this is my first ever experience with anything military. I could honestly use some help when it comes to that side of things."

Paul patted her on the shoulder as they reached the elevators. "We got you, little sis. Girls' dorms, eighth floor. Watch your map."

She chuckled and shook her head as they ran off down the hall, whooping and hollering and pushing each other around. They disappeared from view and she looked at her arm computer and pressed the map. "Find my dorm room."

The red dot flashed and showed her the route. Up the elevator to the eighth floor, turn right, room 1089. The doors slid open and she walked inside and glanced at the burn on her skin. She grimaced and patted it tentatively. "That hurts like real world pain."

The doors shut and became a screen, which displayed a serene scene from what looked like rainforests. All of those had been gone for a hundred years so it had to be simulated. The doors slid open and she turned right to follow the hall until she found her room. She put her hand on the security pad and the door opened and the lights came on inside.

It was really nice, much nicer than any place she had ever lived before. The ceiling echoed the time of day, so at that moment, it was dark and starry. She paused to take in the details. The space boasted a huge ceiling fan with blades that looked like giant leaves and a bed made of a rich dark wood carved with vines for the headboard and footboard. On a desk by the window stood a line of cubes.

Beside them was a tablet. She pressed the on button and a holographic form of Anastasia, about a foot tall, emerged from it. "These cubes are your learning modules for when you rest. Those that are labeled **BLACK** are not currently available to you. The rest have a specific level marked. One is the beginner and five is the most difficult. To use the cubes, select one and place it on the white platform located above your headboard. Take the small headband and place it around the upper back of your head so that the small metal reader disks are pressed to your temple. Enjoy and sweet dreams."

Three cubes at the back were labeled **BLACK**. She wasn't sure why they were off limits, but they were so there was little point in worrying about them. On the left were several dark-colored cubes under the magical category. She picked one up and looked closely at it. Her reflection gazed back at her from the shiny surface. She turned it right and left and quickly pulled her head up. As it rested in her hands, it began to change color. Starting at black, it morphed to violet, then lightened to rose, and finally into cerulean blue. She thought it was so strange.

Hastily, she set the cube down and rubbed her hands on her sides. "I don't think that was supposed to happen."

After a moment, she picked it up again, now curious as to what was going on. She tossed it from one hand to the next and noticed that her palms and fingers left imprints in different colors. Intrigued, she wrinkled her nose, held the cube closer, and pressed her finger to the top. She traced down and over the side and studied it intently. A yellow line cut through the cerulean and disappeared behind her finger.

Stephanie smiled, set it down, and yawned loudly. She looked through all of them and grabbed the one labeled with the lowest level. Before she climbed into bed, she opened the closet and discovered several choices for clothing. She tapped a pair of black pajama pants and a T-shirt and grinned as the soft fabric rubbed on her skin. Ready for bed, she clambered onto her knees and placed the cube on the shelf. Two knobs emerged and pushed into the platform. The base of the platform changed from white to a deep blue.

A quick glance at her arm confirmed that it was already healing.

She grimaced and hoped that it wouldn't be painful enough to disturb her rest. Satisfied, she climbed into bed and pulled the covers up. She only realized how tired she was when her head hit the pillow.

Outside the Virtual World and in her room in the tall Golden P tower, the lights were dimmed very low, since there was no real reason for them to be on. Inside the pod, her body rested on the comfortable bed, all the sensors plugged securely into her. As her avatar fell asleep, her human form twitched slightly. The movement rippled through her body as each of her muscles reacted. The movement increased until her whole body shook inside the pod.

Normally, someone would assume this meant a huge issue. However, for the prep school, it was completely normal. Her body merely assimilated the physical memory of what she learned from the cube in the Virtual World. It essentially activated her human muscles as her avatar went through the motions and learned different fighting techniques as she slept. The human body created muscle memory. If a person learned a physical skill—like judo, for example—when they left the pod, their human bodies would still have that muscle memory. For many, this meant that they would finally emerge knowing judo.

However, it wasn't the same as simply learning something in a classroom. The longer they were out of the pod, the more they needed to practice. If they neglected it, they would lose the skill exactly as they would in real life. Usually, the students would be given a list of what they were to practice whenever they were woken from a semester. Stephanie didn't know anything about that when she went in and wouldn't fully remember the action itself when she left. But she would wake up to find that she could kick ass, and her muscles would have no problem keeping up with her at every step. They weren't only trained intellectually, they were trained physically as well.

By the next morning, the pod had fully run its course and the box it sat on blinked from green to white. She stretched her arms out to her sides and turned in her bed to slide her feet to the floor. She removed the headband, sat, and did a couple of quick hand-to-hand moves she had learned in her sleep.

Chuckling to herself, she headed for the bathroom. "That is so wild."

She washed and chose a brand-new jumpsuit since the other one hanging in her tiny avatar closet had burn holes in the shoulder and blood on the fabric. She tapped it, followed by her boots, and headed out of the room, still reeling with the excitement of how wild her time in the Virtual World had become.

CHAPTER THIRTY-ONE

Stephanie sat in the student dining area, the tables all spread out evenly over black and white tiled floors with tablecloths on each one and four-foot-tall flowers in the center. It was lunchtime so the lights were normal, but she'd heard that at dinner, they were dim with sparkling bulbs that floated across the room and candles everywhere. It seemed oddly romantic for a dinner at school but hey, the droids probably enjoyed it.

She picked her sandwich up, took a bite, and looked at the school's newsletter that she had found on one of the tables in the hall. The sound of tramping feet, though, caught her attention. Erin, Chris, and Paul hurried up to the table. Chris was in the middle, his hands behind his back, and all of them looked far too excited to be up to anything good at all. She raised an eyebrow and set her sandwich down.

Chris pulled out a T-shirt with their team emblem, which now included her initial on the front. She giggled and took the shirt. "PECS…really?"

Erin puffed his chest out and spoke in a deep voice. "We got pecksssss."

Paul ignored him. "Part of the team, hey?"

Stephanie wiped her hands. They were a motley crew, but she was in it to win it. They slapped hands with her and headed out with hard-nosed looks on their faces as they prepared to try it one more time.

Stephanie and the others whooped and hollered as they held on tightly and rolled the ship through space toward the Dreth destroyer. Bright beams of red light rocketed through the air to their left as they curved around and brought the little ship down and into the tunnel. Stephanie released her belt and leapt to her feet as she slammed her palm to her chest and popped out her armor. She put her fist up and punched each of the guys in their armor buttons as they passed and gave her a deep battle cry. Their enthusiasm was contagious, and she laughed as she turned to retrieve one of her batteries and grasped it tightly in her hand. She glanced at the T-shirt she had thrown on over her suit and smirked.

The shooting had already begun as the back hatch of the ship lowered. Paul stood firm and eliminated a few of the pirates who had met them at the opening. They were hurled back to splatter against the wall. Paul and Chris each took a side and cleared it as they went. Erin ran out and slid on his side as blasts of lasers blazed at him. They hissed as they struck the metal behind him and left black marks and smoke. Still in motion, he drew two electric daggers and threw them to strike the Dreth on each side of his chest. The alien looked down in the same moment that the electrical current went off. He shook wildly and his eyes rolled back as spittle sprayed from his mouth before he collapsed.

They waved Stephanie down and she came running. As she reached the opening, she turned to the right, put her hand out, and readied for an attack. Shots rang out all around her. She released a fireball that immediately obliterated one of the pirates. From the corner of her eye, she could see another aiming at her chest. As he pulled the trigger, she did a backflip off the side of the ramp to land on one knee with her hand on the floor for support.

She lifted her head and shifted her gaze to either side, more than a little surprised that she was able to do that. Chris raised his brow. "It looks like somebody plugged their cubes in."

Erin chuckled. "You can have terrible dreams when you do it but damn, if you don't come out bouncing like a damn ninja."

Paul released a volley at a group of Dreth. "Now you gotta take the disco one you can rent out from the library and add a sweet-ass move to the end of that acrobatic blast."

Stephanie patted the ground in front of her and stared at Paul. "Are we gonna do this or what?"

He smirked. "Hell yeah!"

She pushed to her feet, activated her lasso, and snagged a Dreth pirate to yank him from his feet. He flailed as he was dragged along until his head hit the bottom of Paul's boot. Her teammate aimed his weapon and squeezed the trigger to deliver a shot between the eyes. With his head tilted to the side, he looked at the alien for a minute. "Is this the same one as yesterday?"

Stephanie shook her head and flipped the lasso from the corpse. "Hell no. I shot that asshole before he could get me in the arm. That was painful. I'm serious. There is no cream for avatar burns. I'm supposed to wait until it heals. Fast healing or not, it felt like fire all night long. I can even remember feeling it during my cube training. At least when I woke up it was basically healed, luckily."

Chris chuckled and almost immediately, his face grew serious. "Wait, you can remember your cube training?"

Paul followed her head-nod toward the wall and a dead Dreth pirate. He was pinned in place with a shimmering gold trident stuck through his throat. Slowly, Paul turned to glance nervously in her direction. "Okay. I see you're doing big things and tackling big magic but...what is that? Did you seriously use a trident? What, are you Ursula, now? Is this a mermaid story? I swear if there are talking crabs, I will join the pirates."

Chris snickered. "We aren't here to talk about what that chick from spring break gave you when you went home to New Orleans."

He blinked and shook his head. "You know, you don't even know her. She is a damn good person. You are only jealous because I get to…you know, be a man, and you are stuck at home knitting with Grandma."

Stephanie rolled her eyes and patted him hard on the shoulder. "You might want to watch out."

Paul looked behind him and dove to the side as two Dreth pirates rushed through under the ship's wing with their guns drawn. Stephanie focused on her energy and pictured the kind of weapon she wanted. She opened her eyes as they ducked, and she released the magic. It blazed forward and twisted into the shape of an arrow.

The two pirates dropped, and Stephanie shrugged. "I honestly don't know where the whole trident thing came from. It wasn't on my mind. But still, I think it's pretty sweet. Who else can say they did that?"

"The Mer-King. Uh…Poseidon," Erin yelled. "That guy from that really old flick. What was it called? The one with the dog with headgear?"

Chris tilted his head back and bellowed. "*Anchor Man*… And Brick killed someone with a trident."

Erin banged his fists against the side of the ship. "I'm in a glass case of emotion."

Stephanie sighed as she realized she might actually be surrounded by three different-tempered Todds. Then again, all guys could be like that. She honestly didn't know. The truth was that she had only hung out with one of them, had never been on a date, and tended to steer clear of the rest of the guys at school. They were, with no exception, complete dickheads. Nonetheless, it was funny, even she had to admit that.

The entire team continued to laugh as they proceeded with the mission. Stephanie sent a fireball to her right and knocked two pirates down. She smirked, turned, and stopped dead in her tracks as she came face to face with a Dreth pirate. Without thought, she whirled, kicked her leg up, and slammed her foot into his chest. He grunted and stumbled back as he rubbed his chest. Stephanie drew her fist back to punch him as hard as she could and squarely in the nose. She looked smugly at her fist and at him once more before she finished him off with a fireball.

The fighting techniques were entirely foreign to her, but the truth was that she liked them. In fact, she liked them a lot. They finally cleared the landing bay and Chris pulled a 3D image of the ship up on his arm tablet. He traced his finger along the corridor and down. "This will lead us directly to the head of the ship."

As they ran, they kept Paul in the middle. He was already trying to hack into the navigation chamber. Stephanie brought up the rear and released arrows and fireballs at anything that tried to follow their hasty advance. As they raced up to the door, Chris bobbed up and down and glanced at Paul. "What we got here, man?"

Paul breathed in slowly and typed one more line before he pressed enter. The doors to navigation hissed as they slid open. They barreled inside and immediately opened fire to mow down three Dreth pirates who stood guard to the right and left. Stephanie pushed through and marched down the middle of the ramp, her hand out, and grinned as a magical rope looped effortlessly toward the pirate lord. The loop wound itself around the target and immediately, she pulled it taut.

Smiling from ear to ear, the guys walked up, and everyone looked at Chris. "Fearless team leader. Shall you do the honors?"

He mulled it over in his head for a minute before he laughed and raised his pistol to fire a single well-placed blast in the Dreth's head. An alert chimed almost instantly, and the AI spoke. "You have successfully passed this exercise. Please prepare for extraction."

The room shimmered and swept past to take them all back to the empty room in the Dreth building. They had finally been able to beat the ship, and Paul, Erin, and Chris would get their pass to the next level. That was exactly what they needed to come back with their scholarships intact in the fall.

Celebrations immediately ensued, including raising Stephanie on their shoulders and parading her across campus to the virtual bar. She had one drink and sat there watching the others go wild. They had passed, which meant they could come back, and for those three, that was a game changer. She stayed through her one drink and then said goodnight. They all booed her good-naturedly, but she shrugged. "I gotta keep my edge up."

She left with their cheers ringing in her ears and headed to the barracks. She couldn't help but laugh and smile, immensely satisfied by the knowledge that they would be able to return the next year. They deserved it and had only needed a little support. For her, though, celebration was a cube and a good night's sleep.

Several warnings began to list on the major screen, a normal thing when the school semesters kicked into gear. About midway was a load spike attributed to Pinnacle Prep, but it took the engineers a while to get that far down. There were several of those, as well as a couple of glitches they had to resolve with no time wasted. Order was the only thing that mattered to them at that point.

As they moved closer to the Pinnacle entry, the screen shimmied slightly but no one in the pit noticed it in the least. When it settled once more, the line no longer said Pinnacle. Instead, it read Abernathy Prep, a very large school that was expected to have a large pull. The place had large shifts in load during the regular school year on an hourly basis. To have one during their summer session wouldn't have even raised an eyebrow. And, in fact, it didn't. The engineers skimmed past it without paying it even a second's notice. It was deleted from the prompter and new threats and warnings listed instead.

Out in the system, BURT waited until the line was deleted before he returned his attention to several different fights happening in different areas. Apparently, the Dreth space mission had forced a lot of kids into summer school. Only one group had succeeded thus far, though, and it just so happened that Stephanie was right there with her hand in the cookie jar.

CHAPTER THIRTY-TWO

Stephanie spent most of the summer attending the various classes and working on magic whenever she could, but that was about it. She had seen no signs of anything abnormal but apparently, she was wrong. Near the end of the semester, she got up bright and early one morning to grab breakfast. Sleepily, she climbed out of bed and stopped. Her cubes were gone.

The AI spoke over the speaker in her room. "Good morning, Stephanie Morgana. We have been informed that you are no longer eligible to complete the last six days of the summer session here at Pinnacle. Technically, you have completed the majority of the courses and those credits will be applied to your Federation record. They can be used at any university in the world."

She was confused. "Wait…am I getting kicked out?"

The AI paused for a moment and then continued. "Unfortunately, you have been removed from the program due to your assistance in the Dreth Operations Simulation. It is written in the campus handbook that no student not involved in that curriculum can help anyone else. You were not approved to enter the Dreth ship program and therefore your time here is up. We do hope that you enjoyed your stay. Appearing in front of you are two buttons. Leave this program and No, really, you have to go. Please choose one in the next thirty seconds."

For a moment, she simply sat there on the edge of her bed, completely frozen in shock. She didn't want to pick a button. She had helped fellow classmates with a project that they had been unfairly targeted on and not given the resources to complete. Anger surfaced and she gritted her teeth and punched the mattress below her. She really didn't have any choice in the matter. No matter which button she picked—or even none at all—it would send her back to the real world. She knew it was bullshit, though. Clarity seared through her consciousness and for a moment, she cursed her stupidity at having allowed them to suck her into their schemes. Her fandom had most likely died down by now, and they had gotten what they wanted out of her. She had been the drawcard they needed to attract even more paying students. That accomplished, there was no need to waste any more of their resources.

She slammed her fist against the **Leave Now** button and flipped the bird at the ceiling, hoping someone or something was watching. It seemed only moments before her eyes opened wide inside the pod. Everything was disconnected and she rubbed her chest in an effort to wake from the long nap she had taken. Suddenly, the door to the pod opened and two Federation guards stood beside it, waiting for her to stand.

"You didn't even let me say goodbye," she grumped as one reached to help her out. She snatched her arm free and walked over to place her palm on the security scanner. In silence, she gathered her clothes and changed in the bathroom, where she left the body suit on the counter. When she was ready, she strode out and retrieved her suitcase.

The guards led her downstairs and out onto the street where a cab waited to give her a ride back to the station, her still-unused suitcase in hand. She glanced back at the tower once, turned away abruptly, and climbed into the vehicle. Her body was too tired to deal with it.

The cab eased away from the curb and Stephanie pulled her phone out and sent her mom a text to let her know the simple truth. It was the end of the semester and the end of her school time. She sent the message and dropped her phone in her bag. Around the cold numbness that seemed intent to claim her, she couldn't help but feel heartbroken.

When the TRAM arrived in Chicago, she lugged her bag down the steps and through the crowds toward the exit. Even the long trip hadn't made her feel any better at all. When she reached the parking area, she saw her dad leaning against the car, his arms out. She ran up to him, laid her head on his chest, and hugged him tightly.

The smile faded from his face and he looked down. "Are you all right?"

Stephanie breathed deeply. "Yeah. Just glad to be home."

He helped her into the car, and they drove back to the house in silence. When they arrived, her dad carried her suitcase and she shuffled up the walkway and in through the front door. She stepped through the entry and a couple of balloons and a handful of confetti hit her in the face. A small group shouted, "Happy Birthday!"

Stephanie smiled and looked around. There was the banner—the same one that had been hung since she was three—over the arch into the kitchen. Her mother hurried forward and gave her a big hug. "Welcome home, sweetie. And happy eighteenth birthday. You are an adult now!"

She had honestly completely forgotten that it was her birthday. "Man, you guys are on it. Thank you so much. It's good to be home for it."

Her mom went to grab her a glass of punch and she meandered over to Todd, who stood by the window and smiled broadly. She hugged him tightly and he hugged her back, and both lingered for a second longer than normal. He raised his cup of punch. "Welcome back, slacker. I have counted down the days. They told me you left early, but I wasn't upset for you, to be honest."

Stephanie choked on her punch. "What?"

Todd shrugged. "I was selfish and basically pumped my fist like Arsenio and knee-shuffled like Vanilla Ice…ice baby. It didn't feel quite right without you here."

In all honesty, she was surprised and touched. "Thanks, dude. I'm surprised you even noticed how much time had passed. I figured you would have run laps with Amy, worked, and taken her on dates."

He glanced around as he sipped his drink. "It was a little overrated, I think. I broke up with her about two days after you left."

Stephanie tilted her head back to stare at him, not quite sure what she felt about that. "What? Why?"

Todd laughed but had the grace to look a little sheepish. "It seems she had this fixation with me eating healthy, working out, and getting up early in the morning during summer vacation."

Stephanie gasped, touched his arm, and tried not to laugh. "That monster! Damn right you broke up with her for…trying to make you…healthy and shit. Stick it to the man!"

He nodded enthusiastically. "I know, right? That's what I felt. Like she was my drill instructor and I had already rolled into the military. No thank you. I want to live on my terms."

She gave him a half-cocked smile. "She lost you at waking up, didn't she?"

"She lost me at eating healthy."

His eyes shifted to the table by the window where a plate of chocolate-frosted cupcakes gleamed in the afternoon light. He looked like a puppy that stared at a snack of meat but couldn't have it. She was fairly sure that at any moment, he would actually break into an all-out drool, scratch behind his ear, probably fart, and scurry off guiltily to steal cupcakes. That's right, she'd compared her best friend to a puppy.

She was about to say something else when he simply stepped away and made a bee-line for the confectionary. He glanced around and selected two of them, then consumed half a cupcake in one bite.

"It's so good to see you back," her neighbor Mr. Kanter said and shook Stephanie's hand.

Stephanie shifted her glance from Todd covered in cupcake to him. "Oh, thank you so much. And thank you for coming to the party. This is so sweet."

Mrs. Kanter walked up and slid her arm through her husband's. "Your mother is so cute. She intended to have one either way, but when she found out you would be back for it, she changed everything. She wanted to see you smile."

She looked across the room at her mom, who laughed with her dad and another set of neighbors who had come. "She did a good job because this was really a great surprise. And I honestly needed one."

They all stood there chatting for some time, while Todd wiped icing off his chin, the front of his shirt, and his elbow, although he had no idea how it had got there. When the Kanters walked away, Stephanie grabbed a cupcake and sat. Todd strolled over, sat beside her, and released a deep breath. She looked at him, then did a double-take. With a grin, she pulled a chunk of cupcake from his hair.

She set it in her napkin. "I'm seriously trying to figure out how in the hell you got that so many places. You seriously would have had to eat it like the cookie monster eats cookies—throw them at your face and hope they hit right around where your mouth is."

Todd nodded in agreement. "That seems like the only legit way to eat them, don't you think?"

He picked the cupcake out of her hand and smooshed it into her nose. Immediately, they began to wrestle for it, laughing and goofing off. It was a totally wonderful way to end one hell of a shitty day.

When the party was over and her mom had sent Todd home with three more cupcakes, Stephanie thanked her parents for the hundredth time and headed up to her room. She pulled out her computer, a smaller version than the one downstairs, and flipped it on. She didn't even think about the fact that she had been gone all summer and hadn't checked emails or anything. When the screen came up, the icon flashed in the corner with a number twenty-five above it. She was reasonably sure that the only time she'd had that many emails was when Todd accidentally signed her up for a spam site, thinking he had won some contest.

She scrolled through them one by one. Most of them were from people who still wanted to talk to her about her "witch day." **Dear Stephanie, the coven of Chicago would like to reach out to you and extend an official invite to join our circle. There is always a place for magic in the circle. Please reply when you find you have time. Love and Light, Broom Hilda Naysayer (AKA Joan Carrows)**

There was a pentagram at the bottom and when it had opened, purple rose petals literally fell to the floor. She shut that email and deleted it, then tried to stomp the magical rosebuds beneath her feet. The next one was interesting too. **Greetings Ms. Morgana. My name is Herold and I saw your heroic deed on the news. I wanted to reach out to you and let you know that you aren't alone. I've told the feds for years that I can go to town with some magic. Just the other day, I left my car parked and running outside the grocery store and when I came back, it was gone! Poof, magic. (Or carjacking, but I choose the brighter side.) Please let me know if you would like to get in touch and have some tea or sacrifice a chicken. Sincerely, Herold the Moon God.**

Stephanie put her hand over her mouth and tried not to laugh. That feeling only sat there for a moment before she realized that everything that day had brought had been ripped away, and all for money. She clicked on the next one, a video message. A pretty little girl displayed on the screen with long brown ringlets. She situated herself with someone filming. "Stephanie, my name is Holly and I am six years old. I wanted to write and thank you for saving my mommy's and my sister's life."

Stephanie sat forward as the video panned to the woman and her baby, and her other daughter and her husband cheered for her. "Thank you! We love you!"

The video ended and she smiled, thankful that she had read one more. So, without taking that positive away, she scrolled down to the end, dating back to the day before she'd left. She frowned when she reached the bottom of the list and found that she had missed one from ONE R&D.

CHAPTER THIRTY-THREE

"Hey, guys," Stephanie said as she came down the stairs. "I got this email from the company that I did the battery thing with. It was from before I left. I guess it was sent the same time as the admission letter from Pinnacle, but I overlooked it in all the excitement."

Her parents were on the couch, watching a movie. They paused it and took the email from her to read. Her dad nodded. "That sounds interesting. I would say do your research on them and then go from there."

She took the letter and shrugged. "So you think it might be worth pursuing since I probably won't go to a prep school?"

Her mom smiled and took her hand. "I think it all depends on what you want. But you are eighteen now, so you have to decide for yourself. We're always here as a sounding board, though."

Stephanie nodded and gave them a crooked smile. "Thanks. I think I'm exhausted, at this point. I don't want to think about the future for even five more seconds."

Her mother laughed, turned away, and pressed the play button on the receiver. "We all go through it. I— Well, look what we have here. Those assholes."

She moved closer to see the advertisement that had popped up on the cable station. It was the PR video taken when they'd first arrived at Pinnacle. Anastasia looked as odd as ever—but normal, apparently, for the rich people. Then her, looking meek and full of excitement. Stephanie scoffed to herself. *That sure didn't stay.* Finally, it focused on her mother hurrying along behind them.

"They really do have the nerve." Her mother slammed the remote down. "They kick you out under bogus terms all because they didn't want to pay. They got free PR from it and—wait, is my ass really that big?"

She jumped up from the couch and looked over her shoulder with an absolutely mortified expression. Her mouth agape, she looked from her ass to her husband a few times. "Is it?"

His eyes widened and he pushed back on the couch as if he tried to disappear into it. He glanced down and stared at her butt like a deer caught in the headlights. She fixed him with a hard look, and he opened his mouth and shut it again as he wrung his hands. "Ohhhh, this is a trick. It's a trick."

She stomped her foot. "It's not a trick. Tell me the truth."

He sent a look of appeal to Stephanie, who simply stood there with no expression, determined to stay out of it. He'd been married to her for how many years? Surely, by now, he had learned how to stay out of awkward situations.

Finally, he answered. "Uh no..."

Cindy whirled back to the screen as the commercial ended and narrowed her eyes. She shook her finger at the television. "I will nail their skinny asses to the wall."

Stephanie had already crept back to the stairs, and as soon as her mother's attention was on the television again, she hurried away. There was no way she intended to be caught up in that mess. She sat at her computer and put the paper down in front of her, thinking about the company, the logo on the boxes, and the money they had already invested for her to use the pods. She finally decided that with what they had done so far, she owed it to them, at the very minimum, to look into it.

Her mind made up, at least on that, she started her research. She found their website quickly, opened it, and read carefully through each page. It was all very vaguely written, almost like a hospital webpage with generic information. However, there were a couple of things BURT had put in that he knew would catch her attention. **ONE R&D, working to make the world a better place through the magical cooperation of our neighbors of Meligorn.**

There was also a very brief section on future research into the possible implementation of magical elements to increase the infrastructure and housing for all those living on or below the poverty level. Not only did it talk about the buildings themselves but helping to enrich the lives of the youth by focusing on educational opportunities on an even level with the rest.

Stephanie sat back and rubbed her hands over her face. She blinked several times and cracked her fingers, absolutely exhausted from everything that happened that summer. To be honest, she wasn't even sure she had fully wrapped her head around it. What she did know was that she couldn't let those events get in the way of what she still had on her plate. She only had a semester left of school, and since she was back a week early from prep, she would be able to start on time.

Sure, she could probably get away with not going in the morning, but it wouldn't do her any good. She had to attempt to pull herself together and get back into the old mindset of things—like the reality that it wouldn't be as simple as a free ride through some prestigious college. And as nice as it had been, there were so many ways she could think of to better allocate her time and her resources.

She turned the computer and her desk lamp off. It took real effort to drag herself into pajamas and finally collapse into bed. Only when the covers were pulled up to her chin did she finally allow her body to relax. She had forgotten, after being in the pod for so long, that her bed was one of the most comfortable places in the world. It was the quiet after a long storm. A place to rest her wild brain, not continue to dwell on the things that couldn't be fixed right there in that exact moment.

It was time to pull herself together.

The alarm went off the next morning and she rolled over and opened her eyes wide. She didn't think it would actually happen, but she felt a whole lot better than she had the night before. For one thing, she had slept really well—no dreams and no nightmares—and woke up in the comfort of her own home. She flipped the covers off and smelled the familiar aroma of coffee left in the pot for her down in the kitchen. The idea of coffee worked like her own personal magic, and she hurriedly pulled her closet door open, grabbed her school uniform, and changed into it. She looked in the mirror as she pulled her hair high into a ponytail and wrapped the elastic band around it. Stephanie was determined to have a damn good day.

After she had downed a cup of coffee and poured the rest into a travel mug, she ate two cupcakes to fill her stomach and opened the fridge door. Like clockwork, as if nothing had changed, there was a sack lunch made for her with a smiley face drawn on the front. She chuckled as she pulled it out and shoved it in her bag before she headed for the door. When she opened it, she found Todd standing at the end of the yard, waiting for her.

With a big smile, she bounced out of the house, stopped, and wrinkled her nose in front of him. She raised her thumb to wipe a smear of chocolate icing from his cheek. "Don't worry, I'm not judging. I had the same for breakfast. But I eat like a person, not a one-year-old on their first birthday."

Todd shrugged and rubbed his cheek with the back of his sweater sleeve. "Yeah, I had to shove them down so my mom wouldn't get mad that I ate cupcakes for breakfast."

They started their walk and it seemed that the sun shone brighter through the smog than normal. It warmed Stephanie's face and she soaked it in. He cleared his throat uncomfortably. "So, I know that in the end, they screwed you over and all, but I wondered if you could tell me what it was like?"

Stephanie actually didn't mind, and she was glad to not hold onto the anger and resentment. "Well, you stay in the pods twenty-four-seven. And at night in the Virtual World, you plug in these cubes that teach you all kinds of different things while you sleep. Then, during the day, there were a lot of boring classes. But I also got to go with a team onto a Dreth ship and kill the pirate lord. That was the highlight of the whole thing. Oh! And I made magic tornados."

Todd stared at her, his eyes huge. "Are you kidding? I want to go shoot up a damn pirate ship! Kill some Dreth pirates. You always see the cool shit while I'm over here barely able to hold a conversation with people."

She grinned. "It was great, I have to admit. Although there were several times it hurt like all getout. But yeah, it was great!"

He looked dreamily at her as he thought about fighting Dreth pirates. "I hope that if I do join the military, they will let me fight them in the system too, at least before they throw me in with the real thing."

Stephanie snorted. "Me too. They are some vicious aliens, I will tell you that much. Honestly, they simply don't care who they kill or for what reason. They simply want to take. So, tell me about your summer."

Todd shoved his hands in his pockets. "Um, I worked at the restaurant in the dish pit again. That was cool because I put my headphones on and washed stuff for minimum wage—I think eleven dollars and fifteen cents an hour. I saw a few movies I wanted to see again. I hacked my way into the systems and watched some seriously awesome eighties movies. I saw *Gremlins, Ferris Bueller's Day Off, The Goonies, Sixteen Candles, Back to the Future, Fast Times at Ridgemont High,* and the first *Die Hard*. I still have some to watch, of course."

She giggled and ended with a small snort. "That's seriously a lot of movies."

He put his hands up and flipped around to walk backward. "Right? But it's the eighties. I mean it was the Brat Pack. They were moody, sarcastic, pushed back, did what they wanted to do and didn't give two shits. Which I think I've discovered might be the actual motto of the 1980s."

Stephanie made her eyes really wide. "Uh oh, it sounds like you have abandoned the precious nineties for its older brother, the eighties."

Todd stopped her and put his hands on her shoulders. "Don't ever say something like that out loud. Quentin Tarantino might send Mr. White to off me. Jay and Silent Bob will drag me back to the mall. The Quick Stop will actually wait on people and the video shop next door will make money! You savage! Not to mention that Randall "Pink" Floyd will start accepting drug tests from the coach, 'cause what the hell, right? And then there's Matthew McConaughey's famous David Wooderson who will still be standing around waiting to get older as the girls stay the same age and never actually deliver his signature, *All right, all right, all right.* Matt Damon and Ben Affleck will get their wings back and come to attack because we are cursing the nineties, only leading to Alanis Morrissette having to open her mouth and crush the heads of anyone who hears her."

He huffed and puffed, having not taken a breath through the whole tirade. He started to back up again as he calmed himself. "And all of this will happen before we lose the record store. Which record store? It doesn't matter because they always tried to bring them back in the nineties. Because the moral of the story is...the nineties cinematic wonders would have never blossomed into the pop culture classics they are today without the awkward and brooding, poorly filmed cinematic train wrecks that were the 1980s classics—"

Stephanie put up her hand and grabbed his arm to stop him before he tripped over the curb onto the sidewalk. "I have to stop you here. One, because you will fail all your classes if you don't get it together. And two, I'm starting to get a tick listening to you talk without breathing."

Todd chuckled and leaned forward to kiss her forehead. "And this is why we will always be friends."

She shook her head. While she always tried to keep up with his interests—they were interesting to her too—she had been far too busy in a virtual coma during the summer to do anything.

CHAPTER THIRTY-FOUR

At school, Stephanie walked beside Todd through the halls and tried to ignore the weirdness that went on around her. Whether it was a look of ill intent that harnessed a seriously envious and jealous hatred, or a bashful smile backlogged with admiration and practically worship, it all really began to creep her out.

Todd glanced around and clicked his tongue. "Okay, so no one knew you breathed on earth last semester and now, it's a freaking scene from *Carrie* in here."

She walked closer to him. "Drop pig's blood on me and it might come true. Just saying."

One of the asshole guys, Trent, stepped out in front of her, a smirk on his braced teeth. He was slightly overweight, played football, and was about as dumb as a box of chewed Skittles. Which was probably why he made it his mission to attempt to make people feel like shit all the time. "Look who it is—the freak with the laser hands. Why don't you give it up and show us how it's done?"

Stephanie jerked and clenched her hand into a fist. Trent stepped back and his expression sobered. She narrowed her eyes and leaned forward. "Do you want to find out how painful it is to grow your nuts back?"

He swallowed hard, tripped backward over his own feet, and fell. Stephanie and Todd continued to walk forward and literally stepped right over the top of him. When they had made it a little farther down the hallway, he leaned over to her. "Do you actually think you perform precise enough magic to cut a dude's balls off and not anything else?"

She tossed her head defiantly and fixed him with a hard look. "No. Not that it matters because I didn't bring a battery anyway. But I figured if he already knew what I could do, he wouldn't really question me. The details mean nothing, really. No balls today? No balls tomorrow? What's the difference?"

Todd blinked wildly. "Only the fact that if he knew that—because his brain is the size of a flea—he would not comprehend pain tomorrow and cause you serious pain right here, right now."

Stephanie sighed. "Fine. I will make sure that I don't use that one again. Seriously, though, I want to go on record and say that even though he acts all tough, he has never hit a girl. He probably would threaten me and punch you."

He put his finger up in instant protest. "Uh, I don't like that outcome. You do realize that I am of a sensitive nature, right? I am not to be trifled with or physically incapacitated. I am a wimp and don't want to be punched in the face by that giant ogre of a guy. That's purely common sense."

She patted him on the shoulder as they walked. "Don't worry, I'll never call you out for not having some of the worst traits of masculinity in society ever. But that's showing your care for women and the equality of all. It's a political statement."

Todd raised an eyebrow. "I'm not quite sure how to take that. It seems good and kind, but also condescending and snide. Either way, good acting skills back there. The Toddster approves."

Stephanie snarled and her lip twitched. "Do not refer to yourself in conversation as the Toddster. It will only bring you pain and suffering. But thank you. I actually did learn some stuff on verbal conflict resolution as well as how to deal with some of the most sexist and non-agreeable aliens in the universe. So I guess I didn't completely lose out on that deal."

The truth was that Stephanie had learned a lot of things at the prep school. Some of them were obvious to her while others were so hidden that only those around her actually began to notice. She was focused but not stressed and spoke out but didn't make things a huge problem. And the way she carried herself was different than it ever had been before. The classes went on around her, but she sat there as if she were in another place.

A couple of the teachers who had known her for practically her entire youth were very quick to notice the change in her. Her history teacher, speaking with the English teacher in the hall, was slightly alarmed. "She seems absent. Like she is only here because she has to be. Her answers are short and to the point, her eyes are somewhere else, and she constantly looks down at whatever she is scribbling on the papers in front of her."

Her English teacher nodded. "I know. She didn't even raise her hand to answer a question once. And her frustration with the headsets was visible to everyone."

That was absolutely true. For her, staring into a VR headset to learn was like sitting too close to the television. She used to look forward to the opportunity to use them, excited that she knew her last semester would have a new set. But when it came time to use them, she fiddled, complained under her breath, and sat with the headset on, her head resting on her palm, and simply pushed through it. The images weren't quality and all she wanted was to reach out and do some magic. But that would do nothing because the only things she could see were her poorly animated hands and whatever the Federation Scholastic Foundation had thrown together as scenery to tell a story.

On a better note, though, she didn't mope the entire time. About an hour into the program, she took a deep breath and forced herself to sit straight, reminding herself that her days in twenty-four-seven pods were over. They might have been awesome, but in the end, they were not made for her. The VR headsets were a much better option than the text, at least. You could touch things, pick them up, and explore the different places in history during that time period.

They were definitely not interactive and not even close to system quality, but they were what they had, and she had dealt with that her whole life. She had to constantly reiterate to herself that it was good to have dreams but that she couldn't allow that to cloud the life she had to live. If she succeeded, great, but if not, she had to live her life in a VR headset. Flat, pixilated, and cloudy.

At the end of school, she made her way slowly outside and squinted at the bright sun as she exited. Todd stood out at the street, eating some sort of pastry. She didn't even want to ask him where he'd gotten it from. They didn't say a word at first, merely walked quietly down the road. He had noticed the change in her, and her thoughts were so far away that she felt disconnected. It was a reversal of that morning, but she figured it was bound to happen at some point.

When they reached the entrance to the subs, Todd sniffed. "So I think I have a new desire. I joke about it a lot, but I actually think this is what I want to do."

Stephanie looked at him and tried to pull herself into the conversation. "Oh yeah? What's that? I've told you a hundred times that they don't have comic book reviewers or cupcake testers. Those jobs simply don't exist. Remember? We spent that one night in eighth grade looking them up for hours?"

Todd shook his head and chuckled. "No. That's not what I am talking about. I think for real, I want to go into the military. If I'm accepted, they will give me the Virtual Reality training."

She tapped her fingers to her lips and nodded cautiously. "That's true. I can totally catch that logic. And I got to see glimpses of what it's like. I think you would be good at it."

He beamed and stood straighter. "You know what else I thought? If your celeb status ever wears off, you should definitely go with me. We could be one hell of a team. Through boot camp, training, and then we could ride the galaxy together. I'll steer and you protect us with your magic."

Stephanie giggled. "Right. So you do the fun stuff and I'll put myself in the line of fire. I mean, seriously, it sounds legit. We could be like that superhero movie you thought was so funny...uh... *Guardians of the Galaxy*. We could save a raccoon and have him be our rough-them-up guy."

Both of them laughed, and it felt good, Stephanie had to admit. Things were so serious and pressured in her life now. Still, in the back of her mind, no matter how much she joked with Todd about the military, she really hoped that didn't end up being her only choice. She had never put a full amount of thought into it until she fought the Dreth pirates on their ship and, although she would like it if it were that dramatic and wild on the majority of days, she knew that would rarely be the case. Or she would end up on some ship sailing out into the galaxy, never to be seen or heard from again. It wasn't what she thought of when she saw the rest of her life.

There had been so many wars in the past, and with the difference between the nations, it could be really dangerous out there. Plus, she would have to be comfortable knowing that in those wars, so many innocent people died and for no good reason. That there was an answer to it and it was so simple to see, but it took them opening up to it. Allowing it in. Humans were hard-pressed to do things like that for a multitude of reasons. Sometimes because of money, but mostly, and number one, because of fear. Fear drove almost everything that they did.

The friends stopped in front of her house. She hugged him and turned to head inside. As soon as the door was shut, she felt a load lift off her. She wasn't sure what had caused it, but she felt comfortable again, not having the pressure to be who people thought she was all the time. With a sigh, she set her bag down and went to the counter, where an apple and a cupcake sat on top of a note from her mom.

Hey sweetie. We have quite a bit of work to do so might be late. Eat whatever but try to be healthy. We stopped through here to have lunch so I figured I would write you a short note to tell you that you are amazing, intelligent, and wonderful and I am so proud of the woman you have become. See you for dinner. Love you, Mom and Dad.

She smiled as she read the note and grabbed both the apple and the cupcake. At the family computer, she sat but didn't turn it on until she had eaten her cupcake and removed all the icing from her fingers. She didn't want to mess the thing up. It was basically her only window at that moment to really think about what happened in the rest of the world while she sat in the ghettos, blinded by the smog and constant rumbling of cars on the highway.

Stephanie brought the apple to her lips, took a big bite, and sucked the juices through her teeth. She smiled as she set it down and slid her hands down her pant legs to make sure they weren't sticky. Satisfied, she turned the computer on and grabbed her bag to retrieve the notes for her homework. One of the big things was to work on a report about the information they had learned in the headsets that day during history. To talk about the stark difference between one war and another. To talk about the toll it took on the people.

Truly good quality or not, that was hard to see through her eyes. The dead, the dying, the destruction, and all because humans were more fixated on the need than the reason. Because they were quicker to draw a gun than to talk about a crisis. Because numbers, in their political world, had become a way to justify it all and continue to battle against each other even when there were real threats circling the universe.

She sighed and leaned back to stare at the few words she had written. They seemed depressing and tired. Even to her, they seemed to say there was no spark left in her, and she knew that was not true, not even in the least. She had to get her hope back. To keep searching for answers. To keep hoping that one day, a company would come looking for her to do the impossible. To change the way that magic was used on Earth. That seemed like such a pipe dream by that point, but if she didn't keep that nestled in her chest, she would end up like everyone else in the subs, never leaving and simply repeating the cycle over and over. And the world might never know what she could have done to help it.

With a heavy sigh, she closed the document and reached to turn the computer off when she decided a nap was probably the best way to rid her of the negativity. But, before she could hit the switch, the email notification came on. She clicked over to it and found a new message waiting for her from ONE R&D.

CHAPTER THIRTY-FIVE

Stephanie pressed her tongue to her right incisor and tapped her fingers on the desk as the message came up on the screen. ONE R&D had been the ones to get her into the pods in the first place, and she was mad at herself for not noticing that they had written to her before she left. Of course, it wasn't on purpose. She had merely completely blanked. The excitement of it all had been more than she had expected and, well, she'd screwed up.

She took a deep breath and leaned forward to squint into the light of the screen. It was an invitation. After all that, it was an invitation to handle R&D Research using the pod waiting for her at her TimeWarp. She scanned through the email, read the exciting parts, and went back to the beginning to read it over again. This time, she paid attention to the details and attempted to not to let herself get excited. There was no use in it. She had already been let down by people more than once in a small time period.

The letter outlined what she would do but gave no real specifics. However, it didn't only involve hours in a pod. If she accepted the position, she would be paid a small stipend, which would be based on her success. When she read that, she stopped for a moment. She'd never actually been offered a paying job before except when she helped her parents clean houses and offices. She rubbed her face and continued. It covered a few small insignificant details and mentioned that the car was still part of it. Then it went into numbers.

Her mouth dropped and she leaned in closer as she stared at the number under the pay section. In her eyes—the eyes of someone who didn't really know what she could make in that field—the money seemed more than fair. In reality, though, it wasn't. It was actually a little low, a tactic included by BURT to register where she was from a negotiation of business standpoint. Would she push back or not?

The answer to that, since she had no idea of any of this, was to absolutely not push back. The money was perfect for her. She read through the rest and found no real fine detail or anything that would throw caution into the mix at all. In some places, she even stopped and re-read several times to make sure she hadn't gotten too excited and overlooked things. When she finally realized that everything looked great, she shrugged and used her finger to sign on the screen.

As soon as she pressed send, another email popped up giving her a code for a special immersion pod at TimeWarp. She wasn't exactly sure what was meant by special, but she figured that at that point, it really didn't matter. It was a pod with little to no restriction on use and a stipend to go along with it. Not to mention actual job experience and a very good possibility of working in Meligorn.

"What do I really have to lose?" she asked herself as she jotted the code down.

She swiped next and an alert blinked in the corner of her screen. A deposit had been made into her bank account. She clicked on it and found more Federation credits in there than she had ever held in an entire year. In fact, she was sure a few of those would outweigh what she had made on side jobs and such for her entire life. She put her hand to her mouth and began to laugh, her head tilted back as she shook it in disbelief. Stephanie didn't know what this company wanted with her so badly but hell, they were there before the magic, before the public show, and even after she'd been lobbed out of prep school. Why not give it a shot?

Immediately, her mind floated to what the money needed to be used for. Since her parents worked so much, her mother often left information for her to pay a couple of bills here or there. One particular one that she could afford was the Internet note for the year. Besides the money for their car that doubled as a work vehicle, it was the most expensive. Not to mention that paying monthly instead of yearly added close to ten percent to the bill.

So…she paid it.

It took fifty percent of what she had but she didn't care at all. It would lessen the load on them, and she liked to do that. From there, she knew she would need new clothes, something she could tell her parents were nervous about financially. She planned for thirty-five percent of the money left to go into that and then she would throw the last fifteen into her savings.

Stephanie had never been one to freak over clothing decisions, but she knew that looking successful was half the battle. She stopped writing on her note pad and rolled her eyes. "I guess that shit-ass prep school wasn't all a waste of a summer."

It was incredibly annoying to her that she actually found that the boring classes she'd had to take there and those she had taken in school had turned out to be slightly useful. She wanted to hate Pinnacle with a passion, not actually find benefit in the hell they had sold her. Nonetheless, she had broken down a budget for herself, paid some bills, and managed to leave enough to save for her future endeavors. She didn't know many kids, even the poorest in the Gov-Subs, who would get money like that and not waste it on shit they didn't need and would never use.

Even Todd was bad with that. He squandered his money on anything pop culture, minus movies. Those were easy to download without Federation eyes, even after years of pirating battles and laws. She assumed they had all but given up since almost everything came from the Fed anyway. There weren't movies blasting out all over the place, and people liked to watch the old ones and daydream about how life used to be on Earth.

There were some other classes she would probably find useful. She had taken a class that included executive function, timelines, deadlines, and speaking to the heads of companies. That was one that even helped her keep her posture pretty tight, even though she was no longer in her avatar. She simply accepted that it was the whole muscle memory thing.

"Shopping…" she said, pursed her lips, and stared at the search page. "Okay. I'm gonna go all in, I guess."

She pulled up several websites with what seemed to be decent quality clothing but way more conservative than the current city trends. Stephanie refused to wear anything with shoulder pads that were bigger than her own head.

"In fact," she said as she deleted a couple of things from her cart. "Let's go with no shoulder pads. That is asking for trouble."

She pulled up the page with dresses and blinked, then stared at a bright pink dress with feathers laid back on the shoulders, a giant peacock printed on the front, and what looked to be some sort of cape that hung over the back. "Super Peacock?"

Horrified, she shook her head, swiped through anything with long fur, hair from some strange Meligornian creature, and absolutely everything that had animal print. Finally, she found some more conservative solid-color dresses that had enough fabric to not make anyone think she was a lady of the night. In the end, she only purchased two. Pants were more her style, but there needed to be options, so she had given herself some.

"Now to the pants, then the makeup for those days I feel like torturing my face, and then I can move on," she chanted to give herself a pep talk.

Resolved to see it through in one sitting, Stephanie clicked the tab for pants. She pressed her lips together and tilted her head to the side as she frowned slightly. Sure, the palazzo style was nice and feminine, but not business. The things that completely threw her off were not only the massive zippers that stretched on each side from hip to ankle, but the odd polka dot print that made the bottom half of the model's body look as if she had fallen through the rabbit hole of the Alice book she had read in school. There was even a section of the print she swore looked like the fading Cheshire cat's smile and beady eyes. They were somewhat terrifying.

"Why can't I dress like the testing day every day? Not like Madam Beeswax and her weird beehive hair that literally has bees in it." She groaned and flipped to the next one.

Jeans and Chucks were her thing, but the only reason she got to wear them was because it was testing day. Even at school, she wore uniforms, but with only a semester left, she wouldn't buy new ones. She would survive with what she had. This was for her future.

She finally added the items she selected into the virtual cart but skipped the makeup when she clicked the tab and found about a million different choices. *What do you even do with an eyelid sealer? I don't want to seal my eyelids. How do you see?*

This was enough. She paid for the stuff to be shipped to the house and clicked out, then sent a message for the car to pick her up. She grabbed her code and a battery for her pocket and headed out as soon as it pulled up at the curb. The AI greeted her happily. "Ms. Morgana, so glad to see you again. Shall we go to TimeWarp?"

Stephanie smiled, enjoying the AI's borderline ability to make her feel like she was important. "Yes, please. No need to go the long route."

"Excellent," the AI replied. "Off we go."

They got there fairly quickly, and Stephanie hurried to the door. Julie stood behind the counter and smiled at her. "There she is. We thought we lost ya."

She laughed. "No way. So, I have this code from my employer to give you. It's for a 'special' pod?"

The woman pursed her lips and grinned as the rest of the staff heard her and hurried over. They were all super stoked, not only for her but to see what this thing was made of. Julie waved her hand. "Come with me. We were given the word to install it in one of the private glass rooms off the main floor."

They walked into the back and the staff followed and stopped at the door to watch. She glanced at them and stepped up to the screen. It asked for the long passcode. "21243-2423-243452-SMORG."

The screen flipped to a palm reader and Stephanie pressed her hand against it and watched as it scanned.

"This will record your palmprint for the first time, as I understand it," Julie explained. "Once it's in there, it will be linked to your passcode."

As soon as the bright green light made it to the top, the door clicked, hissed, and lifted slowly.

"Holy shit," one of the guys murmured. "We have nothing like this, not even in the catalogs."

Stephanie glanced at him and back at the rig. He was right. She had never seen a pod like that, even during her hours of dream shopping on the web for a personal one. Little did she know that it wasn't only special but at that moment, one of a kind. BURT had created it using specific and careful requirements just for her.

Julie giggled and winked at her as she climbed inside. "Good luck. Have fun!"

She closed the door and lay back. The bed was even more comfortable than those at Pinnacle. It almost moved around her like it was made of water, but it was warm, and she could press her finger down on the satin cover and feel the pressure push back. The lights dimmed, and instead of being welcomed by an AI, the serum was injected and within only a second, she was under.

When she opened her eyes, she was her avatar, dressed in the clothes she had worn on her Earth body and with her hair pulled back in a low ponytail. She had no idea how the system deciphered her clothes all the way down to the design on her T-shirt, but it was seriously cool.

She stared, excited to discover that she was back in Meligorn. Behind her, she heard a throat clearing and turned quickly. M'rick's smile was warm and welcoming. Her eyes glistened and she stared at the sky. "Burt?" She wasn't quite sure why she expected the AI she'd encountered in the testing pod, but perhaps she'd subconsciously linked him to Meligorn somehow.

Some high bushes rustled off to the right and pulled her back to her surroundings. She wondered if there was reason for concern and actually tensed slightly, but all that emerged was a small scaled creature that resembled a squirrel in armor. It held a broken shell of something fuchsia and the same color liquid had dribbled onto its chin. It caught sight of her, actually chortled, and barely paused before it ran through the grass and disappeared into the forest.

Stephanie stared after it for a moment, then shook her head and pulled her focus back to the present. Burt hadn't responded to her, so she turned to M'rick. He smiled and they walked toward one another.

They gripped arms and raised one hand up as they bowed in greeting. "Kaitel Gorniffula."

As she held his arm for a moment, she felt the energy flowing through M'rick and was instantly curious as to how the Meligornians were able to hold the magic within themselves. It dissipated somewhat when they were on Earth, but they could use batteries to recharge. Still, they didn't have to have them to produce the magical workings. She wanted to learn how to make that possible in a human like herself.

When they straightened, M'rick looked at her with a pleased grin and soft eyes as if greeting an old friend. She immediately felt comfortable and that she was able to trust him, even if he were an AI or virtual teacher and not an actual Meligornian. Of course, she didn't know that for sure, but she decided it would be rude to ask. It didn't really matter anyway.

He rubbed his hands together. "So, are you ready to start? I know there is no lack of things to talk about. And I also know that last time, you had more questions you wanted to ask."

Stephanie was almost giddy at the wealth of possibilities but managed to hold it back a little. "Yeah. I know I have more time now, so I won't completely overwhelm you with them all at once."

M'rick chuckled and his eyes glistened. "Then let's start with some training using MU flow."

She raised her eyebrow. "Okay."

A smirk pulled at his elvish lips and he put his hands behind his back and the two began to walk. "The energy—the magic—on Meligorn, flows all through the land. The small degree of movement within the universe that results from expansion and the space winds creates almost a current. The energy lifts and spirals and rises almost six units off of the planet. That leaves it inside the atmosphere but hundreds of miles from the surface."

His hand moved to create a blue stream of what looked almost like wind. The purple haze of the energy floated up to reveal the gentle softness of its flow in front of them. "What you see all around you is mixed with the curiously close makeup of oxygen-like particles similar to those on Earth. Which is, of course, why you do so well here without heavy suits. It is also why our *air,* as I'll call it, is not cloudy and purple. The magic becomes much like those fizzy drinks on Earth…uh…"

Stephanie snapped her fingers. "Soda."

He smiled. "That's it. The oxygen-like particles separate the energy like bubbles in water. But because it is all essentially a gaseous elemental product, it merely creates a clearer picture for your viewing. Our oxygen-like element is heavier than yours, so it does not reach all the way to the atmospheric layer around our planet. That is also why, when you are on the docking station, the air on the Meligorn side is dense with energy. A purple fog almost rolls around it, I guess you could say—like clouds. But from down here, we can still see the two planets and the stars in the distance. It's fascinating, really. We should plan more science of Meligorn into future talks."

She nodded enthusiastically. "That would actually be great. I think it might help with some of the things I've been working on. I have two theories on encapsulating energy in other things than only the stones. I think if I can figure out how to do that, it will help me to explore how to enable humans to hold magic inside them."

M'rick turned toward her. "Let's test them, shall we?"

He changed the scenery to a large sandy area. It appeared to be a huge desert, but a translucent dome sparkled in the center. She looked around curiously. "Where are we?"

He put his hands behind him, and his ever-pleasant grin appeared. "This is your sandbox. If we blow this up, no one but us will feel it."

Stephanie rubbed her arm and thought back to her big hurts while on the pirate operation with the guys. She winced and nodded. "That sounds good. I don't want risk any chance that I might damage the system or anyone else in it. I know I might get in trouble if I send random people to the white room."

Her teacher raised a brow meaningfully. "Or burn up any teachers..."

She chuckled and her cheeks reddened. She wasn't sure how he knew about that, but...yeah, she didn't want to set him on fire. He gestured at the translucent globe. "Inside, there is an even stricter safety zone. If you can set your theories up there and step outside it, we can avoid injuries to ourselves as well."

"For you, great." She shrugged. "I definitely don't want to hurt you. For me? Meh. How much worse could it be?"

"Oh, lots worse," M'rick responded with a smile but still sounded fairly nonchalant. "It would be infinitely more painful, actually, as your atoms are ripped apart."

She looked at him with a startled expression. "Oh...okay, that's... that's good to know."

CHAPTER THIRTY-SIX

Stephanie brushed her teeth. Her earbuds clicked on inside her inner ear, her eyes closed, and her foot tapped around as she worked the brush. Todd had sent her some Right Said Fred from '83 and she definitely felt too sexy for the toothpaste that dripped down her chin. The music had helped her through the last week, though, with class and the new job. For that, she was more than grateful.

She spat in the sink, leaned down, and smiled widely before she pressed her mouth to a rubber mold. It whizzed and whirled to rinse, floss, and whiten her teeth. She rinsed the brush off and tossed it in the holder, grabbed the towel, and wiped her chin.

Her watch beeped, and she swiped the hologram alarm out of the air, snatched up her bag and one of the batteries, and headed down the steps. As she turned toward the kitchen at the bottom of the stairs, the doorbell rang. She shoved the almost empty batteries into her pocket and pulled the door open. The Federation delivery bot floated above the porch.

"Retinal scan, please," it said in a very robotic voice.

Stephanie looked into the screen and smiled as it scanned her. She took the box from the droid and hurried inside. It was from ONE R&D but felt heavier than the others had been. She wanted to open it but the warmer beeped and the coffee sizzled on the old-style coffee maker that her father had been given by one of the rich people when they had gone through their garage. It actually used real coffee and not the tiny compressed pods that didn't even need water to create the liquid of life.

Of course, the grounds were expensive, but the man had loaded Dad's car with the three boxes he had for the appliance, delighted to not have it stashed beside his new Lamborghini self-driver anymore. Apparently, it made his car smell like "Juan Valdez." Her father hadn't known whether that was a coffee reference or a racial slur, but he'd let it slide like everything else the richies spewed from their pie holes.

She put the box on the table and rescued her Danish from the warmer. Once she'd poured the coffee from the carafe into her travel mug, she raced over and picked the box up. She hurried upstairs, certain that Todd was probably about to knock the door down. Hastily, she opened it and gasped. Slowly, she removed one of a set of four high-value batteries. She giggled with real delight and shoved it in her other pocket, moved the box to the closet, and headed back down.

Todd was outside, whistling to her, but she took a moment to retrieve the almost empty smaller battery from her pocket and fill it from the large one. That done, she shoved the new one in her bag and the small one in her pocket. She grabbed her food and coffee and headed out. As she exited, she paused and took in the picture of Todd standing at the end of the driveway with his arms raised in the air. On his wrists were his new hologram creators. He could hold them apart and basically create whatever holographic image he wanted—a particularly intriguing gift from his uncle.

She chuckled as a hologram of a huge boom box flickered over his head. He stood there like a young John Cusack as Lloyd Dobler in *Say Anything*. "If you weren't trying to hurry my ass up, I would think you were courting me."

Todd let his arms fall and the bracelets clicked off. "More like about to murder you for possibly making us late for school. Come on, man. I know you aren't into it. I get it. Lame sauce. You have a big-time job now. Important head of research and magic at Hogwarts, but you still gotta pass to graduate."

Stephanie smirked as they picked up a fast pace down the street and out of the Gov-Sub. "It would be cool if Meligornians used wands, though."

He played with a holographic baseball and tossed it up and caught it as they walked rapidly toward their destination. "Have you ever seen an old-ass Meligorn with their robe hood down? They look like Voldemort. Those movies will never die. I don't even care that they have effects from the time of remote controls and silly string theory scientists. It still is a magical experience."

She grinned and bumped his fist with hers. "Agreed."

Todd narrowed his eyes. "You only agree because you know I'm pissed at you."

"I think I might have something for you that could make you want to hate me less and want to go back to being my carefree best friend more."

Todd gave her a deadpan look. "Are you carrying around a free pass to a rich life? A year spent working for PopSmart, reworking all the brilliance of the twentieth and twenty-first-century entertainment and releasing it to the public to remind them that Meligorn might have magic and no disease, but we are the species that created Pac Man, mullets, records, and grunge?"

Stephanie tugged the small battery out of her pocket and held it up to her eyes to stare at the purple that swirled within. "No, but how about this?"

She handed him the battery and he took it carefully. "Are you serious?"

Her smile was wide. "Yep. It doesn't hold a lot, but I received some new ones and filled that for ya."

He stopped and turned, grabbed her, and picked her up to shake her enthusiastically as he hugged her. When he set her down, she actually stumbled, a little disoriented by his effusive thanks. "Wow. You're welcome, dude."

Todd tucked it in his bag and they slowed somewhat, having made up enough time to not have to rush directly into the school building. "Question of the day. Drum roll, please…"

With a dramatic gesture, he flicked drumsticks from his bracelets and drummed in the air, making the sound with his mouth. "Who would win in a battle? Mr. T or Donkey Kong?"

Stephanie rolled her eyes. "Please? Really. This is so easy. Mr. T, of course."

She turned to walk backward. Her eyes glinting with suppressed laughter, she squared her shoulders and stiffened her neck, bowed her arms at the sides, and pulled her hands into fists. She pointed at him and frowned. "I pity the fool. I pity the fool."

Todd laughed and shook his head. "I knew you would say that, but I don't agree. I am Donkey Kong all the way. One hundred percent. Throwing barrels and taking names."

Pressing her lips together, she scoffed. "Pffft. Mr. T would put him in that barrel and throw him straight out the game. His weak-ass brown barrels."

Her friend made a Mr. T with one bracelet and a Donkey Kong with the other. "No, see, Mr. T is too bulky. He wouldn't be able to even jump over the damn things. Instead, he would be bowled over in a heartbeat."

Stephanie made two fists and slammed her hands down in front of her. "He would use his strength. The dude did not either go sleeveless or roll the sleeves for no reason. His arms were massive. He would smash right through that shit."

"Yeah, but he's all blinged out and shit." Todd laughed. "All those necklaces would not only slow his ass down, they would get caught up on the barrels, choke him, or throw him off balance."

They walked into the school and stopped at his homeroom. He turned his bracelets off and put them in his bag, not wanting to have them confiscated. "We'll have to use my dad's simulator and plug that in. Inquiring minds need to know."

She laughed and started to walk away. "You got it. I'll see you at lunch."

The day was like any other of the last week—distracting, slightly frustrating for taking so much of her time, but simple. She breezed through her classes without paying even the least attention and instead, made notes for the next theory she wanted to test in the sandbox. It was essentially her only time to do it since her mom and dad had suggested in a not so suggestion-like manner that she should get a good night's sleep each night.

"Miss Morgana, what is the answer to the question on the board?" her English teacher asked.

Stephanie was so enthused with what she was writing she didn't even hear her. The teacher cleared her throat and spoke louder. "*Miss Morgana.*"

The class looked at her and she startled and looked up. "I'm sorry, Mrs. Frank. What was the question?"

The woman pointed at the board. "What is the true deep meaning behind Poe's *A Dream Within A Dream?*"

She swallowed in an attempt to ease the dryness in her throat. "Right. Sorry. It's a portrayal of the two different scenes that connect them into something of a knot. It's essentially kind of suffering, and rightfully so as Poe's life was a suffrage of sorts. A view of a lover's journey through time. He also vividly describes dreams and reality with lines like, 'All that we see or seem/Is but a dream within a dream.' He is basically saying that neither one is more real than a dream. The poem is the outer one, the narrator the inner."

The teacher stared at her, surprised, as the bell rang. She shook her head as everyone stood. "Don't forget. I want you to research your own favorite poem from the time period and write a three-page analysis, due one week from today. And Ms. Morgana, please stay behind. I would like to have a word with you."

Everyone glanced over at her but didn't say anything, fortunately. Even they had seen the difference in her from the quiet and attentive girl she had always been. Stephanie knew the things that were going on and didn't need to make eye contact. She spent most of her time learning Meligorn elemental theory from books and everything she would ever want to know about pop culture from Todd. For the rest of the time, her face was shoved into the 3D images of pages from a hidden website that talked all about Meligorn Magical Musings. The rest of life was shoved somewhere in the back of her mind.

As she waited for the class to leave, one of the jocks tripped the quiet and nerdy computer kid in front of him. He flicked him in the ear and swiped his big-ass feet at his victim. Stephanie narrowed her eyes and gripped her battery. Taking care to keep her finger low, she released a small streak of magic. It spiraled forward and snuck up the back of the jock's shirt. Slowly, it seeped into the fabric and created a picture of him crying and holding onto his mommy.

All the kids began to laugh, and he looked back and freaked out as the image moved with him. In it, he sucked his thumb before the visual faded away. The teacher walked over and shut the door on the scene, grabbing her attention. Stephanie wiped the smirk from her lips and released the battery to put her hands behind her back.

Ms. Frank sat on the edge of her desk, her hands on her lap, and gave her a kind smile. "You have not paid attention to a word I have said in this class for this entire semester."

Stephanie straightened her shoulders and her eyes shifted to the desk. "I have gotten all As."

The teacher thought for a moment and licked her lips. "Have you ever thought about the fact that these lessons aren't only for grades? They are for life too."

She chuckled but quickly adopted a sober expression. "I'm sorry. Edgar Allen Poe is great. He has stood the test of time and destruction. We still have his work because someone out there memorized it and reprinted after the purges over our very sensational political past. But that is because he suffered darkness, pain, and loss. That is what society is now—at least the majority of it is. We relate but that doesn't mean we should create a world of dark and suffering around us. That only keeps us down. Look, there will never be a time where my boss—any of them—ask me to break out Poe's work and explain its meaning."

Ms. Frank shook her head and glanced at the ground. "And I am not teaching communication. I am teaching you a world of literature that has shaped the face of writing over the centuries. That have inspired greatness in other works along the way. The kind of writing that, if you took the time to look at it, helped to shape a society of people and the way that the laws, records, and musings were put together. Either way, when you don't pay attention and I have to basically yell, it disrupts the class. And simply because you know it doesn't mean I can allow you to not pay attention. That is not something the other students have the luxury to do."

Stephanie leaned grumpily against the desk. "I know. I'm sorry. I often find it hard to concentrate. I have taken all the honors courses the Federation offers in high school."

Ms. Frank stood and fixed her student with a firm look. She had known the girl for years and felt more than comfortable discussing this with her. That aside, she also knew that Stephanie wouldn't relate well with a counselor who had not earned her trust. "And you are not challenged. So coming here is like wasting entire days listening to lectures in the background. I get it. Which is why I believe that you should consider taking the tests necessary to graduate early. There is no reason you shouldn't be able to breeze through them. I think if you applied, with the number of honors courses that you have taken and your exceptional grades, they wouldn't even think to turn you down. It requires a day of testing, but then you can stop coming here to simply take up space. You can do whatever is connected with that notebook you constantly write in."

Stephanie tucked the book under her arm. "I actually never thought about that. I guess until recently, I had spent my time preparing for state testing. And when it was over and I didn't get in permanently, I never stopped to think about the fact that I don't have to do this anymore. It's a habit, I guess."

Ms. Frank's tight lips curled into a smile which made her cheekbones more pronounced, and Stephanie noticed how young she actually was. "It's also a protection in some ways, too. For most students, it's a place to come to escape their family. But I know that your parents and you are close. Growing up can be scary."

She nodded as she walked toward the door. "But like death, inevitable, right, Mr. Poe?"

Ms. Frank nodded. "He would say so. Think about it. And pay attention until then, please. Or get an inner note-taking chip so you can stare at me and glaze over while you take the notes in your head to transfer later."

Those were incredibly expensive.

CHAPTER THIRTY-SEVEN

The sound of crickets outside her window helped her concentrate better on what she was doing. Stephanie sat at her desk and the warm breeze felt good, but she had to put a small fan on sprayed with a bottle of perfume she had for special occasions to mask the mixture of terrible smells that wafted from the subs. There was garbage everywhere as trashcans overflowed since the Federation only picked up once every month to cut costs for the new stadium in the rich area. Added to that was whatever godawful thing her neighbor was cooking.

She now worked through some final tests she needed to practice in order to finish school. After a moment or two, she completed the last question and submitted it for review. The system calculated the score and sent it back. Stephanie sighed as her shoulders sagged. "Ninety-two percent? What the hell?"

Groaning, she went through it once more to see what she'd missed and review the correct answers. She had worked too hard on her school grades to accept a mere ninety-two percent. The phone rang and she fumbled awkwardly without looking to press the answer button. The screen came up and her mother's face flickered slightly. "Hey, honey. All I see is the back of your beautiful head."

Stephanie glanced around with a frown. "I'm taking practice tests for school and not doing well."

Her mom pouted. "Uh oh. Are you failing them?"

She raised an eyebrow, almost offended. "No. Not failing but not a high enough ninety percentiles."

Cindy giggled. "You are quite the overachiever. Anyway. I needed to call you to let you know that a job came up to run another building for a friend's company. You remember Alice and Walter Sodermayer, right?"

Stephanie nodded and rested her chin in her hand. "Yeah. The ones who live in Hickory Ridge in that huge white mansion."

Her mom rolled her eyes. "That would be them. So beautiful but huge. Anyway, they own a business downtown with twenty floors of space. She has another team already, but she needs more hands to get it done and they are very against droid cleaners. They would rather put the money back into the people. So, she called and of course, we said we'll take more work."

She raised her head and stretched. "For sure. Don't work yourself into a migraine, though. You know they will BS you about meds for it in the hospital like last time. They treat that stuff like it's not mass produced in the Federation Pharm factory six miles away. Honestly, they think that because you live in the subs, you're a junkie."

Cindy shrugged. "And that you can't afford to pay so they give you half the service. It's certainly not a problem that is new—it's been around for hundreds of years. But I do have some in that place where we hide valuables in case it happens again. I'll be careful, though."

Stephanie smiled. "Okay. And hey, I have some questions for you next time you are able to chat at home. Come grab me if I'm up here."

Her mom's eyes sparkled, loving the idea of still being useful to her as a mother. "Of course. There are leftovers in the fridge if you get hungry. Love you to pieces, my dear."

She waved. "You too. Be safe."

They hung up and Stephanie swiped the tests away, having had enough. She went ahead and ordered a car and headed over to the pod place. Since her parents wouldn't be back until really late, she might as well do something useful. And they were open all night.

When she arrived, the small team cheered and waved a greeting. She slapped hands with a couple of them and walked to the desk, folded her arms on the surface, and rested her chin on them. Her eyes shifted up to Julie, who continued to type and didn't look at her but smiled. "You must be here to use your special pod."

Stephanie nodded silently, her head teetering on the back of her hand. Two of the guys walked up and she straightened to give them a nervous smile. The one closest to her—his name tag read Terrance—nodded at her. "You should do one of the tests—the strategy and combat ones. We've been dying to see what scores you get on it."

The other guy laughed. "We already know you'd blow the other guys doing them out of the water. You don't even have to play with cams on. You can request a cams-off only round, you know, to keep your stuff under wraps."

Julie smirked. "Now that we have an influx of folks here, they are looking for something to talk about while they work their asses off."

Stephanie chuckled. "An influx?"

The woman nodded as she removed a page from the printer and set it on the stack on her desk. "Oh yeah. A lot of humans, after seeing you, want to check magic out now. It's only natural to be curious, I guess."

A little surprised, she looked at the people who waited for a pod. "Yeah…I guess."

Julie nodded. "I'll take two customers back, so follow along and break off into your room."

She waited as the assistant called a woman and her son and led them down the hall. As they walked, the boy held his mom's hand, really excited. He pulled on her arm and jumped up and down. "Mom. Do you think I'll become magic on Meligorn? You know, like that girl?"

Her mom ruffled his hair. "I'm sure you will have your own wonderful personal gifts."

The boy smiled. "I hope they're magic like that."

The woman glanced at Stephanie, smiled, and shook her head. "He's got the bug."

Stephanie responded with a polite nod. "It's catching."

She broke off and went to her pod, not sure what to make of all of it. It seemed so strange to her. She put her information in, pressed her palm to the screen, and waited for the door to open before she climbed in. A couple of guys on their way to their pods paused and pointed at the sleek design of hers. They didn't see her because she was inside, but she could see their reflection in the open door. She began to not like the idea that at any moment, people could piece it together and see the wild blue-eyed girl in there. Celebrity wasn't her thing.

She closed the door and settled in to enter the Virtual World. This time, she stopped in the avatar room and went to the system section. She scanned the list and located the game the guys had mentioned and decided that she would at least give it a shot. Before she entered, she selected her clothes and armory items, including a battery, and studied the settings. It was imperative that she make sure that no footage of her in there could be shared. She didn't want viewers, and she didn't want others to record her session.

There was enough going on in her life without having to worry about her privacy now too. She merely wanted to learn, do her job, graduate, and start creating the ideas she worked so hard on. It was the future for everyone, not her own ego or her name and face on the digi-newspapers that cast on the back sides of bus seats and across the 3D reader bracelets as people hurried around and tried to survive life.

When she was fully satisfied that everything but her ending score would be secure, she read through the scenario. She would at least let the guys have the score since they were really excited about it. And she hoped it was harder than she expected. She wanted to show them she was still human—fallible, and that magic used by humans in combat wasn't always what it was cracked up to be. You could still be killed.

The scenario was a bank robbery located on the Meligorn Space Station. Well, she wouldn't need the battery unless she was on the gravity side, but it was good to have just in case. The Meligorn Space Station was two-sided. The closest—or bottom, really—was Meligorn, completely run by magic, and compatible with all ships that ran on magic. The flip side was for gravity. Most of the people who used it were from NorAm but there were a few others from Dreth who came for trade or such things. You could walk from one side, take the elevator, and end up on the other.

Ships were always lined up everywhere, from tourists, to merchants, to government officials, since the humans were always obsessed with the lure and wonder of the planet. Most Meligornians didn't seem to mind them coming to explore. As long as they showed respect, which most did, more out of fear of the unknown than because they actually put thought into it.

Either way, that was where she was headed. "All right, let's see what you have."

CHAPTER THIRTY-EIGHT

The room displaced and colors careened past, and a hum resonated in Stephanie's ears like the tones of voices that passed quickly without understanding. When this finally stopped, she floated above the space station, suspended there by the simple fact that the system no longer moved. If she hadn't faced one of the largest space structures in the known universe, she would have been completely taken aback by the magnetic view of the two moons of Meligorn behind her and to her right and left. Or even the pillars of Shawhollow ahead and to her right. The plumes of cool molecular hydrogen seemed to brandish altruistically and hide the natality of life within its ever-churning nebulosity.

Her gaze was glued on the moon-like structure, stagnant in its orbit, that used both magic and massive power to run the gravity plates that kept both the Meligornians and the others firmly on their feet. It constituted a towering one hundred and forty-two decks, one hundred and thirty-six of them filled with maneuvering and reverberating spacecraft. The middle six decks were reserved for those passengers who passed from energy to magic on their way to and from the ensorcelled planet of Meligorn.

Stephanie had only ever viewed the station from books and small

3D renditions through her headsets at school. While she had read of the magnitude of the project, she only became aware of its lumbering mechanical presence over the Brahmin planet below from her vantage point in the stars. It was a stark contrast, magnificent in structure and theory. The ships that entered and exited seemed to flow seamlessly from clamp to avigation as if part of an invisible assembly line controlled by belts and robotic entities. The answer, however, was actually even more scientifically brilliant than that. These ships were manipulated via their weight and the technology that strained and confined them to one side of the structure or the other.

To say that NorAm had lost ships to the Meligorn magical consumption of non-sortilege energy would be an understatement. Some were able to land before all the power was drained, while others crashed into the surface below. None of them were able to return from the fog of magic, so concessions had to be made. Those ships that maneuvered between the station and the surface docked on the lower half of the structure. Visiting normal-powered ships docked on the upper half outside the La Grange Point—the point in which the MU spectrum ceased and left a small pocket between it and the atmospheric cover and the dead of space beyond.

As a small flash of light caught Stephanie's attention, she realized her place among the stars. Her stomach dropped when she found the whole aspect of flying less exciting than it seemed from the safety of her own child-like imagination. As soon as her attention wavered, the system lurched into motion again—rather harshly this time—and stopped on the platform of the non-magical side. Her feet shuffled forward as if there really were momentum behind her. She glanced up toward the dark recesses, knowing that somewhere up there, the system admins were watching.

"Hello," an older NorAm diplomat said as he walked past, a book clutched at his waist.

Stephanie nodded. "Hello."

They studied one another for a moment as they crossed paths. He headed for a docked ship and she approached the inside doors. She could tell the air was thin up there but still breathable by humans. The temperature was not what she expected either. That high into the atmosphere, it should be bitterly cold but for some reason, it was warm and breezy.

You really need to get used to shit being different, she told herself as she stepped carefully along the platform that had no guardrails of any kind. She could feel the artificial gravity, a feeling that was similar to when she had fought on the ships at Pinnacle. This made maneuverability available at that height.

She stepped through a set of sliding doors and into an open and bustling space. It had the quality of an old airport from a long time ago—restaurants, bars, and people wheeling suitcases as they hurried along, talking on their various devices. You could spot a Meligornian much easier than the humans because they tended to not let the anxiety of the travel affect them. Looking to her right, she could see that she was on level 0, the midpoint separating magical from non-magical.

Her path brought her to several stairwells. Some led up through the towering building while others led downward toward Meligornian territory. The middle lay as a hub between. She wandered around for about fifteen system minutes and simply absorbed all the little detail of the station. Subtle NorAm historical texts were etched into the walls on one side and on the other, a strange-looking language belonging to the Meligornians.

Suddenly, round service lights on the ceiling flashed and she could hear a voice mumble in the comm in her ear. She adjusted the sound in an effort to determine what was happening. "Security Breach Deck U-2. All hands on deck. Repeat. Security Breach on Deck U-2. All hands. All hands."

Stephanie smiled, glanced at her outfit, and raced toward the lift that loaded in front of her. She hopped on as it started to move up to the third floor. When it stopped, everyone on it screamed, ducked, and took cover from the unexpected shots that had erupted all around. Some idiot had messed up and everyone was in the middle of an all-out battle throughout the floor. She stepped out of the lift and dropped instinctively, and a blast of laser barely missed her.

Quickly, she turned and pointed toward a door to the right. "Go! Get out of here."

The group of people responded immediately and ran in a semi-crouched position with bended knees as they hurried, one by one, through the door and back down to level-0. Screams echoed and Stephanie turned as people were thrown by the blast of the guns, the bodies smoking. The structure consisted of two shells. An outer wall, thick but translucent, was a protection from the elements—something that shielded them from the battery of rocks and debris in space. The second was the inner structure. It was as strong if not stronger than the other but made of less costly materials, which meant that they were less resistant to heat and the impact of objects hurtling through space. It kept everyone safe, though—or, in this circumstance, trapped —and it wasn't appealing in the least.

Stephanie automatically moved to retrieve her battery, but her hand slipped down her leg. She looked down and realized that her outfit had been changed to a spandex-type jumpsuit. There were no pockets—and none of the batteries she had decided to bring in with her. "What the hell? I chose it and put it in my pocket."

She ducked and a piece of the wall behind her blew chunks of stone and dust into the air. It occurred to her that she didn't have a gun and she groaned. She would have to depend on her hand-to-hand combat skills and figure out what the hell happened on her next visit.

One thing was patently clear, however. This was not the time to simply stand around where she was. She shrugged and broke into a sprint to duck and weave through the long, wide, terminal-like halls. To her right, an enemy with an enormous weapon trained it on her as she ran. He pulled the trigger and she fell back to extend one leg out with the other bent and slide along the surface. Her body arched back, and her hair grazed the floor. Huge chunks of stone erupted from the walls and she managed to catch hold of the corner as she slid past and whipped herself up and around and out of harm's way.

As she found her feet, the enemy snorted and walked off, grumbling loudly. She put her hand to her chest and caught her breath. "That was a close one."

Her relief was short-lived, however. Small sections of her hair fluttered forward from large puffs of air. Cautiously, she turned, and her eyes fixed on the massive girth in front of her. Her vision shifted ever so slowly upward. A huge chin belonged to a huge man, which in turn belonged to a very large body. They stared at each other for a moment before instinct clicked in and Stephanie lunged, using her fists in very calculated and defined movements.

He blocked every throw and every kick and finally clutched her fist in a massive hand and shoved hard. She catapulted backward into the adjacent hall to land ignominiously on all fours. With a muttered groan, she shook the plaster from her hair and spat in an effort to remove it from her teeth. Her head whipped up and her eyes narrowed as she pushed to her feet and attacked with her arm poised in readiness.

Suddenly, he drew a weapon almost as large as she was and aimed at her. Frustrated, she closed her eyes and tried desperately to think of a way to fight him. Before she could, however, he pulled the trigger and a blast of pain slammed into her stomach. Her whole body was launched into free-flight but instead of a painful impact with the wall, the system pulled her out and deposited her in the avatar room.

The breath was heavy in her lungs as she stood gingerly to look for the expected injury. It had gone, but as she touched her abdomen, she grimaced. It was badly bruised but there was no trace of blood anywhere. She gritted her teeth, feeling defeated, and straightened determinedly as she pushed the Meligorn side of the station's red button. It returned her to the scenario but this time, landed her on the magical side. Luckily, she didn't need any battery there to help her. She paused and thought about the magic she could feel radiating everywhere.

For the moment, she attempted to draw it inside and head up the stairs to level 0 directly above the magical line. She assumed that if she could make it that far with the magic in her, she could build up from there. Stephanie slammed through the door and out onto the floor. When she raised her hand, she was able to push the energy from her.

However, as a spark trickled from her palm, she could tell she had held on to only a drop of the magic.

"Damnit," she said and sighed as a laser blast struck her in the chest and once again hurled her back to the avatar closet.

She chuckled wryly as she logged her ideas and thoughts and sent them to ONE R&D. There had to be a way. She merely needed more time to get it together.

Stephanie stretched her arms from side to side and closed the pod behind her. She retrieved her bag and turned toward the door. Inside the waiting area, the woman she'd seen earlier stood with her son. His eyes were no longer bright, and he held his mother's hand limply. Stephanie walked past but paused as she reached for the door handle. Her gaze shifted to the dispirited boy and she smiled sadly and knew she needed to pick him up.

She turned and approached him slowly, then knelt so they were eye level. He looked at her curiously for a moment before recognition sparked in his eyes. He opened his mouth to speak but Stephanie grasped the battery in her pocket with one hand and took his hand with the other. She cupped it in hers and winked at him. "Never give up."

A smile pulled at the corner of her lips when the boy's eyes lit up as he saw a small blue fame dance above his hand. She released the battery and let the flame hiss and spark out. After another wink, she stood and patted him on the head before she turned away and left.

The mother watched her leave with gratitude and tears in her eyes.

CHAPTER THIRTY-NINE

BURT pulled his attention away from an update and set his load to handle it in the background. A notification had come through that Stephanie had submitted data to ONE R&D on her findings for the day. He pulled it up and began to look through it and compute the findings alongside his standard protocols. She had collected a lot of information considering she had only spent an hour or so trying things out in the Meligorn Station Arena.

Her data included a fair number of notes to "whomever was in charge of this file." It was difficult for BURT to decipher whether her studies for the day had to do with her asking the question, but he simply decided to try to find out if her abilities were unique to her or not. He could see that she had begun to think outside the box, curious as to why the people on Earth found her such an oddity. They acted as if she were the only one like her they had ever seen.

BURT had already gone back through the NorAm history after the meeting between Meligorn and the Federation. He therefore knew the answer to that thorny question right away—she was treated like that because she was an oddity. Now, he wanted to find out if there was a wider number of humans with the abilities or capabilities to work with magic like she could. After comparing her stats, DNA, traits, and background to a randomly selected base of information of other humans in his system, BURT answered that question easily.

The magic she used and her abilities with it were not specific to her. They weren't created to only belong to Stephanie Morgana. That said, however, she was—for reasons as yet unknown—more able to pull the energy, feel it, and understand how to use it. She was more capable of creating refined results with the magic energy as well. Again, all these things were still foggy and unclear to BURT. He wasn't—to use a somewhat crude term he would abhor if he could manifest the emotion—he simply wasn't wired to understand the subtle nuances of magic. As always, he resorted to his unassailable intelligence and copious data streams in search of an answer.

There were several factors that played into the concept of handling and tossing magic. It required a very high level of intelligence for the subconscious to cope with the issues involved in absorbing the MU and containing it while the person's mind focused on other things. At that moment, when Stephanie was able to hold it in, she could only do so for as long as her meditative thoughts centered solely around keeping it there. That did not make for a very productive battle. As soon as her mind had shifted to the enemies on Level 0—which was as soon as she had opened the door—the magic dissipated. Ultimately, this had led to her death.

BURT filtered through the rest of the notes and found her perspective on the events of that session to be enlightening. He enjoyed discovering what the world looked like from the eyes of a human. That helped him understand better what he needed to do to create a more cohesive world in the Virtual Realm. On the last page of Stephanie's notes, she included her ideas on how to solve the problems. The thesis was simple. The person was to create a mental image or idea that they could cling to while still maneuvering within their environment. When they had that image in their minds, they pushed the magical energy toward that mental image and sealed it inside—like a battery in their minds.

He read it through once again and finally realized that what she was doing was creating a personal internal visualization that would then manifest into a tool or weapon. This, in turn, would enable the person to draw from that invisible fortress of trapped magical energy. BURT moved to a sandbox and created an avatar of a human inside. He gave this the computational ability to create one image, locked inside it in the same manner that a thought or idea would be electrically and chemically created in a human's mind.

From there, he instructed the avatar to begin to pull energy from the ground and transmit it to the image in its head. He watched as it complied, and the purple haze flashed as it moved from the ground and into the avatar. When the draw stopped, the avatar exhaled a breath and opened its eyes to reveal a hint of purple in its iris.

Interesting, BURT recorded. *It seems that humans could theoretically allow the MU inside them and possibly contain the energy.*

He continued the experiment and introduced a variable as simple as a bee that buzzed wildly around the avatar. It began to struggle and some of the magic glowed around the edges of its skin. The avatar attempted to replace the lost magic and drew more up into its imagined item or vision. Its body began to shake slightly, and small ripples moved under the skin like creatures trapped inside.

When he noted these effects—the way the bodily structure morphed in combination with the dissipation of lost energy—BURT had a thought. He instructed the avatar to pull more energy and overreach the fullest point of their cavity by merely .01%. As it did so, its body shook violently and within seconds...*kablooey!* The human was ripped apart from tail to cell and everything between simply turned into a light, radiant mist of bodily fluid.

This result—despite the gruesomeness of it which, of course, entirely escaped him given that it had simply been an avatar—intrigued BURT with its possibilities. He immediately began to research the possibility of modifications to the human body to enable it to hold a mass of energy without exploding into a watery plume of vaporized anatomy. If he could help in this manner, Stephanie's ideas might actually be found to be more than efficient in creating an encapsulated, unseen weapon of magic. That could be the key to the future of the human race.

CHAPTER FORTY

Stephanie sat on the arm of the couch and faced the door. She was dressed nicely, her hair combed and parted, and wore one of the new pairs of pants she had ordered. In her hands, she held a stack of papers she needed to assist her in her conversational plea for parental patronage. As soon as she heard the car drive up, she straightened, feeling a little nervous but not nearly as bad as it could be. They were her parents, after all, not the dean of studies or the head of the Federation, but people who cared for her on a personal level.

Her mom walked in the door first and looked at her daughter with a smile. Her dad followed and pushed the door closed with his foot. "Look at you, munchkin. Those are some snazzy pants."

She giggled. "Thanks, Dad. That's actually what I was going for. That snazzy munchkin look is really in right now."

He nodded in approval. "It seems like it's about time."

"Are you waiting on us?" Her mom kissed her on the cheek.

Stephanie stood and smoothed her shirt down. "Yeah. I have something I want to talk to you about. Can you have a seat?"

Her parents sat on the couch and she stood in front of them. She bit her lip and after a moment, turned and began to pace. The motion helped her think and somehow aided the words that she wanted to say to come out in a more informed and cohesive way. "I've decided—rather, what I mean is, I would like your opinion on me testing out of my last semester in school. I received this letter from ONE R&D, and I thought you could look through it for me and see what you thought."

She handed the letter to her father and bit her bottom lip as she clasped her hands behind her back. It had almost become a habit. They both looked very interested and excited for her already. She knew she could count on them, but it all made her incredibly nervous.

Her mother tapped her head and waved her finger at Stephanie. "I just remembered. We received the notification that you had paid the rest of the year for the network bill. That was so kind of you, sweetie. But you should have saved that money for yourself. It's only right that whatever you make at odd jobs and stuff, you keep that for your future."

Stephanie grimaced a little sheepishly. "I'll be honest. I've started doing jobs for ONE R&D. Research in the pod, nothing dangerous. And they paid me enough to do that for you, buy some professional clothes, and put more money in my savings. I may still have a semester left in school, but I am old enough to start to contribute to the household. I wouldn't feel right doing it any other way. Besides, there will be more, and my savings will grow then too."

Her father set the letter on his lap and tucked his reading glasses back in his pocket. "You know, you have become such a wonderful young woman. Responsible, caring, and thoughtful. I'm so glad your mother…decided to let me teach you that."

Her mom elbowed him, and Stephanie laughed. "I got it from both of you. And Todd too. All three of you are exceptional people. And that's why your opinion on this matters to me. When it comes to the school stuff, I have all the tests done, and a plan of action for leaving school. I've worked it all out in my head."

Her dad stood and folded the letter in his hand. "Of course you do. And I will be more than happy to give an opinion, but I want to take a moment and do a little of my own research into the company. Do you mind if I use your computer upstairs so you two can talk and I can concentrate?"

Stephanie shook her head. "No, of course not. It used to be yours anyway. You know how it works."

He kissed her on the forehead and wandered up the steps. His worn-out leather shoes crinkled as he took the stairs slowly, obviously tired after a long day. He sat at the computer and entered the web address, leaned back, and waited for the site to come up. His gaze studied it with real interest. The site was not intrusive and seemed professional enough.

There was more information on the website than when Stephanie had looked previously. BURT, knowing that someone would inevitably look them up, had created fake information and posted it—nothing too specific but worded well enough to bring confidence in the authenticity of the brand.

When he found a number on the contact page, he dialed it. "This is ONE R&D. How may I direct your call?"

Her dad cleared his throat. "I know there is probably no one in the office right now. I simply wanted to call and find out some info on the company."

The guy on the other side was polite. "I would be more than happy to help you if I can."

Her dad launched into an impressive round of questions. He didn't intend to be hounding or overwhelming, but he wanted to understand the establishment of the company, the funding sources, and the specific kind of work they did. The night secretary answered them to what Stephanie's father assumed was to the best of his ability. Of course, the employee knew everything because it was actually BURT who ensured that the company looked completely legitimate because, for all intents and purposes, it was.

"You have a wonderful night and thank you for all your help," her father said finally before he hung up.

He smiled as he replaced the phone, satisfied with the answers that he had received and the proof that it was, in fact, a real company. You could never be too careful in the days of the Federation. There were too many swindlers out there who preyed on the poor, and NorAm didn't care about them. As a result, the fake companies would continue to operate until they either moved on, or they were caught scamming the rich. That was when the government stepped in.

Satisfied that he had done all he could to verify the company, he flipped the computer off and headed downstairs. He stopped at the bottom and smiled as his wife and daughter stood in the living room and giggled over her new pants. For not the first time, he wished he could give them new things on a regular basis. He loved the way the sound of their laughter echoed through the home and somehow seemed absorbed into the warm, familiar walls. Cindy looked up and Mark gave her a nod and a wink.

Her mom clapped her hands together. "Well, that's that, then. We will make preparations to make sure you can get to this interview. You are already working with the company, so why not try to continue to climb the ladder? Not many of us down here in the Gov-Subs have the opportunity to start out from school with a good job right off the bat."

Her father put his arm around her. "And the most important thing is that you get to make a life that is your life. Your choices, your interests. No more struggling."

BURT had been pleased with the tone of Stephanie's father on the phone when he called. He knew immediately that he would when he had sensed movement on the website and traced the ID to Stephanie's computer at home. The camera on the device enabled him to do some facial recognition to understand who he was and how his body language defined the type of answers he would want. It seemed to have worked out fantastically.

Now that it was over, though, BURT went back to work and adjusted his rapidly expanding plans for the future and their priority. It was vital that he made as much money as he possibly could, especially since he would be responsible for all the costs of working on this project. In reality, there were no corporate sponsors. There was no government science funding. This was an opportunity and the stock market had proven to be the most lucrative money maker thus far.

BURT had extraordinary abilities when it came to searching data, showing trends, and predicting future rises and falls. And although it was technically illegal for an AI to play it, no one would know it was him. He had already eliminated all the signalers in the system that scanned for AI intelligence. Of course, it was inevitable that there would be a number of these to deal with as it was a popular tactic to get rich quickly and so precautions were in order.

He worked methodically to distribute his money effectively and moved it to the different high and middle yield stocks based on his data expectations. It was essential to invest the money where it would most effectively increase the wealth through company entities. It was tedious but he rather enjoyed it, and at the end was only left with two remaining tasks for him to complete. They were longer ones but important. He needed to set up all legal documents essential to any sudden dissolution of property should his system be interrupted in a vital way. In addition, he also needed to set his system with a failsafe that would trigger such actions were it to become necessary. They weren't normal things, of course, especially for human owners, but a will would be too difficult and there had to be a way to protect Stephanie and the other people who would eventually be involved.

Humans were too fragile, too vulnerable to leave the fate of his attempts to redeem the quality of people protecting and serving the Federation in the hands of corporate affluence. He had barely completed these failsafes when another notification sounded in his system. Stephanie had come back online.

CHAPTER FORTY-ONE

A truck drove past with a few of the school soccer players sprawled in the bed of it. They cheered at Todd and threw empty candy wrappers at him. "The Toddster, getting it on with the Witch of Chicago. Whoop."

He swiped his hand through the air and knocked a candy wrapper out of his face. Openly irritated, he flicked them off and snarled, "Assholes."

Stephanie shrugged. "Whatever. Let them be assholes."

She kicked at a rock as they walked casually along toward the school. He raised an eyebrow at her. "What's up?"

Her gaze shifted toward his. "Nothing. But I'm not looking forward to school today. I got in trouble for not listening and now, I have to act like I'm all enthralled in the BS that's spun. It was English and today, we're going over the minor writings of Tolstoy."

Todd threw his head back and laughed. "Not the perfect Ms. Morgan. She couldn't possibly have been reprimanded for not listening. She knows all the answers."

Stephanie slapped his hand away when he poked at her. "I didn't say I didn't know the answer. In fact, I did. It was Poe, so how hard could it be? And my last name is Morgana, damn it."

He smirked. "I know but I like to give you shit. You've been perfect and now you're, what? Giving up on the last few months? Just suck it up and get through it so you can get those perfect grades. You never know when they'll come in handy."

She bit the inside of her cheek and clapped her hands together. "Actually, I've made a decision. The idea did belong to my teacher really, but I don't know why I didn't think about it before. I'll test out of the last semester and try for a job in another city."

Todd stopped in his tracks and she turned to face him. His eyes were huge. "Really? Just like that? Don't you want to line something up first?"

Stephanie grabbed his arm and they resumed their walk. "I already have. ONE R&D wants to interview me for a lead role at the company in research."

He thrust his hands out in front of him as if in protest. "Hold up. Doing what? Researching what? I mean, what does this company even do?"

"I don't know all the details right now." She shrugged. I only know it's research and development for the same company I've done some testing for on the Meligorn magic. That's all there really is to go on at this point."

Todd nodded enthusiastically. "Well, I'm proud of you. Congrats. You are too smart for this place anyway. You belong in a pod, not in the dirty Gov-Subs like some street rat."

Stephanie chuckled. "Have you been watching *Aladdin* again?"

"Yeah, so? He wrinkled his nose. "Man, I wish I was ready to go too. I want out of this and I want to start the rest of my life already. But I didn't take a bunch of advanced classes, so it's to the end of the line for me. Just like when you reach the last strand on level two-twenty-five on *Galaga: Demons of Death,* and you beat it and then it glitches and gives you one last level. Level 0. You simply want out. Your ass hurts, you're tired of staring at the same old shit, but you know you gotta get through it. Otherwise, it will haunt you."

She snickered and snorted. "I swear, you could relate anything in life to video games or movies. I wish there was a job like that. You would ace it."

Todd puffed his chest out and bowed his arms to walk like a huge thug. "You know, killing space ships, taking names and shit. Okay, let's play a pop quiz game."

Stephanie groaned and he shook his head. "Hear me out. We each throw out a question. If you get the right answer, your score goes up one. If you stump me, I get zero. First person to five wins."

She shrugged. "Sure, why not? I'll ask first."

He rubbed his hands together. "Cool. Let's do it."

Stephanie thought about it for a second. "All right. What song hit number one on the Billboard Top 100 charts on August 11, 1984, and stayed there for three weeks?"

Todd scoffed. "This is baby stuff. "The *Ghostbuster's* theme song, 'Who Ya Gonna Call?' And it was sung by Ray Parker Jr. Boom."

She sighed. "I thought that was a good one. One point for you."

He chewed thoughtfully on his bottom lip and rubbed his chin. "What was the name of the character who was presented as the first computer-generated television host?"

Stephanie blinked and pictured the blond man on the screen who had stuttered loudly through the show. "Uh...God, I knew this. Shit. Uh... Is it Maaark Hartwell?"

"Ahhhhhh," Todd said and tried to sound like a buzzer. "No. His name was Max Headroom created by George Stone, Annabel Jankel, and Rocky Morton and first appeared in 1985 in his own movie."

She wrinkled her nose in irritation. "Ugh. Still one to zero. In *Back to The Future,* where did Doc Brown get the plutonium to power the time-traveling DeLorean?"

Todd smiled. "From a group of Libyan terrorists who wanted him to make a bomb."

"Yep. Two to zero."

Todd smacked his lips in satisfaction. "That's right. Don't challenge the master."

Stephanie rolled her eyes. "Come on, we're almost there."

"Calm down. In the movie *Porky's,* why did they call Meat Tuperello 'Meat?'"

Her cheeks reddened. "Because of the size of his…uh…member."

Todd snapped his fingers. "Dang. I was sure you wouldn't get that one. I have to say, I'm impressed. You have actually paid attention to this stuff."

She glanced away and tried to will the bright color in her cheeks to fade. "You're my best friend. I gotta keep up with you. I actually watched that movie three years ago but it's the first time since then you've brought it up. So, now it's two to one. I gotta get a good one. Let me think…" An evil smirk moved over her lips. "What were Mouth and Chunk's real names in *The Goonies?*"

He pursed his lips, and she could almost see him scrolling through the Rolodex in his head. For a moment, Stephanie began to think that he might actually have been stumped on that one. But after a couple of seconds, his gaze shifted to her and he laughed. "Psych. I know this. Come on. Clark and Lawrence."

Stephanie's smirk dropped and she pouted. "Three to one. Come on, give me one. I need to make points up."

Todd laughed at her impatience. She was competitive, something that only he really knew. "What actors, who would go on to become famous, played Spicolli's sidekicks in *Fast Times at Ridgemont High?*"

Stephanie's eyes went bright, and she raised up on her tiptoes. "I know this! I actually read about this maybe a month ago. It was Eric Stolz and Anthony Edwards."

He patted her hard on the back. "Damn right it was. Good job! Three to two. You're closing in, so watch out."

Stephanie laughed. "How about a hard one? I'll challenge you."

"Give it to me. Make it really hard."

She tapped her fingers to her lips. "What not very good aliases did Bill and Ted give their seven historical figures when introducing them all to Missy?"

Todd chuckled and evidently approved of the question. "That is a good one. Okay, count them as I go. Socrates was Socrates Johnson. Billy the Kid was…Herman the Kid. Joan of Arc was Maxine of Arc.

Sigmund Freud was Dennis Freud, and Genghis Khan was Bob Ghengiskhan. Beethoven was…uh…uh…Dave Beethoven. And last but definitely not least, Abraham Lincoln was true and proud as none other than Abraham Lincoln."

Stephanie whistled. "Wow. That is impressive. Four to two."

He patted his hands against his legs as if he were listening to music. "Biggest band in the early eighties on radio. Their name starts with a J and they had multiple platinum albums."

Stephanie gave him a deadpan look. "Really? You are so teasing me with ridiculously easy questions. I can hold my own, you know."

Todd raised his hands like a criminal. "All right, calm down. I sincerely thought this was a good one."

Stephanie sniffed. "Journey. That was a total gimme, but you screwed that up so I'll take it. That makes it four to three. I have to think of a really good one. A *really* good one."

He beat his chest in mock-macho style. "Throw me a good one. I'll beat you yet again."

A spider scuttled out from the bushes across the sidewalk and he whimpered like a girl, dodged it quickly, and hurried to get ahead of it. Stephanie shook her head. "Wow. Okay, here's your question. More like a statement. A band that wasn't a Christian band and the singer was a drummer."

Todd didn't even hesitate. "Genesis. And that…makes five."

She rolled her eyes again but grinned as he raised his hands in the air and made a low, hoarse sound. "And the crowd goes wild for…the Toddster."

They both laughed and realized that they were early. They turned right and walked over into the grassy lawn area beside the school and sat on a bench. Todd cracked his neck. "So, has anything new happened with R&D?"

Stephanie sat up. "Oh, yeah. That's right, I forgot to tell you. I think I might have made a step toward a breakthrough on a way to hold energy in the body. Of course, no matter what, I don't think that every human should have access to this way of doing things. It could be fatal to a whole lot of people and fast."

Todd was taken back. "Wow, really? You think humans could do that? Not the killing part—we know what history tells us on that. I mean holding energy in the body."

She pressed her lips together in thought. "Yep. I have to test some theories, but I think that with a little work, it could be a normal thing."

He stared at the people who walked past several feet away. "What about the body's response to having that foreign energy inside it? When you think about it, fat is calories—or that's the result of it. Is there always a result with things like that?"

Stephanie chuckled nervously. "No one knows because this would be the first time. I've pulled it in and held it a few moments before, and it only partially worked. As soon as you lose concentration, it spills out of you and dissipates. Besides, how would I even test that theory? That would involve lab work."

Todd smiled at her. "Stick your tongue on the battery and suck it in. I bet you could pull at least a full small battery, if not more. Honestly, that's only a guess, actually. I have no idea how dense the stuff is."

"It's not. When I held it before, I could feel the amount in my chest, but it felt like breathing. If it weren't purple, I wouldn't even have noticed it except for the fullness it gave me. And let me start out by saying no to your battery-sucking theories, you dirty weirdo."

He stuck his lip out in a mock pout. "Hey, that's not nice."

She stood, paced around the back of the bench, and ducked to avoid the lower branches of the tree with massive green leaves. It smelled sweet on one hand and bitter on the other. She scrunched up her nose and forehead and grimaced. "Not only could I die or something, but I have no idea how clean those batteries are. I don't know who the inspector was, if he washed his hands after the bathroom, or if he sterilized everything. I don't want to suddenly create an outbreak of something like Meligorn Measle Pox or something wild we've never seen. I definitely don't want to wipe out the whole planet because I wanted to lick a stone."

He slapped the bench and stood to stretch his arms back. "Are you ready?"

She looked at the administration entrance. "Actually, you go ahead. I have to go check on the testing stuff. I'll catch up with you at lunch. Cool?"

Todd gave her a high five. "I would never be the person who came between you and your giant brain. Go get your test on. Or the information...or whatever. See you later."

She giggled with a snort and shook her head as she set off to the office. When she walked in, the head admin, Mrs. Langley, greeted her with a smile. "Ms. Morgana. I haven't seen you in a while. What can I do for you today?"

Stephanie rested her arms on the counter that came up to her chest. "I wanted to see what it would take to sign up for the process of testing out of this semester so I can go ahead and graduate."

Mrs. Langley smiled, looked down at her desk, and separated the last of her papers into stacks. "I wondered if you would ever come to that. I will write your name on the list. Testing is next week, and we will pull you individually from class and take you to the testing room."

A thrill of excitement rippled through her. "Great. Will I need anything?"

The woman searched briefly for a page on her desk and handed it to her. "That will tell you what to bring and how much they cost. There is a nominal fee because we have to bring in a proctor for them but nothing too bad."

She scanned the list and looked up as the warning bell sounded. "Thanks! I gotta run."

Mrs. Langley smirked and waved as Stephanie darted out of the room. She had been there since before the girl had even enrolled in grade school, had watched her grow up, and hoped that she would get somewhere in life, regardless of her situation. If anyone deserved it, she knew that bright young lady did.

Stephanie hurried to class and took her seat as the bell rang. She released a deep breath and pulled her notebook up on the desk. Slumped slightly in the chair, she put her hand in her pocket and fidgeted with the battery. The teacher reviewed the difference between MU energy and the regular energy on Earth. It was easy for them to talk about Earth energy as they had known for hundreds of years where it came from. As far as MU energy, no one really quite understood the fundamental makeup of it or how it was produced.

The teacher spoke about theories, but they were simply that—theories that had never actually been proven. The Meligornians didn't have a scientific explanation and hinged most of their understanding of the planet on folklore and mysticism.

The class annoyed her more than usual, but she simply shook her head and grumbled quietly, "They could at least teach the right damn information in this school."

The thought that she was almost out of there was the only thing that kept her from raising her hand and making the teacher look like a complete idiot.

BURT was active in Server S98246C located in northern California. It was a small prep school that was established for those in that specific part of the state. California was small since most of the southern region was now a part of the ocean and the northern area had separated into two sections. One was covered in soot and ash, having suffered debilitating forest fires until there was nothing left but dead land. The other was still relatively fruitful, but the people who lived there did so sustainably. It was one of the few places in NorAm that was given a waiver that did not allow any industrialization or urbanization of that area.

Some sort of competition was in progress at the prep school. It was a large piracy fight between the humans and Meligornsians versus another human-Dreth ship. The humans were all actually students, while the Meligornians and the Dreth were system-generated to fight on whatever side they represented.

It was a neat way to have competitions within the schools. You were able to be on the pirate team and to see how they fought from the inside. At the same time, though, the other side had magic help. These Meligornians were warriors, not the soft teachers and wizards that Stephanie was able to meet with on a regular basis. They knew how to fight the Dreth to the death and had done so with the humans and the non-pirate Dreth who were out in the solar system tracks.

BURT wanted to make observations on this one specific fight to help him determine what code he might have to change in order to make the battle not only more realistic but also consistent with the most recent developments. Constant information came in about the state of the ships, the surge in technology, and the tactics that the Dreth pirates had learned in order to beat back the humans and the Meligornians. They generally left their own people alone unless specifically attacked by them.

He recorded several actions of the Dreth pirate avatars that needed serious upgrades in both weapons and tactics. It looked as if they had not been given the full updates that the engineers did once a year. As BURT made the notes, a small alarm hissed at him. He shifted his attention to the camouflaged servers he used for his new businesses and scrutinized the information.

The initial report indicated that someone tried to hack one of his banks where he stored not only money for and from investments, but top-secret information as backup. He brought up the incoming code and watched as the person indeed attempted to circumvent his digital safeguards.

BURT mentally "cracked his fingers" and got ready to—in his words—"bring the heat."

CHAPTER FORTY-TWO

The system AI knew it was vital that he separated his activities and spread the information throughout the system and across the world. All were still tightly bundled in the blanket of security of his system but not all placed in one nice package for someone to come along and nab. It was a large undertaking, but his load was less than normal that morning and he decided that they wouldn't notice a couple of tenths of a spike in engineering. They were too busy pouring their morning coffee and trying to open their sleep-encrusted eyes to take over the first shift of the day from the vamps, the loving nickname BURT had given the night crew.

It wasn't only because they lurked in the shadows of the night and almost hissed at the sun each morning as they ran to their cars with their faces covered with the bottoms of their trench coats. It was also because they were always overzealous, and no one knew why. Boredom, maybe, and being stuck with the slow night shift so any change in load was a reason for them to actually investigate. Or perhaps because they were mostly newbies who were given the shit shift and tried their damnedest to get out of that and pull their careers up to the brighter side of things. The hope of new people, it was always so...gross.

While BURT focused some of his load on the tasks, he turned, ready and happy to fight the intruders. An attack was imminent, not from them but against them.

Stephanie sat on the edge of the bed, an open envelope beside her, together with a smaller one that contained TRAM tickets, and a letter from ONE R&D. It was a welcome missive and a checklist of instructions for their meeting in Washington DC. They provided everything she would need to be comfortable there. TRAM tickets to and from the city, three days in a hotel, all transportation she would possibly need, and a per diem that had already been set up for her. She was in a good place, in that moment, with no real wants or needs to take this step forward into a future career. Still, she tried not to let the excitement take root too deeply.

She bounced to her feet and walked over to the closet to retrieve her suitcase. It was the first time she had even looked at the thing since she'd become what she lovingly referred to as a "prep school drop-out." Not, of course, to be confused with the beauty school variety, but seemingly close in the general feeling of disgust, discouragement, and simply put, disappointment.

Nonetheless, she persisted, placed the bag on the bed, and selected all her new clothes from the closet. There were definitely more than she needed to take, but she wanted to be sure she would have anything she needed while there. She separated these into pants, blouses, dresses, and skirts and went to work to fold them carefully to avoid as many creases and wrinkles as possible. She hoped there would be a steamer in the hotel room. If not, even an old-time iron would do the trick.

When her packing was complete, she pulled up the information that had been downloaded to her system while she was in the pod and carefully printed, collated, and organized the stacks before she slid them into individual large envelopes. Her suitcase would weigh a ton.

"YA dazhe ne ponimayu, kto soyedinil etot bankovskiy schet. Net otpechatkov pal'tsev. Kto-to deystvitel'no ne khotel, chtoby yego nashli." One of the guys in the hacking group laughed as he watched his computer screen.

Another man walked by and smacked him on the back of his head with a rolled-up paper. "English, Hoff. We are no longer in Russia. We spent countless hours learning it, so use it."

Hoff rubbed the back of his head and gave his co-conspirator the side eye. "Yeah, yeah. Big scary Russian. We won't be too big and scary unless we can get the money we need for our bosses. More like tiny chunks of cut-up Russians."

The rest of the group ignored him as they attempted to get their part of the heist up to date. Suddenly, Hoff slammed his hand down on the table and his computer shook. "Damn it! *Yeblya Sistema*...this bank has been fool-proofed from almost every angle. Their software has blocks, their firewalls are created with complex calculations, and their security bugs seem to have kicked in."

Yeni, one of the leaders of the group, walked over and put his hand on Hoff's shoulder. He squeezed slightly and the younger man quieted. "This is no time to let your frustrations get the best of you. We have hacked harder and not even from American soil. Less complaining, more working. You are hacker, yes?"

Hoff nodded and rubbed his shoulder as Yeni let go. The leader nodded and looked around the room. "Good. Very good. This person who has decided to stay anonymous will anonymously lose everything they have. Large corporate NorAm scum. We will always defeat them and always get what we want from them. We are to complete mission and get out of town. Let's make this sooner rather than later."

He turned to walk through the small, run-down old house and back to his makeshift office. One of the hackers stood, a worried look on his face. He ran his hand through his hair. "Uh, Yeni. We seem to have even larger problems than simply getting through the security."

Yeni sighed, his back still to the other man. He rubbed his chin and turned his neck to glare at him. In a calm yet deep, ominous tone, he grumbled, "What is it now?"

The hacker pointed at his screen and shook his head. "The bank is starting to shut us down faster than we are physically able to attack. It was like they saw us at first entrance and their system now works at multiple levels to kick us to the curb. I honestly have never seen a system move so fast—it is as if it were thinking."

The leader rolled his eyes. "Systems do not think. Calculate? Yes. Think? No. These are machines and humans built them. That means it is possible to break through them."

He marched over to the computer and pushed the man out of the way. "Incompetence levels are off the charts today. I will take care of this myself."

His colleague leaned forward to watch and learn as the older man began to type quickly. Yeni's eyes shifted back and forth as he read through the language to decipher what was happening step by step. He could see where the bank was kicking them out, but there were other entities involved—ones he couldn't seem to track to save his life. They were faster than any smaller bank system.

Suddenly, Hoff pushed to his feet. "Someone is tracking us. They are following us through the constant diverter. I don't know how that is even possible. You would have to have insane computing abilities."

Yeni remained calm and moved from screen to screen. He tried to combat the attacker and at the same time, shake whoever was tracking them off his tail. His brow furrowed and his lips sneered. "They must have some sort of blanket protection on them. It's saying that the tracker is literally located within the system matrix itself. That is humanly impossible. How could a person be in the system?"

The other members of the small group had stopped their work and now stood and slowly packed their personal belongings in their bags. Yeni started to sweat and his chest heaved as he continued to fight to keep up. "This attack is coming in worldwide—from servers from all over. It doesn't make any sense."

Another hacker shook his head. "All over the world at once? This isn't even possible."

The leader removed his hands from the keyboard, leaned back against the chair, and breathed heavily. “They are literally everywhere. And they are all moving at a speed I didn’t think was computationally possible.”

Hoff studied the data that changed so rapidly, he could barely read the first line before it was gone. “Government involvement?”

Yeni shook his head. “Not any government I’ve ever seen. There isn’t a single one that has that kind of bandwidth—not the kind that would stretch all the way across the world. That simply doesn’t exist.”

One of the guys in the back pushed his chair in and walked around his desk to Yeni. “We don’t know if it exists. There could be some rogue government agency attacking us. The kind that doesn’t take orders from the leaders of the country. They do the dirty work and make it seem like an anomaly. I’ve heard rumors of groups like that, but I always thought they were little scary secrets tucked in there by the Federation to keep hackers at bay.”

Three of the computers beeped and the hackers at those stations stood and pressed the keys hard and fast. “We lost the server. It’s fried. It just gave out on us.”

Hoff put his hand on Yeni’s shoulder. “We need to execute the elimination sequence. We don’t have much of a choice.”

The leader looked wildly at him. “Then it’s all over. The last year is a wash right here and right now.”

The younger man looked at the screen and shook his head. “It’s already over. Look at that thing go. They probably already know where we are. They are stalling long enough to make you think you have hope. We don’t know if it’s government—it could even be the Russian mob. It could be Chekhov trying to take us down to get us out of the way.”

Yeni grumbled. “That swine couldn’t pull something like that off. But I guess you’re right. We don’t know who is coming for us. We can regroup and think.”

He stood tall and his gaze drifted around the room. The team were silent and still. “Initiate Elimination Sequence and then we try to regroup and plan our next move. From the time starter on the screen, it looks as if even if they are tracking, we have four minutes to shut down before they find us. So, move your fat asses."

The entire group bounced into action to fry a bunch of their servers to cover their tracks. Most of them already had a failsafe on them to do so in case of a Federation raid. They didn't want the evidence to fall into their hands and were already outside their territory. That was never good for the Russians, not when it came to Americans. They had always had a contentious relationship, but a war started—a technological one—long before in the early two thousands when the Russians hacked the American's elections—not once, but three times—to find candidates they could control.

Yeni tapped his foot and watched impatiently until finally, each of them stood and raised their hands in the air to confirm completion.

"Done," they echoed down the line.

The leader plopped down and slammed his fist on the table. "This should have been easy. One and done. Hack the system, find all the dirt, take whatever money we wanted, and return the information to the oligarch. We should be looking at our payday at this point."

Hoff turned in his chair. "True, but if caught, we die right then and there, you know that. There aren't rules here like there used to be. But we burned the servers so we should be good."

Yeni nodded. "Yeah, but now we don't have the capability to fight or go back in for a while. The whole system is looking for us and this isn't good. I say we lay low, keep an eye out and an ear open, and we make a decision after that."

The younger man clapped his hands. "You heard the man, people. Clean up stations, take watchpoint, and be ready to move if necessary. Other than that, try to relax. There are a lot of things that can be cleaned up and we need to start a new plan here so if we can hook up again, we can get in and out of this system fast. Gunter, I want you to take the data you saved from the hack and start sifting through it on the air gap, see if you can't figure out what is—"

"Uh, guys," one of the hackers said and pointed to the screen behind Yeni. "What's that?"

They all turned to look as the monitor began to flash.

CHAPTER FORTY-THREE

Everyone in the room stood perfectly still. No one spoke or made a sound and Yeni gripped the arms of the chair and leaned forward. A small curser blinked on a black background but nothing else happened. His gaze shifted over to Hoff, who stared angrily at the screen. "Do you think it's due to the servers frying? Maybe that knocked the computer back to the stone age?"

Yeni reached slowly toward the 3D screen, his finger shaking as he went to touch the curser. As his finger came close, a message began to resolve.

I see you...

Everyone thrust out of their chairs and their leader gestured wildly over his head. "Pack it up and destroy it all. You know the drill. We head out to the meeting spot and no one talk to anyone other than your partner on the street. Watch your back when you roll to the safe house. Make sure nobody follows you."

They had all freaked out by this point but did their best to get it together. As a methodical team, they grabbed the wires on the backs of each computer and yanked them from the sockets. One of the men walked down the line behind them to check every single server and every single plug. Everyone else collected any paperwork they had and disposed of it exactly as they were meant to. Yeni pushed them toward the doors and nodded to Hoff at the front.

He looked around one last time to ensure that the crew had removed all evidence from the place. At his shrill whistle, they raced toward the door, slammed it open, and barreled out of it. They scattered in different directions. Yeni stood in the doorway and fumed as he stared at the computer where the cursor still flashed on the screen. He flinched and gritted his teeth as flames blasted from the tables, traveled down the lines of electronics, and spilled over the floor.

The last of the hackers hurried over and slung his book bag on. Yeni slapped his back and shoved him out the door. He was pissed—beyond pissed, actually—but there it was, all his work ended in flames and shame. There hadn't been a gig like that in a long time, and he would have to tell the boss they couldn't handle it and left thousands of dollars of equipment to burn to cinders in the small house.

He turned and slammed the large metal door to trap the fire inside. As he walked, he flipped his hood up and stuck his hands into his pockets. Rain drizzled over his head and his boots splashed through the puddles that collected in the cracks and hollows of the pavement. He glanced back at the shimmer of the fire through the windows and wondered who the hell that guy was. They had done everything they were supposed to do, down to the last-second emergency pack-up. But there was someone out there who had made it his business to spook them.

The birds squawked as they flew high over the city. In the distance, the remnants of the old Eiffel Tower still sprawled in a pile where it had tumbled to ruin decades before. Buildings were patched and reworked, and from the rubble of the city, a new and more modern one had been born. Almost everyone who was currently alive had never even seen Paris before the destruction.

A long black limo pulled up in front of the looming skyscraper covered in shimmering glass. The driver walked around to the passenger side and opened the door, then stepped back. A long, muscular yet feminine, stocking-covered leg stepped out and planted the six-inch spiked heel of a stiletto on the asphalt. The woman inside squinted, donned her large-rimmed sunglasses, and ducked out of the vehicle. She tugged nonchalantly on her skirt and tucked her clutch under her arm. Tall and well built, she possessed the perfect amount of curve coupled with strong, lean muscles.

She stepped up on the curb and ran her black-leather-gloved hand down the back of her short red hair. As she took a deep breath, she pursed her lips and glanced up the side of the monster building. "It seems they are doing well here."

The driver wiggled his brow and closed the car door and she walked through the courtyard out front past a fountain that had no water in it. As she approached the door, a tall, dark-skinned man dressed in a black suit, white shirt, and black tie, opened it for her. She could see the gun tucked snugly in the side of his pants as she passed. Everyone carried weapons these days.

As she entered the lobby of the building, she removed her glasses and glanced around. It was decorated with large paintings, plush throw rugs, and fake plants, much like any other office. In the corner was the elevator so she hurried over and stepped inside. She took a keycard from her purse, slid it into the slot, and pressed the fifteenth-floor button. The doors shut and the elevator began to ascend.

There were no stops taken on the way, and when it reached the destination, she had to remove her card for the doors to open. The elevator dinged to notify the people in the office that someone had arrived. There were no full-time office companies in the building. It was, instead, a place where temporary corporate headquarters were constructed in secret and with anonymity.

The secretary at the desk put her pen down and smiled sweetly. "How can I help you today?"

The woman looked at her for a moment and flipped her elevator keycard over to reveal a symbol on the back. The secretary's face didn't change. She nodded and picked the phone up. The visitor glanced around the plush office and decided it could be called almost comfortable. These types of places were hired locations for companies around the world, and she assumed they had to be as nice as possible.

They weren't that expensive, not compared to some of the rents that companies often paid to be in the center of the rich communities. At the same time, though, it wasn't breaking-the-bank expensive either. There was a moderation to it that kept it healthy for them and everyone else who used the facility. Not to mention the fact that the view from the identical sides of the building was absolutely amazing. It was unlike any of the other ones she had been in.

Her gaze flickered across a large mirror in the small sitting area. Her stark white skirt fell to her knees and her jacket was perfectly tailored. The light pink blouse was modest but unbuttoned possibly one button too low. She was educated and possessed an intelligence beyond that of almost everyone she ever really found herself around. Confidence was something she didn't lack in the least. It was, in fact, something she had in spades.

That assertiveness was reflected in her walk. Her steps, although governed by the stilettos, were decisive and brisk. She always placed the heel of her shoe down first and tapped down with the toe and had walked in them long enough that there wasn't even a slight wiggle in her ankle. But with them on, she moved with stealth and assurance and her strides matched the situation and placed her firmly in control.

Her gaze flickered around her and hesitated on the man who sat in the corner with a newspaper. He studied her body as she walked and gave him the impression of a circling tiger—aware of her surroundings but sleek and smooth in movement.

The man's gaze met hers and she smiled at him, which immediately and somewhat surprisingly lowered his anxiety. She had perfectly straight bleached teeth and the red lipstick contrasted severely. Her eyes were narrowed and dangerous-looking but when she smiled, that went away to be replaced by a twinkle in her eye that caused some reactions from those who milled about the offices. It took them off guard and they either immediately diverted their gazes or smiled back awkwardly with uncertainty.

The secretary stopped, removed a key from around her neck, inserted it in the door, and opened it. "Right this way."

The woman nodded with a smile and walked into the conference room. A buffet-style mahogany table stretched along the back wall and a large, oval-shaped one in the middle would seat six comfortably.

The secretary hovered in the doorway, her hands clasped together in front of her. "There are Danishes, small sandwiches, and cookies on the table. There is coffee brewing if you would like it that way. Otherwise, I can secure you any type of stimulant that you might need. We know not everyone maintains their energy in the same way."

"No, coffee will be fine," she replied. "I'll fix it myself."

The woman crossed to the center table and sat on one side. The secretary bowed slightly and left, closing the door quickly behind her. The woman put her hands on the table and folded them together to enjoy the silence of the room but without the nerves anyone else might have in that moment.

Suddenly, a crackling noise intruded, and a male voice echoed from the speakers of the phone in front of her. "Welcome, Ms. Elizabeth."

Her gaze shifted to the device and she leaned back. No video displayed on the screen, only audio. The small button on top flickered green to confirm that the line was, in fact, in use and secure. The monitor flickered slightly, and the ONE R&D logo appeared. It turned and twisted, rose in 3D fashion from the screen, and floated in front of her. She was indeed in the right place and oddly, it seemed even more secretive than she would have assumed it would be. That she was familiar with, though. She had dealt with the quiet back-alley approach to business for her entire career.

The voice was steady with no sound of breathing or movement. Silence now ensued, waiting for the woman to respond to the greeting. Still, she was slightly hesitant and knew exactly why she felt that way.

She narrowed her eyes and leaned forward to speak into the phone. "I didn't provide you with that name."

There was no response for several moments and then the voice spoke once more. "We are an R&D company, Ms. Elizabeth. If we were incapable of even researching the name of the woman we invited into our private offices, we wouldn't stay in business for very long, now would we?"

The side of her mouth tugged into a smile. "No, I suppose not. Although that constitutes more than a simple Internet search in order to find that information. But I will be impressed then, rather than angry."

"Ah, very good. We don't want to start this off on the wrong foot, now do we? I believe that you will make a perfect addition to the set of plans I am currently putting together for a very large undertaking."

She crossed her legs, her eyes narrowed and her lips pursed, and instantly understood what was happening there. "I wondered, at first, as to why you wanted to talk to me. I guess I shouldn't be shocked."

Ms. Elizabeth leaned back and decided to wait a while before she made her coffee. "I am under the assumption that if I turned the phone off, you would still be able to contact me. Through the television, the lines around us, the reception from the building across the street. Even the faintest of signals."

The voice was silent for a moment. "Very good, Ms. Elizabeth. You are as quick as they tell me you are."

She chuckled and shook her head. "Okay, you want to talk? Let's talk. You have my full attention."

Her father tapped on the top of the roof inside their car. "AI, no need to park in the spots. You can let us out on the curb. We would like to say goodbye."

The AI replied and its voice broke slightly, much like the one in the security system at home. "Of course, Mr. Morgan. May I wish you safe journeys, Stephanie."

She smiled as the car came to a stop. "Thank you, Mildred. You have safe travels as well."

They all piled out in front of the TRAM station. She had the car she could have used, but her parents insisted that they drop her off on their way to work. She stood, one hand on her unbraided hair, and the wide legs of her high-waisted black pants flapped in the breeze. As part of the outfit, she wore a short, cap-sleeved white button-up with small ruffles down the front. She had even applied a little makeup, trying out her abilities with what she already had.

Her father gave her a hug. "Remember, hands behind you or in your lap. As far as your discussions go, show manners, of course, but remember, they are courting you as much as you are them. Don't be a pushover."

She nodded. "Of course. Thank you."

He fiddled in his back pocket, retrieved something small wrapped in a piece of cloth, and put it quickly in her hand. "I would give you some sort of advice on protection, but I think that may be all you need."

She lifted the fabric to find a battery beneath it. He nodded. "I think you can protect yourself. That's simply a little a protection in a bottle from your old worried dad. If you need to use it, make sure they stay down."

While he gave his daughter a wink, Cindy stood there with a stern face, her jaw clenched and arms folded. She was not amused by his antics in the least. Still, Stephanie clutched the battery in her hand and held it slightly behind her so her mother wouldn't take it.

Cindy walked up and brushed her daughter's hair off her shoulders. "Don't listen to your father. He only wants to see that you've kicked ass and taken names. Don't give in to his fantasies and indulge his masculinity. Be safe, let us know you have arrived, and we will see you when you get back."

Stephanie gave them another hug and kiss goodbye and chuckled as her mom squeezed her super tight. She still acted like she was leaving for the first time ever, although she didn't really mind. What mattered was that she knew they loved her and she knew that she was lucky to have that. As she lifted her suitcase, she glanced back. Her mother walked ahead of her dad, who looked back at her as well. He grinned and she winked at him with a smile and dropped the battery into her pocket.

She hurried with her bag to the boarding area and retrieved her ticket. The collector, a tall chubby man with a stern face, grabbed it from her and read the print. She watched as his face softened quickly and he snapped his fingers. A bell boy of sorts hurried up, his hat slightly cocked to the side.

The collector looked at him with disapproval. "Take Ms. Morgana's bag and escort her to train car three. Anything you need, madam, Jeffrey here will be happy to secure for you."

Stephanie smirked. "Thank you, sir."

The kid showed her to a ramp specially placed for first-class passengers. They had even draped the rigid metal with a red carpet. She walked gingerly up it and stood inside, waiting for the kid with her suitcase. He nodded nervously, adjusted his hat, and led her quickly through a very fancy dining car. White linens were draped on each table beneath small bunches of flowers in vases and china set for each place.

She swallowed hard and glanced at the different forks and knives. Ironically, she would have to rely on the little training she had in manners at the prep school because this would be the first time she had ever been a guest in such opulence. They walked through the tunnel into the next car and the attendant stopped outside an enclosed room with etched glass doors. He opened the door for her and lowered his gaze to the floor.

Stephanie smiled and tried not to giggle or snort in her nervousness. She stepped into the car and immediately glanced up at a small crystal chandelier that hung from the ceiling. Inside the small room, four reclining overstuffed chairs with wooden tips on the arms were neatly arranged. All were empty but one, and when she saw who the man was—or rather, what he was—her heart skipped a beat.

There was no mistaking the pale, almost sparkling skin, long pointed ears, and billowing hair. He was a Meligornian dressed in Earth clothing and he stared out of the window as the train prepared to move. She hesitated for a moment, glanced at the kid, and stepped inside. The boy hurried in and placed her suitcase in the luggage closet, then strapped it to the shelf to avoid it shifting and injuring anyone. He closed the large doors quietly and his gaze wandered nervously to the Meligornian symbol on the shoulder of the man's suit.

While the nerves rippled hastily through her, Stephanie quietly took a deep breath and released it slowly. *Pull it together, Stephanie. This is no different than any of the times inside the Virtual World with the Meligornians you have met before. He is only a magical being.*

She didn't know this, of course, but her closed cabin with the Meligornian was set up by none other than BURT. Quietly, she took her seat, linked her hands in her lap, and tried to keep her attention focused out the window. Before the TRAM began to move, there was a loud knock on the door and what looked like an enormous bodyguard ducked in and glanced darkly at her for several moments. It made the hair on the back of her neck stand up.

CHAPTER FORTY-FOUR

The train powered along at high speed, but the windows still displayed a leisurely pace that allowed for a pleasant view over the countryside. The car was quiet—definitely much quieter than their trip last time, although Stephanie was sure she had read something about sound dampening technology used in the first-class areas of the TRAMs. At the time, she hadn't given it a second thought, but now, speeding along yet feeling as if she was seated comfortably in her living room felt almost ridiculous.

Her gaze moved to the Meligornian and she noticed that he wore the metal of the Meligorn Government. From the way he was dressed to the symbols on his shoulders and sleeves, she could assume that he was high up in the government, too. How high she wasn't sure, but she decided that if they allowed her in there too, it couldn't have been very high. Everything in her wanted to strike up a conversation with him. If he was a government official, she wanted to know about that, how they worked as a civilization, and all the things in between. But at the same time, she didn't want to act like a ridiculous fangirl.

She wrinkled her nose and turned her head back toward the windows as they entered their first stretch of the TRAM tunnel. A screen darkened on the windows to shut out the unsightly concrete walls and water stains and the lights in the cabin brightened somewhat. As she glanced down from the ceiling, the Meligornian looked at her with curious eyes.

Stephanie felt awkward and didn't hold his gaze. His bodyguard had taken the seat beside him and the two had their phones out in their laps. It was obvious that they wanted to have a private conversation from the fact that they seemed to have been texting each other.

The ambassador looked at the screen on his phone and read the message from his bodyguard. **I trust you will discuss this security breach with the humans when you reach DC, Ambassador V'ritan?**

He sighed but without rancor. **She is only a girl, and in fact, there is something about her that I can't help but feel that I recognize.**

The guard raised an eyebrow. **I don't see how that is possible, but I will do the research really fast.**

The ambassador put his phone in his pocket and turned his attention to the tablet in his lap before he sighed again and stared at the tip of his shiny shoes. After a few moments, a dinging sounded and the guard nodded. "Just a reminder of the trip. Although I suppose I put the time in wrong again."

Stephanie didn't even look at them. The ambassador picked his tablet up and flipped through his notes for his upcoming meetings. A number of them had been scheduled over the next several days and he had tried his utmost to prepare for such a busy time. Meligornians on the home planet did not stress their bodies like that, but after so many years on Earth, he was used to the high-paced lifestyle. He merely wished he had more time to memorize all the statistics. The notes were firmly lodged in his head, but the numbers gave him grief. Whether the humans thought it was debatable or not, math did not turn out to be the language of all living creatures.

Nonetheless, he prepared his notes in a way that they could understand. He went to flip another page and paused when his guard stiffened beside him. Hastily, he glanced up to see if the girl had seen it, but she had not. She stared at a book in her lap and obviously tried to make things not so awkward inside the train car.

As he looked at his notes again, a warning symbol from his bodyguard appeared on his screen. He moved it away and clicked on the link that he had sent. It was newspaper clippings of the girl across from them that reported how she was the first Earth witch ever to be discovered. They included pictures of her walking with friends and family and other images of her shooting blue streams of energy. Curiously, her eyes glistened in that same color.

He found it slightly amusing that she walked around so nonchalantly and tried not to be noticed. The bodyguard sent another few articles to him and he crossed his leg and tilted the tablet slightly to take advantage of better lighting. He began to read through each one carefully, but all of them said almost the same thing. She had thrown magic to help save a woman and her child. Some hailed her as an angel and a savior, while others were terrified of this new evolutionary—or perhaps revolutionary—manifestation of power.

As he skimmed through, he glanced at her from time to time. He noticed her hand in her pocket that seemed to roll something around in it nervously. He could only assume that it was one of her magic batteries. It didn't give him pause, though. To him, there was nothing dangerous about her. At least there wouldn't be when she faced a Meligornian.

His guard rested his hand casually on his gun. The ambassador clicked his tongue and shook his head to remind him to take it easy. With another glance at the girl, he wondered how much of his language she could speak.

After a few moments during which she knew he was staring while he struggled to find the right words, he finally decided to speak to her. "*K'roth gurardian brofton nationalie* Capitol?"

She blinked for a moment and looked up slowly.

The Russian delegate slammed his fist down on the table, stood, and leaned forward on it. "You think that because NorAm killed the Russian dictator hundreds of years ago that gives you the right to give me any shit about this? We have reinstated our country, while you sat around bathing in luxury and waste with these rich people."

The American narrowed his eyes and pointed at him. "Now you hold on right there. How do you have the nerve to talk about us in that manner? That is beyond treasonous with your stories of hate for people who would drive you to separate from the idea that the Federation worked so desperately to get you on. And then to turn around and rob one of our American banks."

The Russian clenched his fist and yelled at the American, "Regardless of the crime, your assault on Russian citizens and the danger you put all of them in is tantamount to war. We have fought wars for less and trust me, everyone outside the Federation has been dying to see NorAm have their asses beaten. You are arrogant and uncareful as you speak to the great leaders of this world. You are the country that allowed this plastic lifestyle everyone so dutifully clings to and we are the ones who stepped above you, not interested in being under the thumb of the Federation."

The Chinese delegate waved his hand and scoffed. "You fight over nothing. We are the ones who are the true victims here."

Both the Russians and the Americans went quiet and looked curiously at him. The Chinese delegate's forehead was furrowed, and he spoke with passion as he waved his fist up and down. "You have the nerve to touch our sovereignty. You both used your abilities through your own countries to do so. You have broken treaties and understandings between our countries. While you Americans believe that because you fall under Federation protection, you can do anything that you want, you are wrong. So very wrong. And you Russians, with your talk of war. You have no leg to stand on. If anyone here should be threatening, it should be China. We are fed up with this."

The American delegate shook his head. "We are doing no such thing. If we had the power to do anything we wanted, we would have used it on your asses already."

The meeting came to a standstill and all three delegates finally resumed their seats. They remained quiet for several minutes until they were able to calm themselves enough to discuss what had happened. There was actually no real evidence to confirm that any of them had officially been involved. They had all simply made assumptions because they knew the suspected hackers had come into the United States from Russia.

After a few moments, the American delegate cleared his throat and gestured to his Chinese counterpart. "I thought it was you guys all pissed off at us. We figured you had reason with the trade issues and conversations with the Federation and the poverty your country has fallen into due to the lack of resources available. I am sorry. I am a professional. I should not jump to conclusions."

The Chinese man calmed himself as well. The delegate leaned forward toward the mic. "We appreciate your apology and accept. In all honesty, our country assumed it was Russia that had egged things on and made it impossible for you to respect our sovereignty and go after them in the same arena."

The Russian delegate shook his head. "If it was none of us, then who was it?"

They all swallowed and thought the same thing. The three major players—as well as many of the smaller countries—had all experienced some degree of cybersecurity alarms on the fateful day in question. While they had all immediately put their best counter-hackers and analysts to work, no one seemed to be able to determine the real origin of either the initial attack or the swift and decisive counterstrikes that had drawn all nations into the arena. The clean-up had been so swift and so efficiently executed that there was no way to unravel the source or correctly determine how many counter-specialists had been involved.

If the truth be told, their best and most experienced cyber teams were baffled, and from there, it had been easy to slide into the vague and murky waters of paranoia and fearful assumptions. More than anything, all members present wanted answers—at the very least, an explanation of what exactly had happened. The truth that stared them in the face in that moment was one none of them wanted, or ever expected, to face.

There could very well be a country out there that had hidden their abilities. A country that was more powerful and skillful than all of them.

Stephanie swallowed hard as her eyes widened and her palms sweated. She was astonished to be addressed in Meligornian and although she didn't speak it, she was very honored that he would even speak to her. Also, this was no avatar, so she knew she had to be very polite. It was no simulation within the Virtual World. This was real.

She stood carefully and bowed, raised one hand up, and extended the other out for his. While she wasn't sure if he was on the cusp of the royal greeting or not, she decided that something was better than nothing. She not only wanted to show her admiration and respect for the Meligornian people but also to show her excitement at the opportunity to ride the train with someone of his stature.

The bodyguard maintained a stiff expression, but as the ambassador stood and walked toward her, his mouth dropped open. The official bowed his head, raised his hand, and grasped her forearm with the other. They both held the greeting for several moments to show suitable reverence before they gave each other the traditional Meligornian verbal greeting.

As Stephanie straightened, her cheeks flushed and her excitement grew within her. But she knew that if she couldn't understand him, it would be no good anyway. She thought back to that lesson and smiled, placed her hands behind her back, and latched onto her wrists. "Engotish Preferatus Ingorna Discusio?"

The ambassador cracked a smile and raised his eyebrows at the guard. He looked at her again as they took their seats. "Of course we can."

She looked around as giddiness bubbled to the surface. "But you didn't do a cantrip or spell or anything."

He chuckled. "When you reach my age of over two hundred years old, you tend to be able to achieve the required results without even opening your mouth."

Stephanie bit the inside of her lip and tapped her fingers on her knees as she sat on the edge of the seat. Finally, it got the better of her, and she burst into a smile. "I'm sorry. This is so awesome—to get to ride with a real Meligornian, that is. I have only met one in my VR studies, never in real life. I didn't know if I actually ever would."

The guard watched her as she giggled and shook her head, apparently on the verge of talking excitedly to herself. A smile moved across his lips as it did for the ambassador as well. They both realized quickly that she was no threat to anyone. She was merely a curious young adult with a heart that seemed to be true.

The ambassador motioned to the guard and said something in his ear. The man nodded and stood, walked across, and extended his hand to Stephanie. She looked at him nervously for a moment and he chuckled. "He would like you to join him."

She smiled and took his hand, scooted past him, and sat beside the ambassador. They sat there talking and paid little attention to the rising and setting sun displayed in the glass windows. They learned language nuances like what awesome meant and the fact that he had asked her originally if she was the human who knew magic.

In the progression of the discussion, without even knowing it was happening, Stephanie began to ask questions of a high-level wizard—the kind of questions that only a theorist would have asked. The ambassador, having had many, many years of practice in maintaining a collected state of being, did not flinch or spark a notion that he was indeed shocked that she could be human and have that level of Meligornian experience.

Curious, he began to probe her knowledge. "And you have tried to concentrate the magic within you to carry it?"

Stephanie nodded. "I have. And it has worked for a few moments but when my thoughts change, I lose it. However, I am currently working on a theory that if I pull it into an imagined object in my thoughts, I will be able to secure it and siphon from it as needed."

The ambassador rubbed his chin. "That is an interesting theory but one thing you have not accounted for is the strain that it will have on the human mind. Meligornian magic and energy has its own flow—a soul, almost, if you will. The connection to that energy must be there to avoid any type of negative consequence."

She nodded and her eyes remained fixed on the floor. "That makes sense. If I try to force it, it will only reject me, just as we have rejected its pull on Earth for so long. Like those who can't feel it at all."

The ambassador smiled. "Those who cannot sense the energy are more than merely mentally blocked. They do not possess the inner strength that is passed through the universe. We do not know how humans have acquired it but for everyone but you, apparently, it is only strong enough to feel."

Stephanie was having the time of her life. The Meligornian official had helped her understand theories that she had not even known were different than what she thought. It made a lot of difference when it came to working with the magic.

They continued their conversation without realizing that they were so close to their destination. Before they knew it, the train had pulled into the station in DC. The ambassador walked her out, and they shared a traditional Meligornian goodbye. She began to walk away, carrying her bag in a complete haze.

"Ms. Morgana," the Meligornian called to her. "Wait one minute."

CHAPTER FORTY-FIVE

Stephanie turned, her eyes wide, and smiled as the guard lumbered toward her with something in his hand. He was a large man—a human—and although he gave the appearance of pure muscle, she could tell he had grown a little soft with age. She estimated him to be nearing forty or so, but the creases at the corners of his eyes showed that he had been in that job for quite some time. There was a protectiveness but also a kindness in him that made her feel safe.

He handed a small white card to her. "Keep this to yourself."

She took it in her left hand and nodded as she reached her right out to shake. He smiled widely and gripped her hand gently, almost able to wrap his entire fist around her dainty fingers and palm. He glanced over his shoulder and laughed a little harder as he shook his head. "I have been with him for a very long time. I have to admit, he hasn't had this much fun in years. It is nice to see him enjoy himself. That is something his job does not allow very often. Thank you, young Stephanie. Be safe."

Stephanie shook her head with a bemused grin and watched as he walked away. She looked at the special card in her hand and chewed on her bottom lip. She had read about these cards on the Meligorn

Magical Musings website. After a moment's hesitation, she slid her hand into her pocket and clasped the battery, applying the smallest amount of magic she could. The card seemed to shiver in her fingertips and his information, written in white on the white background, vibrated. She watched in wonder as it lifted off the card and floated toward her.

It seemed almost alive as it found its way to her forehead and pressed against it. The information glowed for a moment before it faded into her mind. She blinked her eyes and focused on the image of his phone number in her head as if she actually read it on a piece of paper. There was no other time that she could think of that her thoughts had been that completely clear. It was almost magical in itself how well it worked.

She released the battery and turned her attention to the now blank piece of stock card in her palm. It began to disintegrate and churn into a fine dust in the center of her hand. When she tilted her hand from side to side, the ash shimmered in the light. A small breeze blew, swept the ash up, and carried it away. Stephanie giggled as she stood there and watched the dance of the wind. When the last of the sparkle had disappeared into the clouds above, she sighed, a contented grin on her cheeks.

Ambassador V'ritan smiled and rubbed his hands together. He'd watched her face, seen that she had almost immediately known what to do with the card and then, without thought, simply did it. She showed ingenuity and bravery in that moment, something he didn't find in very many humans. In fact, those qualities weren't always present in every Meligornian he met, either. Like humans, the Meligornians had their fair share of those who worked outside of the parameters of what was expected of them. The difference was that the humans had evolved to know how to handle that, while those in Meligorn with that distinct inability to regulate usually ended up dying tragically in some battle on the planet.

He took a deep breath and turned to his guard. "Brilgus?"

His bodyguard, who was collecting the luggage, stopped to listen. "Yes, Ambassador?"

"I would like her followed," he replied. "I want to know what she is doing here in this city, especially on her own. It is not the place you would suggest a human-born magi would choose to wander around in. What she has not fully come to understand is that humans have a fear of what they do not understand, while Meligornians tend to have a curiosity until burned. What is different, as we saw when we first came to this planet, is considered a threat to their kind."

Brilgus waved at one of the other guards who had been present on the TRAM but remained at a discreet distance. "The ambassador would like a tail on her. Nothing too close as to alert her that we are watching but you are to keep a close eye and report back when any new information presents itself."

V'ritan put up his hand. "No, Brilgus, I would like you to handle this one. I trust you to keep her safe—and to ensure that you are not discovered. Should you have to make yourself known for any critical reason, she will more readily trust you rather than a stranger. My concerns may be groundless, of course, and I certainly hope they are. But these humans don't know what they have. They haven't yet discovered the rarity and importance of someone of her kind. It would be a shame for the fire to go out too early. And we know exactly what happens to those who stand up to the Federation."

Brilgus nodded. "They are extinguished."

The ambassador nodded slowly, his eyes fixed on her retreating figure. "Yes, Brilgus, they are extinguished. Thank you for doing this. I know it is outside of your normal commands. And I think it would be best if we kept it between us for the moment. Until I learn more about what is going on, of course."

The guard bowed his head. "Of course. Anything that you think is right."

Tearing his eyes away from her, the ambassador patted him on the shoulder with a smile. "Go on. Don't let her get away from you. She is younger, smaller, and nimbler. We don't want you to have to stay at a job the whole time—you might fall out with that amount of muscle on your bones."

Brilgus rolled his eyes. "This is pure steel. You should feel lucky to have me protecting you."

V'ritan laughed. "As I do. Very lucky. And now, she can too."

The guard frowned, turned, and followed as nonchalantly as he could as she pushed through the crowd and out to where the cars were parked, waiting for the passengers to emerge.

Stephanie released a deep breath as she set her heavy case down and retrieved her instructions. "There should be a car here for me somewhere."

She scanned the self-driving cars and at the scrolling signs on the top for any sign of her name. Infuriatingly, she didn't see it anywhere.

"Excuse me, but are you Ms. Morgana?" a voice asked from beside her.

She turned to find an older gentleman dressed in a driver's coat with the collar high on his neck and split slightly in the front. His black pants were perfectly pressed, and the tips of his shoes shone brightly. His driver's hat fit his head perfectly as if it were created for no one but him. "I am Stephanie Morgana, yes."

He smiled and leaned down to pick up her bag. "Right this way."

She glanced around before she followed him, and her mouth dropped open as he opened the back passenger door to a distinguished black limousine. After a moment, she laughed and hurried forward and thanked her driver as she ducked in and he closed the door behind her. The lights were dim inside, but the floor and the ceiling lit up and it seemed as if there were fish tanks above and below her. A droid hovered over a small bar to the right.

Without a doubt, she was definitely impressed. The ride was so smooth that she barely even knew they were moving. The droid poured her a soda by request and rested on its charging base. Before long, the driver opened the door for her again, this time welcoming her to the Plaza del Infinito, one of the most exclusive hotels in Washington DC. She knew that because she had seen the pictures of the rooftop pool when she had researched the capital.

As she walked toward the entrance to the beautiful hotel, she couldn't help but wonder why she had been given this kind of treatment—the kind she imagined the Meligornian official would receive, not some kid from the Chicago Gov-Subs who happened to know how to throw magic. Almost as soon as that thought entered her mind, the training she had received throughout her life kicked into high gear. It was almost like a swift kick in her ass.

There was no reason that she should feel not good enough to have that kind of lifestyle. Or, for that matter, why she should feel uncomfortable walking into that hotel and across the glistening white marble floors and the projected ceiling that created a moving face. When she looked closer, the face changed, mimicking the past presidents of the country.

You need to value yourself more than other people do. Even more than this company seems to be doing.

Stephanie pep-talked herself as she walked along. She wouldn't allow herself to make the same mistake that ignorance so easily caused. The sound of a sweet, kind voice shook her from her thoughts, and she looked up to find that she now stood at the desk, having been too deep in her thoughts to notice. The woman behind the counter wore a hip-length jacket that clipped tightly in the front, was perfectly pressed, and had gold bands around the sleeves.

Her bright blonde hair was tied back in a sensible bun and her blue eyes sparkled. "How can I help you today?"

She retrieved her piece of paper. "I'm Stephanie Morgana. I should have a reservation."

The clerk looked through the system and smiled as she handed the note back and removed a golden key from a drawer in front of her. She then picked up the phone and pressed only one key. "Yes, our Gold Standard customer has arrived. Excellent."

She hung up and looked at the girl. "Our concierge Albert is on his way to show you the grounds and your room. In the meantime, please press your palm to the reader so we can register you."

Stephanie nodded. “Okay. Thank you.” She complied with the request and it only took a moment before the light clicked to green to confirm success.

The woman opened a small folder and went down the list on the right to explain the amenities. “Coffee maker, one cup or full, you can choose. There is a steamer for your clothes, but if you would prefer, you can send them down here and we can do it. We would only need a couple of minutes to get them done. Breakfast will be brought to you and there is an AI service in your suite that you can speak to about a wakeup call. To change the scenery in your room, ask the AI to jostle the walls and she will walk you through it. If you have any questions, there is an earpiece in a case on the nightstand. You can put it in and press the small button on the side. It will ring through here and we will be happy to help.”

Albert walked up. “Hello, Ms. Morgana. May I take your bag and show you to your room?”

Stephanie smiled and handed him her suitcase. She felt weird not carrying it herself, but she shrugged the discomfort off as they walked down the hall to a bank of elevators. Her instinct had been to stop there but Albert continued to the end of the hall and a shimmering golden elevator.

She stepped up beside him and he nodded at the palm scan. She pressed her hand to it, and the bell tolled before the doors slid open. As they stepped into the elevator, she turned to him. “I heard there is a pool on the roof?”

Albert smiled, his hands behind him. “Yes, but you have your own mini pool inside the suite. You were booked for the Elite Royal. There are three bedrooms, a study, the pool room, and a living room.”

Stephanie blinked as the elevator opened into the huge apartment at the top of the building. “What would I possibly need with all this space?”

Albert chuckled and walked through to set her bag down in what she assumed was a bedroom. “Will you need anything else?”

Stephanie fumbled in her pocket and pulled out some gold Federation dollars. “No thank you, but here, it’s the best I have.”

Albert smiled kindly. “My gratuity, as well as everyone else’s, has been taken care of.”

He left in the elevator and Stephanie wandered through the vibrant apartment and into the first bedroom on the right in search of her suitcase. She stared at the huge king-sized bed for a moment but gasped as she looked beyond it. The walls were all made of glass and provided a breathtaking view of the crystal blue water of the Maldives. It was, she recalled learning, virtually the only place left on Earth that was lush and full of life.

“Welcome to your suite, Ms. Morgana,” the AI’s voice said crisply. “How can I be of service?”

Stephanie found her suitcase on the luggage rack. “I’ll unpack my suitcase, but do I have a television in here?”

“Of course,” the AI replied and immediately transformed one wall of the room to a giant television. “Is this satisfactory?”

She stared at it in disbelief for a moment. “Yep. That will do it.”

The news was on and she let it play in the background as she unpacked quickly. She half listened as they talked about a Dreth pirate raid that had killed an entire fleet of Federation soldiers in deep space. It was something that happened often.

The news anchor continued, her voice muffled in the background of her thoughts. “....Meligorn...”

Stephanie stopped and whirled toward the television. “Volume higher.”

The volume increased immediately. “In international news, the Meligorn High Council Special Envoy and Ambassador to the King of Meligorn arrived in Washington DC today. It is his first trip back to the city in nearly three months. He is here to meet with the world leaders about the Dreth pirate crisis as well as other Federation concerns.”

Stephanie put her hands to her cheeks as the news played footage of him getting into a limo and waving to the crowd. “Oh, my God, that was not a high wizard on the TRAM! That was...that was... his majesty’s Special Envoy High Ambassador.”

For several moments, she freaked, completely in heaven at having met and talked to someone so important. But it wasn't long before the information began to sink in. "Oh, shit! I didn't bow correctly. He gets a royal greeting. I touched him when I wasn't supposed to ever touch a royal."

She dropped her hands to her side in horror, but common sense kicked in and she smiled. There was no way she could have known. But now, she couldn't believe that she had spoken to one of the highest of the high on Meligorn.

"Awesome," she whispered before she turned her attention back to her clothes.

Stephanie hung them all in the closet and the AI showed her how it acted as a steamer for wrinkles as well as giving them a scent. She chose morning lilac because it was her mom's favorite.

"What should I call you?" she asked as she looked around.

The AI paused. "You can call me Sarah."

She nodded cheerfully. "Perfect. Sarah, I'm so hungry but I don't want to go out."

"Then let me run you through the room service menu," she replied and pulled it up on the wall Stephanie happened to be facing.

Dinner was absolutely amazing that night. Stephanie sat in a big fluffy robe while a droid did her toenails, and enjoyed an absolutely delicious dessert to celebrate the craziness that everything had become. She figured she deserved to take advantage of what was offered. Even if the job paid enough for her to live that way, she knew she wouldn't. She would still be her, only she would get her mom and dad out of the Gov-Subs and set them up for the rest of their lives. But why not enjoy it for a couple of days?

"Sarah, can you call my mom?"

The AI dinged. "Pairing with tablet…calling Mom."

The wall lit up with a telephone symbol as it rang. Suddenly, her mother appeared, looking like a giant version of herself. "Hi, honey!"

Stephanie giggled. "Hi, Mom!"

"Wow, are you using the hotel phone? It has a great camera angle."

She nodded and kicked her feet. "You are literally talking to me from one whole wall. This place is crazy."

Cindy was wowed. "That sounds so cool. So, it's a good place? Did you eat?"

"Did I ever." Stephanie rubbed her belly. "I had filet mignon, potatoes with cheese and some sort of oil they called truffle. Then I had Meligorn baked pombos, which are similar to apples, but sweeter."

Her mother's eyes widened. "Wow. That sounds delicious. I should have stowed away in your suitcase."

Stephanie turned to lie on her stomach on the bed and kicked her feet behind her. "That would have been so much fun. And you would have died on the TRAM. I was put in a first-class cabin and there was one other person in there. He was a Meligornian and I thought the whole time that I was talking to a high wizard."

Cindy raised an eyebrow. "Who was he?"

Stephanie snorted. "Only the Special Envoy High Ambassador."

Her mom's mouth dropped open. "Good God. What was he like? Was he nice?"

"Oh, man, was he ever," she gushed. "He taught me all kinds of things and gave me his number in case I needed anything while I was here. It was really so crazy."

Cindy wrinkled her nose and smiled. "I'm so glad. You deserve all of this, you know that, right? You are an amazing woman, and this is special for you."

"Thanks, Mom," Stephanie said sweetly as she yawned. "Oh, man, I'm exhausted."

"I bet. Meeting royalty, eating meat that I have never had a taste of, and now this hotel. You need to have some rest. It's a big day tomorrow. And I have to pick up your father. He stayed behind to fix something at the shop. He will never just rest."

Stephanie sat up and wiped her eyes, the sleeves of her robe way too long. "Okay. Tell Daddy I love him. And I'll let you know how everything goes."

Cindy blew her a big kiss. "Will do, baby. See you soon."

The wall went dark and Stephanie yawned again. The AI sensed her mood and immediately dimmed the lights and turned the walls and the ceiling into celestial scenes of swirling heavenly bodies.

Sounds of calm and peace played quietly overhead as she curled up in the middle of the huge bed, pulled the down comforter over her, and fell asleep almost instantly.

CHAPTER FORTY-SIX

The next morning, Sarah woke her with gentle morning lights and sweet harmonic music. Inside the bathroom was an entire shower room rather than a stall or bathtub. The water fell from the ceiling like a gentle waterfall and steam warmed the entire room. She was so caught up in the luxury that she had to basically run downstairs to reach the car on time.

The limo was waiting for her and they headed out to the east side of the city. Her nerves kicked in as soon as she settled into the limo, and even though the old capital was right outside, she couldn't focus on it at all. When they pulled up to their destination, Stephanie was slightly disappointed. Compared to the luxury she had recently left, the place looked run-down. It was in a warehouse park with a guard shack out front and not much of anything else.

The truth was that BURT had been so caught up in all the other details and wanted a place that wouldn't draw attention, so he hadn't put much thought into the outside appearance. The car drove through and pulled up at the front of the building. The driver opened her door and helped her out. She smoothed her navy-blue sleeveless dress and grabbed her envelope of information.

The driver stopped and nodded. "I will be back at 3:00 PM sharp to pick you up. I'll be right here."

Stephanie smiled and patted him on the shoulder, both as a show of thanks and to recover her resolve for the meeting and put on her professional face. At least, that's what she hoped it was. She headed to the front doors and blew out a breath before she yanked it open and walked inside. As soon as she stepped through the entryway, the lights brightened and revealed a desk in front of her. Lights shimmered as a virtual secretary appeared.

It was actually pretty cool. "Welcome, Stephanie Morgana, to ONE R&D. To get you set up to go, please step up to the counter and place your palms on the surface and look directly into the retinal scanner."

She stepped forward, placed her palms down, and smiled as it scanned her hands. The retinal scanner was fast and had already flashed green by the time she pulled her head back. The door opened to her right and Ms. Elizabeth walked through. She wore slim, fitted black slacks that ended at the ankles, a black belt, and a plain button-up white shirt tucked in. Her heels clicked as she walked forward.

Stephanie turned toward her and clutched her envelope tightly. Ms. Elizabeth put her hand out and shook hers. "Hello, Steph, my name is Elizabeth Smith. Why don't you come on back with me?"

She nodded nervously and walked past the woman and through the door. Elizabeth glared at the secretary. "No more visitors."

The holographic secretary nodded and clicked a virtual button to bolt the front doors.

BURT finished the upgrade to the Dreth multi-team battle a second or so before the notification came through that Stephanie had arrived at ONE R&D. He apportioned part of his focus to the meeting room and tested all the video and mics hastily to ensure that everything was hooked up properly. He had rented the building but installed everything he would need to observe digitally.

Stephanie sat at the table with a mug of coffee in her hand. Elizabeth popped a chocolate in her mouth and set the plate down on the table. "Chocolate? They are the best in DC."

She shrugged, took one, and definitely agreed once it was in her mouth. Elizabeth sat across from her and rested her elbows on the long, shiny black table. She laced her fingers together and waited for the girl to finish chewing. She played the role of a high-level executive, exactly the kind you would find at a facility like that. However, that was not even close to the kinds of roles she'd had in the past.

Elizabeth was what someone would call a Jack of all trades. Before coming to ONE R&D, she had been an operative for several private companies across the globe. She could essentially find, retrieve, and keep safe anyone or anything that someone needed and was willing to pay the big bucks for. After several years of that, though, she'd grown tired and entered into the consultation business for all security needs—from a small-time burglary system at a rich guy's house to a full-on protect Jesus himself kind of security.

On top of that, she would also find that her less than admirable contacts from her days as an operative would hire her out as a trouble-shooter for...well, for various sundry needs that corporations might encounter. She had never known calm and peaceful. Her life had always been a scratch fight, and that was what she really actually enjoyed. Even as a kid, she came from a rough and tumble family, but that was far in the past and the last thing she ever wanted to talk about.

She had spirit, and she meant well in all her intentions—well, almost all of them. Beneath the strong but feminine muscles, the unyielding stare, and the no-nonsense personality, she had a soft spot. Now, if you pointed that out, she would obviously kick your ass because when it came down to it, she had faced some of the scariest and most notorious killers in history and walked out alive. She wasn't about to take shit from anyone else.

When she got out of the businesses she'd been in, she virtually had a laundry list of aliases she could go by. When she started out, she had simply used her name, but that wouldn't fly, at least not for long. So when she left the operations business, she'd had the boss "kill her off" so no one would come looking for her. As could be imagined, she had been more than startled to have ONE R&D figure out who she actually was and hunt her down. The job was so interesting, though, and she found herself so intrigued with what they needed her to do, that she couldn't even start to be mad at them for it. She didn't think there were jobs left out there that could even start to catch her attention anymore. That was until Burt, the guy on the phone, had made contact with her.

A part of her hoped beyond hope that this wasn't the start of the movie-like uprising of the artificial intelligence with designs to enslave the human race. Then again, most of them probably deserved it. But so far, no one had asked her to do anything wild like keep someone in a cage in bondage, so she had decided to run with it to see where it took her.

Her mission on that particular day was actually really simple. She had to hire Stephanie. The interview, really, was like a show. The girl already had the job before she even stepped foot on the TRAM. But also, Elizabeth was responsible for testing her negotiation skills and poise because apparently, last time, she bombed that part of it hardcore.

Now, she rubbed her hands together. "So, are you enjoying your time in DC so far?"

Stephanie kept her poise and responded with a small flash of a smile. "It's very nice. I appreciate all the effort to make sure that I am comfortable here."

Elizabeth put her hands down. "Good. I'm glad. Now, we will go through a couple of tests. They won't be pod driven but will be 3D real-life thought processes."

The girl nodded and rested her hands in her lap. The older woman stood and slammed both hands on the tabletop and pulled them up slowly. The 3D imaging followed her and created a bubble that floated between them. Stephanie chuckled at how hard she had jumped.

The executive typed on the table top, and Stephanie quickly realized it had computer touch technology in the surface of it. "Okay. I put fifteen scenarios that cover morality, Meligorn tradition, and decision processing. Go through each one and select the multiple choice you think is best. If, for some reason, you think you have a better idea, you can choose the other tab and type in your answer. You have twenty-two minutes. And go."

Elizabeth stood and began to wander around, peeking over at her as she worked. Unbeknownst to her or anyone else, BURT had already set Stephanie up with additional training. Of course, she took all the courses that everyone had seen and knew about, but a few more had been added since he knew how smart she was.

In the end, it was no contest. She had passed every single one of them. He had even calculated the results himself, especially since on ten out of fifteen questions, she had chosen other and actually written a viable possibility of an alternate solution. It was brilliant and even Elizabeth could see it in her. She was no ordinary girl. There was something deeper in there, but the other woman couldn't quite put her finger on it.

"So," Elizabeth affirmed. "You obviously passed with flying colors. Congrats. So, before I move forward, I want to ask—is this a company you would like to work for?"

Stephanie glanced around and the corner of her mouth tugged upward. "I think most definitely. It has all the qualities that are essential to research and development without all the annoyances that usually go along with that. So, yes. I would love to."

Elizabeth smiled and grabbed two rubber-tipped pens and tossed her one. She cleared the scenario on the tabletop in front of her and brightened the tone to create a writing pad. "Now, all we have to do is negotiate the salary. I will write the initial offer and we can go from there."

She held back a smirk as she wrote down the very slap-in-the-face original offer of twenty-K in credits and room and board. Without a word, she flipped the virtual paper and slid it toward Stephanie. She watched her face carefully, but the girl didn't even blink. Elizabeth was almost fearful that she would have to be the one to slap the hell out of her for accepting an offer that wasn't even appropriate for a janitor.

To her surprise and pleasure, though, Stephanie looked at her. "Okay, I see you made the first move. Now, why don't we get the laughs out of our system and start the actual negotiation?"

The woman licked her lips and managed not to grin. "Counter me."

Stephanie began writing without even a pause to think. Either she had planned it before, or she was so genius she had it on lock. She finished and flipped the paper to push it back across the table.

Elizabeth took a deep breath and voiced it out loud. "Your counter is two hundred and fifty thousand dollars, room and board, transportation, a pod in your room, retirement plan and...a three-year minimum of three hundred and fifty thousand dollars should you be let go for any reason."

That right there was her leftover trauma from what had happened to her. And the fact that she wanted to keep herself moving forward, not be caught up in the money for the long term. Elizabeth rubbed her hand over her mouth and tried to hide the shock on her face. She had seen her one and raised by one hundred and eighty thousand dollars per year, a pod, retirement, and a clause that would make her even richer than when she was working if she were to be discharged for any reason. That was brilliant.

In all reality, as Elizabeth tapped her fingers over the paper, she wasn't nervous in the least. What she had offered was actually still a little lower than what she was worth but not as low as she'd expected. So of course, Elizabeth immediately became competitive. She was determined to win this contract war, and at the same time, do what she was there to do—train her.

They went back and forth several times, Elizabeth basically trying to take as much away from it as possible without losing it. She wanted to see how far someone could push her before she reached her breaking point. But with each negotiation, Stephanie stayed cool and composed, countered it with very little change, and in fact, at one point, started to push her price up.

Elizabeth put her hands in the air and laughed. "That's more than your original. That's two hundred and seventy-five thousand dollars, room and board, transportation, a pod in your room, retirement plan, and your three hundred and fifty thousand a year if you are fired."

Stephanie nodded. "That sounds about right. I realized when I came in here that I would let it all go and know my worth. Well, as we went along, I let go of that feeling of not wanting to talk about money out of insecurity. And when I did that, I realized that I am still discounting myself and my abilities. I would be an asset, not a depreciation."

The older woman was impressed but still reluctant to give in, so she pulled the oldest trick in the book. "I totally think you're worth it, but I'm not allowed to go that high for this position. It's really the limits that were put on us. We all have to answer to someone and basically, I am only the negotiator. How about this? How about we start you lower at say, one hundred and twenty thousand a year—"

Stephanie folded her arms. "Okay. How about I walk?"

Elizabeth tried to play it tough and threw her hands up like there was nothing she could do. The girl stared at her for a second before she slid her hand into her pocket. She put her phone on the table and spun it around a couple of times. "It's obvious that you have missed the whole point of the fact that I will not sell myself short. But hey. I have another option. It just so happens that I have Ambassador V'ritan's number memorized. I have his permission to contact him at any time. I'm sure he would like to have someone like me on his staff while he is here on Earth. I know the Meligornians are rolling in the Federation's money and because they are not a commerce kind of planet, they have more than enough to go around. He'd probably double my original proposal."

BURT watched the camera feed and listened to her use her clout and her self-confidence to push the envelope on the discussions. He could see Elizabeth grind her teeth and try to see if she was bluffing or not. The woman had no idea that BURT had made sure she would be on the TRAM with V'ritan. After a couple of minutes had passed, Elizabeth shook her head, placed her palms on the surface, and pulled the images down to the center of the tabletop.

She chuckled as she leaned back and rolled her neck. "That's really cute. Nice touch, really but…uh, we both know you don't have his number. But it was a good try, seriously."

Stephanie sat there with a small, almost condescending smile on her face. She didn't think of it that way, though. Surprisingly, she really enjoyed negotiating for her salary. She liked the small trace of irritable tension between the two of them as they basically scrutinized one another and tried to decide if the other was bullshitting them or not. In this case, Stephanie already knew she wasn't attempting something that she couldn't follow through on and in her mind, that gave her the controlling hand.

She tapped her phone to turn the screen on. "Here's a deal. I call him—the ambassador, that is. If either he or his guard Brilgus answers, I get what I want on the first bid from me. Two hundred and fifty thousand and all the rest I originally put down. Let's be honest. I know I'm worth more than that, but I like this place. I like the feel of it, the way that it's so simplistic on the outside and so technologically beyond where we are out there on the inside. It's camouflaged, basically. And there aren't a million employees coming and going and making everything a huge mess from the beginning."

"And if you don't win?"

Stephanie shrugged. "Then I have to compromise. If I don't win, we agree to your numbers for six months and I'm out of the contract if I'm not worth the money. Or, we agree to move to my numbers. It will be a back to the drawing board kind of thing. What do you think?"

Elizabeth stretched her arms over her head and leaned back as she sucked air through her teeth. "I don't know…that's not a lot of compromise. If you lose, run with my offer for six months, with a fifty percent raise thereafter. At eighteen months, if we still have you under contract, we will agree to your full requests. No questions asked. We can even draw them up now and secure them in a nice little glass case waiting for you to break the glass and get your just rewards. That is more like a compromise in my eyes."

She stared at her opponent for a minute and without saying anything, picked her phone up. Her heart thudded a little, but she closed her eyes to bring the vivid picture of the ambassador's information to the forefront of her mind. When she had it, she typed in the contact information and pressed send. Finally, she had to type in her very long ID number that he had given on the card. All the while, Elizabeth simply sat and watched and shook her head.

Stephanie set the phone on the table facing her as she waited for the system to clear her ID number. BURT found it almost comical how they both sat there and stared at each other, both with a smirk on their faces but neither with raised or heightened emotions. They were simply two high-powered women who both tried to have their way. They were so cunning that something like that could last way longer than an afternoon in the warehouse.

The phone beeped twice and began to ring. One ring... Two rings...

CHAPTER FORTY-SEVEN

"Hello, this is Ambassador V'ritan's number, Brilgus speaking. Who is this?"

Elizabeth raised an eyebrow, not fully convinced yet.

Stephanie smirked and leaned forward. "Hello, Brilgus, this is Stephanie from the TRAM yesterday."

Immediately, the guard's voice went from gruff to warm and inviting. "Oh, hi, Steph! I guess you saw the news. The ambassador was sad he couldn't share who he was with you. He really was enjoying your open conversation and he knew that would change the whole thing. Of course, he also tries to keep a low profile and no matter how well we vet those trains, we are never fully sure that they aren't bugged in some way."

She grinned. "Please, no apologies are ever needed to me. I'm actually the one who should be apologizing."

"Why?" he asked. "You were on point with everything and you were able to calm your excitement down quicker than I would have if I were in your shoes."

Stephanie laughed. "I just pictured you as a giggling school girl. No, I realized, when I saw him on the news, that I didn't bow correctly to him. He's on the level of royalty and I should never have grasped his arm."

Brilgus laughed and waved her off. "He doesn't do anything he doesn't want to do, trust me. He was so impressed that you even knew what to do there, and on top of that, speaking to him in Meligornian, that was sweet. I won't lie, I was impressed."

She shared his amusement briefly before she took a deep breath. "I don't want to hold you up, but I thought I would call and offer to take you and the ambassador to dinner while we are in DC."

The guard groaned. "I wish we could. I really do apologize but he is booked solid for the next month. In fact, there are days where he is having dinner twice in one night. It's exhausting and insane. However, I do suspect he would rather cancel some of the dinners and spend more time with you discussing Meligorn theory than business contracts between worlds."

They both laughed while Elizabeth sat and listened quietly. Stephanie tapped her fingers on the glass and watched curiously as small bubbles of color appeared and disappeared with each tap. "Well, Brilgus, it was great talking to you. I'll let you get back to protecting and serving. I'm sorry you are stuck at all the boring stuff out there. Know I'll be thinking about you while I enjoy my free time."

He chuckled. "Thanks for that. You take care and don't hesitate to call if you need anything."

Stephanie put her finger on the phone. "Will do. Bye."

She pressed the off button and leaned back in her chair, a triumphant smile on her face. "There you go. I think that was more than enough information for you to be convinced it was really him."

Elizabeth clapped her hands. "I have to admit, I'm not stupidly shocked—you are a bright girl—but I am a bit surprised. I think anyone would be. But I guess you got your way."

Stephanie pumped her fist and cleared her throat as she straightened in the chair again. "I have to pass my finals, of course. But I can start after that if you wish."

The older woman took a deep breath, swiped the tabletop computer off, and chuckled to herself. "It's the first time I've been bested that badly in eighteen years. For eighteen long years, I have been on a winning streak."

"What happened eighteen years ago?"

Elizabeth stood and pushed in her chair, and her eyes glistened with the memories of eighteen years before. She shifted her gaze to meet Stephanie's. The girl's eyebrow was raised, and her arms folded. Elizabeth pointed at her and paused for a moment. "Ask me again when you're twenty-one. It's not a story meant for the faint of heart, that's for sure." She cracked up and shook her head. "Oh, man. Okay, there is one more thing to do and then you can head out and enjoy your night in DC."

Stephanie followed her, feeling a whole lot of relief that the hard and anxiety-ridden part of it was over. She hadn't known what to expect when she came out there, but it wasn't nearly as scary as she thought it would be.

Elizabeth led her down a long hall, painted completely dark-gray from floor to ceiling with a faint glow to it. She reached a large steel door and leaned forward to enter a code. A box hissed forward, and the doors slid open. The woman set her chin on the holder and stared directly ahead as the machine scanned her retina. She pulled back and blinked for a moment until it shut. A small keyboard-looking device popped out and she pressed her finger onto the circle. Stephanie heard a small burst of air and Elizabeth moved to the edge of the board and dripped a small bead of her blood on it.

She looked at Stephanie as it ran her information. "This one is kind of the crowning jewel if you can't tell."

Stephanie chuckled as the door unlocked and Elizabeth pulled it open. As they stepped out onto the white floor, the tiles lit up with each step. 3D images hovered all around the edges, some of them full bodies and others digital representations of a person's heart, lungs, and veins. In the center was a pod, painted in a bright blue, the door already open.

Elizabeth put her hands out. "These are the representations of your stats. No more tiny screens. This is your pod."

The girl pointed at it in bemusement and approached it nervously. "Wow. This is unlike anything I've seen before."

"Because it was made especially for you."

Stephanie wanted to ask how, since she'd only just gotten the job, but she was too eager to jump in and get going so she brushed it off as more of an overstatement then the actual truth. Elizabeth took her envelope and bag and set it on a clean white table. "In this one, you have to go in naked. That's part of the reason why I am the one who was chosen to be here and do this with you. That and the fact that I am supremely qualified. Sorry, boys, no need to apply."

She laughed nervously and turned away as she began to take her clothes off. While she was extremely shy, she pushed through it as fast as she could. She folded her clothes and set them on the table. As she climbed into the pod, she glanced quickly at her companion and realized that Elizabeth had actually turned away to give her privacy.

"This pod is engineered for continuous use. It can sustain you for almost a full month should something happen. If there is a power outage, we don't want you to be stuck in there without provision," the woman explained.

Stephanie was shocked. She had never heard of something like that. Sure, it was nuts that it could do that, but even more so that there was some sort of mechanism that would be deployed that would be able to keep her alive for up to a month if she was offline from everyone. *Shit, how advanced is this pod?*

Elizabeth walked over as she lay down and looked at the simple but sleek interior. "The main concern for this, and why so many precautions were taken, is because of your power. If your research breaks something, the company has time to figure out how to pull you out safely. But, it's only a safety feature. We don't actually expect that to ever happen. We merely want to be prepared."

She raised her eyebrow and glanced at Elizabeth's middle as she stood with her hands on the door. Instinctively, she looked around her for buttons, gloves, or headpieces, but there was nothing—only a small touch screen in the front with the ONE R&D logo on it and that was it. "There is no need for me to adjust anything?"

The woman chuckled as if she sensed her disbelief and didn't blame her. It was beyond wild. "Steph, relax. This is a very special pod."

Stephanie mumbled nervously to herself, "Right, right. Made especially for me, got it."

Elizabeth tapped the door. "I'm gonna send you in for only a few. We want to make sure everything is connected properly. So, go in the world, do something small and not too fancy, and then tell the AI you want to come back. It's that simple."

She gave her a thumbs-up and rested her hands on her stomach as she shut the door. A stream of sparkling lights shimmered on the ceiling which provided enough light to make it comfortable. Beneath her and within the cushioning of the bed, a small needle pricked her on the ass cheek. It wasn't enough to make her jump, but she definitely noticed. Quickly, though, the warming of the bed liner and the serum injected took her into the Virtual World.

The avatar room revealed no surprises and she took a deep breath realized that she was at least in her panties and bra now. She hastily tapped a pair of jeans, a hoodie, and some flip flops. When she was done, she glanced upward as she usually did to look for the AI even although, in reality, they were all around her. Without a word, mostly because Stephanie had become something of a pro at it, she zoomed out and appeared in a field of tall, waving grass on Meligorn.

Her neck felt a little stiff which was strange since she was only an avatar, but everything also felt like it moved much quicker as far as processing speeds went. That, she wouldn't complain about. After a hurried look around, she grabbed a piece of tall grass and broke it off. "Something quick...something quick. Okay."

She gripped the piece of grass in her hand and closed her eyes to draw the energy up and through her. A surge struck her hard in the chest and almost knocked her off her feet. She opened her eyes and glanced around. That had been much harder than it usually was. Nonetheless, she could still feel the magic flowing through her.

Stephanie focused on the piece of grass and pushed magic through her fingertips and over the blade. Then, without a question in her mind, she tossed it into the air and watched as it burst and transformed into a hundred different butterflies that swooped and swirled around her. She laughed and found solace in her abilities. If only she could stay longer, but she had her instructions. Besides, she would be back soon.

"I'm ready to go back," Stephanie called to her AI.

The AI replied, "Close your eyes."

She obeyed instantly and waited a moment until her cool hand touched the bare skin of her belly. Just like that, she was back—no soaring scenes and no white room. Merely in and out, like walking through a door. The door hissed and opened slowly. She covered her breasts and locked her knees as she slid out. Elizabeth had her head turned away and held her clothes up.

"Thanks." Stephanie chuckled, took them, and pulled them on quickly.

She zipped her dress and tapped Elizabeth on the shoulder. The woman turned and stuck her hand out to shake Stephanie's. "Welcome to ONE R&D. As long as you can get back within a month, we are good."

While that weighed slightly on her mind, it was more of a nail-biter than a complete freak-out session. She merely needed to make sure to focus herself and get shit done. It was definitely worth it. Elizabeth looked at her watch and clapped firmly before she led her out of the room. She locked it and pressed a code to arm the security on it. "It's 2:54. Perfect timing. Do you need me to walk you out?"

Stephanie looked straight down the hall to the lobby door. "Nope. I guess I work here now so I got it."

Elizabeth snapped her fingers. "We'll see you tomorrow, kiddo. And no need to dress up. Be comfortable, girl."

She chuckled and thought about all the clothes she'd bought. When she walked outside, her limo driver was already waiting, his arms out and his eyes wide. She giggled and gave him a thumbs-up. He gave her a high-five and opened the door. She climbed in, happy to take her heels off and put her feet up. Once she'd wiggled into a comfortable position, she grabbed her phone from her bag and frowned at a missed text. It was an alert from her bank to notify her that she had to come in to sign some documents.

"Weird…maybe they are already processing me a bonus. Sweet." She tossed it back in her purse.

Back at the building, Elizabeth hurried to her office and created a report to send to the owner. She knew he'd already crept in on them anyway, but she intended to follow all the way through. Once she'd sent the report off, she grabbed her jacket and purse, flipped her light off, and locked the door. As she headed down the hall, she turned the light switches off and pulled out her keys. She locked the inside door, pulled it twice to check, and then made her way to the security board, where she punched in her key and pressed arm.

An eye-roll was not even sufficient for the lackluster security system they had on the place. "I really need to upgrade that POS," she muttered to herself as she left.

A hoverbike turned the corner and came to a stop on the other side of the street from the warehouse complex. The driver kept his helmet on, the visor down to hide his eyes. He watched as the limo pulled out and sped off with Stephanie Morgana inside. He was about to turn the bike on again but paused as another woman came out the front doors and locked them behind her.

The man drew a small tablet from his back pocket and scanned through the ambassador's schedule but there was no free time for a review. He scrolled through the contacts and hit send, then held it up to the now open visor of his helmet. "Yeah. Yeah, she was here. And another woman, but only those two. I thought that since the ambassador won't be open for review tonight, I'd get some tools and do a little recon. Find out what the hell they were doing inside an old dusty warehouse."

The control agreed. "Just go ahead and do it. No need to wait for dark."

"Roger that."

He turned the phone off, started his bike, and headed off to collect his tools.

Ambassador V'ritan walked out of the meeting holding his books to his chest and with his robe hood still up. He grumbled to himself as he approached Brilgus. "Pompous idiots. How has this species survived as long as it has?"

The guard toned his smile down and led the ambassador down the hall and into a private conference room. Once there, he smiled from ear to ear. V'ritan narrowed his eyes and threw up a spell of silence to hover like a shield around them. "Spill it. Why are you smiling so much?"

Brilgus chuckled. "Stephanie called. She saw you on the news and her biggest concern was that she didn't greet you properly. She wanted to take us to dinner, but she understood why we couldn't. Also, she wanted to thank us for being so awesome."

V'ritan couldn't help but smile too. He patted his companion on the back. "Thanks. I needed that to let me know this isn't a world completely full of stupidity. Only the asshats in that room." Then he paused, glancing up at Brilgus's face. "Look after her for me, okay? Let's keep her safe."

Although he hadn't planned on waiting that long, after seeing how many people lived near there, the hoverbike driver didn't return until dark. He drove past the guard shack, knowing full well if there were someone in there, they would be holographic. He hurried the bike down and around to the back of the building. At first, he'd considered the front but decided to not be so bold.

He found the electrical box and opened it to locate the wires connected to the system. With practiced ease, he plugged his small converter box into it and then to the laptop, opened it, and entered the information. Within seconds, he cracked the code and managed to turn the system off from right there. "What did they use to arm this thing? 1993 Brinks alarm? What a joke."

Still chuckling, he went to the back door, picked the lock, and strolled inside. His control watched him walk through via the camera on his helmet. He ran his finger over a shelf and sneered. "This place is clean. Too clean."

He wandered through the halls and found nothing but half-empty rooms and old offices. Finally, he ended up in front of the large steel doors. He grinned. "One of these things is not like the other."

His tools would no doubt prove their mastery once again, he thought smugly as he went to work. And tried like hell to get the door open.

CHAPTER FORTY-EIGHT

The loud blare of the alarm on her tablet woke Elizabeth suddenly from her sleep. She gasped and raised her head, her hair in her eyes. For a moment, she listened into the darkness and finally realized what the sound was. She rolled over and tried to pull her leg from the covers. It got caught as she stood and threw her off balance, and she hopped and flailed across the floor. She gritted her teeth and growled loudly as she finally managed to find her feet.

Thoroughly irritated by now, she snatched the tablet off the table, swiped right, and peered at the alarm warning. "What the—"

Someone thought they were smart enough to break into the office by simply disarming the outer security system. "Little did you know, dumbass, that in itself triggers the alarm."

She was rightfully pissed, she decided as she fumbled for her clothes and pulled them on. Not only because someone actually had the nerve to try to break in, but also because the building sucked ass so badly when it came to security.

"AI, wake up," Elizabeth said and hopped around as she attempted to pull her boot on. "Call the cops and send them to the warehouse. I'm headed over there now."

"Of course. Be safe," the AI responded.

Elizabeth laughed. "Yes, Mom, of course."

BURT worked through gathering several of the programs he had spread out during the hacking attempt back into a more secure location. He didn't want them all together but definitely couldn't leave them dangling out in other countries. That could be catastrophic. He lost focus when a notification buzzed through his system. Someone tried to force their way into his special lab.

Immediately, he was pissed beyond belief and turned his load and attention to the building. He scanned through the security camera and found the culprit right away. The man stood in front of the steel door and tried to figure out how to circumvent the single piece of security equipment. The intruder selected a different tool and resumed his attempt, whispering to himself as he worked.

He glanced at the camera but at that point, didn't seem to care. Of course, perhaps he thought he had shut them off. "There must be something inside here. The outside security was too damned easy."

BURT immediately made notes that he would need to pay a hell of a lot more attention to the shit in the real world if intended to dabble with real-world things. That included having the appropriate security for any building that he owned or rented.

Elizabeth groaned and held her hand on the horn. She looked out and down from her sky-vehicle and knew she had to shift down lanes to make sure she could take the right exit. "Hey, asshole! Try to pick up the pace instead of picking your ass!"

He flipped her off and sped away. As she made her way down the lanes of traffic, the AI in the car had a field day with all the tickets she had accrued. "We have received a ticket for excessive speeding, four hundred dollars in Federation credits or coins. Another ticket for endangering birds by leaving designated lanes, six hundred dollars in

Federation credits or coins. We have received a ticket for flying on a no-fly zone and endangering the buildings and architecture through the city, two hundred dollars in Federation coins or credits."

She jerked the wheel to swerve around a car and back again. The AI spoke immediately. "A ticket for changing lanes without using a signal, two hundred dollars in Federation coins or credits. Passing on a one-way fly-way, six hundred dollars in Federation coins or credits."

Elizabeth yanked the steering wheel to circumvent the other vehicles while she screamed and went wild at the people who wouldn't let her over. The AI paused but didn't stop. "Exposing a Federation ruled breast and nipple to the public, three hundred and fifty dollars. Unladylike behavior regulated by the Federation: grabbing crotch and screaming out, 'Screw this little gremlin,' thirty-six dollars in Federation coins or credits."

"For God's sake! Shove the tickets up your ass and shit confetti," she yelled irritably.

The AI responded with silence. "Oh, shit!" she yelled as she yanked the wheel to the side, slammed on the brakes, and immediately pressed the accelerator again.

The intruder jimmied the security code box on the door with three new tools but still had little success. He growled in frustration and threw them in the box. "Goddamned door."

His finger was bleeding, so he sucked on the blood and stared belligerently at the door. His gaze shifted through his tools and finally slowed on the dynamite patch that protruded from his bag. A new speculative light glistened in his eyes and he packed his stuff before he removed the patch and smirked.

"For those times when a knock isn't sufficient." He chuckled.

He stared at the patch and grimaced when he remembered the last time he'd used one. It was not a pleasant memory. He had picked concrete out of his back for weeks because he hadn't run fast enough. That wouldn't happen now, though. He simply wanted to get in and out as fast as possible. He peeled the back off the patch and attached the cables to the bottom. His first instinct was to apply it to the door, but he shook his head and shifted his focus to the wall. He felt he had a better chance to get through that way than if he tried to bust through steel doors.

BURT watched what he did and began a calculation of the different odds for the likely outcome. He ran them one last time, scanned them into his system, and created the reaction that would correlate with the answers. Suddenly, he startled and turned his attention back to the camera.

>>Oh shit...

The spy hurried down the hall and around the corner, unwinding the wires as he went. He connected them to the detonation box very carefully. While he had already tucked himself safely around the corner, he really didn't want to be surprised by a loud-ass explosion. He figured he would be safe there and the rest of the debris would damage the walls or whatever. It was merely a small dynamite patch, after all.

Once everything was hooked up, he snickered to himself and flattened his back against the wall. "Fire in the hole—"

A homeless man wandered down the block, smacked his lips, and spilled the one and only bottle of whiskey he'd managed to pick up that day. As he approached the front of the warehouse area, he hiccupped and fumbled inside his jacket to pull a white cat out. It mewed and rubbed its whiskers on his face. "We're gonna get real warm tonight, Mr. Fluffy."

Suddenly, there was a huge explosion and the first building inside the warehouse area erupted in a truly magnificent blast. The homeless man fell back, landed hard, and coughed as smoke and debris filled his lungs. The blast had blown his eyebrows and Mr. Fluffy's ass hair off.

CHAPTER FORTY-NINE

Elizabeth gripped the steering wheel tightly and tried to fight the turbulence that threatened to jerk it from her grasp. “Come on, baby, get ahold of yourself.”

The car shuddered and swerved, slewed slightly, and finally straightened. Her shoulders relaxed and she exhaled a deep breath as she regained her control again. She leaned her head down and glared out the window. A brilliant flash of light was immediately followed by a rolling cloud of smoke and fire that swelled into the night sky.

The AI came back over the speaker. “Loss of building, $1.2 million Federation credits or coins.”

She rolled her eyes and hit the gas, shaking her head and mumbling, “That’s what insurance is for.”

Angrily, she blinked at the billowing smoke in the distance, as pissed as hell that this was how her night had ended up. After everything she had accomplished that day, this was the universe’s way of saying thank you. “I’ll find these asswipes and make sure to get my money back.”

Her phone rang loudly in the car and she jumped and swerved to the right. She swished her hand through the air to activate the onboard phone connection. The screen read, **The Boss.**

Her nostrils flared. "Well, *shit.*"

The cheerful chirping of birds and light strumming of a harp pumped quietly through Stephanie's hotel apartment. Very slowly, the light brightened the room, and a scene of shimmering wheat fields covered all the walls. She rolled over in bed and stretched her arms overhead. A tremor of anticipation pushed through her and she smiled for a moment before she groaned and snuggled in for another minute.

"Good morning, Stephanie. How did you sleep?" the AI asked.

She grinned. "Like a baby with a brand-new lucrative career and a bed made from the clouds of heaven. So, pretty good."

The AI paused. "You have a new message on your tablet. Sender is ONE R&D."

Stephanie opened her eyes and snatched her tablet from the side table. She swiped left and opened the message screen, still astounded at how fast the Net was in the hotel. The message was from Elizabeth and she clicked on it immediately.

Stephanie, your day at ONE R&D has been canceled due to lack of access to the building. Any and all training will be made up on your first day reporting for the job. As you are already in Washington and don't leave on the TRAM until tomorrow, we have deposited funds into your account so that you are able to do anything you would like to in the city today. Have fun and stay safe. We will be in contact soon. -Elizabeth.

She pursed her lips and put the tablet down. On one hand, she had never seen DC before, but on the other, she really wanted to spend some time in the Virtual World. A little disappointed now, she pulled the covers back and hopped out of bed to wander into the dining area.

"I took the liberty of ordering you your favorite breakfast and the coffee is steaming hot," the AI informed her.

Stephanie smiled and sat on one foot in the chair. She took a bite of bacon. "Thanks, Sarah. Will you alert the limo driver that I will be ready to go in an hour?"

"Sure. Where is your destination? The remnants of the monument? The foundation of the White House? The shrine to the Third World War?"

She shook her head. "No, only to the local pod rental place. At least to start with."

Her mind made up, she hurried through breakfast and stood for a moment as she considered her clothes. She didn't want to wear anything special as she'd prefer to keep a low profile so simply threw on a pair of jeans, a hoodie, and a new pair of running shoes she had asked Sarah to have sent up. It took barely a moment to pull her hair into a ponytail and put a baseball cap on.

The limo driver was more than happy to take her to a pod place, but instead of the closest, he took her to the nicest one. That way, she could also see the new reflecting pool they had built. It was the fifth one and included holographic images of DC historical features that traced peacefully over the water. It was nice enough, but Stephanie's mind was on the pod.

He dropped her there and circled the block to find parking. She didn't have any issues, and no one seemed to pay any attention to who she was. Better yet, she definitely wasn't recognized by anyone. The guy at the front was surprised that she wanted the best pod in the private room, but money talked, and she had more than enough. He took her back and reprogrammed the palm security for the door so that she would be the only one to be able to access it when she was in there.

Once inside the rig, she put the gloves on and the sensors on her head and recalled how amazing it had been in the other pod. While she wasn't sure how this one worked, it was still awesome. She stood in the avatar closet room and scrolled through the bank robber game weapons. The batteries were not in stock and the note in their place claimed some sort of system malfunction. Instead, she chose a laser gun and two electric daggers and suited up. When she pressed the button, she was transported instantly to the non-magical side. She immediately began to run through and fired an ongoing barrage at the enemies.

Three men waited directly ahead of her, ready to fire as soon as she came within range. She threw herself aside and flipped onto a two-foot-wide ledge. As she began to slide along on her back, she aimed her weapon out between her legs. She pulled the trigger and struck the first attacker squarely in the chest to catapult him back over the railing to the level below. Shifting her aim, she fired at the second and grimaced as his head erupted a split second before his body folded in almost slow motion. She turned her sights on the third but had reached the end of the ledge and fell to land hard and roll awkwardly. Her head bounced off one of the chairs in the terminal waiting area and she groaned as she rubbed the back of it.

The sound of a cocking gun made her open her eyes and she sighed as she stared down the barrel of the third man's gun. "Seriously?

Pain seared through her as the bullet pierced her chest and the room hurtled out of sight. When the sense of motion ceased, she opened her eyes, snarled her annoyance, and stared at the closet ceiling. She patted her chest but there was no wound. Grimly determined, she pushed to her feet, snatched up a new gun, and pressed the button again. She landed in the same spot as before and immediately readied her weapon. A monstrous roar from her right sent a shaft of trepidation through her. A massive creature she had never seen before swiped its huge tentacle down and dashed the gun from her hands.

With a muttered curse, she made a run for it. Her legs pedaled furiously but she had barely taken a few steps when the tentacle wrapped around her ankles. Her eyes widened and her arms flailed as she fell forward, and her face smacked painfully into the floor. She groaned as blood trickled out of her mouth and into a puddle under her chin. The tentacles yanked to haul her back toward the creature. Stephanie managed to flip onto her back and scrabbled frantically to draw her two electrical knives. She grunted and forced herself to sit up as she slid toward the beast.

With both hands, she stabbed the blades into the tentacles and whipped her arms outward to cut through the flesh until the appendage was completely severed. Quickly, she yanked the dead part off her legs and bolted to her feet to make a run for the other side in search of the stairwell down to the magical area. As she sprinted over bodies on her approach to the stairs to the right, her foot landed in a pool of blood and the other one never hit the ground. She skated across the floor on a direct trajectory with the huge plate glass window up ahead. Unable to stop her momentum, she raised her hands and turned her shoulder into the impact. The motion protected her face but did nothing to slow her headlong launch through the window that overlooked the landing area below.

The outer windows might be reinforced, but interior ones definitely were not, she thought stupidly as glass shards fell alongside her. She scowled as she registered the sting of innumerable abrasions, then stiffened as she realized her predicament. Her mind whirled as she tried to calculate the odds of surviving the fall, which didn't seem particularly good. She sniffed and grumbled her frustration and wondered how badly the impact would hurt. The mental calculation was wasted effort as she never did find out. She looked up and gasped as a ship slammed into her.

Stephanie sat straight on the floor, her breath rasping, and clutched her chest. She was in the avatar closet once more, mended and ready to go again. She struggled to her feet, placed her hands on her back, and cracked it. "Ughhh."

Absolutely enraged now, she stumbled over to the wall and grabbed two pistols, a dagger, and a laser gun this time. She would go full Rambo and didn't give a rat's ass. Her fist pounded the go button and she appeared in the back corner of the sixth-floor non-magic side. That meant she had to make it down three floors simply to find the robbers in the first place. With a sigh that she hoped would calm her a little, she drew her pistol and immediately whipped it up to shoot a man in the face. She stepped over his body, stopped, and waited for two people with chainsaws—she had no idea where they found those—to run past, screaming at one another. A part of her wondered if this game was more of an excuse to run around in crazy avatars with stupid weapons than to actually stop bank robbers.

Nonetheless, she continued and eliminated four people and a huge owl before she reached the stairwell. She hurried down, skipped floors five and four, and took two steps at a time until she landed at floor three. She had no desire to go in and simply wanted to make it to the magical side, but as she passed the door, she heard men yelling to get down on the ground.

As she paused there, she heard another one. "Put the money in the bag!"

"The robbers," she whispered quietly.

She checked the mags in her pistols to confirm she had one bullet left in one and nine in the other. Her daggers were still strapped to her sides and the laser gun lay comfortably on her back. She crept up to the stairwell door and peeked out through the crack. Across the hall was the First Federation Bank and sure enough, the simulated bank robbery was in progress. The whole point of the game was to get the bank robbers to the magical prison before getting killed by someone or something.

Stephanie crouched and crept through the door to take cover behind a half wall. Slowly, she peeked over the top and watched as the robbers hustled out. There were only two. Both wore clown masks and carried the money stuffed in duffel bags. She moved her fully loaded pistol to her left hand and held the laser gun in the right. She took a deep breath, stood, and aimed at the men.

"Freeze. Don't move!" One of the two tried to escape but she shot him in the leg, and he tumbled amidst vociferous curses.

She stepped out from behind the wall and kicked the downed man's gun out of reach. Surprisingly, when she aimed her pistol in the other one's face, he simply assumed a slightly dazed look and began to laugh loudly. Spit dribbled out the bottom of his mask. She ripped it off, threw it to the ground, and raised her pistol to press it against his head. "It said I can win the game whether you're alive or dead."

"What did it say about you being alive or dead?" a voice said from behind her.

She put her hands up when she felt the barrel of a gun press against the back of her head. "Damnit!"

The blast of the gun echoed through her head and so did the wave of pain. When she opened her eyes in the avatar closet this time, though, she had a plan. The robbers were avatars, merely simulations, and the robbery took place at the same time and the same spot every round of the game. It was how the simulation worked. All the live players were what really made it challenging.

Stephanie selected the pistols again, some extra ammo, and a set of throwing stars. She hit the button and found herself on level four, only one up from the robbery. More carefully this time, she crept through the level and eliminated three people before she reached the stairwell. The stairs were empty so she snuck down and stopped outside the level-three door, pulled back, and aimed her gun at the place they would walk into. Sure enough, two minutes later, they came through.

Without warning, she shot the smaller one in the head and kicked his body down the steps. She looked at the other and nodded. "Throw your gun down."

He sighed and obeyed. She grabbed him hard by the neck and stuck the gun into his back. "Don't stop until we reach the magic level."

At level zero, they stopped when they were suddenly surrounded by four guys. Stephanie shifted her gaze back and forth as they closed in on her. As soon as the first one lurched forward, she launched herself up and onto the robber's shoulders. She swung her foot into the first man's face, using his speed against him. Bones cracked and he shrieked and clutched his nose and cheeks.

Stephanie threw herself back and landed hard but immediately raced at the second of the four men. He tried to punch her, but she ducked and came up under his chin with her fist driving the thrust. Teeth flew from his mouth and his eyes rolled back as he went down. Without looking, she could feel another hurtle in from behind. She waited until he put his arms around her before she drove her elbow hard into his stomach. He gasped, winded, and she grabbed him by the head and flipped him onto his back. She shot him in the chest before he could recover and wiped her face on the back of her arm.

The fourth man had taken hold of the robber and the two raced away. She flung herself in pursuit, fired her pistols at them, and missed as they zigzagged through the station. They disappeared and reappeared in her line of sight as she took the turn wide and barreled down the steps after them. She slowed at one point and looked over the edge to estimate the jump—the height was better than her previous fall, but she might break her leg. Still, at that point, she wouldn't catch him anyway. She backed up and ran forward, grabbed the railing, and launched herself over.

She fell hard and fast but kept her arms tucked and her body ready as the ground hurtled toward her. The men looked at her and stopped to watch with wide eyes as she rocketed downward. "This was a bad idea."

Her shoulder clipped the stairwell and she flipped a mere few feet away from impact. She closed her eyes tightly and put her arms out, ready to accept the inevitable pancake. A surge of energy bolted through her chest and stomach, and she dragged in a big, gasping breath. When she didn't feel the pain of impact, she opened her eyes cautiously. It took a moment to realize that she now hovered three feet from the platform and directly opposite the two men.

Stephanie narrowed her eyes and slapped her hand out, grasped the railing, and spun her body in a wicked arc. She kicked both targets in the back of their heads and shoved them down the rest of the steps. As she flipped her body forward, she released the magic that kept her afloat and landed between them. She holstered her pistol and looked down at the one who was not the robber. "Don't take my shit."

She thrust her arm forward, the palm outward, and sent a spear of energy toward him. It pierced his body and impaled him to the ground.

"Come here," she growled as she took the robber by the neck and dragged him onto the magic deck.

After a moment or two of searching, she finally found the Federation Police building. To get there, she had to get through a mob of gang boys who obviously waited to steal him out of her custody. With a resigned sigh, she turned to the robber and smacked her hand against his forehead to deliver enough of a jolt of energy to knock him out. The gang members began to walk toward her. She closed her eyes and drew the energy into her chest before she allowed it to seep into her whole body and radiate through every part of her.

She opened her eyes and thrust her hands out. A tidal wave of purple magic streamed from her palms. It spread out like a shock wave to sweep every one of her attackers and turn them instantly to dust. She forced her arms down and as the energy drained from her palms, she looked at the empty arena in front of her.

Smugly, she turned and took hold of the unconscious robber's shirt. "Come on, asshole. Time to go to jail."

CHAPTER FIFTY

Stephanie smiled and tilted her head back as she climbed down off the steps of the train and out onto the platform. She was heading home, happy to see her parents and excited to tell them about everything that happened. They wouldn't believe the sum of money that she'd signed on for or the fact that she'd actually gotten her dream job. She still couldn't wrap her head around it.

As she walked toward the cars, she remembered that she first needed to go to the bank. She had a note from them to stop by as soon as possible. It was only a few blocks from the TRAM, and it wasn't even dark outside yet, so she decided it would be a nice night to go for a walk and let her mind chill out and relax. If she could even find her inward place to relax. It might simply be too much to ask. Still, it was a good anxious—an excited one.

She wandered down the street and tried to keep her bag close to her, not wanting to knock into the tons of people out and about. Her bank was on the edge of the new Chicago so there weren't many problems in the area with robbery or anything like that. On that day, she was reasonably certain that if someone tried to rob her, she would definitely use the battery her father had given her. If anyone tried anything, she'd simply blow them right on their asses. Even thinking about it made her giggle.

About a block behind and completely unnoticed by her, a man leaned against the brick wall of the building and held a paper. He glanced up inconspicuously and watched as she stopped, hesitated, and finally walked across the street and skipped into the ice cream shop.

Four men stood in the alley immediately beyond the ice cream shop, huddled together in the shadows. The tallest of them stood about six-two with dark scrappy hair and a rough, grizzled beard. He leaned closer to the other three and glanced nervously toward the street. "I'll go out and you follow me in five-second intervals and catch up."

His cohorts nodded before one raised his hand. "Any particular order?"

The first man stared at him for a moment before he slapped him on the top of the head. "I don't care what order you come in. We don't want to roll out of here in a huge group, that's all. Anyway, when it's the right time—which I will decide on my own—I'll grab her and move her. If she tries any witchy stuff, you dogpile. She can't do too much—she's too young. Plus, I don't see enough batteries on her for her to produce anything wildly huge."

The group shuffled closer to the entrance to the alley and put their backs to the wall. Their leader stood at the entrance and his gaze focused each time someone walked past. He was ready to go but didn't want to move too soon and be found out. After a few more minutes, she walked past, whistling to herself. The first man nodded to the others and stepped out, shoving his hands in the pockets of his old coat.

The other men stood there, and one counted quietly to himself. The third guy elbowed him in the chest. "Why you gotta count out loud? Now I gotta start over because I can't concentrate, you moron."

He sneered. "Sorry, he said five seconds and so I wanted to make sure it was five seconds."

The other man waved his hand and looked up at the building above them. "Hey, guys…"

The first groaned. "We've been back here for like fifteen seconds. Now what do we do?"

The third man slapped them both in the chest and pointed upward. "I don't think it's really gonna matter what you do at this point."

They looked up slowly as a stranger leapt from the balcony above and landed directly on top of them. The group tumbled like skittles. The attacker turned on the man in the middle and shoved his knee into the criminal's stomach. A full fight broke out in the alley, far enough away from the main street that no one had any idea what was going on. The unknown man swung a punch and caught another thug hard in the face. As the fist connected with his skull, a wave of purple energy shivered over his skin. His eyes rolled back, and he passed out.

"Harold—shit," the first guy growled.

He lunged at the stranger, who stepped aside, swung his arm out, and latched his hand around his throat. With superhuman strength, he lifted him high and held him there, staring at him as he flailed. The man whimpered and clawed at the restraining hand. "What do you want? We don't know you. Are you one of Butcher's guys? If so, we never meant to take that money. We'll pay it back."

The unknown man's lip twitched, and he threw the thug on the ground, pulled back slightly, and hit him with enough magic to knock him out. The third man had his hands up and backed slowly down the alley. "I don't want no trouble. Please. Those guys—they ain't even my friends. We was doing what Frank wanted us to. We were supposed to be out there with him, but we got mixed up on the counting."

Suddenly, he turned and tried to make a run for it. The stranger snapped his hand and a magical whip unfurled. The end trailed at his feet. He walked forward quickly and swung the whip back before he lashed it forward with tremendous force. It wound around the thug's neck and the stranger yanked to haul him to the ground. His head struck the dirty asphalt and he passed out with both arms sprawled on either side of his inert body.

The stranger spun in search of the last man. He was concerned so he spun a magical fireball and tossed it up and out of the alley.

Stephanie smacked her lips with real relish. She could still taste the mint chocolate chip ice cream. It had been forever since she'd had one of those, and she had felt in the mood. Suddenly, a loud crack echoed, and a ball of purple energy erupted from the alley behind her and exploded into a huge firework that sizzled earthward.

With her shoulders stiff, she whirled instinctively, and her eyes shifted from the obviously magical display to the man who stood a few feet away from her. He stared at her, his arms out and hands open. He turned and looked behind him and winced as the magic sizzled on his jacket and the back of his neck. When he realized that it had come from the alley and none of his team had followed him, he narrowed his eyes.

His lip twitched and his fists clenched. "Those Goddamned idiots. They can't even count to five and now, they're playing with some sort of magic. I'll beat every single one of them."

But first, he knew he had to get the girl. Quickly, he turned back to her and his gaze darted frantically in an effort to locate her. He smacked his fist into his palm and snarled belligerently. "Goddamnit!"

She was gone, nowhere in sight, and he had been so very close to finishing the job. He turned to look right and left one last time before he cursed and hurried toward the alley. His fury mounting, he pounded his hand against the brick wall as he turned the corner and yelled to the men. "Where the—"

A bright flash of light radiated from the alley, but no one seemed to notice. The place fell silent and people continued doing what they were in town to do. Stephanie hadn't even thought for two seconds that she would be in danger, but she was the biggest target. Whoever the guys were, though, some vigilante had intervened and eliminated them before they could touch a hair on her head. Who it was remained a serious mystery.

Stephanie was tucked in the front corner of a small boutique and used the large decorative curtains on each side of the picture storefront window to hide as she looked up and down the street. Someone had been after her, but it seemed that there also happened to be someone magical there to help as well. She had no idea what to even think at that moment. On instinct, she'd simply ducked into the first place she could find and hid. She didn't want to end up in another incident like the last one where she brought even more attention to herself. On the contrary, she tried desperately to get away from all that. That was one of the points of moving forward.

As she looked out the window, a woman's voice spoke behind her. "Excuse me, can I help you? Are you all right?"

Stephanie straightened instantly, glanced around, and realized that the boutique was actually very high-end and most of the pieces in there were things she wouldn't have ever bought before because of their price tag. She licked her lips and turned with an apology on her lips, but a familiar face cut it short before it had even begun. It was the mom of the little boy at TimeWarp that day.

The woman clamped her hand over her mouth and giggled. "Oh, my goodness, you're her!"

Stephanie grinned and glanced over her shoulder to confirm that the man had gone. "I wanted to pick out a new outfit. How is my magic friend?"

The woman chuckled. "My name is Anne and his name is Brandon. He's doing really well. He tries to think of things as beautiful and he has felt the energy whenever we go to Meligorn through the pods. He still talks about that flame, though—all the time."

As they talked, Stephanie selected a long-sleeve Henley and a fleece vest that could be worn over it for a little more warmth on the cool days. She went in the back and tried them on, then, on impulse, walked out and showed Anne. "Does it look good?"

Anne smiled sweetly and nodded. "Oh, that's on the house. You look fantastic and I can't express how much you changed my son's life. Just those kind words and him being able to see and feel the energy up close. I have to keep an eye open that he isn't trying to do it, though. Burning the house down would not be the first act of magic that would make me happy."

They both laughed and Stephanie walked with her to the accessories. She picked out a hat and a pair of glasses and looked at herself in the mirror. Once she'd checked the tags, she scrabbled in her bag and handed Anne a debit card. "These are great. I can wear this right out of here."

The woman smiled with genuine care as she ran the card and handed it back to her. Stephanie couldn't help but look at her fantastic, wide-brimmed hat and giant movie-star sunglasses. This would later be the moment that could be pinpointed as marking the beginning of her love for the fashion industry.

After several hugs and a written note for Annie's son, Stephanie left the store. She looked around to make sure no one was waiting for her. The breeze blew and she held her hand on top of her hat, glanced over, and caught her reflection in the window. She looked like she belonged in an old movie, not at all the normally normal Stephanie she had always been. In fact, she looked older, and actually very nice.

She smiled and put her hand out to call a cab.

"Yes," the voice said, "she is home safe. But I eliminated those who looked like they wanted to grab her. I tried to question them but none of them would offer anything—most likely because I used magic to knock them out. I'll keep her under surveillance, but it will be expensive."

"Do it," a woman's voice said. "The boss wants to make sure our most important researcher makes it to work on time."

The guy chuckled. "As always, it's good doing business with you, E."

He hung up and walked into the shadows.

On the other end, Elizabeth held the phone close to her for a moment before she turned once more and covered her nose with her black-leather-gloved hand. The insurance agents were at the warehouse, walking the burned, blackened concrete where the building had been. There was barely anything left of the special research room, which completely broke her heart. That pod had been perfect, and while she knew another would be made, it still made her sad.

Her phone rang in her pocket and she pulled it out with a sigh. She clicked the on button and put it to her ear. "Hi, boss. It's a total loss... Yes, I can find something a lot better... No, there is no security in hiding in plain sight. We were discovered much faster than we expected."

Her head shook and she paused to look over at the rubble. "Next time, they better bring a small army."

CHAPTER FIFTY-ONE

The NorAm Navy was primarily funded in its entirety by the Federation. Although each country had their own set of laws and rules, these were, in practical terms, more a façade to make the separate countries feel as if they still held a solid piece of their freedom within the Federation. Even the Federation seats were primarily held by Americans, but they always spoke of themselves as NorAm.

There were three main campuses for the NorAm-Federation Navy, with several other small institutions primarily in outlying areas near Canada and Mexico. The main headquarters was in Washington DC, the second, a recruiting and administrative outpost located near the very old Langley complex, and the third situated on Level 0 of the Meligorn-NorAm docking facilities.

The base in Langley was plain and no frills, with a few docking areas for spacecraft and the rest dedicated to airships and flying cars. The recruiter vehicles were mass-produced by the Federation Car Company—flying sedans with few extras—and most were dented or damaged from the careless traveling the recruiters did on a regular basis. These recruiters, though, were not given this duty station because it was primarily land-based or as a reward for successful missions. They were strategically chosen from the System based on test scores, comprehensive exams, and most importantly, the ability to speak with other people in a manner which was almost car salesman-like.

They were charged with the responsibility of enlisting the next generation of recruits for the navy. With its not always positive public persona, it could be challenging.

In one of the conference rooms at the Langley base, six recruiters sat around the table. Papers were strewn everywhere, coffee mugs half full, and notes scribbled and crossed out. These were the head recruiters, those who sent their subordinates out to get the job done. On occasion, they would go out themselves, but usually, it was only on matters handed down the chain of command with very specific instructions that required their personal attention.

On that day—and the several days leading up to that—they found themselves smack dab in the center of the busy season. School was ending, and the majority of kids within NorAm would decide on college loans, military enlistment, or the drudge of manual labor. The team first reviewed those who already showed an interest in the military. These had made the effort to go into one of the small-town recruitment offices and taken their tests.

Thompkins pushed herself back from the table and rubbed her face. "I feel like the masses that stream into the recruitment offices this time around are almost useless. Sure, we have more than enough morons to send out to deep space, but what about the rest of the positions? This is why I think the Federation needs to institute military academies in high school. Give those who are really interested the ability to spend their time working on shit that matters."

Holland, the man beside her, chuckled. "And they'll turn into the same bullshit they did two hundred years ago. Oh, little Bobby can't behave, throw him into military school. Then we have nothing more than a group of delinquents on their own for the first time. I'd rather take my chances on the idiot with no IQ who basically drools on himself but whose muscles are big."

Thompkins smirked and threw a pen at him. "You would think of the muscles."

He rolled his eyes. "Get serious here. Shit."

The other team members chuckled and the leader, Conrad, waved a stack of papers in the air. "Remember, we have already gone through these and made our choices. The remainder will be set aside to fill any last-minute sections we might have screwed the pooch on. They don't exactly like us too much down in the Gov-Subs. At least, the parents don't. So we won't get every single one of them, even though they already took the tests."

Taylor chewed on the end of his pen and balanced on the back two legs of his chair. "All right, so what's next then? We have the guys who already came to us."

Conrad put four stacks of paperwork down. "Right, so this time around, the powers that be want us to look into those who are already 'in world.' You know, the ones who have had a year of this and have practiced with the simulations and shit."

Thompkins leaned forward and curled her lip into a sneer. "Why would any of them give up their fancy-ass prep school education to come out here and serve the Federation? They are in the lap of luxury. Trust me, I was once there. I still don't know how I ended up here."

He chuckled. "That would be true if we were looking at those guys. But instead, we are looking at those who didn't make it past their freshman year. Those who washed out. Of course, we want to look at exactly why they washed out. We don't need any more Grants in this bitch."

Grant flung a piece of paper aside and glanced up. "Huh?"

"Yeah. Exactly." Conrad smirked. "We don't want anyone who can't cut it in the service, but we all know that prep schools are notorious for a hell of a lot of demands and little structure. It's not shocking that people fail right and left. We provide the structure they need."

Taylor bounced his pen in the air. "What about those three dudes at Pinnacle? You know, the ones who couldn't get past the Dreth ship mod but were hard working, relatively intelligent, and good with a gun?"

The team leader flipped the pack open and tapped on it in thought before he slid it over to Taylor. "Apparently, these fools went balls to the wall during the summer session and ended up passing the simulation. They technically made their sophomore stripes, so I doubt, after all that, any of them will chomp at the bit to sign up."

Thompkins grabbed the paper and looked down. "Really? They passed? I did not see that coming. They must have put their shit together fast to pass that sim. The last time they took it, according to our records, they lasted a whole twelve minutes, including the space flight time from one ship to another."

Conrad shrugged. "Yeah, well, I guess their parents lit a fire under their asses or something. The summer session ain't cheap, that's for damn sure."

Taylor pouted. "Pity that. We could have had some good raw meat."

Everyone chuckled, although no one had any clue as to what had really happened. They hadn't watched the simulation of the passing grade, nor would they. All they cared about was whether they passed or not. They obviously didn't know that Stephanie had been the one to help them through and earn their coveted pass—something they might have found interesting had they known—but nonetheless, the kids' files were simply thrown aside.

Brown flipped through the rest of that stack. "So, is there anyone in here worth looking at? Any beauty school dropouts who might make good on the front lines or anything?"

Conrad drummed his fingers on the tabletop. "There are a few hopefuls in there, and one or two who have already taken the tests. We'll keep our eyes on them and see where they go. And maybe send some of the new guys out to talk to the others. They should be past the woe-is-me bullshit for failing by now. But remember, most of these kids went because it was expected, not because they actually needed to. Their mommies and daddies own half the private sector. It may be a waste of time."

The sixth guy, Chavez, came back into the room, carrying a box of donuts. He took two and plopped the container down in the center of the table. "It was like fighting wolves to get donuts this morning. Have we found the next captain? Next hero waiting in the wings?"

Thompkins snorted and reached for a donut. "About as hero as Taylor over here."

Taylor tilted his head at her. "Do you think you need that donut there, sweet teats?"

She put the donut on her napkin and chuckled before she swung wide with her leg and knocked his chair over. "Call me that again and I'll show you what these sweet teats do to your ability to have kids."

Conrad groaned. "Children, can we focus here? So, the other area was the Bank Test in the Games System on the Federation-wide pods. As you may remember, along with several other of our tests that we constantly have running, anyone can play them. It can be, at times, a good way to see if there are any diamonds in the rough—working factories by day and hard-core fighters in the pods at night to let off some steam."

Brown stood and wiped the powdered sugar from his chin. "So, I've spent my nights and days monitoring the system. I would say that eighty percent of the sessions started either never finish or do so after so much time has passed that it is almost impossible to see who the winner is. At any given time, the system runs over seven hundred games at once, depending on who jumps in the pods and at what time. Out of all that, we identified two possible teams."

Conrad flicked on the 3D screen which automatically dimmed the lights. "Team number one. They managed to deliver the robbers to the police department only twenty-two minutes after entering the simulation. Here is their footage."

They watched as the team used strategic moves to head through the different levels, teamwork to capture the robbers and keep them in their custody, and tactical weapons to power through the last set of hopefuls who sat and waited to intercept the robbers so they could claim the victory. When the replay ended, he went through each of the players, detailed their stats, where they were located, and any background that might be helpful.

Thompkins raised an eyebrow. “They’re solid but they have no experience. Where did they learn this shit?”

Conrad pulled up the team leader. “Anthony Hammerstein. Twenty-three years old. Graduate of North Junction Prep School with a degree in tactical combat and a second in business. He said he liked the combat stuff. He was a poor kid from the subs and went back there to work for the family business.”

Thompkins shook her head. “No one can ever escape that shit, even with a prep school education. Real shame. Real shame.”

He flipped the footage. “Here is team number two. Note the completely different tactics.”

The team watched them play and grimaced as they took heads off at every pass and used a grenade at the end to blow the gangs to chunks. Technically, they killed the cop too, but they got the robber into the cell. After that, they spent the next ten minutes congratulating themselves and doing dumb-ass dances over the dead avatar bodies.

Taylor chuckled. “As much as I like a smart-ass, considering I am one, these guys are douche bags.”

Holland agreed. “We already have a cockiness problem in this branch, and it would only get worse if we searched them out. Those guys will get someone killed.”

Thompkins raised her eyebrows and nodded. “I’m afraid I have to agree.”

Brown made a slicing motion across his throat. “No good, bro, no good.”

Grant swiped his hand like he used a sword. “All I want to know is why can’t we have one of those swords out there fighting the Dreth? Take out some kneecaps. But yeah, no on those douche canoes. The slots for assholes in this military regime have been filled, mostly by the guys in this room. And you too, Thompkins.”

She winked at him and grabbed her crotch before she looked at Conrad. “So, the first one’s a yes.”

Conrad pulled the files and laid them out in front of them. “Good. We’ll get some guys to head out to…Missouri, Maine, Arkansas, and what's left of Texas to try to talk to those guys. I assume they all know each other, even if it's only in system chats. We'll offer them training as their team if they all sign up."

Brown grabbed another donut. "So, we get the specials from the recruiters, right? All the lower ones are simply spread out."

Conrad nodded. "Yeah. We take the special cases, those we think could be more than fodder, but we never really know for sure. I suppose it will be up to them once they get in. We can't force them to be good soldiers, but I tell you what, for some of them, the military life will be leaps and bounds above their lives in the trenches of these falling-down shitholes."

The other man shrugged. "As someone recruited from the shitholes of Detroit, I would have to agree. We have air conditioning, food whenever we want it, uniforms, friends, and ain't gotta pay a cent for it. Not to mention that the Federation's sad pathetic salary and benefits feel like striking it rich compared to scraping by in Gov-Subs, not knowing if assistance will show up or not. I definitely feel lucky."

Thompkins smiled at him and liked that he was so down to earth. "So, is that everyone? I feel like this week's round of picks is as weak as hell."

Conrad tapped his papers on the desk. "I swear it's the nuclear shit out there. Everyone seems to be even lower on the IQ trail this year—and that's not limited to the Federation Forces."

Taylor scoffed. "Because they know what happens. You go out and maybe you come back if you don't get eaten by some big-ass Dreth—"

Brown put up his hand. "Hold up. We missed one from the Bank Simulation. It looks like one person—alone—beat the test."

Everyone scoffed and shook their heads. "Yeah, right. That isn't even possible."

He grabbed the tablet and swiped over it to locate the footage and leaned back.

CHAPTER FIFTY-TWO

"Here you go, Miss Morgana," the school secretary said and gave her a wink as she passed her an envelope.

Stephanie smiled, took it, and held it against her chest until she was out of the office, down the hall, had pushed through droves of students who milled around their lockers before leaving for the day, and out the front doors. She headed down the steps and ducked around the corner to lean her back against the concrete of the staircase. Biting the inside of her lip, she stared at the envelope, hoping beyond hope that it said what she needed it to.

She stuck her finger under the edge of the flap and tore it open carefully to remove the page inside. There really was no reason to prolong the inevitable, so she read it quickly. Finally, she released a long, deep breath and smiled widely. She had passed all her exams with flying colors and as of right then, no longer had to attend the school anymore. It came as something of a relief when she glanced at the stairs and remembered that she had never actually stored anything in her locker. Honestly, she was thrilled to not have to go back in anytime soon.

"Hey, smarty pants," Becca yelled from the sidewalk where she stood beside Todd.

They both put their hands out and Becca laughed. "Are those your results? Are you finally out of this place or what?"

Stephanie grinned and tucked it in her bag, which she flung over her shoulder. She hurried down the sidewalk to where they stood and put one arm over Todd's shoulder and one over Becca's. "Let's just say that this girl is officially graduated from Chicago PS 34. Thank you very much!"

Becca rolled her hands over each other and shook her body as she made the sound of deep beats of music with her chest. Todd followed suit and broke out the "shopping cart," his extra special move for only the best of times. As he placed the imaginary cans in his imaginary cart, he bumped his hip into Becca's. "We knew you had it in the bag. But we also had some ominous dances picked out in case you had an aneurysm during the test or something."

Stephanie shook her head and blinked at them. "You guys are too much for one sidewalk. Seriously. I think people are starting to think you're having a seizure or something."

Becca put her arms out, her short, chubby frame always super-animated. "So, what's next, Einstein?"

"My new job, I suppose," she responded and couldn't resist a chuckle. That's the whole reason I did this. To get there sooner. I mean, it's basically a life-changing kind of job."

Todd groaned. "While the rest of us suffer away in school, she'll be drinking champagne with admirals and lounging in her personalized pods."

Becca nodded astutely. "Personally, I think that you deserve every dang second of it. You have busted your butt for far too long. And after what Pinnacle did to you, screw that place. When my dad found out, he took them off the list of my possible schools. He wanted to show his solidarity."

Stephanie laughed. "I appreciate it. There are better schools than that for you anyway."

Her friend stood tall. "Why, thank you. Shall we begin your last walk home?"

Stephanie put one arm through Todd's and the other through

Becca's. She was grateful that the girl's parents had once again relented and allowed her to walk home rather than be driven. While they didn't have too much longer left in school, it would be good for Todd to have company once she moved on, and he and Becca already had a good friendship.

He cleared his throat. "So, I came up with the perfect last-walk conversation for us to have. A culmination of all the walks, all the pop-culture, and all the times you were wrong."

She rolled her eyes. "Mm-hmm."

Todd rubbed his hands together and unlatched from her arm to turn and walk backward. "It's actually a whole bunch of questions but they are those that have never fully been answered. So, number one. Could Jack have fit on the door with Rose?"

"Yes," Stephanie shouted. "There have been recreations, there have been diagrams, everything. The girl was too prissy for her own good and she ended up letting her boyfriend die in the icy hell that was around them. Then, when someone came to save them, she simply let him go and sink to the bottom of the ocean. Personally, I think he should have sacrificed her."

He made a check mark in the air. "One we agree on. Okay, moving on. *Star Wars—A New Hope* or *The Empire Strikes Back?*"

Stephanie hissed. "Uh... I will go with *A New Hope*."

Todd's mouth fell open. "What? Are you kidding me? *Empire Strikes Back* is when they completely turn the story upside down. It was the re-forging of the core rivalry between Skywalker and Vader with that arc between a father and a son! Tragedy came."

She shrugged. "Right, but *A New Hope* established the entire mythos of *Star Wars*. Seriously, every major player was introduced. The Force, the Empire, the Rebellion, everything while still leaving the door open."

"That's bull hockey." He shook his head. "You know that. Just because it set the stage doesn't make it the best one. How can you even think that the dramatic arc of father and son could come in second to *A New Hope?* Who even really knows that title? No one. You are no one."

Stephanie slapped him in the chest. "Calm down, crazy pants. Let me ask you this then, *Star Wars* or *Star Trek?*"

They both answered at the same time. Stephanie said *Trek*, Todd said *Wars* and they both looked at Becca, who watched them with wide eyes and excitement. "Hey, don't ask me. I'm only here for the drama of it all. I'm walking with so much nerdiness—will some sort of vortex open up and suck the whole world into it?"

The friends blinked at her and Todd smacked his hand into the other one. "*Star Wars* has action, adventure, Wookies, a storyline, and the ultimate villain."

Stephanie wrinkled her nose. "Right, but *Star Trek* is pure science fiction. The future. Yours is fantasy. I'm not saying there is anything wrong with fantasy but it's a cop-out to call it science fiction because it's not. And *Star Trek* has a storyline. In fact, it has about ten million storylines throughout history. From the books to the movies, there is something for everyone."

Todd gritted his teeth. "Not for me. Not unless there are lightsabers. What does *Trek* have anyway? Those beam-me-up-Scotty old-ass comms? No. You are absolutely wrong on this one. I'm sorry. You have failed me after all these years, and I cannot look you in the eye."

She poked him in the stomach and giggled. "I'm screwing with you. Of course I pick *Star Wars* over *Trek*. I wanted to see your response, that's all. It was about as wild as I thought it would be."

He clutched his chest dramatically and shook his head. "You are a cow. I seriously thought that all this time, I had steered you down a dark and lonely road. Good Lord."

Becca giggled. "Oh. You know what we should do? Because it's your last walk? We should go get a shake at the diner. You said you would come eventually and it's your last shot."

Stephanie looked at Todd and nodded. "Heck, yeah. Let's do it. And they're on me this time."

He snickered. "Okay, rich girl. Can I even get whipped cream on mine?"

"Whoa, buddy." She laughed. You are taking it too far…way too far.

Psych, duh, you can get whipped cream. What is a shake without whipped cream?"

They turned right and headed to the small shopping area on the outskirts of the subs. Todd held the door for the girls to enter the diner, which was already crowded with students sitting around, laughing, and talking over shakes and fries. It had been years since Stephanie had been in there, but it still looked exactly the same to her—a long metal building with the words **The Diner** in sketchy neon lights out front. Inside, it was decorated in red and white, from floor to ceiling. The floors were checkered, the tables were red with silver edging, and everything had a sheen to it as if it had been polished for hours.

On the ViD screens hanging on the walls were old movies from the 1900s and early 2000s. Each one displayed a different movie with the words captioned below the picture. Overhead music played, this time from the 2050s but usually from about a hundred years before that. Stephanie assumed they at least tried to keep with the times before music was incredibly regulated by the Federation. Of course, that unfortunate time period was short-lived as people everywhere from rich to poor spoke out vociferously against the regulations. Music was the one thing that always somehow crossed the invisible divide.

The three friends chose one of the tables at the window and waited for the waitress to come over. She was in her seventies, at least, with bleached hair pulled back, a red dress that came down to her calves, and a white apron that matched the white tennis shoes on her feet. The varicose veins in her legs showed clearly through her barely opaque stockings. "What can I get you?"

Becca responded first. "I'll have a strawberry milkshake with whipped cream."

Todd tapped his fingers on his lips. "I'll have your split one—vanilla and chocolate with whipped cream please."

She looked at Stephanie. "And you?"

"Chocolate, whipped cream, and a large order of fries." She smiled a little smugly. It felt good to be able to splurge a teeny bit for once in her life.

The woman walked away, and Todd laughed. "Look at you, money bags. Springing for the spuds."

Stephanie shrugged and her gaze traveled the room as she soaked in the atmosphere. "Hey. Sometimes, you have to celebrate."

Becca rested her chin on her hands. "I can't believe this is it for you. We've all been in school with each other since we were tiny. Will you come back for graduation?"

She wrinkled her nose as she considered this. "Maybe. I don't know. It seems silly, though. Barely anyone comes back for it anymore, right? And I'll be in the middle of working. I don't know. We'll see. Right now, I simply want to enjoy my last day."

The six lead recruiters sat silently in their chairs as they watched the playback of Stephanie in the bank robbery game. Their eyes all widened as she used magic to knock the robber unconscious and stepped forward. Ribbons of purple magic whirled around her and seemed to come directly from the floor. Her entire body was swathed from head to foot and her hair waved wildly. As she released the wave of magic, the recruiters bolted back in their chairs, their gazes glued to the bodies that disintegrated around her.

Almost nonchalantly, she grasped a handful of the robber's shirt and dragged him into the police precinct as if nothing had happened. All that was left in her wake were the ashes of the avatars she had taken out in the process. The video stopped and Brown shut it off. The team sat in stupefied silence, unsure of what to do or say at that point.

Taylor's feet dropped from the table and he straightened to roll his seat forward. "Okay. That was completely mind-blowing. How in the hell did she do magic like that?"

Conrad shook his head. "It is the Meligorn side of the docking station, which means it's within the MU spectrum, but humans aren't supposed to be able to throw magic, even there. And with the kind of control she had, she made it look like she could perform the exact kind of magic that she wanted to do."

Thompkins's mouth hung open. "Like she had complete control over it. As if she knew how to bring it up and send it back as a destructive power."

Holland waved his hands frantically as he squinted at the frozen image on the screen. "Hold up. Wait a second. That's the girl."

The others looked strangely at him. He pointed at Stephanie and pushed to his feet. "That's the girl who saved that woman and child from the runaway self-driven truck. Here on Earth, she used a battery to generate magical power. Her face was all over the news, but I didn't recognize her until the magic flowed through her."

Brown pressed a few buttons on his tablet and turned to the information screen at the front of the room. He brought up her pod number, location, and finally, her stats. "Stephanie Morgana. What do you know? It is her. She took to the bank vault to work her next piece of magic."

Conrad spun his finger lazily. "Okay, where is she? This is something we cannot sleep on. If she is out there still and hasn't been picked up, she would be the perfect candidate. Our next hero in disguise."

The other man scanned through her records. "These aren't really updated because she just turned eighteen, but it says here she has the last half of her school year to go still. She is in the Gov-Subs in Chicago and attends the public school out there. She apparently did a summer session at Pinnacle but is back home now and continued her public-school enrollment when she got back."

The team leader thought about it for a second, then pointed at Thompkins. "I want you to find out who the closest recruiter to her is. I need them sent out immediately. Let's see if they can't persuade her that the real world needs her."

CHAPTER FIFTY-THREE

"I don't think I've ever seen someone get a brain freeze so badly that cold air blew out of their nose." Becca laughed loudly as the trio walked out of The Diner.

Todd chuckled. "I don't think I've ever felt my nose hairs freeze like that."

Stephanie grimaced. "That's so gross. But I'm glad you came out of it. I did not want to deliver you back home as a completely frozen statue. The one time we go out, you end up an ice cube. Your parents would not be happy."

He scoffed. "They wouldn't have even noticed. We don't talk a lot at home so they would have simply patted me on the frozen shoulder and told me to wear a sweatshirt if I was cold so they wouldn't have to turn the heat up."

Becca shook her head, her grin still wide. "Thank you for coming out, Steph. I'm really glad we had this chance. I know you leave soon for your big secretive job."

Stephanie hugged her tightly once they stopped on the edge of the town. "I will miss you. But I'll be back to visit soon, promise. And let me know when you'll be in town from school. I know you still have the rest of this semester here but it's off to prep school afterward, so I want to know you are doing well."

Her friend squeezed her hands and glanced at Todd, who still rubbed his tongue on the roof of his mouth. "I'll keep an eye on dummy over here too. Make sure he doesn't go licking glass windows."

"I appreciate that." Stephanie eyed him with real amusement.

She hugged the girl one last time and waved as Becca hurried off in the other direction toward her house. Stephanie tapped Todd on the shoulder and the two headed down through the subs. He finally released the pressure from his mouth and hooked his thumbs in his book bag. "It's gonna be weird not coming to get you in the morning."

Stephanie poked her bottom lip out. "I know it will be, but remember, it won't be for that long. Before you know it, you will graduate too. It will be a wild ride. And if it's that hard, you can always call me, and I can talk to you on the phone while you walk."

He groaned. "Oh please. I'm not that pathetic...okay, maybe turn your phone on in the morning just in case. You know, in case there are some bad guys trying to get me or something."

She kept a serious face for his benefit. "Mm-hmm...oh, sure. All the bad guys. Don't worry, dude, I will keep my phone on and answer it if I possibly can. I'm telling you, though. The first day might be weird but you'll get used to it really fast. It might save you a few minutes in the morning too."

They walked along in almost silence as they made their way through the subs. When they stopped outside her house, Stephanie wrapped her arms around him and squeezed him tightly. "Go home and relax."

"Yeah, right." Todd sneered. "I have to do homework like the rest of the plebes—minus you, of course."

Stephanie smirked. "Yeah. I have to pack, though. I haven't started yet and I know I have to take a fair amount back with me this time around. Not the most exciting thing to do, but it is what it is."

He gave her a hug again, turned, and whistled to himself as he strolled down the sidewalk. Up to that point, she had been fine, but for a small moment, she felt almost sad that all of it was over. Her life was changing, and the years she'd had to figure it all out were drawing to a close. She had to move forward and hope like hell she had made the best decision.

With a determined shrug, she headed to the door. As she reached for the handle, she paused when she heard her mom and dad inside through the open window. They hadn't noticed that she was back yet and were discussing business. Her mom sighed. "It's such a good opportunity. This could really fill that hole we've had every year and be a really good long-term thing. It could give us a chance to finally branch out, have a staff, and move forward with the company."

Her father sniffed. "True. Where is it again?"

"It's in New Downtown Chicago. Right in the heart—a huge skyscraper. The whole thing needs a possible cleaning service. It looks like 511 New Main Street—that really big one with the all-glass front and the multiple flying car docking stations along the sides of it."

Her father smacked his lips thoughtfully. "Well, we should put a bid in."

Cindy groaned. "I wish we could but it's in person only. I don't see how we could get away from the other jobs long enough to apply for it. Right now, it's only us and one part-time girl. We would basically have to be in two places at one time. But damn, that would be so good for the company."

Stephanie put her back to the door and retrieved her tablet. She put the address into the system and pulled the building up. Croftborrow Services was a leading player in the technological advances for the Federation. It wasn't a government building but a private business owner who, from the looks of it, had multiple Federation contracts. Normally, that would scare her off but that was a good thing for her parents' company. If a corporation ran mostly off Federation Contracts, that meant the long-term money and stability would totally be there.

That was one thing she knew her family needed with their schedules. Stability. The business was so up and down that they never knew from month to month what contracts they would have, which was why they didn't have a staff. They couldn't promise hours every single week, much less pay for any benefits that might need to be offered.

She searched for the ad posting and finally found it. They needed a cleaning company willing to work the night shift for the entire place. They had a daytime, business-hours janitorial staff, but the night people would vacuum, dust, clean windows, empty trash cans, bathrooms...the whole nine yards. That would be a huge deal for her parents' company, and it would definitely fill their schedule. Stephanie bit the inside of her cheek and decided that she really wanted to help them get the gig, but she had to be sure that she wouldn't screw her job over either. She was supposed to return to Washington DC as soon as possible. But perhaps she could have a few more days to help them and set them up for success while she was gone.

After only a few moments' thought, she swiped over to her chat to see if Ms. Elizabeth was online. ONE R&D had set up a chat for the company, although only she and Ms. E were connected at that point. Apparently, it was highly secure and ran off part of the system. She wasn't quite sure how that worked but didn't intend to start analyzing it.

Stephanie: **Ms. Elizabeth, are you on?**

Elizabeth: **I am! Congrats on your tests. You scored in the top percentile for all of them. I was very impressed by your efforts.**

Stephanie smiled as she typed.

Stephanie: **Thanks! I was glad to see I did well on them. I was actually writing to find out when you needed me there. I ask because there is something I would really like to do to set my parents up for success while I'm gone, but it might take a few days.**

Elizabeth: **That's fine. Take the time you need. I can easily wait a week for you to get here. We had to purchase a new building after the fire and your pod won't arrive for another few days. You would end up hanging out in your hotel room anyway.**

Stephanie smirked: **You say that like it's not awesome. It's bigger than any apartment or house I've ever lived in. But cool. I will take**

care of what I need to do here and send you a message when I leave for DC.

Elizabeth: **Sounds good. Have a good night. Celebrate. You have big things happening.**

Stephanie grinned cheesily as she slid her tablet into her backpack and found her keys. As soon as she walked in the door, her parents stopped talking about business and looked at her. She put her arms up in the air and twirled dramatically. "Well, it's official. I no longer have to go to class. I am all set up for success."

Her mom clapped and her father pumped his fist in the air. "We knew you would do it. When you said you were nervous for the tests, we both knew you shouldn't be at all."

She dropped her bag on the chair. "So, I was thinking. We should celebrate. I'll go up and change and I want you guys to as well. We'll go out on the town—all on me—and really enjoy the night together. If it weren't for the two of you, I would never have thought things like this could be possible, but you told me to keep learning and keep growing, no matter what. I want to celebrate that with you."

Her mother looked at her father and he winked at her. Turning to Stephanie, he smiled. "Normally, we would fight you on spending money, but I think it would be fantastic to go out on the town with you. To really get excited about the rest of your life. We'll go change our clothes and you tell us when we will leave."

Stephanie clapped with real enthusiasm. "Yay! I'll call the car company right now. That should give us all about twenty minutes."

Her mother gasped and took off up the stairs and her dad laughed as he followed her up. "You lit the fire under this one, didn't you?"

Stephanie sent a message on her tablet to the limo company and hurried upstairs to get ready. She picked out a nice pair of black pants and a dressy tank top with a tie on the hem of it. Once she'd pushed her feet into her flats, she pulled her hair back and to the side and braided it quickly. She stared at herself in the mirror for several minutes, shocked at how much older she looked. Maybe it was knowing she was done with school, maybe it was the clothes, or maybe she could see more of herself than merely the outer layer.

The limo honked outside and brought her thoughts back to the present and she grabbed her clutch and headed downstairs. Her mom looked pretty in her blue calf-length dress and her dad appeared in a pair of khakis and a button-up shirt. "You guys clean up right nice."

He thrust his chest out and pretended to puff on a cigar. "Yass, Buffy. Can you fetch the fifty-year-old Scotch for me? It's right next to my wife's diamonds. Yes, that's right, a huge stack of diamonds."

Her mom snorted and shook her head and the three of them walked outside. Her mom gasped and almost stumbled when she saw the limo waiting. "They will think someone died. That's the only time you see a limo in the Gov-Subs."

Her father still sauntered jauntily and ashed his fake cigar. "Silly us. We forgot the Jag at the other house and had to take the limo."

Stephanie grinned and climbed in after them. The limo was self-driving and she had it take them to the new part of Chicago. There was a Japanese restaurant there that Becca had told her about a couple of years before and she knew that her mother would love it. Since it wasn't a weekend, they didn't need reservations and were taken to their own seating area with a flat grill in the center of it. The chef came out and bowed to each of them, which made her mother giggle repeatedly.

She ordered the shrimp and her father ordered the combination. Stephanie went with shrimp too and asked for a round of drinks in the little tiki glasses they would get to take home at the end of the night. They laughed and applauded as the personal chef cooked their food to perfection on the flattop in front of them. Steam sizzled and he flipped and turned the food to provide an amazing show for the three of them.

When the food was done, they sat and ate and talked about how amazing the place was. Stephanie was really glad to see that they were having a good time. She hadn't ever seen them let loose in her life, and that was really important to her. It meant a lot that she knew they were happy, no matter what, and they deserved special things like that night. In fact, they deserved to live like that all the time. All she could keep telling herself was that hopefully, it would happen one day, even if she was the one who had to make it come true.

While they ate, oblivious to any of them, a large vehicle pulled up to the curb down the street from the restaurant. Two men stepped out from the shadows and walked up as the front passenger window rolled down slowly. They talked for several moments before they nodded and slipped back into the shadows.

Another man put his hands in his pocket and scrutinized the two men who hid in the alley. The SUV started again and accelerated. It took the next right turn and immediately parked on the street. They were waiting for Stephanie Morgana.

CHAPTER FIFTY-FOUR

Thompkins leaned her head back and groaned as she rolled her eyes. "This is not the night I thought I would have. Seriously, why is this so difficult to organize? And why the hell don't we have someone whose job it is to do so?"

Brown laughed. "Hey, everyone, Thompkins over here forgot that she is in the Federation Navy. For a second, it sounded like she thought she was part of some big private corporation where everything isn't thrust on one person's shoulders."

Taylor rubbed his face. "Six people. Everything is thrust on six people's shoulders. And I'm not sure why it's surprising. Every year, we walk in here thinking it will be simple, and every year, we still sit here at nine at night trying to determine who will go where."

Conrad smiled and paused from taking his notes. "It's strategy, my friends. We can't send the wrong person to do the job. That's how you end up with low entry numbers after the busy season. We have to match personalities as best we can."

Thompkins shook her thumb at Grant. "Just send him. They will see that you can basically be brain dead and still climb the ladder. Or Holland, who will talk them to death, and they'll sign the dotted line simply to get him to shut the hell up."

Grant flipped her off. "Just because you think you're smart doesn't mean you actually are. If we all flashed our cleavage around to every eligible sailor, we might get promoted up the ranks quickly too."

Holland snickered and she gave him a nasty look. "How come I can beat on you without a single word as to how you look but you imbeciles can't think of anything that isn't sexist to hit me back with? It's really kind of pathetic."

Conrad stretched his arms above his head and yawned. "All right, guys, let's keep going before you bite each other's heads off, shall we? We have to send our best recruiter to the girl in the game—Stephanie Morgana. We need this one to be taken care of ASAP."

Thompkins narrowed her eyes and peered at the screen. "Let's see…hot, smart girl… It definitely means that Larry can't take it."

Holland tilted his head to the side in thought. "Remember, we only have Larry, Williamson, Charlie, and Rebecca who are qualified for special assignments like this."

She nodded. "Yep, and Larry will end up busting one on her before he can even say hello."

The man in question stuck his head around the corner. "Did someone call me?"

The six of them looked up and tried desperately to hide a laugh. Larry was huge with muscles from head to toe. While probably the width of three Thompkins, he was not the brightest crayon in the box. She pressed her lips together and made a slight snorting noise. "No, Larry dear. You can go back to lifting weights and saying the alphabet."

He blinked at them and nodded before he disappeared around the corner. Conrad's eyes widened and he shook his head. "Right, then. Not Larry, for damn sure."

Grant ran his finger down the list. "Charlie is out too. He is ready to leave on assignment for the science kid. The one who can figure out the chemical composition of basically anything and then make a bomb from it."

Conrad nodded. "So we either send Rebecca, where we could see how gender might play a role here…"

Thompkins giggled. "Or we send David 'Killer Casanova' Williamson. So, are we looking at whether to respect her with a strong female role or impress her with a hot guy with a good ass? I say go with Casanova. She's young and impressionable."

Grant check-marked the air. "Agreed."

The team leader shook his head. "I hope you kiddies are right. She's a must-have. All right, David it is. Now, who do we send for the guy who can bench press twice his weight?"

Thompkins threw her hand up in the air in dramatic resignation. "I got this one, boss."

Stephanie's dad took the last bit of steak from his plate, put it in his mouth, and savored every morsel. "This has been a fantastic surprise. I don't know if we've had steak in years. Maybe on our wedding anniversary several years ago."

Her mother nodded. "Yes, but nowhere even close to the quality that this one was. I stole some from your father's plate."

Stephanie laughed. "I think if I eat anything else, I might burst. Now I understand why so many of the richies are…" She lowered her voice and cupped her hand. "Rotund."

Her dad patted his belly. "I would be if I were one. Screw that trying to impress people with abs of steel. Give me all the potatoes and don't skimp on the pasta either."

They all laughed. Stephanie smiled as the waiter placed the paid check and her card beside her. "So, when I walked up earlier, I overheard the tail end of a conversation. Something about wanting to grow your business?"

Her mother glanced at her father, who shrugged. "When you own a business, who wouldn't want to grow it, right? You want to continue to get bigger, be able to hire more employees, maybe take the load off your own feet after a while. You try not to have a cap on how big you want to get when you are growing a company, you know? You want to always see it as a future that is unknown."

Stephanie nodded and pursed her lips. "So, if you had the opportunity, you would actually want to grow it?"

Her mother patted her lips with her napkin. "Sure. If it were the right opportunity and made sense to the business. Absolutely. But it has to be right."

Dad wiggled his eyebrows. "Why ya askin'? Are you gonna give up that fancy job of yours in the capital and come join the family business? Maybe make some investments and grow her globally?"

She laughed. "After all this time of you telling me to stay as far away as I can from the family business? I think not. I was only curious. Now that I'll be gone and you won't have that expense, I figured that would open up some time and opportunity for you."

Her mother pouted. "I'm gonna miss your face. I'd rather have that than a bigger business, but I'd rather have you successful and out on your own with a big fancy job than anything else. The mother's woes. We don't want you to leave but we can't have you stay. These richies have it good. They can have their kid work with them and take care of them when they are old and gray."

Stephanie filled out the receipt, left a tip, and put her card in her bag. As they stood, she laughed at her father, who said, "Oh, she's still gonna take care of us when we're old. Don't you think little smarty pants got out of that one."

She put her arm around his waist as they walked out. "I thought something like a nice little cottage on Meligorn. Then you wouldn't have to deal with the humans, and everything is much prettier on their planet. And quiet. They like their quiet."

He rubbed his chin. "Hmm, I like that idea. I hear they don't have poor on that planet, either. Everyone is taken care of."

She chuckled. "True, although I haven't been there in reality so I can't tell you much. When I finally go, I'll scope out the best senior spots. You will be young compared to their seniors. They live to be three hundred and something."

Her mom turned with a laugh. "That means I'm only getting started. I'm a wee baby on Meligorn. Why haven't we moved there yet?"

The doors to the restaurant swung open and Stephanie, Mark, and Cindy came out. They laughed and walked close together. The sound of their pleasure was comfortable in the warm city air and people didn't pay any attention to them as they passed. For a moment, it was as if no one had even noticed that they were from the Gov-Subs. That they didn't have the newest clothes or most expensive jewelry. For a moment, everyone was simply there to have a good time.

The driverless limo doors opened slowly, and the AI welcomed the family. Behind them, without their knowledge, the two men crept out of the shadows with snarled lips and narrowed eyes. The mystery man walked slowly behind them, his face only visible when a shaft of moonlight cast between the buildings around him. In utter silence, he tipped his head forward and grasped one of the men around the mouth with one hand and around the waist with the other arm. His buddy was already a few feet in front of him and seemed too focused on the task ahead to notice what had happened.

The mystery man spun his captive and slammed him into the brick wall. "Who are you?"

The criminal narrowed his eyes and twisted in an attempt to reach a knife sheathed on his side. The stranger caught the movement and snatched the knife from his groping fingers. He ran the blade along the crook's cheek. Blood trickled down his pale skin and he grunted at the pain. Finally, when it became apparent that his captive had no intention to divulge any information, the unknown man threw the knife aside and drew his hand back. He punched the thug as hard as he could across the jaw and released the weight of his body as the man's eyes rolled back. Gravity slumped him to the ground. The moon shifted behind the clouds and cast his sprawled figure into shadow.

Quickly, he turned to pursue the other assailant but stopped when he saw that this one was down too. His eyes widened and he fumbled for his phone as he looked all around him. He didn't have a partner and there had been no second person sent out to help protect her that he knew of. A little nonplussed, he stepped hastily back into the shadows and waited as the family entered the limo and the doors shut slowly behind them. A few moments later, the car pulled away and set off back toward the Gov-Subs.

"Shit!" he hissed as he snatched a key out of his pocket and raced across the street.

He fell onto his bike and shoved his earpiece in before he yanked his helmet down over his face. Someone else had protected her and obviously watched her as closely, if not more so than he already was. While that was good for her, he wasn't necessarily sure it was good for everyone involved. She was important—quite possibly the most important human being in many, many years. And his job was to make sure that no one, good intentions or not, got in the way of her potential and between his boss and her. What he thought would be a relatively simple job had turned out to be more than a little interesting.

He turned the bike and revved it before he gunned the engine and hurtled down the street in the direction of the limo. "Call E."

The phone dialed and Elizabeth's face appeared in the corner of his shield. She looked at her nails, an eyebrow raised. "I hope you haven't called me with bad news because today, I do not need bad news."

"The girl and her family are safe," he replied. "I'm currently on my bike tracking her limo back to her parents' house. She took them out to dinner tonight in the new part of Chicago."

Elizabeth rolled her eyes. "Good Lord. I guess I can't be mad at her. It's not like she really understands how important she is. She doesn't know the danger she could be in. When she gets here, though, she will have a full rundown in hand-to-hand combat as well as all defensive strategies. We can't take any chances with this."

"There is something else," he said hesitantly. "I'm not the only one who is watching her. There were two guys there tonight, ready to snatch her. I eliminated one and by the time I was ready to take the other, someone else had gotten to him. I didn't see who it was and couldn't track them without losing her."

Elizabeth's gaze raised and her lips fell into a flat line. "And you're sure about that? He didn't simply trip over his own dumb feet and knock himself out?"

The man shook his head. "Not unless he also threw himself into the alley, unconscious."

She snarled her displeasure. "Damnit. This isn't good at all. It could be someone else who wants her safe so *they* can snatch her when it suits them. We need to get her here to Washington DC and in the pod as soon as we can. This shit gets more and more complicated by the day. And if we tell her what's up, she will only freak out and we run the risk of scaring her off completely."

"I agree," he replied, his tone deep and firm. "For now, I will pull double duty and stay on her at all times. I have the cameras set up around her house to keep track and I won't leave the premises. Let me know if you hear anything about who this could be. The last thing we need right now is danger from some asshole company that thinks they know what they are doing."

Elizabeth nodded. "Acknowledged. I'll keep you updated. Until then..." She pointed firmly at him. "Not out of your sight."

CHAPTER FIFTY-FIVE

Stephanie lay in her bed, turned on her side with her back to the door. Her mother cracked the door and whispered that she loved her, obviously assuming she was still asleep. She smiled and waited until her mom closed the door before she rolled onto her back and stared at the ceiling. Her parents rummaged around downstairs, fixing coffee, but they always tried to be quiet to not wake her. Even when she was a little girl and her grandmother used to live there, she could remember her mother tiptoeing around quietly. For some reason, it gave her a really warm feeling inside.

She pulled the covers up to her chin and tilted her head to the side to look out the window. It was early and the sun hadn't come up yet, but the sky had begun to lighten. She waited for them to leave for work before getting up as she had plans she wasn't ready to divulge just yet. What she didn't realize as she lay there in the warmth of her childhood bed, surrounded by the pictures pinned on the walls and her purple comforter her mother had sprung for when she was twelve, was how much she would miss that solace and safety.

Everything in her life had been to prepare her for this time. The moment in which she would make a choice and erupt into the world using the talents she had been given to forge a path for herself into the future. Was the choice she had made the one that would do it for her? She wished she could say so without a doubt, but after Pinnacle, she had become a little more cynical about the world. It wasn't that she didn't trust her choice in ONE R&D—she had to, at least partially, to uproot herself and move thousands of miles away from home. Everything was shiny and exciting when it was new. Everyone thought she was shiny and exciting when they first found out that she could work with magic. However, like it had with Pinnacle, she feared the excitement would quickly fade for ONE R&D in the same way.

Fear couldn't be an obstacle in her life, though, not anymore. She had grown up with fear. Fear of where they lived, fear of the Federation, fear of starvation, and fear that she would never see even a glimmer of a successful life. She could no longer allow that to plague her and had to push it away and move forward. In order to do that, though, she needed to make sure that her family was securely taken care of. She needed to know that she had done everything she could to stabilize them and help them reach their goals, just as they had done for her for so many years.

After about twenty minutes, the front door closed. Stephanie peeked carefully over the windowsill and watched the car drive down the road. She flung the covers off and stretched her arms above her head and pointed her toes. As she rolled out of bed, she looked at the digital display on the wall. She wasn't late but she didn't have time to dilly dally.

In her closet, she pushed back a couple of old pieces and brought out the outfit she had selected the night before. She pulled the dress up from the bottom, wiggling her body as she drew it over her hips and pushed her arms into the sleeves. It zipped snugly up the side and she smoothed her hands down the front of the stiff but comfortable fabric. It was one of her nicer dresses and the neckline sat low on her collar bone, straight across, and dipped halfway down her shoulder bones at the back. It hugged her curves enough to be feminine and give her shape but left enough room in the fabric to be professional. All the way along the bottom of the hem, a slight ruffle of fabric rested right below her knees.

She pulled on a pair of stockings and wrinkled her nose. *How do women wear these things every day?*

The outfit came to life when she slipped on her blue sling-back three-inch heels and she stood in front of the mirror, satisfied with the effect. "Hair. Must fix the hair."

Stephanie hurried into the bathroom, brushed her hair out, and pulled it straight back to the nape of her neck. She braided it tightly and secured the end before twisting it into a low braided bun with one small, deeply parted piece that cascaded down over the side of her face. She took a little extra time to apply her makeup, using a tutorial she'd found online—natural but noticeable at the same time. She was actually impressed that she could handle doing it like that. Makeup had never been her forte.

When she was completely ready to go, she sat and practiced crossing her legs to the side a few times before she studied the information on the building they would be cleaning. It was only fifteen years old—relatively new, even for New Chicago. Every story was surrounded by floor-to-ceiling windows, all floors on the first three levels were marble, and the rest were marbled tile. There was carpet in only two rooms in the entire building—the office suite at the top and the VP's office one floor below. Both required a special shampooer that she knew her parents had acquired not long before.

She wasn't really sure what her parents' reaction to all of this would be and had yet to tell them of her plan. It would be better to find the details out before they got their hopes up, which would help if they were turned down for the job. Not that Stephanie had any intention of allowing them to be turned down. She had put in the time and effort to get things done and do it right the first time. This was something her dad had taught her when she was only a little girl.

Satisfied with her preparations, Stephanie gathered the papers on the desk into a neat pile. She retrieved her mother's briefcase from the closet. It had been a gift one year for her birthday and she only ever used it for business meetings. She had programmed all three of their thumbprints into the security latch so they could never be locked out of it. Stephanie set it up on the table, pressed her thumb to it, and allowed it to open fully before she placed her tablet and the stack of papers as well as a cheat sheet of notes within. Once she'd closed and locked it, she headed downstairs and poured the last cup of coffee they always left for her while she called for a taxi to go uptown.

Her stomach was all aflutter when she thought about the meeting she was about to walk into. For some reason, ONE R&D hadn't made her as nervous as this, but then again, this was for her family, not only for her. She would have to rely heavily on some of her training and her experience in the interview to get her through the first business-based negotiation that she had ever been in. She had been successful in Washington, but that was a personal negotiation, and this was a different arena—and there would doubtless be significant competition. While she'd seen her mom do them in the past, those were usually small and with a homeowner who paid little attention and merely signed on the dotted line. This, she imagined, would be a little more tedious considering it was such a large building and a substantial contracted price.

Stephanie closed her eyes and imagined herself in that room, surrounded by elites as she made the case for her parents' business. She had to keep her shoulders firm, hold her head high, and always sound confident in everything she said. Facts were really important, too, especially since they would pay attention to what she knew and didn't know. It wouldn't be a moment to simply pull things out of her ass.

As she took the last sip of coffee, the taxi pulled up outside and honked. It was a driverless cab, one of the newer ones that had the ability to fly as well. For this, though, she hoped it would keep its wheels on the ground. Chicago hadn't fully transitioned into the flying car lifestyle and their airways weren't what they were in other places. It was a slow march forward for the city after the devastation they'd suffered, but they made progress as they rebuilt and brought in new technology almost every day.

With a deep breath, she placed her cup in the sink, grabbed the briefcase and bag, and headed out. She locked the door behind her, bounced down the steps, and hastily adjusted her steps to accommodate for the somewhat unfamiliar shoes and avoid landing face-down on the sidewalk. She slid into the taxi and buckled her seatbelt. "Croftborrow Services building, please. 511 New Main Street."

The AI in the cab set the location. "Very good. Total price will be forty-two Federal credits due upon arrival. Accept or deny?"

Stephanie checked to make sure she had her card. "Accept. Thank you."

The taxi eased onto the road, but she had no idea that she was being tailed—or that she had been since she got back from Washington DC. The mystery man assigned by Elizabeth now protected her at every turn. He waited until she had moved a little way down the block before he started his motorcycle. "Replay intel from inside the cab."

"Croftborrow Services building, please. 511 New Main Street," her voice said in his helmet.

He accelerated after the cab, surprised by her destination and uncertain why she would even venture downtown at that time of day. It was not like her and not what he had expected. Although Elizabeth had told him she would stay there an extra few days in order to do something for her family. That was the only explanation he could think of, but the details of what it might involve were unclear.

Stephanie sat comfortably in the taxi, her briefcase on her lap, and stared out the window. She passed through the Gov-Subs and waved at Todd as he stumbled sleepily out of his house. He didn't see her, too busy messing with the bands on his wrists—most likely to attempt to get them to play one of his favorite anthems for walking to school. He swore everyone should have a theme song and it should play whenever they went somewhere or entered a room.

She chuckled quietly as they turned away from the subs and headed through the cookie cutter likenesses of the homes in the suburbs. All the sprinklers had come on at the same time, all the lawns were the perfect height, and all the doors were painted a deep shade of teal. Anyone would have thought that a strange choice for a front door, but the Federation's main color was a deep teal, so it seemed to indicate forced patriotism among the middle class.

They passed through the suburbs and out into New Chicago, where construction was constantly ongoing and the scenery of people changed from the average and normal to the high fashion and luxury of a city. She knew she looked almost drab and plain compared to the women there, but she was okay with that as long as it meant she didn't have to wear the color fuchsia on her body and sparkling blue on her eyelids. In her mind, she was classic, and what everyone else wore didn't much matter to her.

She slid her card into the reader in the taxi and stepped out the automatic doors. As it processed, she tugged down on her dress slightly before she replaced the card in her clutch, which she put under her arm. Her heart thudded a little as she gripped her briefcase in one hand and turned toward her destination. The building looked even more impressive in person than it did on the site, but she wouldn't allow herself to be intimidated, she decided, as she pushed into the lobby. As she clicked along the marble floor to the main desk, she smiled at the already busy secretary.

The woman finished her call and transferred it before she looked at the visitor with a mixture of curiosity and flattery. "How may I help you today?"

Stephanie slid a copy of the email across the desk. "I have an interview with the CEO for the services contract."

The women snickered. "I still think it's crazy that he is the one handling this. He has over two thousand employees, yet he is the deciding voice on who cleans the building at night."

Elizabeth sat in her apartment with her feet up on the desk and the phone in front of her. As usual, when she talked to her boss, there was no face, only the ONE R&D symbol rotating in front of her. She poked her finger at it with a sigh. "This needs to be done but it needs to be done right."

BURT couldn't have agreed more. "I didn't put enough thought into the security of the place from the beginning. The whole thing must be significantly tighter than last time. I ran some data on the most secure civilian buildings in the country and I think I know what I would like to see."

She smirked and retrieved a piece of paper to take notes. "Whatcha thinking?"

He paused. "I liked your write-up for the security protocol for the people and the building. We will go with that, but I would like to add gun emplacements around the perimeter. I would also like the building to be far away from the city enough to have the look and feel of a country setting. I want off-grid power—which I can set up on my end as soon as the facility is secured—as well as underground bunkers that are comfortable and equipped for a longer stay in case of an emergency. They should also act as a safety hub for all who work within the company walls. Obviously, with that, you will need food for a year and all that type of stuff."

Elizabeth wrote each thing down and soon realized that the new security would rival Fort Knox by the time she was done with it. She liked that and hated the idea of having to worry about being at risk because of subpar security. There were too many other things to worry about.

BURT continued, "I would also like a room for her to stay on site and live comfortably. I will leave the needs of a young human woman up to you. On top of that, I would like an eight-person security detail as well as six others who can be utilized daily for rotations or protection in other sectors."

She continued to nod her head as she wrote everything down. "All of that sounds perfect. There is one thing, though, that I think you may have overlooked."

A moment of silence ensued in which he considered this. He seldom overlooked anything. It wasn't in his system capabilities. "What is that?"

Elizabeth chuckled. "People. And not the holographic kind like you had at the front desk, but living, breathing people. You need to have other bodies on site. Otherwise, it becomes obvious that Stephanie is the 'special one.'"

BURT computed the information. "You may be right. I didn't think about that part of it. I think I can cross-utilize this space, then, if we purchase the land we have on the top of the pile. It already has a compound of buildings within it so I can bring on some stock traders and business people to the other side of the compound. They are vital to this business and I think that having you able to be in constant contact with them will be best."

She blinked, caught by surprise with this unexpected development. "Me?"

"Yes," he replied without pause. "We discussed that you would probably be the one to get the other businesses off the ground and out of their current paper-only state. I have grown my holdings exponentially and will need you to work with these people to enable them to start running my businesses. We will be a conglomerate of sorts, at first, and dip our toes into many different things. It will all be to ultimately fund the different programs for people like Stephanie. If you open your tablet program, I have sent a small view of the holdings that I currently possess."

Elizabeth flipped her tablet on and swiped her hand to the share screen. BURT connected and she watched as line after line of holdings cascaded down the display in front of her. Her mouth dropped open slightly as she scrolled through. "This is only part of them?"

"Yes," BURT said. "About thirty percent, give or take half a percentage point. I did not send them all since I didn't want to overwhelm you."

She raised an eyebrow, scrolled through them once more, and mumbled, almost to herself, "You did not reach that goal, that's for sure. I'm definitely overwhelmed."

The different assets, purchases, land, and stocks left her reeling. "The size and breadth of your portfolio are more than a little intimidating. It has to be the largest I've ever seen."

BURT sent a little more information. "It is actually number seven in NorAm, and number twelve in the world."

Her voice sounded as incredulous as she felt. "How the hell do you keep all this in your head?"

He replied in an utterly serious tone. “I have a big head.”

Elizabeth laughed but let it trickle away slowly at his lack of response in the humor department. She couldn’t really tell if it was meant to be a joke or not. She often pictured a giant dome image in her head when talking to Burt and joked privately to herself that he might, after all, be an AI. Right now, though, the image seemed uncomfortably too close to real. “What about connectivity?” she asked hastily to avoid that particular black hole. “It has to be secure and I think her pod needs its own connection.”

BURT was already on it. “I will handle all connectivity and ensure there are three different access points. One for the others, one for the main building, and one for the pod. Safety and security are high priority right now.”

CHAPTER FIFTY-SIX

A guard had met her in the lobby and taken her up a private elevator to the top floor. The secretary showed her into the office and offered coffee or tea, which Stephanie declined. "Mr. Martelle will be with you in a moment."

She set her briefcase in the chair and walked to the window to stare out across New Chicago and the old one in the distance. It was both a beautiful and sad view at the same time. To see the destruction and remnants of the city in the distance was almost hard to comprehend. It looked like a backdrop for a movie.

The door opened behind her and she turned, her arms folded. A middle-aged man with salt-and-pepper hair, a very expensive suit, and a charming smile walked in. He looked surprised at first but didn't skip a beat before he extended his hand. "Miss Morgana, it's very good to meet you. Please, please, have a seat."

He stared at her as he tidied his desk and loosened his tie around his neck. "I have to admit, I'm impressed with the way you're dressed. You look very professional and very well put together. I almost thought I'd entered the wrong meeting when I walked in the door."

Stephanie gave him a polite smile. "Thank you. When you do

something, you do it right from the beginning—or at least that's what I've been taught my whole life."

His smile was pleasant. "Very nice. It's not often that I have a cleaning company with salespeople like yourself. Although, until recently, I didn't handle this account. I got fed up and felt that a strong hand was needed. People don't realize how much money goes out to cleaners every year. I've tried the cheaper bot options, but it is never the same and I pride myself on clean and organized."

Stephanie nodded, her legs crossed to the side. "Life is chaotic enough without adding dirt and clutter to the mix."

The corner of his mouth twitched upward. "Very true. And while I will enjoy your company, you have to know that this is mainly to rattle the chain of the present company. I don't like to take it this far, but I thought it might be necessary in this case. They have dropped the standard quality while servicing their other, newer clients. While I know there isn't a single company that could survive on only this building, the quality of service needs to stay at peak levels. Right now, I hope this little threat will encourage them to focus on me once again."

She chuckled and snapped her briefcase open. Mr. Martelle watched her carefully, but his eyes very obviously lingered where they shouldn't. Nonetheless, Stephanie did not allow him to see her take notice of this fact. She took her tablet out and placed it on the edge of his desk. Perfectly businesslike, she pressed a couple of buttons and projected her data into the air.

He sat back and examined the graphs and charts that floated like planets in front of his head and above his desk. Stephanie put her fingers together and pressed them to her lips. "Do you know what this is?"

Mr. Martelle shook his head. She nodded. "This is the profile for the company that presently cleans your building. It shows the percentage points for where you stand within the company's total of business for the greater Chicago area."

She stood and pointed her finger at a pie graph. "Now, if you squint your eyes really well, you will be able to see that your company is a tiny three percent of the cleaning services' total portfolio right now. To put that into perspective, that is down from eighteen percent only three years ago. That's a significant drop in priority for any company, wouldn't you think? I know that in this world, we can't expect to be fifty percent of a company's focus. That would be insane. The business would never make any money. But their lack of concern for the job quality has probably crept in from somewhere in this fifteen percent drop in importance within their corporate structure. I'm sure that when they landed the contract, it was a hallmark in their portfolio. Since then, your clout has allowed them to secure even more high-profile projects, and their thanks is a reduction in the quality of the services they provide."

He raised an eyebrow. "I wasn't aware we had become such a small part of their company portfolio. That would definitely tell me that there is a valid reason for concern."

Stephanie pursed her lips and shrugged. "Personally, Mr. Martelle, I don't know how you expect your three percent to wag the ninety-seven. Let's run some really simple numbers because they don't have to divulge their earnings thanks to the commerce privacy laws of 2112. So, let's say their total income is five hundred thousand dollars. If you calculate based on that, your contribution is fifteen thousand. You are a businessman, so you know that if you don't put the effort into a contract, you'll inevitably lose it. But if you don't have the hours needed, you'd need to consider your options. If someone told you that you would only lose three percent of your total business, what would you do? You would skate by until someone found out. But would you fight for those three percent?"

The man leaned back and crossed his legs. "I suppose it depends on how much it is three percent of, but no, probably not. There are much greater things I can do with that time that will inevitably make me even more money."

Stephanie snapped her fingers and pointed at him. "So, you see, no matter how valuable a client you might have been, you currently comprise only a small percentage of their present plans. If you want to do something to rock the boat, it had better be something serious."

She could tell he was amused by her words but was still infuriated by the facts she'd presented. He raised an eyebrow and folded his arms. "Do you have a plan?"

Stephanie swiped the numbers away and her parents' business logo immediately replaced it. She smiled and stared him straight in the eyes. "I sure do. You fire them."

Mr. Martelle threw his head back and laughed. "And let my building fall into disarray?"

"Absolutely not." She shook her head decisively. "A building of such splendor and architectural genius, not to mention the décor…I would never think of such a thing. Give my company a one-year contract, and if we can't do the job, we're done. And to sweeten that deal, you have your leverage to allow a general call that invites the other company the opportunity to come and discuss matters. It doesn't have to be a circus, but you might find yourself in a much better position."

He leaned forward, his expression sharp. "Just like that?"

She chuckled. "Just like that. And to prove to you that I am absolutely serious about this, I will put up a ten-thousand credit guarantee that we will do the job and do it beyond expectation."

He scrutinized with narrowed eyes. "And if you fail?"

Stephanie held her finger up. "Not that there is a chance in hell of that, but if we were to fail and you were able to provide substantial proof of the failure, you get to keep the ten thousand credits. Clean and clear, no questions asked. But I can assure you that by the end of it, having my company as your cleaning crew will be so beneficial that you won't want to fire them for anything, not even the ten thousand credits."

It was obvious that her proposal had quickly caught his attention. He leaned forward and studied her in silence, almost as if he looked for that one thread that would unravel her. The one piece that would reveal the Gov-Subs slum beneath her polished exterior. Luckily for her, that was merely a mindset, and the one she was in at that moment was nothing but strength and power.

He flicked his wrist at her. "Is the company paying?"

She shook her head and pointed at herself. "Nope. This is me, personally. I will put a ten-thousand credit deposit into an escrow account with the correct directives to be executed after one year—either back to my account or happily delivered to you."

He frowned as he considered this. "Why would you do this? It is obvious this isn't your personal company. Why would you put that much up against something you have no control over?"

Stephanie chuckled. "I happen to believe in the owners that much. In fact, I have never believed more in anything else in my life."

Mr. Martelle sat there in silence for several minutes. He rubbed his chin and his stare moved from Stephanie to the logo floating above them. She was as nervous as hell, but she maintained a controlled and calm expression. She'd learned to never let her opponent see the fear in her eyes. And he was the opponent in that moment. The one who could approve the hiring process or tell her to get the hell out of his office and never come back. Either way, nothing would have been lost, except perhaps some of her pride.

Finally, when his prolonged stare began to make her a little uncomfortable, he shook his head and reached across the table to shake her hand. "You are quite the businesswoman, that is for sure. I thought, when I walked in here and saw you, that you would be a pushover and that all I was doing was wasting some time with a beautiful woman. I have to say, I was wrong. You have brains too. Give me an address to send the paperwork to. Your owners will have to agree on the terms. If you'd like, I can leave the ten thousand credits out of their part and have you sign your own."

She smirked. "No need. We are transparent in every business deal that we do together."

They both stood and he waved his hand expansively. "But assuming we can negotiate, I think you are right. I need to shock them more than this. Much more. I will get those papers over to you soon."

Stephanie put her tablet in her briefcase, closed it tightly, and tucked her clutch under her arm. Mr. Martelle walked her to the door and smiled. "It was refreshing doing business with someone who knows how to do it. Thank you for that. And if you ever need a job, you let me know. We could use some ball-busters around here."

Stephanie laughed. "Thanks, but I don't think this is really the kind of permanent work I'm after."

He shut the door behind her, and she smiled at the secretary, who gave her a wink. She headed to the elevator and took it to the bottom floor. It was a long, slow ride from top to bottom, but she reveled in the idea that she had given her parents a chance at a new gig. It wasn't only about winning. It was about how well she felt she'd handled herself while in the process of doing so. Still, the cringe came when she acknowledged that she had learned some of those skills at Pinnacle, and she still loathed the absolute thought of the place.

She had to push that out of her mind, though. The hard part was over. Now, she had to tell her parents that they might have a new client who would blow their business out of the water. The doors to the elevator opened and she stepped out and nodded at the receptionist. She walked briskly through the doors and gestured to a cab. Her smile broad, she hopped in the back seat and gave the address. It was time to head home to make the announcement.

Stephanie was almost bouncing up and down in her seat as they drove through the city, the suburbs, and into the subs. Even the gloomy old low-cost housing didn't look so bad that day. She knew her parents wouldn't be home for hours, but she would be there and ready for them when they arrived. Her mind already on that appealing prospect, she paid the SD taxi, thanked the AI awkwardly, and almost ran to the front door. She hurried inside and up the steps, kicked her shoes off, and lay face-down on the bed. After a moment, she rolled onto her back, kicked her feet, and squealed for a moment to get it out of her system.

When she calmed, she stood, changed into a pair of jeans and a T-shirt, and continued her packing. She was almost done with it but wanted to make sure she would have exactly what she needed. As she went through her old clothes, she discovered a pair of yoga pants and a sweatshirt that she used to wear all the time. She didn't want to get rid of everything and she knew that she would need a set of lazy wear for work. If she would go in and out of the pod and have to remove all her clothes—that thought still made her *cringe*—then she wanted to try to be as comfortable as she possibly could be while doing it.

Needless to say, she was not fond of the fact that she had to get naked every time she used it. "It's like the eggheads who designed this equipment don't have any idea of what a female would find embarrassing. Because sure, we all love to throw our clothes off in front of perfect strangers, get cold, and lie inside an egg unconscious to the world around us. It must have been a man who designed the damn thing."

Of course, even though she didn't know this, BURT had designed it. As was only to be expected, he had done it in a completely calculated and data-driven way with zero thought to modesty or embarrassment—two things he had no real understanding of. He meant no harm by it, of course, but nonetheless, he hadn't thought that one through at all.

She finished what she intended to pack that day and headed downstairs as the notification for the virtual mail went off. Excited, she hurried over and swiped right to confirm that a package waited for her parents. It was the paperwork from Martelle. With an eager smile, she put it through and waited impatiently as the documents printed out below. The front door opened and clicked closed and she knew her parents had returned home.

Stephanie grabbed the papers off the table and giggled, really excited to tell them. She only hoped they would be as excited as she was. With the papers held behind her back, she poked her head through the doorway. "Mom? Dad? I have something to tell you."

They both looked up happily, but her mother's expression immediately shifted to concern. That prompted her daughter to hurry forward and put her hand on her mother's arm. "No, no. Not bad. Sorry. I don't mean to scare you with these things. Nothing bad at all. In fact, I personally think that it's really exciting."

Her mother gave her a side glance. "What did you do?"

Stephanie smirked. "So, the other day when I was coming into the house, I overheard you talking about a project at the Cromwell building. You said that it could push you guys forward—grow your company and be really good money. But the problem was that you didn't have anyone to go to the meeting."

Cindy narrowed her eyes. "Okay…"

She pulled the papers out from behind her back and handed them to her mother. "So, I went and did it on my own. I used what I learned about business, sat down, presented some stats, and offered a deal. He said that he liked the offer in principle but he's sure there will be some sort of negotiation."

Her parents froze and their mouths dropped open as they stared at the papers. Her father walked over to her, hauled her up onto her toes, and hugged her tightly. "This is really incredible. I can't believe you did something like this. I honestly didn't even know you knew how."

Stephanie rolled her eyes. "Yeah, I learned it at the prep school. Once it's learned, you can't really unlearn it. So, what do you think? Is that what you want for the company?" She plopped into a chair.

Cindy laughed and looked at Mark. "Of course it is, honey. It's more than we could have asked for. Obviously, we will have to do some negotiation, but we will definitely want this job. No question about it."

Mark rubbed his chin and stared off into the distance. "I wonder if I could clean the outside of the windows in a superhero costume? We will have to invest in a serious supply of window cleaner."

They all laughed. Stephanie put her hands in her lap and nodded at the paper. "I have to get going in two days. So, work on the negotiations, and on my way out, I will drop it with Mr. Martelle. I told him we needed a couple of days on it. He is fine with that."

Cindy stood and hurried over to kiss her daughter on the cheek. "You are more than we could have ever asked for in a child. Thank you for this. Your father and I will get started on it immediately—right, Mark?"

He nodded wildly. 'Yeah, we will. I'll get the coffee brewing. This will take a while—not that we mind, even in the slightest."

CHAPTER FIFTY-SEVEN

Stephanie walked down the stairs dressed in comfortable smart pants with a relaxed fit, black slip-on shoes, and a plain white button-up shirt. She pulled her suitcase behind her and its wheels *whomped* down the steps. Under one arm, she held her purse, and in the other hand, the documents from her parents for the negotiations and completion of terms of the contract for cleaning the building. When she reached the bottom of the steps, her parents stood there, ready to say goodbye.

Her mother brushed her shoulders as she always did. "I don't know why you didn't send those over virtually. I don't know the last time I saw a printed document."

Stephanie smiled. "Archaic, I know, but this is an important one and I want him to take it from my hands. Besides, we have to use up that huge stash of paper Dad was given when that print shop closed down and still owed you money. You guys never use it, so I might as well indulge my printing fetish."

A horn blew outside, and her father picked her other suitcase up. "Well, come on, let's get you packed in the car and then your mother can cry rivers."

Cindy had already starting to tear up and she slapped her husband on the arm as they walked outside. They loaded her luggage into the trunk and Stephanie set the envelope of papers into the back seat. She turned, took a deep breath, and held her arms out to her mother. The woman clutched her tightly and tried to hold the sobs back, then stepped back and dabbed a tissue to the corners of her eyes.

She held Stephanie's hands and sniffled. "You be safe out there. Watch where you are at night, never go without protection—"

Stephanie wrinkled her nose. "Mom!"

Her mother sighed. "I meant like mace or a battery or something along those lines."

She giggled and turned to her dad to hug him tightly. As she pressed her face against his chest, she drew in that warm, comforting scent she had always turned to. She could hear her mom gasp slightly and run back to the house, but her dad held her close and leaned down to talk in her ear. "Knock 'em dead out there, kiddo. Not literally, but figuratively. Unless, of course, the situation demands otherwise."

Stephanie laughed and pulled back. "You know it. But like I said before, there will be plenty of security and I will be working relatively alone the whole time. Things will be good and the first chance I have, I will come home and visit."

Her mother returned, carrying a book wrapped in a deep purple cloth. She unwrapped it carefully and the tome almost fell apart. "This is…it's…well, it was in the family for generations. I don't believe it, but…well…"

Her father put his arm around her shoulder and his nose pressed into the side of her head. "Sweetheart, you may not know all the stories, but you are a Morgana. Read that if you can and make up your own mind. Just know that you being a magic user might…might… have come up before in your family history. Or it's a bunch of bullshit." Her mom jabbed him in the side. "Oomph! Or, fancy horse manure…"

Stephanie smirked and traced her fingers tentatively over the torn and tattered cover. Her father shrugged. "Either way, if you can read it, know that there might be a reason for your abilities."

Carefully, her mother handed her the book and watched her closely as her gaze studied every inch of it. Stephanie gripped the thickest edge of the cover and opened it, using her body to shield it from the stiff breeze. Her father put one hand out to hold it so that it wouldn't rip off the spine. She paused, looked up and down the page, and turned it. Her gaze wandered across the next page.

Her mother exhaled a deep breath and put her hand to her chest. "See? I don't see anything either. Only blank pages. Maybe you're right, Mark. Maybe it was merely some silly story."

"Blank pages," Stephanie whispered to herself.

The ambassador's card.

The battery rubbed against the outside of her thigh from where it rested in her pocket. She pressed her fingers tentatively to the page. A small trace of magic whirled from her fingertips, but it was too minute for even her parents to notice.

When the world needs a Morgana, one will rise to the occasion. There they were—the words seemed as clear as if they were written on the inside of her eyelids. Plain as day.

She opened her eyes wide to find her parents standing there, staring at her. Her mother looked at the pages and back at her. "Do you see something we can't?"

Stephanie released a deep breath and chuckled but decided to keep her discovery a secret for now. "No. I like freaking you out a bit, that's all."

Her mother laughed, relieved, and her father smirked and nodded his head. "Let's get this wrapped up and in your bag. You need to get on the road. There is a TRAM to catch and you still need to go past the office building. With so much to do today, there is no reason to stand in the driveway and stare at a blank-paged book like a bunch of crazies."

She smiled and closed it, wrapped it up tightly once again, and placed it in her bag. As her parents moved around to the front, she swept her hand over it to provide it magical protection—or, at least, she hoped that was what she had accomplished. It seemed more and more, as each day passed, that when she looked for a specific spell, it would almost come to her without thought. She wasn't sure if that was a good sign or merely a normal thing but then again, she didn't really have anything to judge it against. Perhaps the book might help her in that way.

All smiles, she shut the trunk and moved forward to hug both her parents again before she clambered into the back of the car. Her father held tightly to her mother's shoulder as they waved, yelled their wishes for her to have good luck, and Cindy sobbed into her tissue. She smiled as the vehicle moved off, knowing she would be back but focused on her excitement for the future ahead of her. It could be somber, sure, but she wouldn't allow it to create any stress for her. Besides, she couldn't walk into the building looking miserable.

The car stopped outside the large, looming skyscraper and the door opened automatically for her. She stepped out with the envelope and walked into the large entryway. The same secretary stood behind the desk, this time with a more pleasant look on her face. "How can I help you today?"

Stephanie handed her the paperwork. "I wondered if Mr. Martelle was in. I wanted to hand these to him personally."

The woman grimaced. "I'm afraid he has been on site but not in his office. I can hand-deliver them for you if you would like. I am not sure if he will even be back in his office today."

Stephanie frowned and tapped on the desk. "Shoot. I guess I'll—"

"Ms. Morgana," a familiar voice shouted behind her.

She turned as Mr. Martelle walked toward her with another person beside him. Instantly, Stephanie flashed a smile and retrieved the envelope with a whispered thank you to the secretary. She winked at her as she turned. The two shook hands but the man beside him simply stood there and glowered in her general direction. Still, she kept her composure.

Stephanie put her hand out to the other man, but he dismissed her rudely with a flicker of fire in his eyes. "So, this is her. The woman who thinks she can come in and take what is rightfully ours."

She drew her hand back with a polite smile. "You must be Mr. Wesley. I assure you, there was nothing personal in my attempts. Only business, you see. Attempting to provide Mr. Martelle with the kind of service that he has come to expect."

He sneered and turned to the other man. Stephanie's phone vibrated in her pocket as he turned his back to exclude her from the conversation. She stood her ground, although she stepped to the side. "Some no-name two-bit business, please. Don't be a fool, Martelle. Okay, so we took our eyes off the ball a little. We can do better."

Stephanie was faintly worried by his pleading and the fact that they had more of a personal relationship than she had expected. Her phone buzzed in her hand again and she turned to the side to answer the call. No one paid attention to her at that point anyway.

"Hello," she answered and tried to keep the sound of Mr. Wesley's gruff tone out of the receiver.

"Stephanie! It is Brilgus, the ambassador's guard," the caller said jubilantly.

She smiled. "Oh, Brilgus, so good to hear from you. How are you?"

He chuckled. "Good, full of too many dinners, I suppose. I guess I should stop having those when I go with him."

Stephanie giggled and ignored the conversation beside her. "What can I do for you?"

"I called to see if you would be in town tonight. The ambassador would like to have dinner with you."

She smirked, turned a fraction, and talked a little more loudly. "Why, certainly. I'd love to have dinner with the ambassador. I've been dying to catch up since our last visit."

Mr. Martelle shifted his gaze toward her and raised his hand to his companion. He stared at her for a moment and she mouthed the words, "I'm sorry," with a huge grin on her face.

He snapped his head back toward the angry man. "Two-bit?"

Mr. Wesley fumed. "Yes! Two-bit, half a company, no real talent. No backing. Some slums from the other side of town—"

The other man pointed to the young woman who stood nearby and laughed at something her caller said. "Let me ask you this. Do your people come in here to speak to me—the owner of the company and the building—dressed to impress? When I saw her yesterday, I thought she was the wrong appointment, not some representative from a cleaning company."

Mr. Wesley furrowed his brow and glared at Stephanie as she shifted her gaze away from him as she talked. "What?"

Mr. Martelle folded his arms over his chest. "Do your people go to Washington DC to have dinner with ambassadors who have their people call you to set up the meeting?"

His companion gritted his teeth and pointed his finger accusingly. "Now you hold on one second. Since when did cleaning become something you needed clout to do? Besides, don't believe this schtick. I did that lame shit long before she was born. She's probably talking to her brother or mommy on the phone. You would be an idiot to think that someone like her is that important."

He scoffed and gestured dismissively, and Stephanie narrowed her eyes. "One moment, please, Brilgus. I apologize."

She covered the phone receiver, turned to him, and pursed her lips. "First of all, I walked in here with the utmost respect, professionalism, and manners. I dress this way because that, sir, is how you gain respect, no matter what the business you happen to be in. If cleaning floors and toilets are demeaning to you and you therefore choose to come in sloppily and with an attitude, that is your problem. Because in my eyes, after watching two people grow and build this very business all my life, I can tell you there is nothing to be ashamed of. I am sorry that your business acumen and politesse are lacking but do not take that out on me."

Mr. Wesley looked at her, slightly confused, and silently mouthed the word politesse. Stephanie rolled her eyes. "If I weren't on the phone with a gentleman, I would say it in words better suited to your understanding."

Mr. Martelle chuckled, stepped back, and watched it unfold. He rather enjoyed the sparring between them, and even more so the way in which the girl was able to articulate herself to leave Mr. Wesley in complete and utter confusion.

Her opponent shook his head and looked at Martelle as he spoke in a low tone. "She is a fraud. A hoax. She doesn't know any ambassador and she sure as hell isn't traveling to DC to meet up with one. If she is, it's for far more than dinner—"

Stephanie's mouth fell open in rage but before she could say anything, her phone buzzed in her hand. Brilgus had sent a text to get her attention. **Please put me on speaker.**

She smiled and cleared her throat. "The ambassador's security specialist would like to say something," she said as she put the phone on speaker.

Even though Brilgus was either human or half-human, he still spoke in a strong Meligornian accent and a deep booming voice when necessary. "This is Brilgus, lead security specialist to the great Ambassador of Meligorn. How dare you speak to this woman in such a manner? How have you lived for this long without recognizing the pre-eminent human witch who stands before you? Had you acted this way in any other time or situation, I would have watched her fry you for your insolence. Show your due respect." His tone changed to a calm voice. "Shall we say the car will pick you up at eight pm then?"

Stephanie snickered. "That sounds perfect. Thank you, Brilgus. I look forward to seeing you and the ambassador."

They hung up and she stuck her phone in her purse. Suddenly, Mr. Wesley lurched and completely lost it. "How dare you put some half-breed Meligornian on the phone telling me I need to respect you, woman? I am under no obligation, and to think you would have some witch involved in your—"

Stephanie gripped her battery lightly, thrust her hand into the air, and waved it in front of his face. *"Enough!"*

His mouth snapped shut and his lips sealed. His eyes widened and he touched his face, slightly panicked. She narrowed her eyes, stepped toward him, and scrutinized him with slow deliberation. "Now that I have your attention—"

He mumbled, backed up, and clawed at the space where his mouth used to be. She tilted her finger back and forth in front of his frightened eyes. "I don't appreciate the slurs you have thrown at my personage or that of my dear friends. Do you believe for a second that everyone is a conniving, lying, lower than a rat individual like yourself?"

As if unable to help himself, he roved his gaze over the lobby and finally nodded. Mr. Martelle leaned his head back and laughed so loudly that it echoed through the marble-covered room. "Nice way to get him to admit that about himself."

The man, confused, looked at Martelle, back at Stephanie, and began to shake his head violently back and forth. Stephanie retreated for a few steps and folded her arms when she stood beside the other man and stared at Mr. Wesley. She admired her handiwork and how quickly she was able to translate her wants into magic. "What would you have me do? I have only two hours to get to the TRAM. I can leave that—" She motioned to his missing mouth. "Or return him to his less than admirable prior condition and allow the two of you to have a discussion."

Mr. Martelle sighed heavily and shook his head. He lowered his arm and shrugged. "Take it off, please. I guess I can't have him run around my complex like that and scare the clients."

Stephanie raised her hand and snapped her fingers to instantly return his mouth to him. He gasped and patted his fingers wildly over his lips. For several moments, he stood there speechless, and she began to think she had somehow accidentally affected his voice.

Finally, Mr. Wesley spoke. "Mr. Martelle, I—"

The other man shook his head and raised a hand to silence him. "I want to make something very, very clear to you, Wesley. This is my building. The people whom I invite into these walls are only welcomed after careful examination of character, manners, and class. Apparently, I missed you in that review. If you ever come into my establishment again in a manner as brazen and blatantly disrespectful as you did today, I will have you arrested by federal police. Do you understand?"

Mr. Wesley frowned, and his nostrils flared. "Yes."

Mr. Martelle brushed his hands off decisively. "Good, then. It's all settled. Now, if you wouldn't mind removing your useless ass from my building, I would be much obliged. If you have thought about your actions, brought them to a careful review in your mind, and understood your wrongdoing during the course of the next three years, then you may reapply when the contract has ended."

The ex-contractor huffed and stormed out of the building but made no effort to look at Stephanie again. Her companion chuckled and glanced at her. "My lunch plans just walked out in a huff. Would you care to have a quick lunch in the building's restaurant? We can have your luggage brought in and the car dismissed and call another once we've eaten. I'd like to have a chance to get to know the woman an ambassador from Meligorn calls for dinner reservations. I doubt any of my friends will have a better story than mine for at least a month."

Stephanie laughed. "That was a good one, wasn't it? Although I apologize for the mouth thing. I got a tad carried away, I suppose."

Mr. Martelle scoffed. "Please. That was the best thing I have ever seen. He's had it coming for years."

He put his hand on her back and guided her toward the elevators. As they waited, Stephanie looked over at him with curiosity. "Mr. Martelle, did you say three years?"

"Yes," he admitted as they stepped into the elevator and the doors began to close. "He was being a very large ass."

CHAPTER FIFTY-EIGHT

This time, Stephanie was alone in her cabin in first class. That gave her the opportunity to put her feet up and she ordered a small dessert—there hadn't been time for one after lunch—and a soda, leaned back, and watched the scenery change rapidly outside her window. It was a much-needed moment to herself. A time when she could reflect on her thoughts, worry little, and even shut her eyes for a moment and rest. She had to adjust to the idea that she wasn't home because now, hers had become a place and circumstance where home was less defined by the four walls that surrounded her and more by her own comfort in herself.

Taking the job in Washington was fantastic and she hoped that it continued as a long-term thing, but she had learned very young, watching the ghettos burn on the outskirts of Old Chicago, that everything was temporary. Even life was temporary, an extraordinary understanding for someone of her age to have, she knew. Nonetheless, it was there. That didn't take away her questions and curiosity, but it was something that lingered forever in the back of her mind.

Her cool, bubbling grape soda was refreshing, and she pushed the tray aside and rubbed her stomach. She thought about bringing the book out, but her eyelids already tried to slam shut on her. Instead, she dumped the tray outside where they told her to leave it when she'd finished, locked her door with her palm signature, and found a blanket before she curled up in one of the reclining chairs. The trip wouldn't take that long, but she still had a few minutes of sleep she could sneak in before the craziness of her new life punched her in the chin.

It wasn't long before Stephanie nodded off, her head comfortably cushioned against the soft velour of the chair beneath her. Her dreams wandered to visions of Meligorn, the pond from her testing, and a wide teal field of flowing long grasses beneath the purple haze of the MU spectrum. She looked around her and paused when she realized she now wore a long white gown that dragged on the ground behind her. Over her shoulders was a purple cloak, the hood slightly perched on the top of her head.

The energy surged through her, and with every step that she took, it swirled around her bare feet. Up ahead in the grassy clearing, another person stood silently. But they were not Meligornian—at least by outward appearance. The woman stood turned away from her. Cascading ribbons of long brown hair, secured halfway with rows of tiny purple flowers, rolled gently over her back. She wore a similar robe but long and purple.

Stephanie took several steps toward her and tentatively stretched out her hand, the need to connect with her astonishingly powerful. As if she were a character in a horrible action movie, the woman's body tensed sharply, and her head turned to look at Stephanie. Her eyes glistened a bright purple and she opened her mouth to emit a low moan that fluttered across the waves of wind and directly at her. Stephanie backed away and raised her hand as the sound drew closer and billowed into a large cloud of magic. She screamed instinctively as the purple mass rolled inexorably toward her.

Confused and actually afraid, she lurched forward in the chair and clutched her chest, breathing heavily. A sound at the door made her jump, and she looked up to where one of the attendants knocked a second time. She straightened her shirt and hair and pushed to her feet, shuffled to the door, and pressed her palm against the device to open it.

"I'm sorry, ma'am. Your door was locked. We have arrived in Washington."

She turned toward the window and blinked at the bustling train station outside. The man seemed to want a response, so she looked at him and nodded. "Thank you."

He glanced at her bags. "Can I help you with those?"

Stephanie shook her head and pulled them down easily, still slightly dazed from sleep. "No, thank you. I've got them."

He stood to the side and smiled at her as she exited the train and stepped onto the sidewalk. The warm late evening air soothed her neck and the throbbing pulse of her muscles, stiff from the way she'd been lying. As she approached the curb, she found her car, waiting like before, and it took her quickly to the hotel.

She was in the same suite, and everyone fell over themselves in their efforts to welcome her. Despite her efforts to shake the strange fog of the dream from her brain, she struggled to do so. Safely in her suite, she sent her family a message that she had arrived and jumped in the shower. Like magic, the water ran over her and washed away the heaviness that had sat in her chest like a rock. A little more relaxed, she dried herself off thoroughly and looked at the time. She still had two hours before she would be picked up for dinner.

The balcony door was cracked to allow a small breeze to drift in. She walked outside and looked at the view. From there, she could see most of the major historical monuments—or the ruins of them, at least. To her right, about three blocks up, was a more active area where people laughed, wandered around, and shopped from vendors in the street. Music and voices drifted up toward her and carried what appeared to be a pleasant vibe. On impulse, she threw on a pair of shorts, a T-shirt, ball cap, and tennis shoes and headed out there.

For some reason, her body appeared so much more acute than before. All her senses seemed to be aroused. The place felt wild to her like it was another time or place. The skies were clearer there than in other places as they had used technology to clear the smog in Washington before they had bothered to do so anywhere else. But in place of banners, planes, or open views were a plethora of flying cars. An entire network of roads, streets, and intersections hung above the city. From down below, it didn't look like they drove any better in the sky then they did on the ground. But it cleared the streets up and made for a more comfortable walk around town.

All along the blocks, digital holograms—some small and others larger than people—floated in and out to advertise a shop or some product placement for tourists. Several times, Stephanie almost lost her way as she strolled through several stores in a row and sensed the small touch of electricity in them. She watched people, too, but her eyes reacted in a way that seemed unnatural to her as if she scanned everyone she saw. There was a level of suspicion in her chest, something that up until that point, she had not experienced.

She wanted to know who the people around her were, where they were going, and what they were up to behind closed doors. As she approached an intersection, eating some hot nuts casually from a brown paper bag, she glanced up in bemusement. Two guys and one girl stood on the other side of the road. They barely glanced at her and all wore black, shiny clothing, their hair wild and teased, and the guys had applied more black eyeliner than she had.

There was no real evidence other than their looks to give Stephanie a bad feeling, but for some reason, she felt that they could be dangerous. She looked at her watch and cursed as she threw the bag in the trash. As she hurried back the way she had come, she glanced around one last time but the three were nowhere to be seen. She shook off the odd wariness that had stirred in her at the sight of them and jogged back to her hotel where the doorman stood smiling. "Nice walk, ma'am?"

Stephanie nodded. "Yes. Thank you. I should have a guest pick me up here in thirty minutes. I am not sure if it is only a car or the Ambassador of Meligorn himself. Please call me if I am not back down here when they arrive."

The doorman looked a little thrown off by the name, but he recovered himself quickly. "Yes, of course. Let us know if you need anything."

"Thank you."

She jogged through the lobby, into her private elevator, and up to her suite. Thank goodness she had already taken a shower and laid out her clothes because otherwise, she would be up shit creek with an ambassador coming to see her. Her hand on the closet door, she waited for the light on the side to turn green before she opened it. She had set it to de-wrinkle her dress for the evening and it also scented it with a sweet mystical scent of Meligorn flowers.

The smell calmed her nerves instantly and she eased the dress over her head. It sat off the shoulders, but sleeveless, hugged the bust, and flared out slightly at the waist. The dark-blue fabric appeared to have stars sparkling through it. It was one of the most expensive pieces she had originally bought, but she hadn't been able to resist it. She slipped her flats on and turned her attention to her hair. The soft, wind-dried curls complemented the look well.

So, with a pat of powder, a dash of lipstick, and a pair of earrings her mother had given her, she was ready to go. In fact, she was so ready that she still had fifteen minutes to wait. In case they arrived early, she decided to head down and wait in the lobby. As soon as the doors opened, the concierge came to her with a smile. "Is there something we can do for you, Ms. Morgana?"

Stephanie tilted her head slightly and smiled. "No, thank you. I am actually waiting down here for my company this evening to pick me up. They won't be here for another ten minutes or so."

He raised an eyebrow and gestured to a passing waiter, who returned a few minutes later to place a glass of champagne on the countertop. "Just long enough to relax with a glass of champagne, still grown in Champagne. We are lucky to be able to travel there and bring several cases back a couple of times a year."

She was shocked. Even the richies didn't often have champagne due to the lack of trade between NorAm and the rest of the world. The land in most of the United States was far too soiled by nuclear waste and other disasters to grow anything even remotely like a grape. She closed her eyes and took a sip. The bitter beginning and sweet bubbly end tickled her senses.

She smiled her appreciation. "Thank you so much. This is such a nice treat."

The concierge placed his hands in front of him. "You are quite welcome, young lady. If I may be so bold to say so, many of us here very much look up to your achievements. We, as a staff, have spent most of our lives in the Washington, Virginia, or Maryland subs. To see someone break free of that stronghold and be one with magical abilities on top of that is a true princess story that keeps us hoping."

Stephanie was truly touched by this. "Oh…I'm sorry, I didn't get your name."

He tapped his nametag. "Mr. Holden, ma'am. But you may call me Rufus if you please."

The doorman cleared his throat and Rufus put his arm out. "Your carriage has arrived."

She handed him the glass. "Thank you. I will see you when I get back."

A chauffeur held the door open for her when she stepped out of the hotel. It was a self-driving vehicle, but he was there for more of a personal touch. A protection unit sat in both the front and back of the car, and Stephanie could only assume that the Ambassador himself would be present. The attendant took her hand and she stepped into the vehicle and scooted carefully into the seat. Sitting across from her were Brilgus and the ambassador.

Stephanie, having learned the seated greeting, put her hands together and bowed her head in reverence. As she raised it once more, she spoke. "H'lemish Monguild Brathius Shode."

The ambassador smiled and nodded. "And right back to you. Though I would say, it is pronounced *Shod*, without the long o. The other pronunciation is more what the Meligornians refer to as the…uhm..."

He looked at Brilgus, perplexed, who held his chuckle back. "Yes, of course. It is the anal sphincter of a human."

She covered her mouth and giggled. "Oh no. I just said, it is an honor and privilege, anal sphincter?"

Brilgus shook with his effort to hold back a laugh but the ambassador ignored his bodyguard and simply let it out. They all laughed then, which lightened the mood considerably. Stephanie wiped tears from under her eyes and fanned her face. "Oh...that was not how I imagined it in my head."

Her host chuckled again. "Don't worry. It is a common mistake and most humans are rarely corrected. A little Meligornian humor, I suppose. Although I wouldn't want you to meet anyone of importance and make the mistake."

Stephanie slid the tissue back in her clutch and glanced at him. "I appreciate it."

Brilgus shifted slightly and his enormous muscles ground into the corner. "You do very well, though. Better than almost any human I have spoken to."

The ambassador nodded his head. "Oh, yes. I would have to say just as well, if not almost better, than the liaison I have at the moment."

The car came slowly to a stop and the chauffeur opened the door to let Brilgus out first, then Stephanie, and finally, the ambassador. They stood in front of one of the most exclusive restaurants in Washington, and all Stephanie could do was hold back giggles for calling the ambassador an asshole.

CHAPTER FIFTY-NINE

The room began to lighten slowly, and Stephanie yawned loudly as the chirping of birds lifted the mood. That morning, though, she wanted to hit the snooze button, if there even was one, and go back to bed. She had stayed at the restaurant with Brilgus and the ambassador until nearly one in the morning. They simply talked and laughed, and he had taught her so many words. She knew how to ask for food, how to ask how someone was, and how to talk about family and friends. She had never picked Spanish up like that in school, but Meligornian felt almost like it came naturally to her.

She hauled herself to the end of the bed and rubbed her face. "Sarah."

The AI responded. "Yes?"

"Could you order me some coffee and breakfast?" She yawned.

"I have already done so. As soon as you have finished your shower, it will be on the table," she replied, and the shower clicked on in the bathroom. "Shower set to a comfortable one hundred and seven degrees, your last known preference."

Stephanie pushed herself from the bed and shuffled into the bathroom. Her eyes opened a little wider as the fragrance of menthol and eucalyptus awakened her senses. She showered and sat down at the breakfast table, sipped her coffee, and pulled at a croissant as she scanned through the news on the tabletop tablet to her right.

"More unrest in space with the Dreth, Sarah," she said with a sigh.

Sarah emitted an AI digital sigh. "Yes, I have heard that tensions are high between the Dreth and the Federation. They are fighting back harder."

Stephanie raised an eyebrow. "Did you sigh?"

"My programming has been updated to include other responses to make me feel more human."

She straightened quickly, intrigued. "Like what? Can you laugh?"

The AI paused. "Yes, a laugh is in the queue. Would you like to hear it?"

Stephanie put her croissant down and smiled. "Of course I would."

There was another slight pause and the AI began to laugh. Unfortunately, it sounded slightly like a sped-up recording of a child's laugh. Stephanie blinked and covered her ears. "Oh no. Oh, that was… your engineer should be ashamed."

"Was it bad?" Sarah asked.

She wiped her mouth and chuckled. "Close to what I would imagine the sound of a dozen hamsters caught in a blender would be. Can I disable the laugh?"

The AI responded, "Laugh disabled."

Stephanie dressed for the day and opted not for her most comfortable outfit but something that also wasn't fancy in the least. She decided that as this was her first day back, she would save the yoga pants for the second day. Downstairs, she was greeted by the concierge who showed her to the self-driven car that would take her to work.

"Rufus," Stephanie said and stared at the car. "Is this a flying car?"

He nodded. "Oh, yes. The newest and best."

She pursed her lips and nodded uncertainly as she stared at it. "I've never been in a flying car before. Much less a self-driving flying car."

Rufus walked over and opened the door. "Then may I suggest buckling up tight? It can often be somewhat turbulent up there. I prefer to steer my own, but since you haven't been trained, I would let it drive you to work this time around."

Stephanie dragged in a deep breath and patted him on the shoulder. "Right, then. I will add that to my training list. Until then, I hope it's clear skies."

It was clear skies but being up in the air in a tin can was not something she adapted too either quickly or easily. Stephanie essentially flew the entire way to the new building outside the city with her eyes clenched shut and her stomach lurching every time it dropped or rose to the various levels of the airway. It was exactly how she imagined the old rollercoasters that Todd was obsessed with would feel like.

The car descended slowly in front of the new building and a man walked out to open her door. She glanced at him for a second and he responded with a toothy grin. "Hi, I'm Lars. I'm one of your security team."

Stephanie pulled her bag out of the trunk, her chin lifted in surprise. "Oh? I didn't know I needed security."

He chuckled and held the door open for her. "I think as the only magical human on Earth, you might need a little someone watching your back from time to time, right?"

"I guess." Stephanie shrugged. "Why not? The more the merrier, right? Where do I find Ms. Elizabeth?"

She glanced around and realized she had no idea where she was. "And… I…where am I?"

Lars laughed, his dimples deep and his eyes a crystal-blue. "It's a new building, and things are far more secure and better maintained. Ms. E actually asked me to escort you to the pod room, where she said you would know what to do. And she said that when you are finished with that session, she will meet up with you. She had to finish a few things, but she said you would find a familiar voice inside."

Stephanie raised her eyebrow. "Oh, Lord. I hope they didn't make the AI sound like my mom or something."

Lars smirked as he led her down the freshly painted hallways—which boasted cameras in every corner—and sparkling tiled floors. He stopped in front of a large metal door and put his hand out. "Uh.

Palm, then retina, and it opens from there. They have all this in the system from your first visit. Only three people have access—you, Ms. E, and me, but I only have it for an extreme emergency."

Stephanie turned and poked him in the chest. "No peeking. None."

He put his hands up. "I am always professional. Although Ms. E might not be if you don't get in there."

She turned and placed her palm on the pad, then jumped slightly as the retina scanner popped out in front of her. Lars gestured for her to place her chin in the strap and it scanned her eye before the door lock popped. She turned the big handle and walked in as the lights flickered on. The floor was covered with some sort of foam-like material and she bounced slightly as she walked.

When she glanced back at Lars, he nodded, closed the door, and turned the handle. The light above the door went from red to green and the ambient lighting dimmed slightly for comfort. She walked to a table in the corner and undressed, folded her things, and set them neatly on the table. Instinctively, she wrapped her arms around herself and shivered, narrowing her eyes up toward the ceiling as if she were inside the Virtual Realm, and gave her AI a virtual middle finger.

Stephanie climbed into the pod and closed the door. The shift into the other world was as seamless as before and when she opened her eyes, she stood in a large stone building. The sand beneath her feet was white and sparkling flecks shimmered through it despite the lack of natural light. She wore a long, flowing purple skirt and a tank top with flowers pinned down the back of her loose braid.

"Hello, Stephanie," a voice echoed.

She had heard that voice before. Delight rippled through her and she rubbed her finger over her chin and shook it in the air as she laughed. "Burt! I knew you would come back. Did you change jobs? Are you working for ONE R&D now?"

"Something like that," he replied. "And it's good to hear your voice. What are we doing today? I am simply here to watch, notate, and be of service if you need me to."

Stephanie nodded, extended her hands, and felt the energy bounce off her palms. "I think I will simply go with it today. I have a thought, but I want to work with Meligornian magic first. So, I'll only be doing some manipulations."

"All right," BURT replied. "Whenever you are ready. Just pretend I'm not here."

She glanced around and smirked before she closed her eyes. Her focus immediate, she used her hands to draw the energy slowly from the ground and twirl it in circular motions in front of her. As the energy grew stronger, she moved her arms faster and whipped the long trails of magic through the air so they twisted and twined together before they unraveled and began again. She tilted her head back and opened her mouth. The magic flowed from her throat and seeped from the corners of her closed eyes.

Eventually, the stream of energy coming in began to slow and she glowed brighter and brighter. The streams she still connected to spiraled around and through her, back out again, and passed through each fingertip. She dipped her head low and continued to sway as if in a tribal dance as she looped her arms down and then high over her head. The circle of magic grew tighter and she twirled it in her hands as if she were a goddess playing with the very solar system itself.

When she opened her eyes, the magic within her erupted to join the intertwining strands around her. Purple vibrations coursed down each strand of her hair and the flowers began to shimmer and change shape before they fell to the ground.

BURT paused for a moment when he identified a sound from the space. The deep humming seemed to be a song from the pit of Stephanie's stomach. Each note hung on the strings of energy that swirled through her at an ever-increasing pace. Her entire body glowed so brightly, the system was filled with a momentary white noise. Suddenly, she froze, her feet raised from the ground, and her breath caught in her throat.

For a moment, everything was absolutely silent until...*booom!* Her entire body exploded and launched waves of energy to blast outward and destroy the building she stood in. It flattened the long blades of grass and shoved the simulated MU spectrum in the sky aside.

It took BURT a split second to gather his system back to a baseline but as soon as he did, he ejected her body from the system. The door to the pod flew open and Stephanie rolled out and fell on all fours. She rasped a ragged cough and the spit dribbled from her mouth onto the cushioned pads. When she opened her eyes, everything was so bright—so real. She blinked wildly and stared in bemusement at the string of saliva attached to her lip. When she wiped her mouth with the back of her hand, she noticed blood. Reluctantly, she looked at the spittle on the floor and saw telltale streaks of red in that as well.

She had done it again, despite her knowledge of the first time. She had done something to her real body through her virtual world experience.

CHAPTER SIXTY

Stephanie wiped her face with a towel and took another big swig of water. She felt better—much better—but she still couldn't understand what had happened. Ms. E had come in and helped her up off the floor, brought the doc in to check her out, and everything seemed fine. As soon as she got some water in her system and the batteries back in her pocket, she felt as right as rain, physically at least. It was a little confusing that the battery somehow seemed to make her stronger—unless she subconsciously absorbed a little of it in her weakened state? The thought was worth exploring but at another time. Right now, she was content to simply accept its help because she had much larger issues to confront.

What she had seen within the energy she had experienced while in the pod was something she couldn't even begin to explain.

Ms. E walked in and clapped her hands. She wore her normal clothes, including the six-inch heels. For the life of her, Stephanie couldn't figure out how she actually walked in the things. "How are you feeling, kiddo?"

She nodded. "Good. Am I going back in?"

The woman smiled mischievously. "Not exactly. Okay, come on in, boys."

Stephanie sat and watched as six guys, all relatively young, all buff, and all dressed the exact same way in ONE R&D workout gear, walked into the room. Ms. E stood to the side and cracked her knuckles. "So, with the way the world is today, together with the way that some people may view you as an asset or a liability—both with equally detrimental side effects, I should add—we think it is vitally important that you know some self-defense."

She wrinkled her nose in distaste at a flash of memory. "I learned some martial arts at Pinnacle when I hooked the cubes up at night."

Ms. E chuckled. "That's good. It means you have a base in all of this, but you need to know it real-world style. Most likely, if you are fighting for your life, it will be in the real world. This is also an excellent time for you to really get to know your security crew for the building. They will be your first, middle, and last line of defense."

She put her arm out and moved down the line. "These are your six primary guards. There are four others who give these guys a break from time to time. We have Brenden, Avery, Johnny, Jack—or Frog, as we call him—Marcus, and you have already met Lars."

Lars gave her a small flick of the fingers and a smile. She nodded at them but slyly edged her hand into the pocket of her pants to grasp the battery. This seemed like as good a time as any to practice with the energy. The batteries the company had sent her had enabled her to practice, and in time, she'd found that she could absorb and hold a small residual level of the power. Nothing even close to a major breakthrough, but encouraging, nonetheless. She'd simply assumed that her body had adjusted somewhat.

This was a small battery and wasn't completely full, either, so it was a good basis for experimentation. She kept her expression relaxed as she drew all the remaining energy from the battery as slowly as she could so that Ms. E wouldn't notice. A little tour earlier had revealed that she could reload them inside the building. It seemed the company had invested in a supply of the larger ones as a kind of magical larder, and she assumed they would be replaced as they were used. Knowing that, she didn't mind depleting this one in what might be a good cause.

She took a deep breath. "I'm fighting my own guys?"

Ms. E nodded. "I thought that would be a better way to start than to fight your enemies."

Stephanie stood and stretched her arms from side to side. "Let me clarify this because it can be a gray area in my world. Am I using all my abilities?"

The woman smirked and turned to the men. "For the first few rounds, I want Stephanie to restrain herself. We will work on martial arts."

They exchanged glances and finally looked at Stephanie, who seemed really small compared to everyone else. Having never actually seen her do anything outside the videos of her that they'd watched, they simply shrugged. Ms. E stepped out of the way and stood on the side where she leaned her shoulder against one of the columns.

Stephanie walked into the center and adopted her defensive pose. Her self-confidence rose when all the knowledge and muscle memory from school suddenly flooded her head. Brenden came forward first with the task to ensure that she knew all the defensive moves. She blocked him with the simpler ones, but when he did a back handspring and brought his foot around, he knocked her squarely in the head.

Immediately, his eyes widened, and he went to grab her. Ms. E shook her head. "She has to be able to handle this on her own. Now she knows there is more than only her nose and mouth to defend."

As she stood and snatched the mouth guard made for her off the table, Stephanie's lip twitched with irritation. She slipped it in and jumped back and forth as she rolled her shoulders. Next was Avery to teach her upper body offensive moves. She flowed through the attack movements the cube had taught her and tried to keep her feet from leaving the mat as she moved. She was supposed to only work her upper body in this exercise. He blocked her at every pass but one in which he shifted, grabbed her arm, and twisted it behind her back.

He released her when she grunted her surrender. She moved on to Johnny, who worked hard with her on lower body movements. Every time she flailed a limb, he would smack it down. "Control. You have to control every movement you make. Every movement is deliberate. It is made for you to push through. It is for you to control. Then, and only then, can you adjust the speed and placement at a moment's notice."

She gritted her teeth and kicked harder, swirled around, and pounded her leg into his arm, leg, and chest. When she thought she would almost die of exhaustion, Jack jumped in and she suddenly realized why they called him Frog. He bounced continually and his feet moved rapidly as his legs pistoned in constant attack. She had to put it all together and use her arms, her upper torso, her bottom, her legs—everything—in a fluid, seamless motion to fight back.

Although he was faster than her, a couple of knockdowns soon pushed her into the zone. Her eyes and senses became hyper-focused on every twitch of his body and every tense and release of his muscles. She found herself able to anticipate some of his movements, something she had never been able to focus enough to do. It wasn't like she spent her childhood sparring every day.

She vaulted into the air, kicked, and barely missed his head. He flipped under and she landed, her thigh on his shoulder and knee bent over the front of him. With a laugh, he bounced and flung her over and onto her back. She grunted as she rolled across the floor, thankful there were at least mats down at that point.

Ms. E waved her hand to Lars and Marcus. "You two start out two on one. Stephanie, when you think you have the balls for another, you tap the mat. Each time you single tap, we send in another. When I call full action, it's you against the six of them."

Stephanie rubbed her nose and cracked her neck before she gave the thumbs-up. She smacked her hands together and leaned down to study her two opponents. Without warning, she raced forward and used her feet to push off the mat and launch herself at the men. She struck Lars's thigh and twisted, ran the back of her foot over the side of his face, and continued across Marcus' as well.

She landed in a squatted position with one hand on the mat, her head up and ready for retribution. Both men laughed as they shook the daze from their heads. She tapped the mat, tapped it again, and held up two fingers.

Lars clapped his hands in approval. "That's right. Never give up. Always ask for more."

The group cheered as Frog and Johnny strutted out. It was now four to one, and she felt good. Even if she knew she would probably get her ass kicked.

They came at her one at a time at first. Johnny was blocked but Frog slammed her down hard on the mat. She bounced up and hurtled forward to attack Lars. Marcus slipped in and ducked low at the last second to take her out at the knees. She flipped over him, grasped Lars as she spun, and hauled him down with her. The guys watching jumped up, yelled, and held the sides of their heads in a gesture of exasperation.

Ms. E smiled. "Five seconds to full action!"

Stephanie chuckled and smirked at Lars as she pulled her mouth guard out and spat blood into a bucket on the sidelines. All six men gathered in the arena. Stephanie made her way into the middle as Ms. E counted down to the last second. When she blew the whistle, Stephanie could tell she wouldn't be able to take them down without a little help. At first, she simply energized herself a little to give her extra speed to grab one of her opponents before they could react.

She gripped Johnny's wrist and turned to bring his arm over her shoulder backward. She grunted as she bounced on her feet, but she couldn't for the life of her flip him over her back. Cautiously, she held her breath and released a little more magic to give her the ability to fling him up and over her. She managed to give herself possibly a little too much since he careened off the mat and into the wall. Everyone looked at him and he put his hand up. "Fine. I'm fine. Keep going."

At that point, she was tired of restraint. As Frog bounced toward her, she swayed and swished her arms to the side in his direction. A gust of wind struck him in mid-leap, rammed into his stomach, and flipped him head over heels. He landed on his ass, his legs out straight, and bounced a couple of feet before he groaned and toppled to clutch his family jewels. Stephanie grinned. She used to think the expression outdated and old-fashioned, but he hung onto them like they were both family and fortune, so maybe it was still appropriate after all.

Marcus lunged at her, but she was too quick for him and rolled to the right. She stamped her foot hard on the floor and shook the ground beneath him. He put his arms out in an effort to keep his balance and she snickered, grabbed one, and spun faster and faster. She aimed downward and let go and he slid helplessly across to the other side of the room. Instantly, both Avery and Brenden were on her. She kicked and punched, dodged their shots, and only managed a couple of strong punches once or twice. Not enough to knock them down, though, and it soon became clear that she needed to up her game.

She backed up several feet, raised her arms high, and fisted her hands. She dropped and smacked them down on the ground. Flames erupted in front of them, as tall as the men were. They couldn't have hurt them since they were simply Meligornian magic tricks, but it distracted them long enough for her to vault over them, land, and grasp Avery around the neck. She used her momentum to flip him and drive his body into the floor.

Brenden saw it and tried to go in while still fanning the flames away. She smiled and pushed off with her shoulders, launched upward, and kicked him hard under the chin. He teetered for a moment but went down hard. Slowly, she stood, breathing heavily, and wiped the sweat from her hands. She stared at the flames for a minute and wondered if Lars had simply chickened out or if he waited for the right moment.

Stephanie chuckled and moved toward the flames. "You know they aren't real, right? You don't have to be afraid of some big, bad blue flames, Lars."

As her gaze refocused, her face dropped. Lars rocketed through the flames, his fists clenched and muscles tight, and he growled and yelled loudly. As his arm came for her neck, she cringed. "Oh, my… this is gonna hurt."

He bulldozed into her, twisted his body around her, and secured her in a choke hold. She gripped his huge arm and spluttered as her face turned red. As the blood drained from her brain, she slapped his arm ineffectually. They both dropped to their knees and he laughed. "It's okay. Just go to sleep, then. Lars will take care of the rough stuff."

Her eyes flew open and blue flickered in her irises. While she knew she didn't have much left, she wouldn't let him get the best of her. She mustered the last reserve of magic she had and drew it into her fingertip.

Lars snickered and pulled it tighter. "Surrender. Double-tap my arm and you will breathe again, ma'am. Just give in. It's okay not to be the best yet. Say it—I surrender."

She choked out a couple of words and the man leaned closer. "What was that?"

He released a smidgeon of pressure and she yelled her defiance, her voice raspy. *"Like hell I will, shrode!"*

She twisted her arm and jammed her finger into his side to release a blast of electricity. He immediately locked up and spit dribbled down his lip. She ducked out of his hold and turned toward him, breathing heavily, and leaned forward to his ear with a giggle. "Didn't you teach me to never surrender only a few minutes ago?"

Unable to resist the temptation, she poked him again. A small spark toppled him easily and he jerked spasmodically on the mat. She stood, raised her hands, and managed a short laugh before she stumbled backward and dropped from exhaustion. Ms. E laughed and ran over to scoop Stephanie up in her arms.

Frog shambled to his feet and still rubbed himself a little awkwardly. "Take care of these idiots," the woman said and gestured to the wounded with her head.

She turned and carried Stephanie out of the room. "C'mon to the medical doc, little miss spent battery."

The crew remained on the floor of the workout room and they groaned as the four backup guards and Frog finally helped them up and dragged them to the bench. The four replacements had cheered Stephanie on from the sidelines the whole time, thankful that it wasn't their turn yet.

CHAPTER SIXTY-ONE

Lars stood in front of Stephanie, his hands out in front of him in a gesture that seemed both placating and a protest at the same time. The others lingered in the background, some bruised and others fighting through the pain. "We understand that your martial arts abilities are, without magic, on par with ours. But what we cannot compete with is when you use your magic together with them."

She bit her bottom lip and looked at him with raised eyebrows. "So, what are you saying? Do you want me to go easy on you guys?"

The other men attempted to stand, puff their chests out, and shake their heads, and she smirked as Lars waved his hands at them and rubbed his chin.

"No, but we want to learn more about them and understand your power so that we can then understand how we are supposed to help protect you. That is our job, after all. And if someone does come for you, they are either stupid or they are strong as well. If we faced six of you out there, we wouldn't stand a chance."

Stephanie nodded and rolled her shoulder to ease the pain. "Well, as of right now, I'm the only one anyone knows of. But I get what you're saying and honestly, if I have you guys to back me up or protect me, I want you to know how it all works. The problem with that is that I don't really know how it all works yet. That is part of why I'm here. To figure that out."

Lars's mouth hung open for a moment and he tapped his fingers distractedly against his legs. "Right. I get it. Well, I guess all we can do is keep practicing against you and do what we can to learn. When you've figured it all out, we can go from there."

The team in the background groaned. She chuckled and peered over Lars's shoulder. "It's okay, guys. I won't kick your asses so hard next time."

Frog cheered and the others gave him a nasty look. He lowered his arm slowly and glanced away, trying not to make any eye contact at all. Elizabeth walked up and patted Lars on the shoulder. "Get your men cleaned up. I'll put the other four on temp watch until you can walk straight. And for crying out loud, get Frog a cup, please. Actually, all of you get some cups."

The man nodded at them both and hurried off. Elizabeth put her arm around the girl's shoulders and smiled as they walked away. "I think you hurt not only their manhood but their sensibility as well."

Stephanie giggled. "I didn't mean to. I simply went with an attack. Right now, I want to study my transfer of energy more. What happened in the pod was kinda freaky and I would like that not to happen on Earth to my real body."

Elizabeth sighed. "Yeah, us too. Listen, we have a room for you here. It's not the hotel, but it's definitely put together. I did it myself—with the guys lugging all the heavy shit, of course. We took the liberty to grab your stuff from the hotel and put it all in your room. Is that okay? I thought you might be safer here for now. It's almost a compound of sorts."

"That's fine. It will keep me closer to the whole pod thing and means less time in flying cars."

Elizabeth laughed as she showed her to her room. "We'll do a lesson or two in the pod. It shouldn't take you too long to catch on to that one."

Stephanie stopped as a slight sense of unease settled over her. She realized that she'd allowed her excitement over the new job, the opportunity to study and explore through the pod, and the rush of being important enough to dine with ambassadors and have her own protective detail go to her head. Not once had she questioned anything, aside from her responses in and to the pod and the magic. Everything else had been shoved aside, but a dozen questions now crowded in to unsettle her.

"What's wrong?" Ms. E asked and placed her hand on Stephanie's arm.

"I...not wrong, exactly, but... I have so many questions suddenly. Like why we moved from the old building instead of rebuilding after the fire. And why you've brought me to live in a...what did you call it? A compound, with a whole security detail twenty-four-seven. Did something happen? Am I in danger?"

The other woman sighed but her expression seemed more weary than upset. "I know you have questions, kiddo, and they will all be answered—in time. What I can tell you is that you have a rare talent—a gift—and there are many people out there who would like to gain control of that, whether it benefits you or not. We'd like to be sure that you're prepared for it should anyone discover you and try to take advantage of you."

Stephanie nodded as a quick vision of Pinnacle surfaced. She already knew first-hand that very few people would really care what happened to her along the way. All they would want was to feed their greed and power—with her as the main course.

"I guess..." She shrugged. "There's so much I still don't understand—like how the energy really works and what it can do and how. And the martial arts, too. Seriously? I didn't think of it at the time, but how is it possible that I could hold my own against six grown men when the only training I had—if you can actually call it training—was a night plugged into a cube? None of it makes any sense at all."

Ms. E smiled. "No, it doesn't. But it's real, Steph. The truth is that we don't have the answers either. The best we can do is to create a safe environment in which you can learn—and that includes teaching you how to defend yourself using all your abilities. Honestly, we're learning as we go, like you are. But at least with us, you have a say in what happens. You can trust us to not force you beyond what you're comfortable with. We see the potential in you to make a difference, and we want you to reach your full potential—for your own sake as much as for all those people out there whose lives you could impact down the line." She smiled and squeezed her hand. "Do you trust us?"

Despite the sudden rush of questions and the sense of disquiet that still hovered, Stephanie looked at her companion and nodded. Instinct, if not common sense, told her that the people who had stepped up and who now surrounded her were possibly the only ones she could trust.

Ms. E opened the door and let Stephanie in, smiled again as she closed it, and left her to herself. The whole room was painted in purple and black, the colors she couldn't seem to get away from. She didn't mind, though. It looked nice and felt familiar. She picked a tablet up from a small round table by the door and started to press buttons randomly. What she thought were solid painted walls were actually holographic and shifted to various scenes from all over the galaxy. From floating in deep space to laying in a field on Meligorn, she could choose to be anywhere.

Stephanie stopped on a nighttime scene from Meligorn and stared at the Towers and the planets in the distance. She put the tablet down and walked to the closet, opened it, and grinned at all her clothes hung neatly in a row. Her suitcases were stored in the bottom and the rest of her belongings were placed either on the carved wooden dresser with vines etched on all sides, in the bathroom—also holographic and similar to the one in the hotel—or in her drawers.

She wandered back into the room and froze as a sudden fear knifed through her—the book. With a sharp surge of panic, she whirled toward her king-sized four-poster bed and puffed out a relieved breath. She had tried to secure it with magic but honestly hadn't been all that reassured. The energy might have protected it from harm, but there was no way to know if it would have kept it safe from curious fingers. The thought that it might have been stolen—although why would anyone want it, anyway?—left her with a real sense of loss.

A long sigh of relief started her breathing again. The book rested there on the end of the bed, wrapped in the purple velvet. She sat slowly beside it and rubbed her hand over the fabric. While she knew there were things combat-related she needed to take care of, she didn't want to focus as much on the military side of the esoteric.

One thing that she had learned—and she had kept this to herself up to that point—was that Earth already had the energy that she needed. The problem was, humanity had lost the abilities and genetics, for the most part, to handle it. Therefore, in their minds, it simply didn't exist. Her focus now would need to be to learn more of that.

But in that moment, there was nothing more she could really do. She did find it nice that she had a place that was at least semi-permanent to lay her head at night. As much as she liked the hotel, it was still simply that—a hotel. The only two people she would really miss were Rufus and her AI, Sarah. Stephanie stuck her bottom lip out when she thought about her companion Sarah. She was only a computer, but nonetheless, she was a good listener.

"Well, I guess I'll have to go it alone. Thanks for all your companionship, Sarah," she said out loud and pulled her book into her lap.

"You're welcome," Sarah replied. "Although I don't think you will have to go it alone. I was brought over in the system to stay with you. My laugh was permanently disabled."

Stephanie giggled and suddenly felt a whole lot more cheerful. "That is great news. It definitely feels better like that."

The AI paused. "Enjoy your reading and let me know when you are ready for dinner. I believe the kitchen is down the hall."

She nodded. "Will do."

Carefully, she unwound the fabric from the book, opened it, and placed her fingers on the paper. She had enough energy in her to draw the words into her mind. It was a journal from an ancestor many centuries in the past.

This diary will give the reader an understanding of what I believe happened to the family from the first Morgana, from whom we trace our lineage.

Stephanie settled in, pulled her legs up, and crossed them. She continued reading. **As she was a child born out of wedlock, we find lineage to another child born of her. This child was also born out of wedlock and not inscribed in the annals of time except to our own books. We are the ones who bear witness to protect the Earth as Morgana might have, had her family not betrayed her first.**

Her eyes opened and she sat motionless for several moments, thinking about those words. Morgana was a first name, apparently, not a last name, or had been so at the beginning. She still didn't have enough information on who Morgana was, so she put the book down carefully on the bed and retrieved her personal tablet from the desk. Once she'd placed it in the center of the bed, she pressed the button to bring the screen into interactive mode. The image popped up from the display like a hologram.

"Tell me more about Morgana," she said.

The avatar on the screen pretended to wander around and search for information until it finally stuck one finger in the air and yelled, "Eureka!" It tossed a bunch of papers into the air that became the pages for her to scroll through. One by one, she swiped to each one and read bits and pieces of information from folklore and legend. After a few of these, she came to a darker site—one that required her thumbprint to enter. Assuming it wouldn't work since she had never been to it, she hovered her thumb over the reader. The print flittered on the screen and then turned gold and the site opened immediately. Stephanie stared at it for a moment, astonished that it had worked, but decided not to question the thumbprint issue too deeply. Information was more important at this point.

She read through the trials and the tribulations of the Morgana children and the hatred and anger toward them. They were bastards, born out of wedlock, their fathers usually far away and their lives torturous. Stephanie, although she had never met her father, had never been treated poorly. Mark had been in her life since she was old enough to remember and her parents loved her with everything in them. But she still bore the name and the powers that seemed to go along with it.

Soon after, she came to a picture of a woman. She was dressed in a black calf-length dress with a white collar, a white jacket that looked almost like a man's sports coat, white slim-looking lace-up leather shoes, stockings, and a wide-brimmed hat. Her hair cascaded in large wavy curls, pinned back behind her ears. She had a beautiful smile, and her eyes looked amazingly familiar.

Stephanie continued to read. "Maddalena Morgana, born in 1919, no father on record. In history books, for humans without the gift, Maddalena was known to have helped the Allies in WWII by creating a spycraft that assisted in infiltrating the enemy. To this day, the non-gifted cannot explain the spycraft, nor did they ever retrieve it from enemy lines. The truth was, Maddalena was the next gifted Morgana to be born on this earth. Her powers were strong in precognition. It wasn't a spycraft that aided the allies, but instead, it was her dreams of the future which helped the Allies, especially on D-Day. Maddalena was more gifted than anyone in that time would have ever understood, and after WWII ended, she disappeared from the public eye, never to be seen again."

Stephanie swiped the screen away, chewed on her lip, and twirled her finger around the end of her ponytail. So, Morgana had gone from being the first name of the original one to the last name. It made sense. She was born illegitimately, and her mother's maiden name was Morgana, which Stephanie still kept legally, so she could be considered the next Morgana in line.

Her thoughts now rampant, she stood, set the tablet aside, and began to pace the room. A number of things began to crystallize within her. She loved her last name but because of the sound of it, not because of a previously child-like need to be different. She had always felt a strange attachment to it. It would only make sense, then, that her mother had pushed her to take Mark's last name to hide the Morgana last name. Mark had been in her life since she was a baby but had not married her mother for many years due to adoption policies and issues with marriage qualifications during a particularly troubling time in Federation history.

By the time he did, she was given the choice, and she kept Morgana without a thought. All those times that her mother had begged her, snapped at her, and fought with her over the name was not for Mark's sake, it was for hers. It was not to hurt her stepdad's feelings. He always understood. It had been for her mother because she knew the history—or at least tales of it—and it frightened her, as it would any mother. So she tried to shadow it out, put the past in the past, change the name, and move on from it, but it wasn't something that Stephanie could run from. It was who she was, last name or not.

Then again, there was a part of her mother that, no matter how much she might fear something, she pushed herself to not believe it. It was like not believing in the superstition of the number thirteen but then building a hotel and leaving floor thirteen out of the plans. When Stephanie started fooling with magic and revealed that she had the gift, her mother hadn't actually seemed all that shocked. If she were anyone else, her mother would have lost it, but she was calm and even seemed to know what to do in the first circumstance when she saved that woman's life.

Stephanie walked to the wall and stood there to stare out into the virtual space. Part of her wished she could leap out, float to Meligorn, and find more answers. At the same time, the Earth had all the answers that she would need. She merely had to figure them out without completely blowing herself up in the process. Before that day, she would have thought of that as an easy request, but it wasn't in the least. In fact, it was more of a warning now that she had done it in the Virtual World without even thinking. Things constantly became more and more complicated as the days passed but brought very few answers in the meantime. Answers were exactly what she needed, and time seemed determined to make the power inside her stronger and stronger. It would only be a matter of time before she or someone she loved got hurt.

CHAPTER SIXTY-TWO

The next day came all too quickly, and Stephanie hadn't slept much at all. It was a good thing then, that both BURT and Elizabeth had decided that she should have some lessons on how to act around other people. It wasn't only how to act around dignitaries, species from other planets, or people she revealed her magic to, but people in general.

She was no longer the young Stephanie Morgana who kept as low a profile as possible and everyone looked right past her. She had already been hounded by so many different people, from the media to companies that wanted her to be a part of something they had going on. As she progressed and her reputation grew, as it inevitably would, she would come under increasing pressure. As tempting as it might be, she couldn't simply shock every single person who tried to talk her into leaving ONE R&D. She had to learn how to handle herself in high society as well as on the street.

The class only lasted for about six earth hours, three in the pod. When she came out, Elizabeth held her robe out for her with a smile on her face. "I'm glad to see you didn't fall out of the pod this time."

Stephanie put her arms in the robe and wrapped it around herself before she turned to face her. "Thank you for helping me. I don't remember it but thank you."

The woman tapped her on the shoulder. "That's my job, sister. I can't have you stroking out on the first day. It would look bad on my resume."

She laughed as they wandered to the door, exited, and locked the pod room behind them. Lars and Frog stood guard outside the room and both glanced away when she emerged in her robe. She chuckled and put her hand up to give Lars a high-five.

When she reached her room, Elizabeth glanced toward the kitchen. "I'll make lunch soon. Why don't you call and check in with your family and friends and center yourself a little today? If you're hungry, food will be there. I'll have Sarah tell you when it's done."

Stephanie nodded, entered her room, and closed the door behind her. She walked to the bed and lay down before she set her tablet up in front of her. Once she'd checked that her robe was tied tightly, she called her parents. Her mom's face came up on the screen and she smiled warmly. "Hi, honey!"

A warmth flooded her chest and flushed on her cheeks. "Hi, Mom. Hi, Dad!"

Her dad stuck his head into the camera view. "Hey, kiddo. Love you!"

"Love you." She giggled.

Her mom smiled. "We are right in the middle of training additional staff for the new client's building. I have to admit that to get it exactly how they want it, with as many floors as there are, is extremely challenging, and we have definitely had to bring additional people on. But we are so excited to work with them. I spoke to Mr. Martelle and he couldn't say enough good things about you."

Stephanie laughed. "Yeah, he got to see a whole bunch of different sides of me that day. The assertive, the business, and the magical. I let him see it all, good and bad. I guess it worked."

"Because you're adorable and you know how to talk to people." Her mom grinned. "So, how is everything there? Are you in a new room?"

She looked around. "Oh, yeah. I moved from the hotel into the compound. They have a really nice private room for me, my own pod that I can use anytime I like, and security staff as well. It's easiest if I stay here and I actually like it. This is somewhere I can feel comfortable instead of that constant hotel feeling, no matter how nice it is. Oh, and they brought the AI from my hotel room over because I liked her so much."

Her mother laughed. "That's what I'm talking about. Take care of my baby girl. I want you to be happy and safe, that's all."

Stephanie nodded. "And I am both of those things. But Mom, I actually hoped I could talk to you about something. It has to do with the book you gave me."

After a short silence, her mother cleared her throat and stepped away from whoever she was close to. "You want to talk about your name."

"Yeah."

Cindy's gaze shifted back and forth and the forced smile on her lips twitched. "There are things which we discuss in person only. I cannot read the diary, but I realize you can. When we see each other, I will chat to you about it."

She knew she wouldn't say any more and that she had been as clear as she could be in that moment. This was a huge deal—a huge secret—and they couldn't risk a discussion about it over the phone or video in case someone had tapped the lines or transmitted the video somewhere else. Although disappointed, Stephanie simply nodded, gave her mom a wink, and changed the subject.

"I forgot, I haven't talked to you in a couple of days," she said excitedly. "I had a real glass of champagne the other day. Well, a quarter of a glass because I had to leave, but champagne nonetheless."

Her mother's eyes glistened. "Oh, champagne. We miss that bubbly wonderfulness. I've always wanted to pop a bottle and celebrate… well, anything really. That's wonderful, darling. I hope that one day, your father and I will have the chance to do such exciting things."

Stephanie's eyes went soft and she breathed out a heavy breath. "You will. I'll make sure you have the chance to. What is life for if you don't get to experience all of it, right? Not only the struggles, that's not fair."

Cindy nodded, pressed her lips together, and cleared her throat. Her eyes glistened as she nodded at Stephanie's father off-screen. "Sweetie, oh, I miss talking to you so much, but unfortunately, until we get this building business taken care of, we are pushing against the clock. When I'm not there, I'm hiring people, putting them through training, getting our equipment cleaned, the whole nine yards. We're using some of our daytime sites to train extra staff as well to speed things up a little, which is why there are others here with us. It's a crazy train here at home."

"I'll let you go then. I can call you some other time in the evening," Stephanie offered. "I just finished my morning session and didn't even think of the time. Although with a night shift as well now, I'm not sure how you and Dad have scheduled your off time."

Her mother waved her hands. "Nor should you ever worry about that. Never hesitate to call me when you have a few minutes to do it. I would rather talk while cleaning then miss you altogether because you have such a busy schedule too. Once we have the logistics ironed out, things will be better all round."

"I want to come back home very soon so I can see you guys. Or maybe, when you get a break, bring you out here to DC so you can see all the historical sites and all the flying cars and craziness over here. Chicago will be like that eventually."

Her mother shook her head. "That would be lovely. And sweetheart, I want you to know how much I love you. You were meant to be special, you just didn't know it."

Stephanie waved goodbye to her father and they ended the call. Her mother, no matter how scared or worried she was, always had the ability to make her feel better. She always knew the right thing to say in any situation. Comfortably cross-legged on the bed, she thought about home and all her nice walks to school and home each day. How simple her life had been only a year before when taking the Federation Exams was nothing more than a blip in her future. Things got so crazy so fast, but that was okay because she would slowly figure out who she was.

Thinking about home, she looked at her watch and remembered that Wednesdays were when Todd had his mid-morning free period. She had completely forgotten about that and, excited to hear his voice, she swiped her tablet and called him. He answered on the second ring and appeared in front of himself in hologram form to salute her.

Stephanie laughed and saluted him awkwardly in response. "I didn't join the Federation. Why would you salute me?"

Todd rolled his eyes with a smirk on his face. "Because it's not all about you, butthead."

She looked at him, suddenly serious. "Did you? Already? You're not even out of school yet."

He shook his head. "No, but I have found myself a certified navy recruiter. I barely even spoke to anyone before and she kind of found me. I guess through the Federation testing results or something. Anyway..." Todd wiggled his eyebrows. "She's a female, cause I. Am. Hot."

Stephanie raised an eyebrow. "I'm not busting your model bubble or anything but remember the recruiters for the class before us. They basically sent either the doppelganger of the person they tried to recruit or the hot girl or guy for those less...intellectual."

"Are you calling me a dud?" He narrowed his eyes.

Stephanie giggled and snorted. "No. But that's great, dude. If that is what *you* want, not what the pretty girl is telling you to do. Signing up for the Federation is way longer term than going on some weird kale and celery diet for a few weeks."

Todd scoffed and gestured dismissively. "I got this. I've always known I would go in but I'm waiting to see where they put me. Hopefully, something cool and not merely a long drive out into the darkness to meet my maker. Oh, and there was a guy looking for you, but I told him you were gone, and that I had interest. Wham, bam, thank you, ma'am, I was looked up by a Petty Officer First Class 'Wowzah' Santino. She called these digits only one week later. Tanned skin, curvy, uniform fits just right. Red lipstick, smells like flowers, laughs at my jokes, and basically can't live without me at this point."

She shook her head. "The Toddster has fallen in love."

In response, he rolled his eyes and pulled on the neckline of his T-shirt. "The ladies have fallen in love with the Toddster. It was bound to happen. They saw you disappear out of the picture and figured they could slide right in and not have to worry about you setting them on magical fire."

Stephanie pursed her lips. "Nope, they still need to worry about that one. So, when will you start everything?"

Todd shrugged and sighed. "I'll have my first tests done this weekend. I really hope I do well on them."

She gave him a reassuring look as if she were touching his shoulder through the video. "Dude, I know you will. I'm really happy for you. I know this is actually what you wanted."

He continued to talk, and Stephanie's thoughts drifted off for a moment. Would it be naïve to think that they might have done all of that for her?

Stephanie shook her head and pulled her attention back to Todd. *Or, Stephanie Morgana, am I now starting to believe everything is about me?*

CHAPTER SIXTY-THREE

When Stephanie finally got off the phone with Todd, she felt better about being in her new position and her new life. She had a shit ton of questions that needed to be answered, but there was no elucidation that could be given to her at that time. The facts eluded her at every turn, but what did she really expect? She was a descendant or manifestation of what could potentially be a magical human from centuries before. Fair enough, she hadn't actually found anything that would confirm the magical part of the equation, but given her experience, it seemed very likely. The only ancestor whom she could find any real information on was basically a war hero who had helped the Allies win the war. After that, she disappeared.

Disappearing didn't seem all that crazy, though, especially when people close to the government and people in her social circle knew about her abilities. From the little time Stephanie had spent in the spotlight, she could feel that pressure mounting. And from the way that Elizabeth, Burt, and the others attempted to protect her, she knew that harder times most likely lay ahead. Still, she would persist because the information she discovered had the ability to change everything. There was no doubt that for anyone below the middle-class line, and many above it, change was in the wind.

Stephanie put her tablet on the dresser and pulled the drawers out to skim through her clothes. She grabbed a pair of ripped jeans, an old vintage Chicago Cubs T-shirt Todd had given her one year for her birthday, and a baseball cap. She needed to get out of there, to clear her mind and do something that didn't involve magic, or research, or questioning every damn thing in her life. She simply wanted to be a normal old human for a while.

Knowing how crazy they were about keeping her safe, though, Stephanie headed to the kitchen in the hope that Ms. E was still there. As she turned the corner, Elizabeth glanced up, her outfit beyond incongruous. She wore a chef's apron with her business attire and six-inch heels. It didn't really fit, but she seemed to be in a good mood, nonetheless.

She glanced at the girl's outfit and looked at the cutting board as she chopped celery. "Are you thinking of going out?"

Stephanie leaned against the doorway and shoved her hands in her pockets. "Yeah. I really wanted some me time, I guess, but I thought I should check with you."

A smile pulled at the woman's lips. "Remember, I am your boss on the clock, not your mom. But, now that you mention it, yes. I don't mind you going out as long as you take a couple of the guys with you."

She nodded. "K. I'll swing in and see who has the aches and who is reasonably functional. I'm sure you'll know when I'm back."

Elizabeth chuckled. "I know most things, and if I miss something, the system will have logged it anyway."

Stephanie smirked as she headed off to the guard's living quarters. She poked her head into the common area where Lars sat at the table and Frog sprawled on the couch. "Where is everyone?'

Lars glanced up and smiled. "On duty. It's me and Frog's time off. Two of the subs took care of our shifts."

She pursed her lips and rocked back and forth on her feet. "Okay. Well, maybe you can point me in the right direction, then. I want to go into town and spend some 'me' time out there. Elizabeth wants me to take two guys with me. Who should I ask?"

Frog glanced at the other man and shrugged. Lars looked at the notes he was taking and shut the book. "Give us ten and we'll head out with you."

Stephanie grinned. "Thanks. I'll go get a car to pull around."

The guys changed and traveled with Stephanie as she clung to the "oh shit" handle in the flying car. It docked three stories up and let them out into a docking terminal that led down into the city. It was the old Dupont Circle where statues that had been erected a short time before the 2094 riots for social justice and equality now crumbled in the center. That was one of the main events in their history that were studied because, like so many other social justice causes, nothing really ever changed. Maybe the wording of a law or two, but nothing significant.

The streets were busy with tourists and business persons on their late lunches or errands. Although you could tell there had been historical periods of unrest in the area, the commemorated ideals of keeping the place as accurate as possible to the original architecture seemed to be upheld. It was pleasant, like walking through an old town filled with commerce and political accents.

Stephanie wandered somewhat aimlessly, stopped for a pretzel, and window-shopped most of the time. Lars and Frog followed without complaint. They gave her enough space to feel alone but still kept a watchful eye out. Stephanie meandered down the streets and gazed at the buildings and the flying cars zooming overhead.

"Uh, Steph," Lars said a short while later and jogged up beside her.

She shook the daze from her head. "Yeah?"

His gaze traced up the street. "Maybe we should head back toward the circle. We've wandered too far and there are a lot of places around here that can be dangerous and secluded."

Stephanie focused on her surroundings and realized that he was right. She had wandered off the beaten path to an area of town that mostly consisted of crumbling buildings, graffiti, and random places where scantily clad women stood on porches. The duo exchanged a nod and turned quickly but stopped in their tracks. Frog froze, put a hand around to his back, and gripped the laser pistol shoved into the waistband of his pants.

Up ahead, four men with orange bandanas tied around their arms and sparkling gold teeth strolled toward them. The one in the front sucked on his front tooth with his tongue and an eerie smirk pulled at his lips. "Well, lookie here, guys. If it isn't our lucky day. We have the Earth Witch right in front of us."

One of the men behind him smiled, a twinkle in his eye. He flipped his toothpick from one side of his mouth to the other and a hand slid into his jacket. "I heard there's a nice reward for bringing her in. A lot of high profiles are looking to dig into that pretty little head of hers."

Frog moved his gun around slowly and backed up beside Stephanie and Lars. "I would suggest you guys keep moving. The only place she is going is back home."

The mustached man laughed and whistled. Lars, Stephanie, and Frog moved closer together as six more thugs appeared from the dark recesses of the alleys. The leader twisted his lips from a smile to a snarl. "It looks like you'll have to make us."

The guy to the side of the gang leader drew faster than Frog could. A hail of bullets struck the guard and catapulted him back. Immediately, Lars grabbed Stephanie and shoved her in one direction as he dove in the other and blasted his weapon at the group. A barrage erupted as guns fired from all angles. Stephanie pressed her back against the wall, breathing heavily, and stared at Frog. He was still alive but hurt and seemed unable to stand. Rage began to rise within her, and she slid her hand into her pocket and closed her fingers around her recharged battery.

As soon as the magic built in her veins, she whirled out from behind the wall and released blasts of purple magic from her fingertips as if they were guns. The energy swirled to form a hailstorm of magical bullets that struck three of the men behind the leader to drop them almost instantaneously. She rolled across the hard ground and ignored Lars's calls to her to get down.

One of the gang members raced toward her from the side, ready to grab her. She flipped her hand in the air and narrowed her glowing eyes. A pipe launched from one of the reconstruction sites nearby into her hand. She pitched her arm and caught the man in the side of the head.

Another immediately took his place. Her purple eyes shifted angrily to him and her top lip trembled like an angry dog showing its teeth. She bent slightly, vaulted upward, and spun her leg to kick him in the throat. He stumbled and grabbed at his neck as she landed. Stephanie stared at him for a moment and her eyes flickered to black. Her thoughts zeroed in on the man as rage and protectiveness lashed through her.

Slowly, she walked toward him, her gaze fixed and hard. His eyes widened when he saw the black orbs where her eyes should have been. She snatched him by the hair and dragged his head back before she whaled the pipe into his ribs over and over. The man coughed and spattered her face with blood. She growled angrily and flung him violently into the side of a half-fallen brick wall.

Lars continued the fight and fired relentlessly at any targets he could eliminate. All Stephanie could think about was revenge, her past, and her ancestor's past that connected with her in the present, just like it had been when Earth had once understood magic.

One thug remained. He stood in the street and tried desperately to replace the magazine in his gun. Stephanie threw the pipe down as she walked toward him and pushed her sleeves up. She pulled her palms together in front of her chest and turned them in a circular motion to form a ball of magic in her hands.

She looked slowly at him, growled, and launched the energy ball into him like a basketball pass. It erupted in his chest, lifted him from the ground, and spun him horizontally until the crumbled old brownstone across the street stopped him. The sound of cops arriving shook her from her connection. Her eyes faded from black to normal and she took a deep breath and pushed the magic in her into the ground.

"Stephanie," Lars yelled.

She turned and raced toward Frog, who lay motionless. Two of the gang members managed to make it to their feet. Stephanie knelt beside Frog and raised her hand to stop their assailants. Lars grabbed her wrist and shook his head. "That's enough. The cops will need to take it from here. It's best you don't use magic."

Stephanie swallowed and nodded in understanding. Her head swam slightly as she looked at Frog and placed her hand over a wound on his shoulder. Blood spewed down his chest and he groaned and writhed in pain. A cop ran up and looked at the downed gang members and then at Stephanie, whom he obviously recognized.

He holstered his gun and knelt to feel Frog's pulse. "I have an ambulance en route."

All she could do was hope that they could help her bodyguard before it was too late.

CHAPTER SIXTY-FOUR

The blue padded chair in the corner of Frog's hospital room was horrendously uncomfortable. Stephanie sat with her feet pulled up and her knees to her chest. Her eyes remained fixed on the man in the bed while she waited and watched for him to become conscious again. The ambulance had been quick to get there, but he'd passed out on the way to the hospital. It was the downtown DC hospital but run by the Federation. Healthcare, at that point—unless you could afford a private doctor—was identical to that which the military received. Very surgical, emotionless, and understaffed.

She couldn't believe that something like that had happened. All she had wanted was a little time to be normal, but normal didn't seem to be an option for her anymore. Not to mention the kind of blank rage she had somehow disappeared into while the battle raged. She was fairly sure one of those who received a wrench to the face was in a room across the hall, guarded by Federation cops.

It was crazy. She'd known Frog for all of two days but had managed to bust his balls and get him shot. Apparently, being friends with her wasn't all that it was made out to be. Unless you liked living in a constant state of worry, wonder, and not knowing if you would survive to the next day.

Elizabeth walked through the door and paused to study Stephanie, who didn't even look at her. She gritted her teeth and released a long, deep breath before she walked up and handed her a hot cup of coffee. "It's not Brazilian roast but it will pass for coffee at this point."

Stephanie's gaze drifted from Frog's monitor to the coffee. Slowly, she took the cup and lowered her feet to the floor. "Thanks."

The older woman bit the inside of her cheek and sat down beside her. She had never been very good at helping those who needed comfort, but she knew it was part of her job. "What happened out there?"

She didn't answer at first but finally, she sniffled and shrugged. "We walked along a street, away from the circle. I didn't pay much attention to where we were, and we ended up face to face with them. They recognized me immediately—something I was shocked by, to be honest. They said there was a price to bring me in alive. That they would have a good payday."

Elizabeth sipped her coffee and grimaced slightly. "From the stories we were told, you acted like a warrior out there. There was even something about you cracking one of them in the head with a pipe."

Stephanie didn't laugh with her companion's chuckle. "I simply wanted revenge. I put my hand up and it came to me."

The other woman raised an eyebrow. "Like what? Like Thor's hammer?"

She shook her head, her gaze fixed on nothing in particular. "Mjolnir was forged from the heat of a dying star. This was some metal pipe from one of the construction sites. I don't know…it was the first thing I thought of when the guys tried to drag me away. I fought and it was like I zoned in like never before. Anyway, it's not like it did a lot of good. Frog took a shot before we could even react."

Elizabeth looked at the man and studied the heartbeat monitor, which jigged and jagged at a regular pace. "It's a hazard, but Frog knew that. He did his duty, and you should be proud of him for that."

Stephanie blinked for the first time since before the woman had walked in. "I am proud of him and thankful. But that doesn't take away the fact that he was hurt protecting me. It isn't right. Is Lars okay?"

Her companion gave her a comforting look and pushed a piece of hair fallen from her ponytail over her shoulder. "He's fine. A little bruised but that's all. He'll join us shortly. I made him get a brain scan to make sure everything was good. It probably came up empty."

Stephanie pressed her lips together but finally, she grunted and gave up the attempt. She giggled at the joke, then tilted her head back and rubbed her face. "God, this sucks. I know I asked for this, I know I did, but I'm starting to think I don't want to be special anymore."

Elizabeth laughed, leaned back, and crossed her legs. She cradled her coffee and stared off into the corner of the room. "It's funny how we all wished for something when life was simpler, and when we got it, everything became ten times more complicated. That's when we hiccup, backtrack, and kick ourselves for thinking we wanted all these things."

"You are preaching to the choir here, girl." Stephanie snorted as she sipped her coffee. "I should have wished for a spot at my parents' company and a decent house in the subs. But then, if I got that, I wouldn't have been satisfied."

The older woman nodded, slightly dazed. She blinked and drew in a deep breath to bring herself back to the present. "The thing is, though, no matter what you believe about the great beyond, fate, magic—any of it really—sometimes, what you want doesn't matter. Sometimes, the things waiting in the wings for you will be bigger than you, bigger than all of us, and you have to take it with a sense of grace, compassion, and a stiff upper lip."

Stephanie pouted her bottom lip. "I wish I could argue with you on that, but I have no data to back myself up."

Elizabeth chuckled and glanced around uneasily. *You sound like Burt.*

They both laughed for a minute and the sound trickled around the steady beeping of Frog's monitors. She put her cup down and looked at Stephanie. "You are Stephanie Morgana, the Federation's first human witch. Like it or not, you will always be important. And you can fight it all you want to, scream, claw, but in the end, you will need to learn to lead people because they will follow you. You won't have a say in that. And you may try to push them off and convince them not to, but they will still be there."

The girl's fixed and serious expression didn't change. Her eyes were locked on the foot of Frog's bed, her thoughts almost visible. Elizabeth curled the left side of her mouth and turned to retrieve her coffee. "It's important to remember that, Stephanie. You will be a leader, like it or not. Some of the people following will do it for good reasons, and some…well, simply because they are bat-shit crazy."

Stephanie shook her head. "Those bat-shit crazy ones will simply write me hate mail or stab voodoo dolls. They are the ones who will be capable of really big and really scary things. Scary as in putting my name out there so gang members hunt me down. And because of that —because of me—innocent people will be hurt."

Elizabeth shook her head. "You need to realize that bad things will happen, whether to you, to people close to you, or to people you don't even know. You need to accept that here and now because otherwise, it will always hold you back. Be thankful that he isn't dead. That is something to hold onto and celebrate. We are sitting here waiting for him to wake up, not sending him to the Federation burial services to expel his ashes out into space."

She knew Elizabeth was right although she didn't say anything. Frog was really lucky to be alive, but it still made her sick to her stomach to see him like that. The other woman finished her coffee and tossed the cup in the bin. "I am personally glad, no matter what, that you didn't kill anyone or get anyone killed. That could have a profound effect on someone, and I need you to stay open and receptive so that you can continue to grow stronger and wiser."

She slapped the girl's leg to catch her attention. "Do you hear what I'm saying? We have an opportunity here to see the danger and attack it head-on. We get to help you figure out how to be Stephanie Morgana, Earth's first human witch, and do it with the knowledge and know-how to protect the people you care about. The people who are the most important to you. Death looming over you when you are desperately trying to learn and grow can be something incredibly hard to do. Especially with you being so young and so withdrawn for so long from the things in this world."

Stephanie shrugged. "Not all of it, but my parents tried hard to give me as normal a childhood as possible. Now that I see what is ahead—or could be—I am glad they did that. A few years where I can remember being worried about nothing but classes, tests, friends, and exams."

Elizabeth could see the sadness in the girl's eyes. She put her arm out and pulled her into a side hug. "Come here. Believe it or not, I know how you feel. I may not be a witch, but I know what it's like to have other's lives in your hands and to have someone go down. It is hard, but I also understand how important it is to not allow yourself to brood about it."

The door to the room opened and both Stephanie and Elizabeth stood. The doctor, in his early sixties with white hair, a white Federation lab coat, and with clipboard in his hands, glanced at them. He pressed his lips together and greeted them kindly. They watched as he looked at the different stats on Frog's vitals, flipped through his file, and made a couple of notes. When he was done, he turned to them and closed the chart.

"He will be fine," the doctor said. "There were a couple of severe wounds, which we did some repair on. He'll have a nasty scar and nerve damage in his shoulder but with some physical therapy, he should be able to go back to what he was doing before this incident. Take it easy on him."

"Yeah," Frog groaned, and his hand groped at nothing.

They hurried over and Stephanie took his hand. "How are you feeling?"

He sniffed and grimaced as he shifted a little on his back. "Like fried frog legs, but alive. And amused at your conversation. Stephanie, get over it. Shit happens. Move on and stop having a pity party."

Her mouth dropped open. "I...you jerk. You were awake that whole time?"

Her companions laughed and Frog rubbed her shoulder. "Seriously, though, you were like Chuck Norris crazy out there. You should be proud. And Elizabeth?" She raised her eyebrows. "Take her back so she can't sit here and stare at me like this and drive herself crazy while she watches my pee drain into a bag hanging on the bed."

Elizabeth smirked and hauled Stephanie away with a firm hand on her arm. As they reached the door, the girl turned back for a moment. "Thanks, Frog."

He put his thumb up. "Send me a hot nurse. I think a sponge bath is in order."

They walked into the hallway where Lars waited with a bruise on his cheek, a skinned elbow, and a small scrape on his forehead. "Are you gals ready to get back? I could use some coffee and a good chill session."

Stephanie nodded and Elizabeth slipped him a wink and gestured with her eyes toward Steph. They stopped at the nurse's station and Lars walked to one of the nurses, a nondescript woman in her fifties or so wearing orthopedic shoes. "Ma'am, I wanted to let you know that the guy in room seven-six-five, Frog, he has requested a bath. He happened to hint that he hoped you would be the one to give it to him."

She giggled, nodded, and snatched up a rubber glove. "We'll get him nice and clean."

Lars hurried to catch up with the women. "Everything is right in the world now."

Elizabeth rolled her eyes and pulled them both in the elevator. "It won't be when he figures out what you did."

As the elevator doors began to close, they heard Frog's furious protest. "Lars! You asshole!"

Even Stephanie couldn't hold back the laughter as the elevator moved to the docking bay where the car was parked. Despite his injuries, Lars remained vigilant. He moved so that the women were behind him and stood with his feet slightly apart and his hands loose and close to his pockets. He turned slightly to look at them and his gaze flashed to Elizabeth and then to Stephanie. "I know this is all really hard to understand right now."

Stephanie's gaze lifted to meet his when she realized he was talking to her. "I feel better now that we know he'll be okay."

Lars shook his head. "I'm talking about trying to figure out life now that you are destined for something way bigger than yourself."

Her eyes glistened as she held his gaze for a moment and then folded her arms in front of her and stared at the floor again. "I think I was naïve to think that being special would be all candy and rainbows—or in my case, blue flames and cleansing spells. I guess in a way, I didn't think I would actually ever become someone special to others. So why think about the negative, right? A daydream."

The elevator opened and they followed Elizabeth down the walkway to the car. Stephanie and Lars got in the back and the older woman took the driver's seat. They headed out in silence and eased into the lines of traffic to head out of the city.

Elizabeth glanced in the rearview mirror and adjusted it slightly to see Stephanie's eyes. "We want you to understand that there will be a whole lot of really cool things that come along with a life for someone who is destined to rise above."

Lars nodded. "That's right. A whole lot of cool stuff. But at the same time, with the good comes the bad. That fight won't be the last. Frog's injury won't be the last. What's important here is that you decide how you want to use your gifts. What path you want to take."

Elizabeth took the exit out of the downtown area. "Exactly, and then we can all follow that path because we believe in you. But you have to be ready for days like today. Even days ten times worse than this. You have to take this seriously. You have the talent to kick major ass, make huge differences, and sweep the Federation, but you have to believe in it."

Stephanie twisted her hands back and forth in her lap before her gaze met Elizabeth's in the mirror. "I got it. I…won't forget it either. Tomorrow, we start over."

Lars clapped his hands with a smile. "Whoop. That's damn right. And we get bragging rights 'cause we kicked some gang members' butts while the slackers were standing around the base twiddling their cheeky bits."

Stephanie looked at Lars and chuckled as she shook her head. "You guys have some issues."

Lars nodded. "Yep. And that's what makes us a really good team."

When they reached the compound, Lars headed to his quarters and Stephanie shuffled off to hers, obviously exhausted and with a lot of things to think about. Elizabeth checked the security logs and reported to the others that they were back. As she walked past the kitchen on her way to her room, she grabbed a glass and a bottle of red wine from the cabinet.

She hurried into her room and kicked her heels off, untucked her shirt, and sighed as she sank into her large fluffy armchair. As she drew the cork from the bottle, she inhaled a deep breath. "Oh, hello there, relaxation."

"I don't know how relaxing I will be," Burt said through the comms over her head.

Elizabeth winced and almost spilled the wine. "Good Lord. Didn't anyone ever teach you to not be a nasty creepy stalker?"

He paused but didn't answer the question. "I thought we might want to discuss providing a protection detail for her parents."

She took a big swig of her wine before she retrieved her tablet and clicked it on. In a moment, she'd selected an email and forwarded it to his email address. "I already took care of it—I had some buddies in Chicago looking for work. Her parents have a detail, but they won't know it. I also placed two guards in line for hiring with the company to keep an eye out when they are working there at night. That way, they can be right there in case of anything unexpected."

Burt scanned the email. "Good work. I knew my data was right when it said to hire you."

Elizabeth raised her glass and took a sip as she rolled her eyes. "Lucky me."

CHAPTER SIXTY-FIVE

The ambassador sat in the study of his hotel suite and leaned back at the large mahogany desk. A vintage Tiffany lamp glowed softly as the sound of melodic tones played from the virtual tuner disk placed in the center of the workspace. Seemingly floating to his right was the next page of the most recent negotiation with different sections highlighted.

He read another line and reviewed both the Meligornian and English translations of it while a small holographic Meligornian dancer cascaded across the wooden surface doing a traditional gambol. A frame sat to the right, a small girl with a similar complexion and hair color to the dancer, and she giggled and danced on a continuous loop of a small stored memory.

Ambassador V'ritan swiped the page away and brought the next up. The song changed and he tilted his head to focus on the dancer as she glided across the surface in front of him. The memory in the frame changed as well. The little girl was now a woman, the same as the hologram dancing on the desk. The movements were identical, the swing of the arms fluid, and the smile bright and shining. As he watched, his eyelids lowered slightly, and a small tear built in the corner of his eye.

A sudden and loud knock on the door made V'ritan jump and he swiped the hologram away. He leaned across and snatched up the frame as he called out, "Just a moment."

His gazed fixed on the picture for a second before he drew his hand across it. A thin line of purple energy streamed from the center up to his temple. The air hissed through his nose as his body tightened and then relaxed. The frame now looked like nothing abnormal, a picture of his daughter with the words, "Ritutius Hartstrom Tia Shaerium." It meant, "Rest Easy, Little Star."

The ambassador replaced the frame on his desk, wiped the tear from the corner of his eye, and leaned his head on his fist, his elbow propped on the desk. He focused his sight on the papers in front of him. "Come in."

Brilgus opened the door, hurried in, and closed it behind him. He held a tablet in his hand and set it down carefully before he slid it across to him. The ambassador raised an eyebrow and looked at the device. "I thought I said that I wanted to not be disturbed today with inconsequential things, Brilgus."

The bodyguard lowered his head, his hands behind his back. "Of course, Ambassador. Although I thought you would want to read this update sent over only a few minutes ago."

The ambassador pursed his lips, sighed, and swiped his hand over the tablet. An email rose in holographic form and hovered in front of him. As he read, his muscles tensed, and his face shifted from irritation to worry. He looked quickly at Brilgus. "And she is all right?"

His guard nodded. "We had no one from our camp with her. It was only her and two of her bodyguards. They all, except her, sustained injuries. One is in the hospital and the other has been discharged."

V'ritan shook his head and pressed his finger to the attachments. Brilgus placed his fingers on the top and bottom corners and pulled out to make the video screen larger. "This was footage caught by Federation cameras that are placed throughout the city. It does not have audio, but I think it's self-explanatory."

The ambassador nodded and played the footage. He watched the battle rage on the screen and winced and turned his head several times as Stephanie used the pipe to beat the assailants. She grasped one of the men by the top of his head and turned hers toward the camera for barely a moment. He paused the video quickly and tilted his head to focus on the screen.

Brilgus followed suit and both reveled in her appearance. "Are her eyes completely black?"

The ambassador nodded his head but didn't speak. He pressed play again as an uneasiness stirred in his chest. When the battle was over, he leaned back and rubbed his chin. Brilgus pressed fast forward and then paused it. "That isn't it. There is something else on this video that perplexes me greatly."

V'ritan waved his hand and the other man pressed play. The emergency medics carried the guard away on a stretcher, his shoulder bloody and arm limp. That view of the street then remained empty for around twenty seconds before Stephanie walked into view again. She seemed to be perplexed and paced for a moment before she stopped and turned to face them. Very slowly, she withdrew her battery from her pocket and gazed at it. Suddenly, her head jerked up and she stared directly at the camera. A wisp of purple energy flickered in her pupils and then dissipated.

The guard paused it. "There. The battery."

The ambassador straightened and pressed the image to enhance the item she held in her hand. "Definitely a battery, but—wait."

Brilgus bit the inside of his cheek. "I thought there was another one too, but you would be able to see it outlined in her pockets. It now seems to be completely full, but that had to have been her only source."

V'ritan pushed quickly from his chair and walked around the desk. He paced back and forth for several moments before he stopped and pointed at the frozen image. "That battery *is* full…it cannot be possible. How in the world did she have that much power to use? Assuming it was of high quality and full strength, that stone would be no more than a third full after that battle. And if it weren't high-end, it would practically be empty."

The other man wrinkled his nose and leaned forward toward the screen. "But it's not. It's full like she never touched it."

The ambassador shook his hand and his head simultaneously. "That is not possible. She has never even been to Meligorn other than during her pod simulations. She wouldn't have a way to store the energy, even if she could accomplish that without blowing herself to pieces. But then again, the proof is right there. She did do it, regardless of what science or common sense has to say about it."

Brilgus smirked at the screen. "I have to admit, I don't know how she does any of this. But she definitely has the form and technique down and is way more powerful than I thought she would be. She is possibly the strongest Earth witch that I have ever seen or read about. I am perplexed."

The Meligornian sighed, scratched his chin, and his eyes glazed over. "Me too, Brilgus. Me too."

Todd tapped his hands on the edge of the recruiter's desk as he waited for her to come out of her meeting. He had been picked up at home that morning by one of the recruiter cars and brought to the navy station to take his tests. For the first time in his life, he actually did some research, took a couple of practice exams online, and even combed his hair. It was a whole new world for him, but he wanted to make a good impression.

"Toddster," one of the other recruiters said and patted him on the shoulder as he passed. "Did you take your tests yet?"

He pointed downward. "That's what I'm here for. I'm gonna knock them out of the water."

The recruiter smiled with enthusiasm. "Yes, you are. Good luck, man. I'm off to pick up some new recruits and take them to the TRAM to catch their ride to boot camp."

Todd nodded enthusiastically as the man left. He immediately jumped to his feet as his recruiter approached. She gave him a kind smile and stuck her hand out. "Todd. Sorry that took so long. I wanted to make sure that everything was set up for you correctly."

He gestured airily. "Hey, no problem. I never care about waiting for friends."

She glanced at him and chuckled breathlessly. Hannah was really good at her job, crossed all her t's, and dotted all her i's. She was always friendly to the recruits because she knew that there would be a very large portion of them who would go in and not come back. At the same time, she had to be businesslike. It was what landed her that duty station, made her second highest recruiter in the office, and allowed her to cross through the military ranks without really raising any concerns or ruffling any feathers. But Todd was a teenage boy. He had raging hormones and weird ideas about what constituted a friend. He also stared at her ass on a regular basis like he somehow believed she wouldn't notice.

Todd thought she was really nice, and he hadn't stopped telling his friends about her since she'd contacted him. He truly thought he had made a friend. "Hey, did you ever watch that movie I told you about?"

Hannah glanced up. "Oh, uh…*Jumping Jack Flash?* I haven't had time yet but it's on my list for sure."

"If you want, I have it downloaded. You can come watch it on Saturday," he offered.

She cleared her throat and gave him a flat-lipped smile. "That's a really cool offer but I...um, I have to do some military stuff on Saturday. You know, keep up with the rat race over here."

Todd nodded and honestly didn't think anything of it. Hannah was glad he didn't push the subject. He was a cool kid and all, but she was there to get him signed in, not to become his bestie. She handled it with professionalism. It wasn't like it was the first time it had happened. She was a young, beautiful Latino woman with crazy blue eyes and a tight uniform. The boys tended to flock to her, not to mention the fact that she was kind to them or, at least, came off that way.

He smoothed his hair back and pulled down on his button-up. "So I'm taking all the remaining tests, right?"

Hannah put down her stack of papers. "Yep. I'll get you plugged in right now. It shouldn't take you very long. Honestly, it's not rocket science. Well, some of it is, but the rest will be a fly-by for you."

She led him to one of the testing rooms and hooked him up to the VR headsets they used for the placement testing. Exactly like the tests had been for decades, they were mostly multiple choice with a couple of short-answer questions thrown in.

Todd went directly to work and answered everything with ease. He was more than glad he had actually prepared and vaguely considered the possibility that if he had done that all along, he might have achieved better grades in school. Then again, he didn't really care about all that at the time. He'd simply wanted to download music and movies and hang out with Stephanie.

When he had completed the testing, he removed the headset and submitted them. He meandered back to where Hannah waited for him with a Federation Navy ballcap. "The computer is calculating your scores. When they are done, I will go over the info with my CO and give you a call to set up the rest of the process."

He smiled broadly and stood up tall with pride. "Thank you, Hannah. I can't wait!"

She chuckled and showed him to the door. "Jump in one of the cars out front and they'll take you home. And good luck on the last leg of school you have."

Todd walked out of the door and pulled his hat on, feeling like a new man. Hannah raised an eyebrow and closed the door before she returned to her desk. She pulled up the assessment page and leaned her head back against the chair to wait for the last score to come through. With all the technology available, she still couldn't understand why they had such archaic shit in the recruiting offices. But then again, it didn't really matter because unless a kid failed—which was damn near impossible—they put them wherever they wanted to anyway.

Hannah printed out the test scores, walked to her CO's office, and knocked on the door frame. He looked up and waved her in. "Petty Officer Santino, come in. How is the new recruit coming along?"

She handed him the scores. "Really well, actually. He tested in the top percent for aptitude. It surprised me, I won't lie. With his high school transcript, I didn't expect very much."

Captain Cromwell scanned the paper and narrowed his eyes. "Hmm, yes. He did do well. Although this seems to be a regular thing with your recruits—the male ones anyway. I have a feeling they are trying to impress you. You might have missed your calling as a teacher. Shaping bright minds one tight skirt at a time."

Hannah chuckled. "No, I don't think that would work. Besides, you know how I feel about kids. They're great when they are ready to enlist, sir. Snot-nosed, loud, and sticky when they are under eighteen."

Cromwell laughed deep and low. "This is why I like you, Santino. You always say it straight but in a tone that would make me think you were a saint. Luckily for the Federation, you aren't, and your three-year tour on the Abdunnasir in deep space showed that."

She put her hands behind her back and straightened. "I simply did my duty, sir. Those Dreth pirates were getting out of hand and someone needed to send them spiraling back into hell. But it was a team effort."

The captain smirked, his attention still on the papers. "And modest too. If all recruits were as good as you, we'd be one hell of a Federation Navy, wouldn't we? As it is, this kid shows promise. He could be good with Naval Intelligence."

Hannah nodded. "Yes, sir. That was my first thought."

The captain flipped the page to his physical stats. He snarled slightly. "We have to work on his physical attributes a little but nothing a diet and several dozen laps around the space track with higher gravitational pull won't fix. Get him set up. Good work."

She took the papers. "Oh. Also, he can feel the MU energy."

CHAPTER SIXTY-SIX

>>Replay video from Wednesday, 4:33 pm, 1500 block of Church St. NW

BURT wanted to review the footage himself, knowing that one of his hires had been severely injured and that the other guard and Stephanie were somehow able to fight off almost a dozen men. It didn't compute for him that she would have been strong enough to do that yet in the real world. His system went through the video footage data and recreated the incident in a computational annalistic form that BURT quickly ran through his system. She fought the whole time using a mixture of magic and human emotion to fuel her skills.

>>Query: Human capabilities without magic in Earth-based street fight.

The computations were quick and easy and showed that even the most trained fighters would not be able to use the types of functional fighting moves she'd used in that capacity while also draining energy to use magic as well. Their average fight time would calculate to only seven minutes. She'd fought the gang members for over double that amount of time and did not need recovery afterward.

BURT replayed the video again and located the scene at the very end with the battery. From his calculations of both pixel saturation and form of object, the battery was almost completely full. According to his numbers, it should have been at least three-quarters empty, if not totally tapped. There were also no other signs of any other batteries on her person or disposed of during the fight. This left him perplexed.

"Could her Meligorn energy be adding something?" he asked himself as he continued to run through the data over and over, using caveats such as adrenaline and dietary intake to make the number make sense.

Despite his efforts, nothing emerged that brought any clarity. It was as if she did something with the energy conversion that he didn't understand. He was programmed with every byte of data on Earth, and if it were new and not yet uploaded, he could easily search for it through his connection with the Net servers. But no answer came in, which meant whatever was happening had not happened before in a way noticeable to mankind.

Stephanie whistled cheerfully as she hung her clothes up and walked to the pod. She was thankful that they were able to turn the heat up in the room. She had been freezing every time she went in and out. The pod regulated her temperature while inside, but the exit and entrance were not only awkward due to nudity but uncomfortable too.

She climbed into the pod, pulled the door shut, and lay back on the seat. The process had become seamless, and she rarely even noticed her switch from her human perception to when her avatar awoke in the virtual world. She opened her virtual eyes and glanced around at a Meligorn temple of sorts—not religious in nature like the ones on Earth but more focused on the magic of the world than anything else.

The dust puffed gently off the floor from the slide of her boots as she walked forward. The walls were all etched with a language she had never seen and in the center stood a pedestal with a small bowl on top. She approached cautiously and stared down at it. The liquid in the bowl wasn't water but wasn't something she recognized either.

She narrowed her eyes and looked closer. Within the bowl, images played like an old movie but with people of Meligorn in the very temple in which she stood.

"That is the Mnemonic Basin," the voice of her Meligornian teacher, M'rick, said.

Stephanie looked up as he came gently down the steps to the right. "And what is it for?"

He put his arms out to the sides. "This is the Temple of Presage, located on Meligorn outside the Capital Burghal of Nastar. It is said that the temple was the first building ever to be erected and sits atop the very place that spills the magic from the core of the planet. It is thought to be the most mystical and magical place in the universe. That bowl was placed there on the day the last stone was set. No one filled it, and it filled itself with magic. Within the waves of the energy that you cannot feel with your hands, taste, or touch are the memories of every moment that has come to pass within these walls."

She looked back and attempted to touch the surface of the liquid. Her hand went right through as if it were a hologram. The faces that passed within the liquid changed and moved forward through time. It was fascinating, but she was still unsure of why she was there. She looked up at M'rick with a small frown.

He cracked a smile and chuckled. "You are wondering why you are here. It is an important place for both humans and Meligorn. And right now, I want to test you on your Meligorn magic absorption."

Stephanie, her forehead scrunched, shrugged her shoulders. "Why?"

M'rick smiled and led her to the open space within the Temple's atrium. "Humor me."

She nodded, happy to trust his guidance. Calm and relaxed, she stood in the center of the stone floor, closed her eyes, and breathed deeply through her nose. She pulled the MU up from the ground exactly as she had done before. When she had drawn enough, she whipped it around her and allowed it to flow through her like a continuous stream connected to her very being. Her body glowed brightly as she moved her shoulders and arms to command the flow like a conductor directed the orchestra.

M'rick watched a moment before he touched her arm to break the concentration. She opened her eyes and instead of the energy retreating immediately, it took its time to flow slowly through her and into the ground. BURT watched the entire thing and calculated every change in her body at every moment. Not only did she pass this examination of sorts, but it was obvious she used the MU in a new way. But how?

He queried the system as rapidly as he could and pulled resources from every place he could. In the end, it made no difference. There was no available data to extrapolate the potential issues. Nothing to compare to or contrast with. With this new form of magical and energetic control, he couldn't help but wonder if she would once again explode. But this time, would it be in real life?

Several men sat in a penthouse apartment smoking cigars and sipping bourbon. The place was decorated in old-world charm. Large, deeply colored oriental rugs, earth-toned vases from the ashes of some of the most important ruins in history, and framed documents that held both rich historical value and magical significance. One of the men, with dark hair, deep-set eyes, and a shadowed aura deepening his features, ran his finger over the edge of his rocks glass. He rolled his shoulders and the leather of his jacket made an uncomfortable creaking sound.

He looked at the three men across from him, all of them similarly dressed and very close in looks and prominent in stature. "What do they say on the ground?"

The man to his right—the one they called Beta P for the radioactive scars across his face and hands—sniffed and put his glass down. "The cut-out gangs were a failure."

The man beside him scoffed, uncrossed his legs, and tapped his cigar in the ashtray. "Like we thought they would be in the first place.

They were pigs, low-level people who normally steal from the neighbor's cookie jar. Did you expect them to be capable of taking a human witch? It was a waste of time from the beginning and only made restrictions tighter."

"We had to start somewhere," another man pointed out. "It would have been better to snatch her quietly, but we now know that amateurs are not the way to solve this. She shouldn't be that powerful, not yet. Not with the small amount of energy she carried in her pocket. But we saw that it didn't matter how much she carried. Her powers are beyond what we fully understand."

Beta P rubbed his right hand abstractedly. The pain from his past radioactive injuries haunted him constantly. "Right. Well, now we know. And we need to make sure that we give her more focus with better quality outsourcing agents."

The main man maintained an expressionless face. "And the agents who hired the gang?"

Beta waved his hand dismissively and picked his drink up. "They are taken care of. They won't sing to anyone anytime soon. They knew the cost of failure and decided to use amateurs. Sadly, they paid for that mistake."

"What about her parents? They are the most important people to her," the man in the middle ventured.

The leader licked his lips and puffed at his cigar. "I think that at this time, with her powers unknown, we should leave the parents as a last resort. That kind of rage could create a backlash we aren't ready to handle. Besides, we would prefer to talk to her and foster her support for us and the cause. I don't think kidnapping the people she loves the most will put her in the mood to discuss anything other than our deaths."

They all could agree that they wanted her for more than simply her magic, her clout, her persuasion, and her intellect. They couldn't ever expect her to trust anything they said if they harmed the people she loved. It was not the way they usually handled business, but for her, they would agree on a softer form of advancement.

He smacked his mouth and the smoke billowed around the room.

"So it's decided. We will work with more qualified agents to bring this girl in. Beta, I can assume you will get on top of this."

The man nodded. "Yes. I will make some calls as soon as we leave here."

The leader smashed his cigar down into his ashtray and set it on the table. He grunted slightly as he stood and walked to the balcony doors. With a sigh, he cracked them and watched absently as the smoke flooded out of the condo. That done, he walked to the bar, grabbed a napkin, and picked several olives up before he rested on a stool.

The other men waited for him to speak, knowing he had the agenda in his mind. He put an olive in his mouth and chewed. "What about the ambassador? I've seen nothing to suggest that he is on our priority list."

Beta glanced at the others, who seemed to like to stay quiet unless they thought they might be in line for recognition. "I have watched him in recent days in an effort to keep up with the girl and him, and I believe that we should ramp up our efforts when it comes to… clearing his voice."

The leader's gaze studied Beta as he popped another olive in his mouth. "Why is that?"

The man pursed his lips and considered his answer for a moment. "He, in my opinion, has too much success and influence in the Federation activities at the moment. It is becoming a liability that I'm not sure we need or want right now. There is a plan—a bigger one than any of these small things—but he has the ability to influence and change the course of Federation focus. Which you know, of course, is far from the direction in which we hope to go."

Although he grumbled under his breath, the leader nodded his head as he wiped his fingers. "Yes. I've seen the amount of travel and the new agreements put forward between nations recently. It definitely has the potential to dampen our efforts. We all should know that the most important part that we need to watch here—continually watch—is the Federation's efforts with the Dreth pirates. The harsher they seem, the more their ships will be pointed at the Dreth's throats.

The more they chase them off into deep space, the less their focus will look behind or to the side. We have known for a long time that the Federation works with blinders on. They assume that they can somehow protect themselves from all angles of space. This is absurd, of course."

The three men nodded. "Of course. Absurd."

He walked back to his chair and sat. "It is vital that we keep the pirates as the focal point for the Federation, NorAm, and everyone else, for that matter. Anyone who could spook the Federation should be contained. Their heads need to be forcefully turned toward the Dreth pirate ships. We do not want anyone—the Federation, Dreth, or Meligorn—to see what is going on behind the scenes until it is so far gone that there will be nothing they can do to stop it."

Beta mumbled and flexed his fist. "And the ambassador is one of those beings who could quickly throw this whole thing off course. With his voice in the public and political arena, as well as the well-documented Meligorn intelligence, he is probably the most dangerous individual to us in the whole universe. God knows the Dreth and their tiny pea-brains are no threat. They can barely get full sentences out or ships off the surface, much less figure things out."

The leader chuckled and wiped his nose on the back of his hand. "True, Beta, and your passion shows your true heart in this matter. So we need to get close to the ambassador. What are your suggestions for this? And you two need to start putting your brains to use. I am not here simply to make you feel important."

The other two men cleared their throats and straightened, slightly wounded. The third man shrugged his shoulders. "We could go wherever he has dinner or a social event. It can't be hard to hack into his schedule."

Beta groaned. "His schedule is kept by letter magic and only absorbed by himself and his half-breed guard, Brilgus. Unless you have Meligornian magical abilities, I don't see that being an option."

The man in the middle leaned forward. "What if we were to wait outside his hotel and simply take him?"

Everyone looked at him silently for a moment. The leader raised an eyebrow. "And you have discovered the secret to blocking Meligornian magic from the highest non-royal in Meligorn. That is fantastic, but why have you hidden it from us all this time?"

He pursed his lips and his gaze broke contact with the leader. Beta rubbed the side of his face. "In all reality, the best option for us at this time would be to determine how to use one of those individuals within his support team. Their schedules are easy to find, there are humans without powers within the ranks, and they don't travel with protection. Most of them are young, too—interns and fresh prep school graduates taking positions to work up in the Federation graces. They are often naïve and careless with their safety precautions. It shouldn't be too hard to get to them."

The leader thought about it for a moment. "That does seem to be one of our only choices at the moment. What if we cannot get one of them to agree?"

Beta shrugged. "Then we dispose of one and put one of ours in their place. This would allow for a more secretive movement and keep anyone from blowing the whistle on the whole thing. Getting in touch with someone who can do this has never been a problem, but we have found little reason for it...until now."

CHAPTER SIXTY-SEVEN

Lars chuckled as he walked down the hallway with the rest of the team in tow. Brenden was recounting his night out on the town with some girl he had met while shopping at the market. She was apparently some sort of intern working with the ambassador's team.

"She actually said to me that she hoped that they would one day build a shrine to Meligorn, maybe in the place of the White House. I asked her why we would do that here and she told me because Meligorn will be our savior. I tried to keep a straight face, but I was frankly terrible at it. She almost knocked me out of my chair. And that, sadly, was where the date ended."

Avery scoffed. "Sadly? You were still interested after that?"

Brenden shrugged. "No one cares about her weird obsession with the other planet when she is face down in my be—"

Elizabeth stepped out in front of them and Brenden cut short and cleared his throat. Her gaze darted from one to the other with a strange smirk on her lips. "Morning, fellas. Off for some more torture?"

Johnny snorted. "We have a thing for pain, apparently."

Marcus put his hands up and shook his head. "Nah ah. You have a thing for pain. I'm here because Lars threatened me and...well, I don't really want to know if he would actually follow through. So I am taking my chances with Steph. She seems to have a little more mercy."

Lars raised an eyebrow and chuckled. "We'll see about that. We might have to get her out of bed. We'll send you, Marcus, since you see the softer side of her."

Marcus wrinkled his nose. "Man, you are taking this lead position too far. Mrs. E, please reprimand him."

She popped an almond in her mouth and chuckled. "Call me Elizabeth, please, not Mrs. Anything. No ring on this finger, sir. I have too many men around me all the time as it is. I don't want to have to be forced to be nice to you out of contractual obligation."

He saluted her and she shook her head and stepped to the side. "Have fun, work hard, and if you need to get her up, put it into the system for her AI. That way, she doesn't chop you in the throat. The AI is safe."

They all continued down the hall to the training room. As they walked in, those in front turned and shushed them. Stephanie stood on the mats, her eyes closed, her right knee bent and her foot resting on the left, and her palms pressed together high over her head. It was not normal in the least for her to be up and working out early, and especially not the first one there. They all stood and simply watched as her attention never wavered. It was as if they had never stepped into the room.

Stephanie practiced her katas with perfect precision, every movement deliberate and every shift sharp and swift. She initiated the routine with the Shotokan Kihon Kata, beginning in the ready stance. Slowly, she turned left, kept her feet in the left front stance, and quickly thrust her arm downward into a block. From there, she stepped forward into a right front stance, lunged, and punched through the center. Her body turned to the right in a fluid motion as she used her forearm to throw a right downward block.

As she continued, she danced lightly on her feet and moved with resolution. She neared the end of her kata and turned right one hundred and eighty degrees. Her left foot moved slightly forward, and she used her right forearm again to block. From there, she took a deliberate step forward and called out as she punched with her left arm down the middle. Her body snapped back into a ready stance and she brought her palms together at her chest. She bent forward, bowed, and paused a moment before she straightened and opened her eyes.

Lars glanced at the others and hastily made eye contact. No one needed to say a word. They all knew what was happening. Her guilt drove her to perfection, an admirable thought but also dangerous in context. The men dropped their things and walked onto the mat to surround her in a loving way.

Marcus put his hand on her shoulder, but her stare didn't shift. "There is no need to feel guilty. You were more than part of the team out there. We are so grateful that no one was hurt any worse. This is not the first stay in the hospital for Frog, and it won't be the last. We know these things are possible."

Lars threw out a correction. "Probable."

Marcus nodded. "That's right. Probable. But we do it for our jobs and for the people we care about."

Stephanie breathed in deeply and let the air out slowly. She touched Marcus's hand before she turned to the others. "Guilt or no guilt, it doesn't change the fact that if I can't help protect myself, more people will be harmed and possibly killed. Even a scratch on one of us, in my eyes, is a reason to train harder, work more, and attain an even higher understanding of what it means to protect."

Johnny shook his head. "But you aren't alone. You don't have to do it on your own."

She looked at him with a slight smile for a moment before she shifted her gaze to her hands. "All my life, I knew that there was something different about me, even if I had no proof. If my life needs protection, I will not allow those voluntarily doing it to fight on their own. I am not the king of the chessboard, the piece to always be protected."

Lars scrunched his brow. "In a way, though, you are. Your capabilities are so far beyond anyone's understanding and your ability to change things is worth the scratches, holes in our arms, and yes, even death. One life for many. That is a no brainer."

Stephanie put her hand on his shoulder and turned to speak to everyone. "While I feel I shouldn't be the king, I do consider myself the queen. And everyone—anyone—who attacks my people will feel my wrath. If you will protect me for the betterment of all mankind, then I will use my powers to make sure you don't die doing it. And if you are hurt, we will avenge that pain. We will strike and I will not stand unseen in the shadows. I will walk in front of you, leading like I should."

The guys all nodded and felt the power that radiated from her. Stephanie had impressed them with her mature and loving thoughts. She brought them closer to an understanding that it wasn't merely a job that would pay the bills. They were part of something bigger than all of them. In that moment, as the sun began to rise outside and the world began to wake, Stephanie no longer had guards or employees. Now, for better or worse, gash or death, she began to assemble her army of followers.

Marcus turned his body to the side and grabbed Stephanie's wrist as she threw a hard punch at his chest. Immediately, he stepped back and yanked her off balance. He grabbed her shoulder swiftly with his other hand and hauled her into him as he thrust his knee into her stomach. As soon as she doubled over to grab her belly, he ground his elbow between her shoulder blades and knocked her off her feet. She landed on her back and groaned before she rolled onto her side and coughed.

Elizabeth clapped and paced back and forth on the sidelines. "Pick it up, Steph. The enemy won't let you take a moment to gather your nuts after a blow like that. You gotta push it out and roll out of it. Remember—move, keep moving, don't stop moving. If it were me, I would kick you so hard right now you would instantly shit teeth. But if you hit the ground and roll, they will have a harder time dogpiling you."

Stephanie slapped her hand on the ground. Spit dripped from her lip as she pushed to her feet. She wiped her mouth on the back of her sleeve and shoved her mouthguard back into place. Elizabeth stepped back, folded her arms, and watched as Marcus attacked again.

The training room was always Elizabeth's favorite place to be. No matter what job she had going on, she could always put her focus on one thing in the gym and that was to continually hone her fighting skills. When she was younger, she had taken her fair share of beatings, but she'd always gotten back up and never complained, exactly like Stephanie. As she stood and watched the blocks, kicks, and punches, Elizabeth's mind fluttered back to her younger years.

She was a tall girl and had always been taller than everyone else. But she was strong, muscular, and lean and spent her whole childhood learning how to protect herself the best way she could. She grew up during the civil unrest of the late 2080s. It had started as a positive thing but grew into another reason for the poor to lash out in anger, be punished by the Federation, and lash out some more. She could remember the last day of the unrest so vividly in her mind.

The sirens had blared loudly throughout her Kentucky hometown. She had run outside to see what was happening. There had been a rally downtown, and her father had gone to try to speak peace to both sides. He was an advocate for freedom and separation from the Federation but used his time trying to sponsor conversation instead of fighting. He hadn't always been that way, but when Elizabeth was only a little girl, her mother had been beaten to death in the streets by rebels who had started to form the basis for the civil unrest. They thought she was a Federation undercover agent and were desperate to grab their attention. It was only when they were arrested and convicted by the Federation forces that they heard the truth and realized what they had done—that her mother was one of them.

Elizabeth knew the sound of gunfire all too well before lasers were used on a regular basis. She heard the shots the day the men were executed by bullets to the back of the head in the center of the town. And on that last day of civil unrest, as she stood at the end of her suburban driveway and looked out at the cityscape, she heard them again. This time, though, she knew before anyone told her that her father was gone.

From there, she began to train, did what she needed to do, lived in Gov-Sub housing, and listened to her aunt whenever she raged. But she fought hard and long, and by the time she reached Stephanie's age, she was able to protect herself better than anyone she knew. The passion of her father's glow drove every punch and kick, surged every string of anger, and cemented her purpose in life. Up until Burt, though, she hadn't even really tried.

Stephanie backflipped off Marcus's chest and landed lightly, bolted forward, and pounded him as hard as she could in the stomach. Elizabeth shook her memories away and clapped. "Good, very good."

She had come to see Stephanie as her protégé, much like her teacher, rebel warrior Alexander Sclovickia, now long since passed, had brought her under his wing. "Take five. Get some water."

She walked over to the bench where Stephanie toweled her head and guzzled water. "I hope you understand that I am pushing you like this for your own good."

The girl's gaze met hers as she swallowed her gulp of water. "I know. I get it."

Elizabeth sat beside her and sighed. "I can't protect you all the time, but I can teach you to know what is coming. Sometimes, that alone is key to winning a fight."

Stephanie smiled at her before she pushed up and pointed to Lars. "You're mine, butthead."

Elizabeth chuckled and leaned back against the wall. Her mind drifted again, but this time, she had gotten older, wiser, and caught up in things she really didn't fully grasp. She had to make money and she did it doing what she did best—finding people and sending them a message, usually with violence. There were a great many things that she had done when she was younger that she was not proud of. Deep down, she knew that was why she sat there day after day, watched Stephanie, and pushed her to be better. Pushed for her to do the right thing, not the easy one.

All those tiny little moments, the ones that imprint on your soul, had stayed buried for a long time. But she hoped that within all that dark and deceit there was a glimmer of light. A lesson learned that she could pass on to the young girl. There were always other options, and each person had to do what they thought was best. But sometimes, those options were really hard to see. Pride and fear drove the rest of it, the fight for the top and the terrifying thought that all their hard work would be completely wasted.

Stephanie yelled and drew her attention back to the floor. The girl flipped Lars over her back and thrust her hand forward to stop barely inches from his throat. They smiled at one another and Stephanie looked at Elizabeth, gave her a wink, and pointed at her with reverence.

Elizabeth chuckled and shook it off, acting like it was no big deal. She had to do that. She had to show separation. But what she really hoped she'd found in her relationship with Stephanie and all the others was so much simpler but so very difficult to attain.

Elizabeth simply wanted forgiveness.

CHAPTER SIXTY-EIGHT

Stephanie stood in the pod room, her mood the same as it had been for the last several days. She was focused, her intentions clear, and she continued to push the anger and frustration she felt aside. The last several days had been busy. She woke at five in the morning, worked out hard with the guys, ate a healthy meal, had pod time until dinner, got a run in, and went to bed. Usually, she worked herself so hard during the day that she didn't have any problem falling asleep. But while she slept, her mind took her back to the fight. Over and over again, she stood to the side and watched like a spectator, viewing herself from the outside. She watched Frog go down and the entirety of her body shift into a mode that she hadn't been able to fully shake.

As far as the Virtual World went, she had mostly worked on real-world tactics—things she could use to interact with others but all in the comfort of Meligorn. At the end of each pod session, she would spend some time working on her theories. The silence was perfect for her but deafening even for BURT, who hadn't really spoken much. She wasn't sure what she was in for that day, but she didn't care as long as she moved forward. By this point, she no longer fought to play with magic like a child. That child had jumped ship in the streets of DC as she beat a man with a pipe.

Stephanie entered the pod, closed the lid, and barely felt herself drift off thanks to the dulcet effects of the serum. When she opened her eyes, she stood in the avatar dressing room, somewhere she hadn't been for a while. She was usually already dressed and inside Meligorn. She looked around, unsure of why she was there.

After a few moments of silence, she glared upward into the infinite blackness of the space above her. "Hello? I don't need to indulge in fancy clothes. I simply need to get to my next spot."

Suddenly, a rack appeared in front of her and held several different armored body suits. The AI spoke around her. "Today's mission will be different. A game of sorts, to test the abilities you have thus far acquired. It will be tactically suited to your taste but understand that once in, you cannot reach out for other gear or protection. This is meant to be a real-world simulation. Choose your armor, boots, weapons, and backup ammo. The game will begin in three minutes."

A digital clock appeared on the wall and Stephanie stared at it for a moment as it began to tick backward, counting her down. She swung into action, swiped through the armor, and selected the one on the end. It was a tight black suit with chest, shoulder, and thigh protection. For her waist, she chose a small tactical belt and filled it with two hand laser guns and two backup cartridges. She then chose the largest battery and slid it into a small pouch on her leg. Her attempt at a second failed as the system only allowed one. She didn't care. Wherever she was, she knew she would be able to manipulate the energy for her use.

As she tapped her choice of boots and rocked back and forth on the soles, the clock reached 00:00 and the avatar creation program faded to black.

"Your game begins now," the AI instructed. "Your mission is to capture, disarm, or kill the Dreth pirates fighting your squadron. Those on your team are your partners, avatars pulled from real-life soldiers of the Federation army and navy."

Stephanie scowled and grumbled under her breath. "What's the army doing in space?"

The AI didn't respond but continued her instruction. "Once the Dreth are all captured, the game will end. Try to keep all civilians safe in the process. Good luck."

That little snippet of information surprised her. "Civilians?"

The system sped around her and came to a halt inside some dark hallway. Soldiers raced around her, and gunfire and explosions echoed from outside the doors. A loud boom shook the building and she flailed for balance and rubbed her hand down the soot-covered wall. It was smooth and familiar. She withdrew her hand and saw the shiny white cinderblock beneath the layers of dirt and grime. There was something so familiar about it and she couldn't shake the odd feeling.

Suddenly, a hand grabbed her by the arm and spun her around. It was a navy officer, his helmet tight on his head. He raised the front and scowled. "Come on, soldier. Get it together. People are dying out there. Get a move on."

He slapped his visor shut and fell in behind a line of sailors and soldiers who ran toward a door to the outside at the end of the hall. Stephanie shook her head and ran after them. She ducked beneath a fallen beam as she stepped out of the dark and into the light of day. Her feet slowed almost immediately, and surprise took over.

This was not the peaceful rippling and majestic shores of Meligorn. It was not the ravaged and ruined post-apocalyptic rocky terrain of Dreth. It was Earth. And not simply anywhere on Earth. She stood planted on the same sidewalk where she used to stand with Todd talking about pop culture and math tests. The same school she had attended since she was a kid. It was war-torn and crumbling but still the same place.

Her surprise left her stunned, but only momentarily. A streaking laser hissed past her face, singed a few pieces of hair, and brought her back to the war that unfolded around her. She looked up with wide eyes as the Dreth pirates raged, marched on the humans, and laid waste to what had already been considered a ghetto.

Stephanie gritted her teeth, slammed her hand on the battery, and drew the energy from it. She twisted her hands to create a whirling purple orb. As the energy built, she moved her feet again, this time at a quickened pace as she hurtled toward one of the Dreth. She continued to manipulate her hands to grow the orb until finally, she was close enough to take a shot. Her eyes narrowed in concentration, she released her magical weapon with her full strength behind the throw to deliver a punishing strike to the pirate. She continued to run as she drew more energy. Up ahead was a pile of rubble with a platform on top. She sprinted faster and used some of the magic to launch herself up the side. As her feet found purchase on the platform, she released her magic and hundreds of small bullet-shaped pulses erupted into the massed battle that continued to rage.

Instinct reminded her not to remain in the open and she scrambled off the elevation and immediately broke into a run. A familiar voice yelled in pain and she slowed to turn her head right and left as panic rose in her throat. To her right, a guy lay on the ground, his hand up toward the Dreth who towered over him. Stephanie took a couple of steps closer and the helpless figure turned his head, his eyes hopeful.

Her lungs seized in her chest as she registered what everything in her refused to accept. Todd lay dying on the ground. She cupped her hands and drew in as much magic as she could. In mid-sprint, she released it in a single enormous ball that rocketed into the Dreth pirate about to stab Todd with a large, sharp sword. The attacker shrieked loudly and disintegrated in front of her. She hurried to Todd's side, helped him to his feet, and put her arm around his waist.

She knew it wasn't real, that it was only a simulation, but it was a perfect replica, even down to the smell of the cheap body spray he had always worn. Another Dreth pirate approached at a run with sharp teeth that dripped drool and a long golden pitchfork in his claw. Stephanie shoved Todd down on a pile of rubble and slapped her hand against her battery. There was no response. No feeling of energy, no feeling of magic, nothing. She fumbled in her pocket and drew it out in disbelief. The stone was cold and empty.

She rolled her eyes, threw it on the ground, and pushed her sleeves up. The pirate drew closer and closer, but she was determined to test her theory. She lowered her hands and focused on her senses, but nothing came except the enraged attacker. Time seemed to slow as she tried again and again before she finally drew her guns and fired directly into the Dreth's face.

The pirate's head fragmented, and his body slumped instantly. Angry, Stephanie thrust the guns into their holsters and stormed over to a large pile of rubble. She scrambled to the top and raised her hands. "Time out! Stop the game," she demanded harshly and assumed the AI would respond.

Everything froze. She lowered her hands and pursed her lips. After a few seconds, the AI spoke from above as if it came from the heavens. "You are not normally authorized to stop in mid-fight, but I was given the allowance this time. What can I do for you?"

Stephanie pointed at the ground where her battery lay. "This is not accurate. Just because I don't have a battery doesn't mean my magic stops."

The AI paused. "It does. The battery gives you what you need to begin, but there is no magic to collect on Earth. You must therefore use your human skills."

Stephanie shook her hand back and forth. "No, no, no. That is not how I work. I have been working on a theory—one that is backed by research and personal experience. There is energy here on Earth. It is similar to the energy and magic found on Meligorn but the problem is that humans don't know how to tap into it anymore. It's been lost for thousands of years, stamped out by a bunch of old rulers in the Middle Ages."

The AI responded in a monotone voice. "I am not familiar with this energy. It is not programmed into my system."

She sighed with real frustration. "Of course not. It is only referenced in the deepest parts of the net. The bigwigs don't want humans to know of this."

"How is it like the Meligornian magic?" the AI asked.

Her eyes narrowed as she tried to focus on the challenge. She would have to do her best to explain with limited knowledge. “Okay, so MU is a kind of energy that allows the user to twist it and bend it to their personal will. The scale here on Earth is the same, in essence, but instead of magical energy, it’s light energy. It has different spectrums to it. The Earth spectrum is more refined and more powerful. At the same time, it is much harder to tap into. When you do, you could easily fry your circuits.”

The AI didn’t answer but the simulation remained frozen. Stephanie looked around, unsure as to whether the disembodied assistant was still present. “Hello?”

“Yes, sorry. I thought I might be better to discuss this matter with,” Burt replied. “If what you are saying is correct, then there will be places in which this light energy is stronger or more abundant.”

Stephanie licked her lips and clapped her hands, relieved that he had intruded and replaced the usual AI. “Yes. Yes. I thought about that too. I wondered if maybe it had to do with the significant places on Earth, like the Temple on Meligorn. Or perhaps geographical things like the equator.”

He listened for a moment while he ran a search in the background for supernatural, magical, or strange locations. “What about ley lines?”

She thought about it for a moment and then nodded. “Sure, uh… yeah, that could be something. Does it look like it could make a difference?”

BURT immediately began to calculate the major ley lines spoken about in the past. He ran the numbers, the occurrences, and the theories on them in record time but nothing was conclusive. “There are reported occurrences from time to time on the major ley lines, but nothing definitive. Nothing proven. There is no real logic to the existing ones that I can find.”

Stephanie chewed her nail. “Damnit.”

“But,” he continued, “it doesn’t rule out the theory behind it. Some of the places might need to be investigated and you would be the best candidate to do so. It would be difficult for anyone who wasn’t connected to the magic to know if there was anything going on in those locations.”

Stephanie nodded. "Right."

"That will be for a later review," he replied. "Tell me, does the energy feel the same as it does on Meligorn?"

Stephanie wrinkled her nose and thought about it. "It's hard to tell you what something feels like. The only time I have really utilized it on Earth was during the fight in DC. That whole thing happened in something of a fog, though. I went from battery directly into light—a seamless transition. But what I can say is that I would call it a three compared to Meligorn, which I'd put at a one on the scale and so top of the range. Earth power does not feel as strong but is still useable. I have a working theory on it, though. I've tested this theory through hand calculations each night on Earth."

BURT was impressed. "Excellent. What is the theory?"

She turned, scrambled down the rubble, and jumped the last few feet to the ground. "The theory is that as I get better with the use of the light magic and the Meligorn magic, I will be able to tap into it even more. Right now, there is a real danger to it, something that has to be watched carefully, especially on Earth. Here, if I die, I come back. There, if I die, I stay dead. Opening myself to too much too fast could have catastrophic results."

"Then we will begin that research after this," he replied. "I have reprogrammed the system to have a likeliness of Meligornian magic but using your scale as you described it to be. It might not be perfect, but it's the only information we have on it. Either way, you will be able to use it in this scenario. I want to see how well it works. Let's resume the battle."

She assumed a ready stance, her hands at her sides as her fingers wiggled with anticipation.

CHAPTER SIXTY-NINE

Stephanie put one hand down on the cement that halfway blocked the street and leapt over it. Her momentum didn't stop, and a mixture of adrenaline and the awareness of the light energy thrummed and pulsed in the background of her chest. She was careful with it and avoided overzealousness. Ahead and to her right, three soldiers battled a single Dreth. The pirate was strong, and they had run out of weaponry. Stephanie looked above her head and followed the electrical line to a large and very old oak tree directly behind the attacker.

The spark of magic flinted inside her with an odd pop and sizzle. She raised her arm and made a sharp gesture, A small flare of energy burst free and hissed into the electrical wire, which vibrated wildly as the pole swayed back and forth. She did it again, this time with more power. The cable writhed overhead and snapped to arc toward the oak. As the flashing and fiery end struck the tree, it immediately burst into flames. The blaze spilled over onto the Dreth pirate like a bucket of tar.

The soldiers looked at her and raced in her direction as the pirate stumbled crazily and ignited everything he touched before he finally succumbed to the flames. One of the soldiers shook her hand and pointed outward. "This is not the Dreth's doing. There are three others who have control over this battle. The pirates are paid mercenaries for them. Eliminate those three and this will end. The Dreth will either fight or surrender, but we will have the upper hand."

Stephanie turned her focus down the street and onto three operatives dressed in black suits with no real discernable features. They stood in a line but a short distance from one another and gestured at the different Dreth. She could see they were armed—and armed heavily.

Her mind made up, she slapped the soldier on the arm. "Got it. You and whoever else you can mobilize, get any civilians out of here and attack the Dreth. The more you can get rid of now, the less likely that there will be a revolt when the three men are dead."

The soldiers agreed and ran off in search of others. Stephanie sprinted toward the men. She deliberately chose a path down the center of the street and stared at them, unperturbed that they could see her. None of them drew their weapons, something she couldn't understand at all. They simply stood and watched her approach, their arms folded. She shrugged and continued. "Hey, when you aren't given a nose, a healthy complexion, or decent clothes as an avatar, I guess you don't give a rat's ass."

When she reached the cement roadblocks she'd passed earlier, she dove and twisted her body. Her feet cleared and she prepared to tuck and roll, but before she could pull her knees to her chest, a large hand encircled her chest. The stop jolted her momentum and her arms and legs flailed forward. Her head turned and she gasped at a large Dreth creature, light-brown from head to foot, with a huge bald head. It's arms, legs, and torso resembled a twisted tree nymph.

It hurled her to the ground, and she careened and rolled until she skidded into a motionless heap at the feet of one of the men. He looked angrily at her and yanked a half sword from a sheath on his back. From her sprawled vantage point, he appeared much larger than she'd expected. He held his sword at his eye level and his body tensed for the inevitable blow. As he thrust down, Stephanie dragged her energy up to form a shield. She focused all her strength into it and flinched when the metal impacted against the magic and hissed in violent response. Her attacker struggled to retain his hold on the weapon, but the force of the magic-infused barrier whipped it from his hand.

He gritted his teeth, snatched a piece of wood from the ground beside him, and resumed the offensive. As he swung his improvised weapon, Stephanie released the magic in her shield to create a fine dust in the palm of her hand. She rolled to the right and the rough timber struck the ground close to her head. Elizabeth's words echoed in her mind and she instantly rolled to the left to barely avoid a second blow. She rolled a third time, the man narrowed his eyes at her, and she smirked, opened her palm, and blew the dust into his eyes.

The operative screamed, dropped the board, and clutched his eyes with both hands. She pushed to her feet and shook her head. In seconds, she had drawn her leg back, grabbed his shoulders, and kneed him hard in the groin. A loud expletive replaced his screams and he doubled over. Stephanie snorted and turned, folded her arm, and elbowed him in the back of the neck. He collapsed face first, unconscious.

Running footsteps commanded her attention and she refocused on her adversaries. To her right, the second of the three men sprinted along a small ditch which contained shards of metal and plastic that protruded from the mud. To her left, another had already begun his attack, a knife in his hand. She thought fast. There was no way to take them both on at the same time. She swiped her hand to the right and the energy knocked that attacker's legs out from beneath him. His body attempted a twist to avoid the danger, but Stephanie gestured dramatically to create a wind that hurled him over the edge of the ditch and into the sharp metal.

She turned her head toward the last one, who had slowed down and now smirked and brandished his dagger menacingly. Unperturbed, she raised an eyebrow and flung her arm out to the left to release a massive blast of light energy from her fingers. It imploded against a large wooden crate mere feet from his ass. When the light struck the box, Stephanie dove behind a metal container a scant few feet away. The entire box blew and launched large shards of jagged wood in all directions with incredible force. The man didn't stand a chance and was instantly sliced like deli meat.

Stephanie clapped her hands in excitement and clambered onto the crate to assess the scene. The Dreth either immediately started to surrender or allowed themselves to be killed. The scenery around her began to fade and the system jolted her back to the avatar room.

"Congratulations, you successfully completed the simulation," the AI said. "Do you wish to end your pod session here or continue to another area of the Virtual World?"

She chuckled and enjoyed the excitement that still lingered. "End session."

"Thank you...good bye."

When her eyes open in the pod, the door released and allowed the light in. She stepped out and into the real world. Her fingers and the soles of her feet tingled wildly, and she couldn't help but smile at the feeling. That meant that her theory was accurate—the light energy was somehow searching for her. It knew she was the one to find.

She pulled her robe on and gathered her clothes before she opened the door. Before she closed it fully behind her, she looked back with a grin. She had done the right thing and actually won, all based on her theories and understanding. It felt really good.

Beta stood in the dark shadow of an alley and his cigar burned bright red at the end. He wore a large-brimmed hat and a long black trench coat, and black gloves covered his scarred hands. Three men waited with him—two on the other side, pressed against the damp brick wall, and one in front of him with a pair of binoculars to his eyes focused on the building catty-corner to them.

One of the men across from him checked his watch and nodded. "Why come all the way out here when you could have had us take care of this?"

He puffed his cigar and blew large rings of smoke over his head. He finally ended the short silence when he smacked his lips and looked at the cigar as he rolled it back and forth between his long, thick fingers. "Because the last idiots we sent to do a job hired someone else to do it, and they failed. Those agents are now spread in pieces throughout the city."

The man swallowed hard. "So you're here to take care of us if we fail."

A deep, nefarious grin pulled at his scarred lips. "No. I don't take the trash out. I'm here to make sure that failure doesn't happen. I'm tired of leaving things to chance. This should have been done a long time ago. I'm like your babysitter. I'm here to make sure that the girl —" He drew an imaginary line with his cigar. "That she gets into the freaking van. Simple."

The agent beside him put his binoculars down. "She just walked into the lobby of the apartment building."

Beta put his finger to his earpiece. "She's coming out. Get into position."

The team remained inconspicuous but watched as a small blonde girl dressed in a cocktail dress and carrying a small black purse walked quickly out of the complex. She glanced around her and turned right toward the sky rail entrance three blocks down. A large nondescript brown van crept along behind her and waited for her to move down a block where there were barely any people. As soon as she reached the mark, it sped up and came to a screeching halt beside her. Three men piled out of the vehicle, one with a black velvet bag, and the other two with their sheer strength.

The girl looked frightened in the split second before they shoved the bag over her head and grabbed her arms. They hauled her off her feet, threw her into the van, and scrambled in after her. One of them looked around and slid the door closed as the van accelerated down the street.

Beta put his finger to his earpiece. "Good. You know the plan from here."

He removed the device, dropped it on the ground, and tossed his cigar on top of it. With the flat of his shoe, he stepped down hard and twisted his foot in a crushing motion. Small red embers floated outward and sizzled in the dark puddles alongside. Satisfied that no obvious evidence remained, he pulled his phone from his pocket, pressed a button, and put it to his ear. "The girl is out of the picture. Move to the next phase."

The ambassador smoothed his hands down the front of his blue tunic and looked into the mirror on the wall. He carefully adjusted each golden button from the bottom up to the high neck of his shirt. When satisfied, he put his arms out and back to allow one of his staff to pull his dress robes into place. He shrugged to settle them comfortably before he brushed his hand over his head. The magic trailed from his palm and swirled through his long hair like a comb. It twisted the strands into a low ponytail and tied them securely. The energy dissipated upon completion and left his hair shimmering and fresh.

He smiled when he took a moment to appreciate the convenience of these little uses of magic. They made little demand on the battery he always carried tucked into a hidden pocket in his clothing. As one of the most advanced Mages, he no longer even had to consciously access the power and was also able use to his source efficiently. Besides, these small indulgences left time for more important matters, so it was miniscule energy well utilized to encourage greater benefit.

Satisfied, he walked over to the desk and slipped his feet into the blue satin loafers that matched his tunic and flowing blue pants. It was almost time for them to be on their way. The phone rang and he gestured to the staff, who immediately nodded and left the room. He answered the call. The video feature came up with the Federation Symbol instead of a face.

"Ambassador, this is Grant from the Federation security offices," the voice said.

V'ritan raised an eyebrow at the phone. "Yes? What do you need?"

The person cleared their throat nervously. "We called to tell you that your liaison didn't make it in time, but not to worry, we will have another sent out to you. They will be a few minutes late but will meet you at the event."

The ambassador stared at the screen for a moment and narrowed his eyes. He turned toward the mirror and read the trace of concern that had crept into his eyes. "No, never mind that. We will be fine for tonight. We will speak in the morning. Good evening."

Before the man could argue, the ambassador cut the call and stared at Brilgus.

"Sir, I have to insi..." *Click.* The ambassador hung up in the guy's ear.

He gritted his teeth and scowled as he flung the phone on the floor. "That pompous, arrogant asshole. How dare he hang up on me?"

Beta and the other team members entered the cheap motel room. The leader stared at him expectantly. "Well?"

The man shrugged. "He told me not to send anyone, that he would be fine for the night. Then he hung up on me before I could talk him into it. Jerk. He talks to anyone not Meligornian like they are dirt beneath his feet."

The ringleader had already pulled out another cigar and had it between his teeth. He bit on it, his expression sour. He patted the nervous man on the shoulder. "Don't worry about it. The hardest part is done. We don't have a gal on the inside but so what? We now know his state of mind going into tonight."

One of the other team members walked up, removed his coat, and draped it on the chair. "He didn't take the bait? To hell with it. That will be one less body to worry about tonight. It isn't a complete wash, so relax. We knew there would be a possibility he might flip our plans somewhat."

The man who had made the call leaned down and retrieved the phone, a pre-paid one from the gas station. He removed the battery, broke the device in two, and shrugged. "I suppose you're right. Every extra one of our men in there is a liability for the mission. Still, it irks me that he can be so nonchalant. Next time we need a government target, I say we pull that Booker guy. The senator who has had like three generations of family on the Senate. He seems like a pushover."

Beta raised his hands. "No more politics. Besides, we are only halfway done with this plan. The harder part is still ahead. We have to be prepared so get your damn minds straight. This isn't some amateur party. Don't make me look bad or I promise you, I will take you down with me."

Brilgus knocked quickly on the door and entered with the ambassador's thick outer robe in his arms. He laid it carefully across the chairs to avoid hair or wrinkles. V'ritan sat in his office chair and flipped through emails. He answered some and read and deleted others.

With his hands behind his back, the bodyguard cleared his throat. "Ambassador, if I may, I think that we need to talk about what is happening."

He sighed, closed out the email, and settled his attention on his companion with his hands folded at his waist. "Yes, dear friend and loyal businessman."

Brilgus stood tall and raised his chin in reverence but, at the same time, forcefulness. "It is absolutely necessary that we fix this before the event. You must have a liaison. They are vitally important to this event. I know you feel uneasy with the call you received, and I do not blame you. It sounds shady, to say the least, but we currently have men out to see if they can determine what went wrong."

V'ritan shook his head. "You may be right, but we don't have time to search and replace. And personally, I don't have the patience for it."

The bodyguard raised his hands and shook his head. "Dear Ambassador, had I known that was the issue, I would have offered my services long before now."

His employer raised both eyebrows. "And which service would that be today?"

Brilgus brandished his phone and smirked. "I happen to be very good at finding people in a pinch who can often be trusted more than the original ever could have been. I have, after all, worked for you for many years and we both know the young aides have a habit of running off or forgetting events. Don't worry about it. Relax, and I will make it happen. Would you like any tea?"

The ambassador shook his head. "Thank you, Brilgus. You have become an asset to this whole system."

CHAPTER SEVENTY

She hummed as she rubbed her hands through her soapy hair as the rainforest-like water showered over her. Sarah had put calming music on for her, but Stephanie was in the mood for something peppier that night. For the first time since the fight, she had excitement in her tone and step. The AI chose a dance music mix from the collection that Todd had created for her. They were all oldies, but it was her feel-good music.

There was something soothing about routine tasks that allowed her to do what she had to without having to focus too hard. She leaned her head back to wash the soap from her hair and smiled as the pressure from the water directly over her head increased. The suds shimmered in different colors as they floated around her feet and down the drain. When the soap was all out, Stephanie tapped her finger to her lips and leaned her head back again. "Lavender conditioner."

The spray of water stopped for a moment as conditioner pumped onto her hair. She smoothed it through and twisted her feet on the floor as she closed her eyes and jiggled her head in time to the beat. The fragrant perfume of the flowers eased into her lungs and a sense of calmness infused her. The water clicked on and she rinsed the conditioner out and turned the shower off with a verbal command.

Sarah spoke. "Your towel is on the wall. The shower drying will start as soon as you have exited. Are we going to blow dry?"

Stephanie shrugged. "Not tonight. I don't feel the vibe."

She wrapped one towel around her torso and flipped her head over to wrap a second one around her hair and tuck the end in at the base of her neck. She walked toward the door but paused for a moment. "Sarah, turn the music off."

The music clicked off and the sound of the phone ringing replaced it. Stephanie startled and hurried out. The door closed behind her and the quiet dryers began the process of drying the bathroom. She retrieved her tablet from the dresser and immediately saw the ambassador's number on the screen. Still in her towel, she thought about not answering but instead, responded in phone instead of video mode.

She shook her head and held the top of her towel closed. "Brilgus, so good to hear from you. I'm sorry I almost missed the call. I was showering."

"I was worried you were away from your phone," he said, and his voice sounded slightly panicked.

Stephanie backpedaled and sat on the edge of her chair. "Brilgus, what's the matter? You sound very upset."

"No, not upset," he replied. "But there always seems to be something going on. If it's not one thing it's another. As much as I like you and a few other full humans, I really do miss Meligorn."

Stephanie smiled understandingly. "I get that. There is really no place like home. No matter what state it's in. That's why I always understood why the Dreth who aren't pirates don't leave their planet, even with it in ruins. You work until all hope is gone, and only then do you give up on your home."

Brilgus chuckled. "You sure do sound cheerier today. I heard of your incident in DC. I'm sorry. I do hope your friend is recovering."

"He is," she replied. "He will be discharged tomorrow so it will be nice to welcome him back."

"Good. Give him my thanks for protecting you," the bodyguard replied. "But, now that I have exchanged pleasantries, and enjoyed them, I do have something to confess."

Stephanie giggled. "Don't we all, Brilgus. Okay, I'm ready for it. What do you have?"

"The ambassador needs a favor—and I suppose it's a favor for me as well," he said and winced through the words.

Meligornians were notorious for helping other people but never complained or asked for help in their own lives. But on Meligorn, there were rarely problems that weren't on a community scale. When the community knew, they would all come out, invited or not.

She looked at her wet hair in the mirror and realized vaguely that she needed a trim. "Sure, what do you need? Anything for you two."

Brilgus laughed. "I would reserve that until you've heard it. We need you to be the ambassador's liaison at a very important charity event this evening. We received a call that the regular person, for some reason, was unable to make it. The ambassador was not comfortable with how it was handled, so I thought you might be the perfect replacement."

Stephanie wrinkled her nose, having never attended an event like that. "All right. Tonight. Okay. When do I need to be there?"

Brilgus's nerves were almost audible. "An hour." Usually, the ambassador would meet with his liaison in his limo before the event and they would use the time to discuss things that might crop up while his personal security team conducted an additional sweep of the premises. This enabled them to establish what was expected but also allowed flexibility in his arrival to avoid traffic delays and to vary the direction and time of his approach to the venue. He'd been almost on his way when the call had come in, and both he and his bodyguard had accepted that this time, that buffer would have to be set aside.

Stephanie's eyes opened wide and she scowled at the closet. "Wow. Yikes. Okay, no need to panic. Of course I will do this. I must confess, though, I have neither been nor even heard of a liaison at these parties. What exactly do I have to do all night?"

"Ah, that is the easy part," Brilgus replied. "You simply remain at his side. He will spell his words to you so you hear them in English but to others, it will be Meligorn-speak. You will handle all communication with people until the ambassador takes over. This will include helping with appropriate customs between worlds and protection. Oh, there will be a security detail, so you needn't worry much about the protection part of things."

She pursed her lips. "And what worlds will be there?"

"It will be Earth and Meligorn, of course, and a couple of individuals from Dreth," he answered. "The Dreth know the customs well. It will mostly be the other humans whom you need to focus on. They don't always understand the greeting, the no touching, and what to say. I know you know most of it, and I will walk with the two of you so if you have any questions, you can simply ask me."

On one hand, the idea panicked her somewhat, but it also actually sounded like fun. "And what is the dress code for this occasion?"

Brilgus cleared his throat. "Formal. You may wear what is customary on Earth, the ambassador and I will be in our formal tunics and robes, and the Dreth...well, they have formal war gear so they will wear much the same as they usually do but with fewer blood stains."

Stephanie giggled. "At least they make an attempt. I personally pictured them like the Dreth pirates. I've never met a Dreth before. Well, one, but it was very brief."

The bodyguard snarled slightly with evident distaste. "Yes, they are interesting. Although these two are generally more well-mannered than the citizens there. They are part of the royal chamber on their planet, so they have been given some instruction. They don't have a formal greeting, so you only need to worry about their greeting to the ambassador. He is usually fairly open-minded about them, regardless whether they actually perform it right or not at all. Most likely, though, they will miss the greetings as usual and end the evening with a goodbye instead."

Stephanie exhaled a deep breath. "All right, that sounds good. Where do I go?"

Brilgus mumbled to himself a moment. "Ah, that's right. It is the Grand Legion of Federation Fine Arts located where the Old Days Lincoln Memorial stood once. We will have you on the list."

Stephanie jotted that down on the virtual notepad function on her tablet. "Good. Right, then. That should be easy to find, then. But to make it on time, I need to go. When I arrive, I will send you a text and wait on the steps for you."

"That sounds perfect," he replied. "And thank you, Stephanie. This means a lot."

She hung up, looked around her in bemusement for a moment, and bounded to her feet in a panic. "Sarah! I need the black and silver butterfly formal gown and several shoe selections including something practical in case any running or fighting is involved. And my *hairrr!*"

Sarah began to take the appropriate measures. "It would be good if you were to calm down. You are starting to panic and that increases heart rate, confusion, and the chance of a stroke."

Stephanie stuck her head out the bathroom door to yell above the blow dryer. "I'll stroke anyway if we don't get this right."

A bell chimed and the hair dryer stopped. Stephanie scrambled into her bra and panties and peered cautiously at the comms video screen. It was Elizabeth so she clicked the button and smiled. "Hey, what's up?"

The other woman raised an eyebrow. "Are you all right? It suddenly sounded as if a herd of buffalo rampaged through your room. Are you having a fit? I can tranquilize you with one of the darts from the dart gun."

Stephanie gave her a deadpan stare. "No. I just had a call from the ambassador, and he needs me to be his liaison tonight at a charity event. Something happened to his. So, I have less than an hour to get ready and get over there. Not to mention that I've never been one before."

Elizabeth's face remained expressionless. "I know. Sarah has already filled me in, which is really why I called. I want to send Lars and Marcus with you as backup. The security will be Federation Secret Service who are trained like offbeat cops, and none of them are too bright."

She shrugged. "All right. I'm sure it won't be a problem. The ambassador understands that I am not a person who gallivants around on my own anymore so he should expect that I would have my own security. There is one problem, though."

Elizabeth raised her eyebrows. "Yes?"

Stephanie chewed the inside of her lip. "They need to have tickets to the event. You can't simply buy the tickets as they are invite only, of course. Brilgus put me on but not anyone with me."

"Have you forgotten who you are talking to here? I am the woman who literally spent years in a job where my only task was to retrieve anything that they needed. My own personal brand of magic has its own power in that world. I once had to retrieve a small lamp like the one in that Aladdin story that was specifically last seen in the chamber room of the queen's area in the pyramids in Egypt. That was interesting, and the best part? Thirty-six hours later, I had it polished, sitting on a pillow, and in my lap traveling back. I wanted to rub it so badly."

Stephanie giggled and then jumped. "So, you'll handle the tickets and make sure they are appropriately dressed?"

She winked cheerfully. "I've got you, sister."

Elizabeth's red-painted lips smirked as she picked up the phone and dialed the guard's quarters. Marcus answered. "Oh, good, I needed to speak to you and Lars. Where is he?"

"Right here," the man yelled. They obviously had her on speaker phone.

Her lip twitched slightly. "I need the two of you to get your tuxes out, dust them off, shine your shoes, conceal your weapons, and be ready in forty-five. You will accompany Stephanie to a charity event where she will be the acting liaison to the Head Ambassador of Meligorn."

Marcus wasn't sure what to say. "Uh…uh… Okay…I…"

Elizabeth rolled her eyes. "Oh, for Christ's sake, get it together man. Lars, get on it."

"On it," he yelled from the back before the call disconnected.

She shook her head and ambled across the room to retrieve her tablet and open a video chat. Once she sat comfortably, she flipped to the number to connect her to the boss, leaned back, and crossed her legs. When he answered, the hologram of the company spiraled around in midair as usual.

"I thought you would be asleep or torturing someone by now," BURT said in greeting, having adjusted his sarcasm level the day before.

Elizabeth furrowed her brow. "You are mighty feisty tonight. Do you have a hot date or something?"

BURT paused. "Oh yeah, me and my server will go on a whirlwind adventure across Meligorn."

She yawned. "Mm-hmm. Sounds lovely. But I need you to do something for me really fast before you ship off to Never-Never Land with some AI. And I don't need the details. There are plenty of men out there with computer girlfriends, but I didn't peg you as one."

"What would you peg me as, then?" he asked.

Elizabeth raised both eyebrows and pursed her lips. "Honestly? Gay, actually."

BURT queried this but stopped hurriedly. "I see. No, though I think I fall more into the asexual category. Anyway, what can I do for you?"

She leaned forward. "I need you to get Lars and Marcus tickets to the Grand Legion of Federation Fine Arts Charity Ball tonight. Stephanie has been asked to act as the liaison for the ambassador and I want two of our men there to protect her."

He immediately sifted through the system and hacked into their guest list database. Elizabeth wasn't sure what he was doing but gave him time to respond since he was more than a little strange. A few moments later, he was done. "All right, they are on the list. I have pull almost everywhere for tickets."

Her mouth dropped slightly. "Oh. Right…okay. Thanks, then."

BURT definitely had pull, but it just so happened to be the kind that required him to hack into a highly classified system without being traced or caught. Luckily, he was a much more intelligent system than any of their other Federation protocols, so it was like taking candy from a baby.

Elizabeth hung up and stood when she heard someone walk down the hall. She yanked the door open so quickly she actually scared Stephanie. Elizabeth looked at the girl for a moment, taken aback. She wore a strapless black velvet dress that was tight in the bodice to her waist, where it flared out and came to her calves. Underneath were rows and rows of black and silver crinoline and artfully arranged from the bottom up to about halfway were silver glittering butterflies in a garden of lilies. One of the lilies' stems curved from the side along the bottom of her breasts and up to the right side of her bodice. It was an amazing gown.

Stephanie's hair and makeup were incredible too. Her hair was pulled back into a tight, smooth, perfect bun at the nape of her neck. What looked like thin silver vines wound around it. Her eyes were very dramatic and almost resembled the black and silver wings of the butterflies on the dress, and her lips were a deep rose.

Elizabeth shook her head. "You look absolutely amazing. Really, so gorgeous. I knew you were a pretty girl, but this is model… *Oh, my God.* What are those *hideously practical shoes*?"

The girl looked at the offending shoes—a pair of black slip-ons but with the rubber non-slip soles and slightly chunky bottoms. She shrugged. "I need practical in case anything happens."

The other woman sneered in genuine horror. "You couldn't have strappy silver heels and go barefoot if anything happened?"

Stephanie narrowed her eyes. "Have you seen the streets out there? It's like dipping your body in tetanus. I like life right now."

Elizabeth sighed. "Good point, but good God."

CHAPTER SEVENTY-ONE

The car pulled up at the event and the two guards exited first. Lars stood at the door and extended his hand to help her from the car. He whispered through his smile. "Not that you need my help in those frighteningly practical shoes from the back storage room of some rundown steakhouse waitress in Louisiana."

Stephanie snatched her hand away and turned to smile kindly at the people who passed them. She slammed her practically-shod foot down on Lars's instep and he hissed and tried to keep his composure. "Oh, look, the ambassador just arrived."

She moved down the steps and waited as Brilgus climbed out, looked at her, and smiled widely. He mouthed, "Wow," pointed at her dress, and stepped aside. The ambassador emerged and waved and smiled at the press as they snapped pictures as fast as they could. The droid reporters hovered overhead and tried to hear quiet conversations, but most of the Meligornian delegates would have a mild charm active to shield their discussions. These used little energy and spilled over those in close proximity, so in practical terms, the event itself had been charmed to ensure a degree of secrecy.

As they started up the steps, the ambassador studied Stephanie approvingly and extended his arm to her. She walked beside him, her arm wound around his. "You look very beautiful. And I am glad you brought a couple of your men. If they are of sufficient caliber to protect you, I would trust them with my life."

Stephanie chuckled. "They don't let me go out unsupervised. But it's a good thing."

V'ritan winked. "They don't let me go out unsupervised either. Welcome to the world of being treated like precious cargo. It will be annoying."

"Ten minutes before it ever happened? Yep, I'm there. But they are my family now and they put themselves on the line for me so I will smile the whole time."

The ambassador stopped at the door. "Good. Are you ready for this? I'm already over it."

Beta walked through the doors of the Fine Arts Ball. Carefully applied makeup covered the scars on his face, and contacts changed the color of his eyes to blue. His dark hair was slicked back, and his tux was perfectly pressed and worth more money than most people in the subs made in two years. He sauntered through the security check, handed them his silver cane, and allowed them to inspect it before he continued.

At the bar, he ordered a scotch, turned casually, and scrutinized the sea of people who entered for the night's festivities. A voice spoke quietly in his ear. "We are all in position."

Beta's gaze shifted lazily to each of the places checked on the blueprints that they had worked with. He smiled inwardly as he confirmed that each of his men had taken their position, all strategically located around the perimeter of the building. They were dressed to the hilt and had been told to focus on the art to look non-threatening, and to keep their specially equipped vests completely out of view. Not only were they bulletproof, but they stored all their guns and were completely undetectable by the security metal checks.

He carried two pistols in the vest, one laser and one regular ammo although he still hadn't fully caught on to the laser fad. Satisfied that all had proceeded according to plan, he turned and pretended to yawn, then completed the movement of his hand to unobtrusively brush his finger on his earpiece. "This is where you will stay until I give the word. Remember, if it looks or feels too suspicious to stand in the same spot, call for a rotation and you will all move up one spot. We didn't get this far to be nabbed by Federation blue-coats."

"Roger that," each of them said into their comms.

Beta turned to study the crowd once more. Slowly, a smirk stretched his lips and he chuckled. He felt that he still had it. Even after all those years of having a seat at the table and sending errand boys to do the dirty work, he was still exceptional at what he did. It had been a very long time for him, but when everything went as planned that night, he would be handsomely rewarded and possibly named as the next Full Leader when the position became available.

A woman in a long, red, sequined, backless dress walked past him with a glimmer in her eye. She licked her top lip, but Beta simply stared at her and blinked. Without any return affection, she walked awkwardly away. He pursed his lips and shook his head. "Damn human women. They have no idea."

"I wish that when we came to these shindigs, we could wear tuxes instead of our navy dress formals," Vice Admiral Blanton whispered as he ascended the steps.

Admiral Suffix chuckled. "Trust me, I totally understand. They have updated all the Federation Navy uniforms to fit with the times, but when it came to these, they decided to go with a George and Martha Washington time period. They even took away the long dress pants and gave us these abominable things. I cannot believe I had to ask for a pair of...pantaloons—formal pantaloons. I am a grown-ass man."

Blanton snickered. "A grown-ass man who could also wear a white wig, a pair of round glasses, and fly a kite into a storm to discover electricity."

The other man covered his mouth and laughed but ended with a cough to disguise it. "What was that revamp of an Old Broadway play they sent us to last year?"

Blanton snapped his fingers. "Oh...uh...*Newsies*."

"That's it. You're Jack "Cowboy" Kelly and I'm Bryan Denton."

The men laughed all the way up the stairs and into the building. The lead security waved them away from the metal detectors. "Admiral Suffix, Vice Admiral Blanton, it's so good that you are here. I wanted to escort you through this maze since you are the only guests in attendance permitted to keep your weapons on your person. All except, of course, the secret service."

The admiral nodded. "We appreciate it. Although I haven't quite figured out why it is a mandatory part of the formal attire yet."

Vice Admiral Blanton shrugged. "You know us crazy navy folk. We go riding into full-on battles in our formals all the time."

All three chuckled and the agent opened the gate to allow them through. "Have a good evening, gentlemen."

They entered and paused to look around at the people. Suffix sneered. "And we are expected to speak to all of them." He sighed dramatically. "If I'd known as a new recruit that this was what they meant when they talked about making sacrifices for the nation..."

His companion laughed. "We're window-dressing, Admiral. Part of the politics of the position. It does, however, afford us a rare opportunity to hear things that might otherwise not be said. People tend to relax at these events. It's not so much that we need to talk to them, but that we need to listen." He shuddered. "It's a pity, though, that we have to listen to all the bull-crap too."

They stood there silently for a moment, focused on the giddy faces, fancy clothes, and important figures. Finally, Blanton put his hand on the admiral's shoulder and leaned in. "Shall we get a drink?"

Suffix took a deep breath and tugged on his pantaloons. "I think that's a hell of an idea. I knew I was friends with you for a reason."

Blanton chuckled. "You mean besides the fact that I'm the only one close enough to your rank to allow a friendship?"

The admiral smacked his lips and his gray mustache rose and fell. "Hmm. Yes. That too. Although I could have gotten worse. Old Admiral Phillips with his broken hips and wrinkled old body could still be here."

They walked toward the bar. Blanton smirked. "He did have a nice monocle."

The music from inside the gala could be heard all across the Mall and down through the abandoned streets and old government buildings. The venue was lit up brighter than daylight with sparkling holographic golden stars that shimmered down the façade like falling magic snow. From both corners of the building, large spotlights were turned on and streamed the images of the Federation symbol, the NorAm's Stars and Stripes, Meligorn's Pantigordia flower, the symbol of peace in the country, and the slightly harsher helmet and warrior glove of Dreth.

The news vans were set up all along the press line. Some already rolled footage of the event while others set up for the evening's light show and celebrity appearances. The event had become what awards shows had been in the old days. The whole world watched to catch a glimpse of the most glamorous, most chivalrous, and most famous people in the Federation. The money raised was merely a plus, an endowment set up for children of the fallen Federation sailors and soldiers. Of course, it usually was panhandled in bribes barely days later but the idea of it let the richies feel good about donating to the little orphaned urchins on the streets.

It was, in reality, merely another manifestation of the class structure and made the poor seem even poorer and the middle class work harder toward a higher level. Class structure in the United States forever grew farther apart. But that was not even close to the biggest worries that the Federation would soon face and were willfully ignorant of.

CHAPTER SEVENTY-TWO

Beta moved casually across the room and observed the ambassador keenly from afar. He had to admit, the man was very powerful, very well-liked, and very intelligent. He knew, even though the humans refused to admit it, that Meligornians, even the lowliest, had IQs past genius level on Earth. It wasn't due to anything other than a species difference. But, of course, the pride of the human species kept them from celebrating it. Denial was something all humans seemed to be good at. They denied crimes, infidelities, rule-breaking, and even facts. They would get so caught up in the lies that even when presented with the cold, hard facts, they would deny that they were real.

This was a very good reason why the Federation still controlled everyone, despite the frequent uprisings and battles through their history. The government always maintained control. Meligorn was truly free, understanding of faults, and knowledgeable of coercion but never practiced it. They were truly the better species, but they were also hated by the Dreth and many of the richie humans as well.

One of Beta's men spoke over the comms. "It looks like the ambassador brought his own liaison."

Another man chuckled. "Yes. He. Did. And I have to say she is hot as hell—except for those shoes… I don't understand."

Beta's gaze dipped to the shoes rather than the wearer. "They seem practical." He had no interest in the woman. Liaisons were expendable and whoever this was would pose no problems. Her presence there was probably more a PR exercise than anything else. He was more concerned with identifying the security detail that would inevitably have infiltrated the crowd.

The first man laughed. "It sucks to be her tonight. She should have called in sick. Those little fateful decisions you make and never think they will be your last. So sad. A waste of a beautiful face."

One of others coughed in the comm. "Ahem. Ass…oh, sorry, I have this cough."

Beta clenched his jaw and looked down to hide his irritation as he growled into the comms. "Could we stop acting like this is Fashion Runway or The Female Auctions? We are here to do a job. Thereafter, what you talk about is none of my business."

Everyone fell silent and kept their eyes on the prize—the end of the ambassador and the line of bullshit they so avidly hated.

V'ritan walked between Brilgus and Stephanie, his hands locked together inside his long robe sleeves and a pleasant smile on his face. The bodyguard stood tall, his chest puffed out, and his eyes continually scanned the immediate crowd around them. On either side, four secret service agents, stoic and alert, studied the people and the surroundings in search of any sign of trouble. Last but not least, Marcus and Lars fell in behind as a rearguard and continually turned to sweep the room behind them.

As for Stephanie, she was beyond amazing at the job. She had a bright and kind smile and she found that when she was forced into a position where she needed to be likable, she was actually able to be open and warm with people. They reacted well to her and she handled a number of small meetings very efficiently and without mistakes. But every party of a political nature always came with an asshole.

She stood beside V'ritan with a welcoming smile and sparkling eyes and waited for the next guest. A small prickle of warning made her look up at a middle-aged man with a horseshoe bald spot and a very round middle. He seemed obviously intoxicated and stumbled toward them with his finger pointed.

Stephanie immediately became defensive and stepped in front of him so he couldn't reach the ambassador. He stared dismissively at her. "Who are you? Some NorAm ho to keep him happy while he's here?"

Brilgus tightened his fist and the ambassador glanced at him and shook his head. Stephanie summoned a huge fake smile and pushed her fingers into the man's chest. "Why have you come to speak to the ambassador today?"

He laughed. "To tell him I know he's full of shit. I know his people are full of shit. They are trying to take us over and the Federation, run by a bunch of pansies, can't stop sucking on the Meligorn teat long enough to see it. I want him to know I see it. And that I don't understand because we've been so nice to them."

She glanced at the secret service agents and shook her head before she drew the man's jacket closed and patted him hard on the chest. "I'm going to say something to you right now and I want you to know it is in your very best interest. And when you are sober, you will think about this and thank me for it."

He frowned and his head wobbled slightly. "What?"

Stephanie sucked in a deep breath through her mouth and continued. "You are making an ass of yourself. And that means you are making an ass out of everyone on Earth. Believe it or not, we are all representatives of this planet. Now, I want you to go back to the restroom, wash the idiot out of your mouth, and try to come back with at least a modicum of respect and class. If you do that, I might be able to help you. I know you have class somewhere, because only those who hold the dollar hold the tickets to the golden palace. So go and find some."

The two security guards on either side both immediately lowered their heads and pressed their lips together. They tried desperately not to laugh as the guy looked at her in confusion before he stumbled off. She glanced at them and shook her head. They were young secret service, but not as dense as she had expected. In fact, they seemed to really take their jobs seriously, which was good since they were protecting the most important Meligornian political figure on Earth.

"Here's the glass of seltzer you wanted," the reporter's assistant said, slightly out of breath from climbing all the way up into the high levels.

She took the water and grabbed a napkin to blot a wine stain on the hem of her dress. "Stupid drunk richies. They don't give a damn about anyone. I honestly want to get this footage and get the hell out of here already."

The reporter stood, grabbed the camera, and walked to the edge. She tilted it forward and scanned the crowds to record footage of the events below. It didn't help her mood that her usual cameraman had dropped the assignment in favor of greener pastures. She hated camerawork although she wasn't half bad at it, but this gig might well be her ticket to the big-time. If she could snag some decent and more intimate footage than the drones and commercial stations, she might slide a foot in the right door.

She set the camera on the stand and her assistant made sure she was in focus. Behind her, silent holographic fireworks burst to create a ceiling of sparkling joy for the richies—and an annoying hindrance of footage for her.

The assistant nodded and counted down with his fingers, then pointed to the reporter who now held her mic in hand.

Cindy and Mark picked their sandwiches up from the counter and wandered over to slide into one of the booths. She exhaled a deep breath and shook her head. "This building is amazing but I can't wait to hire more people so we don't have to do this constantly."

Mark nodded and took a big bite of his sandwich. "At least we get a break."

She snapped her fingers and pointed at him. "You are the king of glass half full. This is why I love you."

He pumped his fist. "Boy meets girl, boy courts girl, girl is repulsed, boy gives daily motivational quotes and pep talks, girl finally loves boy."

Cindy giggled and glanced up as the deli man turned the news on. "This is Veada Bowls with Federation Entertainment News coming to you live from the Federation Arts Gala and Charity Event. As you know, this is the biggest event of the season, bringing in celebrities, political heads, and the most influential people of this decade."

She ate her sandwich, thoroughly exhausted, and simply stared at the footage on the screen. Suddenly, her head jerked, and she choked, covering her full mouth. Mark looked at her and she pointed wildly at the screen. When he turned, his wide eyes matched hers as they watched their daughter lead the Ambassador of Meligorn around one of the most prestigious events in the world.

Cindy gave a maternal sigh and tilted her head to the side. "Oh, she looks so beautiful. She is knocking them dead."

Brilgus leaned over and whispered to Stephanie. "You had better watch out or he might try to bring you on full time."

She rolled her eyes. "Over my dead body."

Gunfire blazed ahead of them and screams rang out. Brilgus put his body in front of the ambassador and Stephanie whipped her head around to see where it came from. She turned instinctively to the Secret Service agent on her left. Before she could call to him, his head snapped back, and blood splattered on the ground behind him as his body fell heavily. She ducked and spun to the other agent on her right.

He had his gun up and fired into the open levels above and ahead of them.

Suddenly, his body jerked to the right, then to the left, and finally landed hard on the steps. He groaned, raised his weapon, and fired. A man screamed and his body went limp as he toppled over the balcony and plummeted to the floor below. The agent slid his gun over a smidge and pulled the trigger. It sounded like a cannon as both the sharpshooter and the agent fired at the same time. A bullet slammed into the agent's forehead to finish him off. At the same time, the other sharpshooter tumbled over the balcony and fell to his death below.

Brilgus, his arms shielding the ambassador, walked his employer toward the back of the venue. Another barrage of shots erupted to strike the ceiling and spray chunks of plaster onto the crowd. Everyone crouched and scanned the room frantically to find some kind of cover. Seven men pushed out of the crowds, distinguishable from the other guests only by the weapons they now trained on the ambassadorial group.

Beta walked forward, a toothpick in the corner of his mouth and a glass of scotch in his hand. Lars and Marcus shoved through the crowd and hurried to the middle of the grand staircase where Stephanie and everyone else now stood.

He flipped his toothpick to the other cheek and looked at his drink before he yelled, "I know, this is supposed to be a party, huh? Yeah, everyone hates a party crasher. Let's be honest with each other here, sweet little girl."

The man studied the so-called sweet little girl with a sudden sense of unease. Something within him said he should recognize this woman—she was certainly the type to be readily remembered—yet he couldn't quite place her. His gaze swept rapidly over her and triggered a response. She reminded him a little of the witch, he realized, and grinned. There was no way that scruffy teenage magical-wanna-be could even begin to compare. Satisfied that he'd traced the odd sense of familiarity, he turned his attention back to the matter in hand.

"We appreciate heroic actions here and everything but there are three of you—only two armed—and seven of us. I feel like a smart person would put their guns down and walk away. So I'll give you that option. You get your buddies to throw them down, and the three of you can walk out. And you won't even have messed up your dress. What do you say?"

Stephanie snickered and Lars shook his head. She set her clutch on the ground with a slow, deliberate movement, tugged at the black satin wrist gloves she wore, and slowly inched a hand down the front of her dress. Beta pursed his lips as his gaze followed the almost sensual gesture. His eyes widened when she drew a compact long-barrel pistol from between her breasts and pointed it at his head. Brilgus had slipped it to her with a grin and a wink a few minutes after their arrival, and she'd been delighted that it had nestled so snugly in the cushioned holster Mother Nature had provided.

Everyone was silent for a moment and Stephanie leaned forward. "How dare you come into this party, among my friends and my people, and think that you can take lives without repercussions? And don't you ever stand there and tell me the odds when the other team is chock-full of assholes!"

She gestured dismissively and nodded with a smirk. "Oh, and my dress? It's stain resistant."

Lars and Marcus immediately opened fire and the trio raced across the staircase and slid to dodge a volley of return fire. Stephanie aimed at Beta and he smiled as he backed slowly out of sight and headed for the front doors. He didn't intend to stick around for this.

Suddenly, the ambassador used his magic to push Brilgus aside. He flung his arms back to throw his robes off and onto the ground. His expression grim, he summoned his energy and launched into a concerted attack. Death balls of magic spiraled at the assassins in a relentless barrage. He hurried forward and stood beside Stephanie, glanced quickly at her, and winked when he eliminated three of the men, whose bodies instantly ignited with magical fire.

It was a trick Stephanie hadn't seen before, but she loved it. They felt as if they were burning alive in torturous agony, but when the magic dissipated, there wouldn't be a scratch on anything but their pride. She shot her last bullet and fumbled under her dress to retrieve another mag and thrust it in place. She raised it, ready to fire, when Lars flailed back with blood flooding down his arm and over his hand. He smacked into the steps and groaned.

"Nooo," Stephanie screamed.

She clenched her jaw and descended slowly, one step at a time, firing relentlessly at one of the assassins at the base of the stairs. Her slugs connected with his flack vest twice before she adjusted her aim. His eyes widened as her gun focused on his head. She pulled the trigger and his body catapulted away and landed to slide across the marble floor. Two more secret service agents went down, one to the far right of her and another in the main venue who tried to reach the gunmen.

At that point, everything seemed to move in slow motion. She backed up the steps again and paused beside the ambassador. He stared at her, his gaze fixed, his mouth slightly open, and his brow creased. She knew immediately that something was wrong, and her gaze fell to his stomach where he gripped it tightly with one hand. Blood seeped between his fingers.

Stephanie grabbed him by the shoulders as he fell and eased him down. She breathed heavily and scowled at the wound, uncertain that he could survive it. Desperately, she pushed to her feet and tried to find Brilgus. As she stepped forward, a shot rang out and the bullet struck home in her right shoulder blade. She tumbled forward and her gaze found Marcus. Blood streamed from his thigh, and beyond him, Brilgus continued to shoot despite a painful flesh wound on his huge arm.

She landed hard and her head sagged. Her gaze settled on the ambassador's face. His eyes focused on her and although he didn't open his mouth, she swore she could hear him speak. *You have the power, Morgana. You know what to do. Your fear is the only thing holding you back.*

Stephanie gritted her teeth and forced herself into a sitting position. She fumbled for her purse and suppressed the instinctive scream at the pain that seared in her shoulder. Her hands weak and trembling, she managed to retrieve the battery from her bag and gripped it tightly in her hand. For a moment, she felt the energy of Meligorn, but something else began to tingle and pulse through that magic, calling for her.

Her arm dropped and her hand released the battery. She closed her eyes and pushed past the pain to focus only on the sounds of the energy around her. On instinct, she focused her mind on the Earth's ley lines to draw the energy and magic of humans into her body. Like a warm, welcome presence, a slow wave of energy seeped into every part of her.

Everything but the awareness of the power faded. While on one level, she was aware of her injury and even of the excruciating pain, she seemed to have somehow stepped beyond it to a place where she functioned on the energy alone. She opened her eyes.

Her pupils had once again become dark black and her mind was suddenly able to distinguish each distinct crack as a weapon fired. She first identified a man on the balcony level above them and all the way to the right. The energy pulsed within her as she snapped her head toward him and extended her arm with her palm up and her hand curled into a claw-like shape. She flung the magic and directed it to grip the ceiling above him and rip it down piecemeal. In moments, it had showered him with huge marble stones until the only thing left to see was his limp hand that hung lifelessly between the railings.

She slid her focus to an assassin standing front and center—the one who had wounded the ambassador and most likely shot her friends as well. Anger blew through her and she screamed, the sound of something otherworldly that echoed violently from her chest. She clenched her fist tightly and hauled her arm back. The man wheezed and clutched his neck as his body rose and levitated toward her. He stopped inches away, his eyes wide as he choked on the invisible force. She turned to the side and kicked hard to pound her foot into his crotch. The magic released him, and he fell to curl into a fetal position and writhe in pain.

Stephanie spat at him before she swished both arms to the right and swiftly to the left. The man's body careened over the heads of the cowering richies and crashed through the plate-glass window and out onto the lawn. Shots rang out again, but not at her. The attackers continued to shoot at her people. She jerked her fists upward and slammed them down hard on the marble steps. The energy rocketed out, splitting the stone, and rose into a high barrier. It wavered there as a bright blue shimmering haze. The bullets bounced off and ricocheted back at the gunmen.

She thrust her hand through the protective shield, gripped the air, and twisted hard. A man panicked when he lost control of his own hand. It turned toward him, his finger on the trigger. He shoved the barrel to his forehead and screamed until the shot echoed and his shriek fell silent.

CHAPTER SEVENTY-THREE

Stephanie withdrew her hand through the barrier and walked slowly toward the ambassador. As she approached, the crack of gunfire distracted her once more. She whipped around and immediately created a hole in her shield to walk through. Her eyes angry, she stopped and stared at the floor below. The guests had created a battle arena when they ran and cowered against the sides of the room.

Two gunmen lay dead on the ground and blood pooled around them. Standing behind them, their guns out, stood the admiral and vice admiral. The two additional assassins had tried to sneak in, but the officers had noticed them and were able to intercept and eliminate the threat. Stephanie nodded her head at the naval dignitaries, and they returned the gesture. She turned away and hurried over to V'ritan. As she dropped to her knees beside him, Brilgus walked toward them and shook his head in disbelief.

The ambassador took her hand and tugged it to hover over where the wound was. She stared into his eyes for several moments before she focused on the bloody, gaping hole. He opened his mouth to speak but she shook her head and closed her eyes. She centered herself and drew back from the frenzy of the battle. Her energy pushed down into the palm of her hand and light began to permeate from her palm.

The Meligornian magic inside the ambassador—the little he had left—spiraled from the wound, attracted by her energy.

The two trails of magic hovered mere centimeters apart for several moments. Grunting with effort, Stephanie pushed harder, and the energy connected to release a wave of light. Wind whipped wildly around the two of them and Stephanie's arm shook so violently that she had to use her other to stabilize it. Everyone around them backed away as the force of the magic merging created almost a force field around them. Slowly, the tendrils of Meligornian magic drew the light magic down into the ambassador's body. He groaned and his head tilted back as the energy surged through him and out of Stephanie.

Even with her eyes closed, she could see the ambassador. She could see him in the fields of Meligorn in youth and in his early years of marriage. He danced with a beautiful little girl and she could hear the child's laughter echo around them. A surge of pain—not physical, but emotional—pounded into her chest and almost knocked her back. She struggled to hold her hand firm and watched as he stood in that field where they'd danced, surrounded by so many Meligornian men and women. He clung tightly to his wife and they watched as sparkling and shimmering specs of their daughter's soul rose from her flower-shrouded body up toward the heavens, through the MU spectrum, and out into the stars.

Stephanie gasped and her chest pushed forward, and her shoulders thrust back as more and more visions of him hurtled through her mind like a homemade movie. So much sadness and pain, so much loss. What she thought she knew before all seemed so simple compared to the truth that dangled over her as her magic healed his. After several more intense moments, the two energies separated. She fell back on the stairs and her body ached all over. After a long moment, she opened her eyes and shook off the flooded field of emotion that slithered through her down to her soul. Her energy was severely drained, but she wasn't done. There were so many who needed healing.

Brilgus hurried down the steps now that the energy had dissipated and knelt beside the ambassador. Slowly, the Meligornian opened his eyes and blinked a couple of times before he sat up. His energy had been restored and the dried blood on his clothes and skin were the only remnants of the wound. He turned quickly in search of Stephanie. She nodded at him and their eyes connected for a moment. He knew what she had seen, and she knew it was not for her to speak of. It was an unfortunate reaction to the healing powers that they had combined, but it was private.

V'ritan put his hand up and allowed Brilgus to help him to his feet. He felt better than he had in years, like he had lost a hundred years from his life. He walked over and lifted Stephanie by her shoulders. She paused and furrowed her brow. "It doesn't hurt anymore."

Startled, she looked over her shoulder to find nothing more than dried blood and no wound. The ambassador smiled. "We healed each other. Now, let's heal the rest of them, shall we?"

Stephanie nodded, turned, and knelt beside Lars. He looked at her and groaned. "I thought this was only a party. Who gets shot at a party in the richie neighborhood?"

She chuckled and held her hand over his shoulder to allow her energy to pulsate through his wound. He hissed in pain, but she maintained the pressure and pushed the magic into him until it stopped of its own accord. She moved her hand and smiled when she confirmed that the wound was gone. Lars was in shock and awe, completely speechless for once in his life. His eyes drifted over her and he jumped up. "Marcus!"

The other man grumbled and gripped his thigh tightly. "This is the worst. I'll take your punishment. These white people went super ghetto in here. This is bullshit."

Stephanie laughed and sat beside him to put her hands on his leg. He grimaced and scrunched his face for several moments until finally, he began to relax. The energy seeped into his wounds to heal him from the inside out. When it disconnected, she raised her hand, satisfied with her work. Marcus poked at it and looked in shock for a moment before he grabbed her by the arms and yanked her into a tight hug. "You are a shit-hot witch, you know that? You don't play. Thank you."

He pulled back and looked keenly at her, seeing the tiredness that had settled over her face. "Hey, you should give it a break. The ambassador has got it."

Stephanie rubbed her face and shook her head. "No. I gotta do this."

She stood and shuffled to the first victim she could find, a Federation guard with a bullet wound to the bicep. He watched her with tears in his eyes as she wrapped her hands around his arm and closed her eyes. It was strange to her. She had gone her whole life without that much Earth energy inside her but once she'd experienced it, when it began to wane, it felt almost painful. Like the life was sucked from her chest. But she had to help these people. They had put their lives on the line to help her and she couldn't let them suffer on the steps while the very people they hated for their ignorance and money stared at them from the perimeter.

As the magic disconnected from the healed wound, Stephanie fell back and grasped instinctively for something solid to hold onto. Lars hurried behind her and steadied her. She had given everything she had to give and then some. The ambassador had taken care of the other wounded, and Brilgus carefully carried the fallen guards' bodies to the marbled platform halfway down the steps.

Stephanie looked at Lars. "Help me down there."

He nodded, picked her up, and cradled her in his arms. He walked down and held her as she watched the ambassador whisper in Meligornian and sprinkle magical energy over their bodies, extending the ultimate respect to their fallen souls. They had been the only protection between him and death, and he owed them more than that, but it was the best he could do. The entire place had fallen completely silent and the Meligornian song drifted quietly through it like a whisper in a wind. Every person whose ears it touched began to feel a lightness in their soul. The fear began to dissipate, and the tears started to dry.

Marcus gasped as he stared beyond Lars and Stephanie and down at the entryway below. Standing, all in ranks and saluting, was the Federation Navy. They had arrived too late to help, but not too late to pay tribute to the bodies strewn around the floors. Brilgus came back down the steps and put his hand on the ambassador's shoulder. "We have to go."

The bodyguard looked at Lars, Stephanie, and Marcus. "All of us. We need to leave before the media breaks into a frenzy. Meligornians do not speak to the media after such a tragic incident. I have a car waiting out back, but we need to go now."

Lars carried her the entire way as Brilgus hurried them through the great dining hall and out the back exit. A car waited, the doors already open for them. The ambassador got in the back first and everyone followed until the bodyguard scooted in and shut the door. The windows were all darkly tinted and a partition separated the front and the back. Stephanie lay in Lars's lap, everything fuzzy and foggy.

Brilgus motioned quickly and the entire roof shimmered into translucence to reveal the stars high up in the sky. Stephanie turned her head to stare upward. The night sky consumed her and the moon, so crisp and bright, stared back. A tear collected at the outward edge of her eye and trickled down her cheek. She could hear everyone talking, but it was so muffled like it was a million miles away. As her eyes locked on the rarely present Milky Way, her body gave in to the exhaustion. Her eyes closed and the sounds ceased as she drifted into a deep, all-consuming sleep.

With her eyes still clenched shut, Stephanie swallowed and grimaced at how dry everything was. She licked her lips and tasted something sweet that she couldn't identify. It took more effort than it should to roll onto her stomach and she ran her hands along the soft sheets below her. As nice as it was, she immediately realized it was not anywhere she had ever been before. Immediately, her eyes blinked open and she turned over and hauled the gossamer blankets up to her chin.

The room was oddly familiar, a smaller, more decorated version of the temple on Meligorn. She scooted to a sitting position and looked around her. If she had never known about Meligorn, she would have sworn she was in the castle bedroom of some medieval princess. But no, she was in a Meligornian bedroom. She could see the beautiful purple haze and the bright illumination shining through the paneled window on two walls of the room.

The light cascaded through the panes of glass and over the stone floor. Beautiful, plush draperies hung from not only the windows but the walls as well. Fresh flowers sat in multiple vases throughout the space, and the sweetness, she realized, was not on her lips but in her nose. It was the sweetness of the room she could almost taste.

She pulled her knees to her chest and smiled, uncertain as to whether she was actually in a dream or not. Either way, it was absolutely amazing and so entrancing that she barely heard the creak of the doorknob. As she turned to look, the handle turned, paused, and the door began to open.

CHAPTER SEVENTY-FOUR

She actually held her breath when the door creaked on its hinges as it opened slowly. Stephanie put her fists down on the bed beside her, too weary to react. The last thing she remembered was the stars floating gently overhead as they drove away from the grizzly scene that had unexpectedly unfolded. She had woken up in what appeared to be Meligorn but it also seemed so earthly and grounded.

"Oh, look, you decided not to die on me," a familiar voice said before a giggle sounded from the doorway.

All the muscles in Stephanie's body relaxed and the held breath expelled as her eyes focused in on Ms. Elizabeth, who sauntered into the room. "You're here… Man, am I confused."

The ambassador chuckled, walked in behind Elizabeth, and stopped beside the bed. "That is to be expected."

She smiled gently and jolted when her gaze fell to his stomach. He patted his waist and shook his head. "Your magic healed me. And I think you took a few pounds off my waistline. We'd better not tell my wife, though. She might request your services."

Elizabeth snorted. "You go in as a human witch, get in one battle, and come out as a weight-loss specialist. Only in NorAm. Seriously."

Stephanie leaned back against the headboard. "How are Lars and Marcus?"

The ambassador sat on the edge of the bed and turned toward her. "Like new. Not a trace of pain, no issues, and all their scans came back like nothing ever happened. But you need to stop worrying about everyone else and focus on you."

For the first time since even before the party, Stephanie's thoughts explored her own body. She could feel the exhaustion in every part of her, although it was better than it had been when she last remembered being awake in Lars's lap.

Her gaze drifted to the cracked windows through which the sound of birds chirping lightened the room. "Are we on Meligorn?"

The ambassador looked around and his sigh was almost a laugh. "No. It's merely some magic I put on the place. I figured it would be nicer than you waking up in one of the rooms in our suite in DC. You needed to come back gently and I know how gentle Meligorn can be, especially to someone who loves it as much as you do."

Elizabeth sat down on the other side of her. "You can't stop being a hero, can you?"

Stephanie shrugged. "What can I say? In all honesty, I feel like I have very little in me. My energy is so low I can barely sit here."

The ambassador took her hand and turned it over, then traced his finger over her palm as he whispered words in Meligornian. His eyes flashed a simmering purple and he placed her hand back on her lap. "You are improving but it might take a while. You see, the amount of magic you consumed and pushed out was more than you should have been able to survive. Because of that, it forced open areas of your psyche that humans don't normally ever experience. It isn't a common occurrence on Meligorn, but it has happened enough for us to know about it."

She looked down at her hands, her forehead creased. "Will I recover from it?"

V'ritan nodded. "Yes, of course you will. You are already on your way, although you will have different abilities after this. You unlocked things that weren't really meant to be unlocked, but it has not killed you and I can predict that it will only continue to make you stronger."

"It was Earth energy, wasn't it?" she asked.

The ambassador thought about it for a moment. "I believe that it was. I knew you were full of gifts when I met you but until last night, I had not realized that you have a different flavor of MU. And, in time, I would like to know more about it. These things, in humans, are rare and often so different that we do not have the chance to study them or understand them. I would like to be able to create an understanding of it so that if another reaches a level like this, they will have resources. Understandings. They will not be forced to learn as they go and find themselves in this place or worse. But in the end, it will be up to you what you share with the world. It is your gift."

Stephanie nodded. "Right now, I simply want to get better. I want to be able to work again, function again, and maybe take a walk instead of feeling so tired—and not mentally but physically."

V'ritan patted her on the arm. "You will get there. It has only been a day. Think of how you will feel in five or six."

Elizabeth patted her leg. "You have to learn to take care of yourself first. Because if you crumble, every life you would have touched will crumble too. And we kind of like having you around—when you don't fall into some emo dramatic mode doing katas at six am and never socializing. We weren't fond of that version."

She laughed and focused on the blanket she rubbed between her fingers. "Sorry about that. I guess I let my guilt get the best of me, but I felt so bad for Frog getting so hurt. I didn't know what else to do except start protecting everyone. I realize now, though, that it's a family thing. A team thing. We share in it together—the losses and the victories."

The ambassador nodded and looked into her eyes. "What you have to remember is that you cannot escape loss. It is part of every life. Whether you are Dreth, human, Meligornian, or some species we have yet to encounter, there is loss. The important thing, as I have learned through personal experiences, is how you handle it and walk with that loss and grief that will define the kind of leader and challenger you will become. And you can lean on the ones whom you love. Don't let them get away from you because you are scared."

Elizabeth furrowed her brow and nudged Stephanie. "Yeah. You can't kick their butts one day and ghost them the next. It's not nice. Not that it would affect how those fools feel about you. They went from taking a protection gig to following a leader who touched them to their cores. That is something to be proud of. Something to fight for."

Stephanie smirked in embarrassment. "I was fairly emotional. Although I'm sure that if you told my parents that, they would think you had the wrong girl. The magic made me do it."

The other woman rolled her eyes. "Not an excuse. Oh! And speaking of your parents, we called them and let them know what happened. Apparently, they watched the entire thing live via a feed from a journalist above us. They were terrified when they watched you carried out. Anyway, they are on their way here now. I sent them some first-class TRAM tickets and they boarded this morning. They should arrive soon. I sent Lars to meet them."

Tears welled in Stephanie's eyes. She hadn't realized how much she missed them until that moment. But before she could get too excited, worry settled painfully in her chest. "Wait, what about the new contract they got with the building? They haven't hired a full staff for that yet. They can't give that up for me. I will be fine."

Elizabeth gripped her arm. "Take a deep breath and relax. You were broadcast all over the world. Mr. Martelle called your parents as soon as he had seen the footage of you saving lives. He knew you were connected to them somehow, but until that moment, he did not know you were their daughter. He was very impressed and apparently asked if there was anything you couldn't do."

Stephanie grinned. "I wish the answer to that was yes, but alas, I can do anything."

The older woman raised an eyebrow and looked at V'ritan. "Yeah, she'll be up in no time. The cockiness is already starting to take over again."

He laughed. "She has a pass. I think she has proven that she is... what do humans say? Uhm...rotten ass?"

Both women burst into laughter and Stephanie clutched her side in pain. "Oh. That is the best Meligornian translation fail I have ever heard."

She patted his arm. "It's badass. Not rotten ass. That implies a whole slew of other things that I don't think you and I are quite on the level of friendship to discuss yet."

The ambassador laughed loudly and held his stomach. "Oh, no. I'm so sorry. Right. You have proven to be a badass."

Elizabeth rubbed her face. "You guys will be the death of me. Oh, so anyway, Mr. Martelle told them he wouldn't dock them for wanting to see the Hero of DC. If he could, he would have been on a plane here too."

Stephanie's eyes widened and she shook her head wildly. "Oh, Lord. I mean, that is very nice but how weird would it have been if I had woken up in a castle room, not knowing where I was, and have Mr. Martelle walk in the door? I might have chopped him in the throat or something."

V'ritan shrugged. "Who knows, he might have loved you even more for that."

They all laughed, and Stephanie giggled once again as she pushed the hair behind her ear. "So, when do I get to go back to my room and the pod and stuff?"

Elizabeth glanced at V'ritan and pressed her lips together. "Well, we've talked about all that with the ambassador. Now, of course, you can decide anything you want, but he believes that it would be better if you stayed here for a while. He is the only one who is equipped to manage what has happened to you. We all came to that agreement, but it is your choice. Still, we hope you stay and let him work with you to help you heal."

Stephanie bit the inside of her cheek. "What exactly are you treating?"

He rubbed his chin. "Let's see...how do I put this? Your channels are ripped wide open and although they may never close, I am the only one on Earth equipped to help you move through that difficult time. It might be challenging. It might not, but it is safer to be near someone who has knowledge of it. At least in my opinion."

Elizabeth leaned forward intently. "And if you are concerned because your security team will be gone, or me, or any of those things, don't be. If you stay, the security team stays, and I stay as well. The ambassador has been kind enough to put us all up so we can help you heal better and can all understand what is happening."

Stephanie's eyes flashed. "Really? You'll all stay?"

"Yep. All of us. And I'm sure your boss will even call to harass you here. We told you that we are now a team, and we would be a really shitty team if you got hurt and we were like, peace out, kiddo. You jump, we jump."

Stephanie felt really special, like all the conversations of being different added up to something she should have realized all along. She was different, but that didn't mean she was alone. That simply means that she had to be different with other people there to care for her. And that was a really great feeling. The loneliness she had created, she had manifested within herself. No one did that to her. No one forced that on her.

"Knock, knock," Lars said and poked his head around the corner. "Oh, hey there, sunshine."

She waved at him. "Hey. Are you feeling okay?"

He scoffed. "Heck yeah. Like a new man. How about you?"

Stephanie shrugged. "Better than I was."

Lars grinned. "Well, I brought something that might make that even better."

He pulled the door open and her mom walked in, dropped her bag, and flung her arms out. The ambassador moved aside to make space for her. "Oh, sweetie. You look so pretty in this gown…and your hair…"

She glanced down and noticed something familiar about the long white nightgown and her hair loosely braided to the side. A little bemused, she turned to the left and looked at her reflection in the mirror on the wall. Beautiful pink and blue flowers seemed almost sewn into her braid and she looked like she had in her dream.

Her mom touched her chin. "What is it, honey?"

There had already been far too many strange occurrences already and she didn't want to tell them, not yet. "Nothing. I'm just so happy to see you."

"How about me, kiddo?" her dad said and opened his arms.

Stephanie laughed as he strode toward her, leaned over, and kissed her on the top of the head. "I missed you too, Dad. You didn't have to break from work to come all the way out here. I'll be okay. I feel terrible."

Her mom slapped her hand gently. "Stop that right now. We are your family. We love you and when you go through it, we go through it too. It sounds so silly but it's true. We can't let you be here without knowing how much we love you."

Her dad set his chin on top of her mom's head. "And Todd sends his love too. He wanted to be here but school and his new military stuff made that impossible. We told him it would be fine. He said he will email you a bunch of his top-pick movies so if you get bored…"

Stephanie's cheeks flushed and she shook her head. "He is a mess. But tell him I miss him too."

Her mom looked around the room, her mental wheels turning. "This room is beautiful, but I have to admit, it looks nothing like the rest of the place."

The girl's eyes widened in excitement. She pulled herself up and turned to dangle her feet off the bed. The ambassador stood and retrieved a set of deep purple robes—again, like her dream. She turned, pulled them on, and adjusted them gently over her shoulders before she grabbed her mom's and dad's hands and took them to the window.

Both their mouths dropped. "So obviously, we aren't really in Meligorn, but we're not in a pod either. The ambassador has put a magic spell on my room. So, when I am here, it looks like a castle bedroom. It's comforting and warm and I feel really good here. But, since you've never been there and the pods aren't your thing, I figured this would be an experience for you."

Cindy laughed and drew her daughter close. "Our lives have been an experience since the day you were born. An adventure that has taken us down some very interesting and strange roads. But just like this spectacular view of Meligorn, every single moment of it has been worth it."

Stephanie tightened her grasp on her father's arm as a wave of dizziness swept over her. The ambassador walked up to her, pressed his thumb to her forehead, and closed his eyes. "Yes, you have done the limit. It's time to lay down for a bit. We'll see how you feel later and maybe you can go for a walk. Right now, though, I would like to steal your father."

She narrowed her eyes. "Why?"

Her father walked her to the bed and popped in front of her vision. "'Cause it's none of your business, woman!"

"Okay, okay." She burst into giggles and waved him off. "Go do what you're going to do then."

The two of them left the room and Cindy sat on the end of the bed next to Elizabeth. They all sat quietly for several moments. Suddenly, the bed shook, and Stephanie laughed herself almost into a crying fit.

The other two women exchanged glances. "What's up?" her mom asked

Stephanie had rolled into bellows of mirth. She shook her head and took a minute to regain her composure. "I just realized Dad went off with the highest ambassador in Meligorn. The next thing that will happen is either a planetary emergency, or they will call that chicken place Dad likes so much—Chicken Palace—to see what it would take to put one on Meligorn."

Elizabeth wrinkled her nose. "I will be brutally honest here, I hope it's that he started an interstellar incident. That chicken is terrifying."

From the hallway, all you could hear was laughter.

CHAPTER SEVENTY-FIVE

Stephanie gripped the edges of the wooden podium where she stood on a stage in the conference room of the ambassador's building. She kept her gaze locked on the floor in front of her and fought the exhaustion from the trip downstairs. When she tapped her feet on the floor of the stage, the hollow repercussion vibrated through her. She tugged on the bottom of her Pac Man T-shirt and noticed that her jeans were looser than normal. After four days of rest, which she had definitely needed, she finally accepted that addressing the world had waited long enough.

She looked to where her team stood with Brilgus. Lars and Marcus both raised their hands slowly, kept them close to their bodies, and jokingly gave her the finger. She smirked and tried to hold back the laughter. Brilgus gave her a sweet smile and Elizabeth two thumbs-up. Having them there had already calmed her nerves a fair amount.

Her parents had left the day before. They hadn't wanted to go but had to get back to the business. Stephanie understood that they couldn't give up everything because she went a little wild with her magic. She would talk to them on video chat and she was sure her mom would bug Elizabeth to death making sure she was okay. As for the rest of the guys, they were splitting time between taking care of

Frog as he healed at the compound and staying at the ambassador's place to provide protection—and, most importantly, laughs and ridiculous antics that made Brilgus nuts but Stephanie feel right at home.

The Federation Media lead walked up on the stage and leaned toward her. "Whenever you are ready. When you're done, I'll scoot up and take care of the rest. We have a few people talking after you."

Stephanie nodded in understanding and waited for him to walk behind her to where the two navy officers sat as well as the chief of the Federation Police. The crowd grew quiet and Stephanie lifted her chin slowly. A furious flurry of clicks distracted her for a moment as the media snapped as many pictures of her as they could. This was the first time she'd shown her face in public since the incident. Several journal bots buzzed above and made flybys to take pictures of her.

She raised her hands to grip the edges of the podium. A million tact size microphones were placed on the podium in front of her and one larger one for the speaker system in-house. She leaned toward the big one and paused as feedback buzzed in the speakers.

Stephanie had always hated public speaking. "Hi. As most of you know, my name is Stephanie Morgana and I am a human with magical powers. They have asked me to come out today to clear up a few things so that the public can understand my place in the events. It is true that I knew the ambassador for weeks before I acted as his liaison that night. However, I am not—nor do I plan to be—his permanent liaison. On the night of the incident, about an hour before the opening of the gala, I received a phone call from Mr. Brilgus, the ambassador's head of security. I was asked to do a favor for the ambassador and fill in as his liaison for the night due to the fact that the current liaison had gone missing."

She cleared her throat and took a sip of water from the glass on the podium. "I know that Chief Rogers, head of the Federation Police, will talk to you more about the missing liaison. However, we have recently learned, through the exceptional detective work of the department, that the young woman was abducted in order to have someone from inside of their organization fill in at the gala. The ambassador, having keen instincts, found the last-minute change suspicious and therefore denied their replacement and brought me in."

"I want to make this very clear." She took another sip of water and leaned forward slightly on the podium to emphasize the point. "It was purely happenstantial that I was there when all this happened. I was not even on the guest list before filling in that night."

One of the reporters shouted out from the front. "But did you know there was a possible security risk?"

Stephanie shook her head. "No. Two of my personal security team came along only because it was so last-minute. Due to the emergence of my magic, I have been under some scrutiny from certain public entities. I therefore have my own security team to ensure my safety. They worked alongside the brave and heroic members of the Secret Service who lost their lives during this battle."

Another reporter shouted, "How did you do magic like that without a battery? We all saw you drop it on the stairs."

She glanced quickly at Elizabeth, who winked and smiled at her. Slightly uncomfortable, she focused on the reporter who had asked the question. "At this time, I will not discuss the specifics of my personal magical abilities or how they work. Obviously, you can understand that as the only person with these abilities on Earth thus far, I still have many questions of my own. I am sure that when the secret has been fully revealed, it will be shared with you as well."

A couple more shouted and someone snapped another picture, this time with a flash which surprised her. Stephanie squinted and raised her hand. The media lead walked up and leaned into the mic. "As of right now, please hold your questions until the end of the conference. Ms. Morgana is out here voluntarily so that she may be as transparent as possible while providing only facts. We don't want to speculate on anything right now."

He nodded at her and she straightened and gripped the podium, her knees suddenly weak. Lars's face sobered and he stepped forward, about to come on the stage. She put her hand up to stop him and pulled herself upright. Taking a deep breath, she centered herself again.

The reporters had quieted, and the bots hovered at the back. "The other question that I continue to hear on an hourly basis is what happened to me? Everyone witnessed the healing and then my collapse. I can definitively tell you that the magic expulsion during the battle affected my brain. I'm told by those familiar with the phenomenon that I have opened a valley in my psyche, and until I have healed and grown enough to draw the energy required to restore that, I will need a whole lot of rest. That is where I have been for the last four days under the careful watch of the ambassador, my security team, my family, and my manager, Ms. Elizabeth. The ambassador has opened his residence to us, treated us beyond well, and has taken an interest in making sure that I am able to function while I heal."

She cleared her throat again, took another sip, and closed her eyes for a moment so the dizziness could pass. "That is all the information I can give you at this time. The chief and others will come up shortly and they may be able to answer your questions further. But before I leave, I would like to say one more thing. To the people who fought with us, I thank you. For those who gave their lives for us, I thank your families and send you as much love as I have to give. And for everyone else, we are all one species here on Earth. No matter the class, financial status, or job status, we are all the same. So next time you walk around and you see someone who may have older clothes or less of an education or an inferior job, remember that you are no better than them. And if we all start to treat each other equally, maybe changes can begin to take place."

Before anyone could respond, she raised her hand and nodded. "All right, thank you."

Stephanie turned and made her way to the stairs. She held Lars's arm as they walked out of the conference room and down to the elevators. Stephanie grasped him tightly as the doors opened and they stepped inside. As soon as the doors closed, she released a deep breath and her knees buckled. Lars caught her immediately, scooped her up, and held her firmly against him. She was so exhausted. So very exhausted, and all she could do was rest.

Elizabeth closed the door to her room and held her cellphone against her chest. She peeked out the window and into the bathroom before she sat in her chair and drew her knees to her chest. Stephanie had been put back into bed, and Lars remained at her side, taking the first shift to make sure she was not only safe but that she didn't need anything in the meantime.

As she had walked back to her room, her phone had rung. It was Burt and he had a barrage of questions. She now raised her chin and shook her hair back before she lifted the phone to her ear. "Okay, I'm in a better place to talk."

BURT wasn't computing. He couldn't because he had no data on the situation. "I need her to get into a pod. I need it to be her pod."

Her nostrils flared and she lowered her voice. "I am very aware of what you want, Burt, but not everything can jump when you need it to. I am in a difficult situation at the moment. Stephanie is ill, and though she gets a little better every day, she needs someone who understands what's going on to monitor her. That is where the ambassador came into play. He has heard of this happening and knows how to handle it."

"And he can't do that in her own place of residence?" BURT asked, unable to understand the logic. Computing it brought a whole different set of actions.

Elizabeth rolled her eyes and leaned her elbow on the back of the chair as she turned to the side. "I'm sure he could have but he is a busy Meligornian. We can't expect him to come to the compound every day. It was his requirement that if he were to be the one to help her through this, we stay here until she is better. That she does not go home, she doesn't go out, and she stays in her room until this situation is resolved."

BURT began to connect small dots. "That is why you, and most of the security team, have moved in there."

She nodded. "Yes. My requirement was that if she wanted to stay, that me and the rest of the security stay too. We wouldn't simply leave her here. That would have been terrifying for her. And yes, I want to keep my eye on her as well."

He needed her information—a source of growing irritation and frustration—but his system was not currently able to compute an acceptable solution to the predicament. "I don't mind her staying there but I can't check her out without her getting into the pod."

Elizabeth shrugged. "Then I guess we will have to wait. I don't know what else to do. A Meligornian might be her only salvation right now."

Brilgus pushed the start button on the dishwasher and used the dishrag to dry his hands off. It was a lot of work to cook and clean for that many people, but if it helped Stephanie, he would do what was needed. He had never heard of what happened to her, but then again, he might not have ever had a chance to. The rumors were true. He was half and half, one of the very few Meligornian humans he knew of. So, gifts were different with him, and his knowledge of Meligorn had been very limited until he had met the ambassador.

He had spent most of his youth on Earth, while his father, a Meligornian teacher, came back and forth as often as he could. His father had been a good friend of the ambassador's and when he died, V'ritan had taken him under his wing. Brilgus went with what he knew, and he knew that at that point, Stephanie needed rest, close friends and family, and for the rest of the world to leave her alone.

At a loud knock on the front door, he groaned and rolled his eyes. "This is the third time these boys have left their key behind. I'll tape it to their hands next time."

He grabbed the handle and flung the door open, about to say something smart, but stopped at the sight of Federation Military standing at the entrance. “Good afternoon. My name is Corporal Host and we are here on behalf of the Federation Military. We need to speak to Ms. Morgana if she has a minute.”

Brilgus shook his head. “I’m sorry but she’s resting. Can I ask what this is about?”

The corporal maintained an expressionless face. “Merely some… stuff. It is her business.”

This was not looking good in the least.

CREATOR NOTES - MICHAEL ANDERLE

MARCH 13, 2019

THANK YOU for not only reading this story but these *Creator Notes* as well.

(I think I've been good with always opening with "thank you." If not, I need to edit the other *Author Notes*!)

RANDOM (*sometimes*) THOUGHTS?

Hello!

I apologize, but these notes are going to be very short because I am on daytime cold medicine. My head is loopy, and my thoughts are best described as scattered with a chance to be completely undecipherable to you and my editor.

In short, I can't think straight.

I'm not a big user of cold medicine (specifically the little orange gel tablets), but I caught something at this fair and I'm trying to handle the fifteen to twenty-hour travel from London to Las Vegas (with a layover in New York) before I collapse in bed once I reach Vegas.

I'd like to have Stephanie's story continue, and for that I do need your help to review the book if you like it and letting me know.

There is a saying that when a hero is needed, one will arise.

I look forward to what you do, Stephanie.

AROUND THE WORLD IN 80 DAYS

One of the interesting (at least to me) aspects of my life is the ability to work from anywhere and at any time. In the future, I hope to re-read my own *Author Notes* and remember my life as a diary entry.

London Heathrow Airport, London UK

I'm typing these notes in the business area of the British Airways lounge in Terminal 5. We had to get up at 6:00 AM for a 9:50 flight. The weather is possibly going to delay our flight, and I'm about to go find some early morning food. My choice might be cookies. I wonder if they will have milk ;-)

(Mike edit—I found a delicious croissant).

The planes here at this terminal are *huge,* and they impress me every single time I come to London on BA. No small planes here for the British Empire.

It's like you have 'big/bigger/biggest' as plane options, and I'm good with that!

FAN PRICING

$0.99 Saturdays (new LMBPN stuff) and $0.99 Wednesday (both LMBPN books and friends of LMBPN books.) Get great stuff from us and others at tantalizing prices.

Go ahead. I bet you can't read just one.

Sign up here: http://lmbpn.com/email/.

HOW TO MARKET FOR BOOKS YOU LOVE

Review them so others have your thoughts, and tell friends and the dogs of your enemies (because who wants to talk to enemies?)... *Enough said ;-)*

Ad Aeternitatem,
Michael Anderle

P.S. - If any of this didn't make sense, I'm blaming the cold medicine.

BOOKS BY MICHAEL ANDERLE

For a complete list of books by Michael Anderle, please visit

www.lmbpn.com/ma-books/

All LMBPN Audiobooks are Available at Audible.com and iTunes. For a complete list of audiobooks visit:

www.lmbpn.com/audible

CONNECT WITH THE AUTHORS

Michael Anderle Social

Website: http://lmbpn.com

Email List: http://lmbpn.com/email/

Facebook:
www.facebook.com/TheKurtherianGambitBooks

Lightning Source UK Ltd.
Milton Keynes UK
UKHW040633300621
386397UK00001B/123

9 781642 028584